Praise for *Enchanted, Inc.*

"A totally captivating, hilarious, and clever look on the magical kingdom of Manhattan, where kissing frogs has never been this fun."
—Melissa de la Cruz, author of *The Au Pairs*

"With its clever premise and utterly engaging heroine, Shanna Swendson has penned a real treat! *Enchanted, Inc.* is loads of fun!"
—Julie Kenner, author of *Carpe Demon*

Enchanted, Inc.

Enchanted, Inc.

A Novel

Shanna Swendson

Ballantine Books
New York

A Ballantine Trade Paperback Original

Published in the United States by Ballantine Books, an imprint of The Random House Publishing Group, a division of Random House, Inc., New York.

Ballantine and colophon are registered trademarks of Random House, Inc.

Library of Congress Cataloging-in-Publication Data

Swendson, Shanna.
    Enchanted, Inc. : a novel / Shanna Swendson.
      p. cm.
    ISBN 0-345-48125-9
    1. Young women—Fiction. 2. New York (N.Y.)—Fiction. 3. Women—Employment—Fiction. I. Title: Enchanted, Incorporated. II. Title.

    PS3619.W445E53 2005
    813'.6—dc22

                                             2004059460

Printed in the United States of America

www.ballantinebooks.com

9 8 7 6 5 4 3 2 1

First Edition

Text design by Meryl Sussman Levavi

acknowledgments

To Rosa, for the feedback, faith, and, most important, the chocolate. I can't give you your very own Owen, so this will have to do.

Thanks also to Mom, for the "holy nagging" that got the book done; to my agent, Kristin Nelson, and to my editor, Allison Dickens, for believing in my wacky little story; to Tracee Larson for Punk 101 and shoe-shopping companionship; to Barbara Daly, for New York location research assistance; and to the Dead Liners and Browncoats for encouragement during the tough times and celebration of the happy times on the path to publication.

Enchanted, Inc.

one

I'd always heard that New York City was weird, but I had no idea just how weird until I got here. Before I left Texas to move here, my family tried to talk me out of it, telling me all sorts of urban legends about the strange and horrible things that happened in the big bad city. Even my college friends who'd been living in New York for a while told me stories about the weird and wonderful things they'd seen that didn't cause the natives to so much as blink. My friends joked that an alien from outer space could walk down Broadway without anyone looking twice. I used to think they were exaggerating.

But now, after having survived a year in the city, I still saw things every day that shocked and amazed me but didn't cause anyone else to so much as raise an eyebrow. Nearly naked street performers, people doing tap-dance routines on the sidewalk, and full-scale film productions—complete with celebrities—weren't worth a second glance to the locals, while I couldn't help but gawk. It made me feel like such a hick, no matter how hard I tried to act sophisticated.

Take this morning, for instance. The girl ahead of me on the sidewalk was wearing wings—those strap-on fairy wings people wear as part of a Halloween costume. Halloween was more than a month away, and while I couldn't afford designer fashions, I read enough fashion magazines to know that fairy wings were not a current fashion statement. She must be some neobohemian trendsetter from NYU, I thought, or maybe in the costume design program. She'd done a really good job on the wings because the straps were invisible, making it look like she had real wings. They even fluttered slightly, but that was probably just the wind currents from walking.

I forced my attention away from Miss Airy Fairy to check my watch, then groaned. There was no way I'd make it to work on time if I walked, and my boss was usually lying in wait for me on Monday mornings, so I didn't dare come in even a minute late. I'd have to take the subway to work, even though it would take a precious two dollars off my MetroCard. I'd make up for it by walking home, I promised myself.

When I reached the Union Square station, I was surprised to see Miss Airy Fairy head down into the subway ahead of me instead of continuing toward the university. People who work downtown tend not to dress like that for work. As I followed her down the stairs, I noticed that she wore what must have been platform shoes with Lucite soles, which gave her the appearance of floating a couple of inches off the ground. She moved remarkably gracefully for someone wearing what had to be pretty clunky shoes.

As usual, no one on the platform gave her a second glance. I'd been here a year, and I'd yet to exchange one of those knowing "only in New York" glances with anyone. How could everyone be so jaded? Surely there were people around who were newer to the city than I was, and then there were the tourists, who were supposed to stare at everything.

But then I noticed a guy looking at Miss Airy Fairy. He didn't seem shocked or surprised, though. Instead, he smiled at her like he knew her. That in and of itself was odd because he didn't seem the type to spend his weekends wearing a cape and playing Middle Earth in Central Park. He looked like a typical Wall Street type, wearing a well-tailored dark suit and carrying a briefcase—the kind of Mr. Right that just about every career girl in New York hopes to snag. I'd guess he was a few years older than I was, and he was quite good-looking, even if he was a little shorter than average.

Mr. Right (if he wasn't mine, he had to be somebody's) glanced at his watch, then up the tunnel, like he was looking for the next train. He muttered something under his breath—probably something like "Where is that train?" or "I'm going to be late"—twitched his wrist, and next thing I knew, I heard the rumble that signaled an approaching train. If I didn't know better, I would have thought he summoned it. I wasn't complaining because I needed the train myself.

The waiting passengers shoved their way onto the train, then the conductor's voice came over the PA system, saying, "Attention passengers. Due to a onetime situation, this Brooklyn-bound N train will stop next at City Hall. If you need stops prior to this, please exit the train here and board an R train or another N train. Thank you."

There was a chorus of mutters and groans as passengers poured out of the train. I took a now-empty seat and looked at my watch. At this rate I'd be early to work. This wasn't a bad way to start the week.

Mr. Right was still on board, as was Miss Airy Fairy. Mr. Right exchanged a grin with the guy sitting next to me. I turned to look at that guy and then wondered if there was a polite way I could move to another seat without it being obvious that I was avoiding him.

He looked like the kind of guy who spends his lifetime defending against sexual harassment charges, the kind who thinks of himself as so irresistible that he can't imagine his advances being unwanted. Unfortunately, that type is never as attractive as he'd like to think. This one wasn't exactly hideous. With a little effort and the right personality he might not have been so bad. Unfortunately, he made no effort at all, so that his hair was poorly styled and greasy, while his skin would have made my mother, the Mary Kay representative, faint in horror. But he acted like he thought every woman on that train should be drooling over him, which made him even more unattractive to me.

The funny thing was, all the women on the train were looking at him over the tops of their books and newspapers like they thought Pierce Brosnan had joined us on the subway car, and he grinned at them like he was totally used to that kind of attention. Maybe they could tell he was particularly well-endowed. Or maybe he was a famous rock star I didn't recognize. I wasn't hip enough to know what most rock stars looked like. He had the kind of smug slickness you'd expect from a famous rock star who didn't have to do anything to make women fall at his feet.

As for me, I'd rather look at Mr. Right, who was getting his fair share of admiring glances but who looked shy about it, not like he expected the attention. That made him infinitely cuter in my book.

"On your way to work?" Slick asked. It wasn't among the top five pickup lines I'd ever heard. Not that I heard a lot of them.

"Actually, I just like being crammed like sardines in an underground tin can to head to lower Manhattan in the morning," I said.

He stretched his arm out along the back of the seat, like he was angling to put his arm around me. I'm from a part of the world that still has drive-in movies, so I recognized the move and edged away as subtly as I could. "You're obviously not a native New Yorker," he said, oozing charm like my dad's old tractor oozes oil. "I love your accent."

Little did he know, but he wasn't paying me a compliment. As effective as the steel magnolia routine could be when I was asking for something or trying to get my way, it was a liability at work, where everyone seemed to think my Texas drawl meant I was dumber and less educated than they were. I'd been trying to lose my accent, but it kept slipping out when I was being particularly sarcastic. I guess I inwardly thought the drawl took the sting out of whatever ugly thing I'd just said. In this case, it seemed to have worked, just when I didn't want it to.

I wished I'd brought a book to bury my face in, but I'd planned to walk to and from work when I left the apartment, so I hadn't brought anything to read. In fact, the only things in my oh-so-professional-looking briefcase were my sack lunch and my dressier shoes for the office. Instead, I just gave Slick a glare and turned my attention to Mr. Right. Maybe he'd have a Galahad complex and feel compelled to rescue me from the subway stalker.

Then I noticed that Slick was looking at Mr. Right as well, and suddenly his face was totally serious. Mr. Right, also serious, nodded his head slightly. Miss Airy Fairy was also staring at me. Now I couldn't help but wonder if this was a conspiracy. Were they going to rob me or try to scam me? Goodness knows, I might as well have been wearing a big yellow button saying "Hick from Out of Town! Please Take Advantage of Me!"

Just then the door between cars opened and a giant chicken entered our car. To be more precise, it was a bored-looking man in a chicken suit—and how sad was it that he was more bored than embarrassed to be wearing that costume in public? I added to my mental list of jobs that were worse than mine. He shook a little plastic box in his left hand, and clucking sounds came out of it. I felt a pang of homesickness, for I used to have one like it on my desk back in Texas. I wouldn't dare put it on my desk here. It would only reinforce the hick stereotype. At the clucking sound, everyone looked up, reacted with mild amusement, then immediately went back to reading or avoiding eye contact. The chicken man then tried to hand flyers to

everyone in the car. I hadn't yet learned the technique for avoiding flyers that most New Yorkers seem to have honed, so I took one from
him. A new fried-chicken restaurant was opening, which gave me another moment of homesickness as I remembered family Sunday din-
ners. I tucked the flyer into my briefcase.

This incident didn't do much toward helping me understand
New Yorkers. Fairy wings on the subway weren't worth noticing, but
a guy in a chicken suit got a slight reaction. Both outfits involved
wings. Why was one humdrum while the other was at least a little bit
amusing? I noticed that Mr. Right had also taken a flyer. He was smiling and staring at the chicken man, which made me like him even
more. Or, it would have if he didn't seem to be in cahoots with the
other two, who were still looking at me funny. I forgot about the giant
chicken as I remembered why I felt ill at ease.

The train screeched its way to a stop. "City Hall," the conductor
said. I wondered if I should get off now and get away from these people. The walk from there to my office would make me late for work,
but better late than dead or robbed.

But before I could get to my feet, I noticed that the three weirdos
were congregating around the door. I relaxed with a sigh. They were
all getting off here, which meant I was being paranoid about them
being out to get me. I still had too many New York scare stories in my
head from my family, and they crept to the surface at awkward mo-
ments, even though I'd never been mugged or even seen a mugging
in my whole time in New York.

Besides, I had plenty to worry about without concocting subway
conspiracy theories. It wasn't like this morning's events were all that
extraordinary in my life. Weird stuff like this always happened to me,
or at least, it had ever since I moved to New York. I was always seeing
things that shouldn't be there, like people in fairy wings or pointed
ears, people who appeared to pop in and out of existence, and things
appearing in strange places. I knew it was likely the result of an over-

active imagination and my family's scare stories about New York, but it was almost enough to worry me. I figured if I still noticed strange things that no one else seemed to find odd after another six months in the city, I might have to talk to someone about it.

In the meantime, I had to get to work and survive the day. Fortunately, due to the train's timely arrival and the unexpected express nature of the trip, I was ahead of schedule. To add to my run of good luck, the up escalator at the Whitehall station was actually working. I emerged topside among the soulless modern glass skyscrapers, went into the lobby of my building, and paused to change into my work shoes. Then I put on my employee ID badge, got cleared by the lobby security guard, and headed for the elevator bank that served my floor.

I was seven minutes early when I stepped off the elevator into our lobby, and I was five minutes early when I reached my cubicle, but my boss Mimi was already lurking. I wondered which Mimi had shown up for work today, the best buddy or the evil beast from hell that would rip me apart with her hairy-knuckled hands. Mimi was about as stable as Dr. Jekyll.

Okay, so I'm exaggerating a little bit. Even on her bad days, her knuckles weren't all that hairy.

"'Morning, Katie!" she called out as I neared my cubicle. "How was your weekend?" It looked like the good Mimi had shown up for work today. There was no telling how long it would last, so I kept a safe distance and looked for something heavy to use for self-defense, just in case.

"It was great. And yours?"

She sighed blissfully. "Fabulous. Werner and I spent the weekend at his place in the Hamptons." Werner was her richer-than-God (and almost as old) boyfriend. She leaned toward me and added in a whisper, "I think he's getting ready to propose."

"Wow, really?" I said, faking enthusiasm as I edged past her and got to my desk.

"You never know. See you at the staff meeting."

I sat down at my desk and turned on my computer. I'd hoped for a Mimi-free morning before I had to deal with her at the torture exercise we called the Monday staff meeting, but my luck for the day had apparently run out, even if that encounter had been fairly benign. I sincerely wished that Good Mimi was still around when the staff meeting started in fifteen minutes. Otherwise, I might find myself wishing the trio of oddballs in the subway had kidnapped me. Whatever they might do to me would likely be more pleasant than Mimi at her worst.

Although Mimi was my boss, she wasn't that much older than I was. While I'd been running the business affairs of my family's feed-and-seed store in a small town in Texas, she'd been earning her MBA at some fancy upper-crust school. I'd learned very quickly after getting to New York that the degree and related credentials and contacts counted for a lot more than real-world experience, especially the kind of real-world experience I had. A BBA from a public university in Texas and a few years actually running a small business didn't get me much credit in the New York business world.

In fact, I wouldn't even have this job as assistant to the marketing director (in other words, Mimi's personal slave) if one of my roommates hadn't worked her own business network on my behalf. I'd looked at this job as a temporary fix to tide me over until I found something better, but I was still here a year later. I suspected I'd have to gnaw my own arm off to get out of this trap.

My computer finally finished booting up, and I checked my e-mail. The top message, received just minutes ago, said, "Excellent Opportunity for Kathleen Chandler." Excellent opportunities were few and far between, and they seldom came in e-mail. I suspected that, in spite of the seemingly personalized subject line (which probably came from my e-mail address, anyway), it had something to do with enlarging a body part I didn't have. I deleted the message and scrolled down to find the message I always had waiting for me on Monday mornings: Mimi's staff meeting agenda.

I fixed the typos, printed it out, then skimmed over it while I walked to the copier. This one didn't seem to have too many mine-fields in it, just the usual status reports. I might survive, after all. I made copies of the agenda and returned to my office. There was a new e-mail waiting for me, probably a revised agenda from Mimi. But when I clicked over to my e-mail program, it was just another "great opportunity" spam, this time adding the words "don't delete!" to the subject line. With a sense of perverse satisfaction, I deleted it. It was probably the only act of rebellion I'd get away with all day.

I knew better than to be late for one of Mimi's meetings, so I put the agendas inside my notepad, got my pen, coffee mug, and lunch, and headed for the kitchen. There, I put my lunch in the communal refrigerator and poured myself a cup of coffee before going to the conference room. I reminded myself that after surviving the meeting, the rest of the day should be easy.

I wasn't the only one who looked like I was attending my own execution. April, the advertising manager, was already in the conference room, and her face was an ashy shade of white. Leah, the public relations manager, looked serene, but I knew that was just because she was taking prescription tranquilizers. Janice, the events manager, had a nervous tic. The only person who didn't look stressed or medicated was Joel, the sales liaison, but that was only because he didn't report directly to Mimi. It was the last Monday of the month, so it was just a managers' meeting instead of the whole staff, or else the room would have been full of a lot more anxious bodies. I was, by far, the lowest person on the totem pole, but I was there in my capacity as Mimi's brain. Apparently, when you have an expensive MBA, you lose the ability to take notes for yourself in meetings and remember what was discussed.

I handed agendas to everyone at the table. We didn't talk to one another while we waited. That was too risky. You never knew when Mimi would make her grand entrance and hear something out of context that would set her off. Nobody wanted to be responsible for bringing out Evil Mimi. Instead, we all studied our agendas, looking for potential trouble spots.

As usual, Mimi was ten minutes late for her own meeting. I knew enough about nonverbal communication to know she was sending us a not-so-subtle signal that her time was more valuable than ours. She opened both of the conference room's double doors, then paused like she was a talk-show guest waiting for the studio audience's applause to die down before she took her seat on Oprah's couch.

"Good morning, Mimi," I said, even though we'd exchanged morning greetings not all that long ago. But she would have stood there all day waiting for someone to acknowledge her presence, and as her assistant, one of my unwritten duties was to make her feel special. The others all mumbled greetings. She finally closed the doors behind her, then swept to her usual seat at the head of the table. I handed her a copy of the agenda, which she studied like she wasn't the one who'd written it, before she looked up and addressed the group.

"We'll keep this short because we all have a busy week with a lot to get done," she said brusquely. Her tone was different enough from her earlier chatty friendliness that I grew nervous. "First item on the agenda is departmental reports. April?"

April went a shade paler. Even her lips were white. "We have a meeting with the agency later this week to discuss their ideas for the next campaign and review their suggested media buy."

"Is that meeting on my calendar?"

"Yes, it is," I told her, trying to give April a break. "Remember, I checked with you about that last week?" As soon as I said it, I knew it was a huge mistake. Everyone else in the room tensed. They all knew how badly I'd goofed. Mimi couldn't handle being questioned or criticized, not even something as mild as pointing out something she'd forgotten.

I got even more nervous when she didn't immediately turn into Evil Mimi. Instead, she just nodded and said, "Okay. Be sure to send me a reminder. Leah?"

In her drugged calm tone, Leah said, "We should get last week's clips from the agency by close of business today. And we'll get the first draft of the new product release tomorrow."

Mimi nodded. "I want to see those as soon as you get them." I made a note of Leah's report and the action item as Mimi turned to Janice, who visibly flinched. "Any news from events?" Mimi asked. Janice had been on her hit list for a long time, thus the nervous tic and the fact that Mimi never called her by name. None of us, not even Janice, was sure what Janice had done wrong.

"We're still getting estimates on locations for the product launch. There isn't much within our budget that's large enough but still nice."

Mimi turned to the rest of us. "Does anyone here have any ideas for the launch? The events staff needs all the help it can get."

I had an idea, but I hated to get Janice in trouble by bringing up something when she didn't have any ideas. Still, in this department it was every man for himself. I had no doubt that every one of these people would be willing to throw me to the wolves to keep Mimi off their backs. "I—I think I may have something," I said. Every head snapped toward me, and I had second thoughts about speaking up. Technically, I wasn't even present at this meeting other than as a note taker.

Fortunately, Mimi didn't look displeased at my breach of protocol. "Yes, Katie?" she said. I suspected she was enjoying Janice looking bad more than she was mad at me.

I took a deep breath and forced myself to be conscious of my accent. One hint of drawl and my idea would be shot down like a clay pigeon. "I've found that if you try to do something too fancy-looking without the budget that goes with it, you just end up looking cheap. Let's face it, serving low-budget shrimp puffs is just asking for food poisoning. What if we do something that's supposed to look cheap? Instead of doing a ritzy cocktail party, have a picnic or cookout. Grill hot dogs and serve beer and have a few nostalgic picnic-type activities, like sack races or bobbing for apples. Adults get a real kick out of an excuse to act like kids, and you can give a lot of people a good time they'll remember without spending much money." We'd done customer appreciation days like that at the store, but I knew better than to mention the store. It might be real-world experience, but it would detract from my credibility.

They all stared at me in silence when I was through. Finally, Mimi said in her most acid tone, "That may work down in Grover's Corners, or wherever it is you're from, but we have different standards in New York." I knew now wasn't the time to point out that the play she'd referred to took place in New Hampshire, not Texas, or that my idea would probably be even more successful in New York than in Texas. Why else do so many easterners pay outrageous sums of money to vacation at dude ranches? It must be a huge relief to take a break from trying so hard to be jaded and sophisticated.

I glanced around the table to see if I had any support, but they were all rolling their eyes or snickering. Once again I'd branded myself as a hick who was totally out of touch with the New York business world. I silently prayed for a surprise fire drill, but the meeting went on as if I hadn't said anything.

Joel had the final report. "The sales force met last week to prep for the launch. We've got our collateral printed and ready to go. We'll just need to see the news release so we'll know what the press will be seeing."

Mimi fixed him with a killer glare. "Why wasn't I at that meeting? And why didn't I get sign-off of the collateral?"

Joel stared her down. "Because last time you were invited to one of our meetings you said it was a waste of time and told us to leave you out from here on. As for collateral, that's not your responsibility."

The rest of us looked for cover. I wouldn't have been at all surprised if Mimi's eyes had turned red, her skin had turned green, and little horns popped out of the top of her head. Collateral was a sore spot with her. In most companies it fell under the responsibility of the marketing director, but ever since she signed off on a brochure that misspelled the company's name and the product name on the cover, that responsibility had been transferred to Sales. She had never recovered from the slight.

"I don't have time for your little sales meetings, anyway," she said stiffly before abruptly dismissing the meeting. She was out the door before the rest of us could collect our wits and make our own escapes.

"Nice going," Janice muttered to Joel as we trooped out of the conference room. "You just had to stir her up, didn't you?"

"It's funny when her eyes pop out like that," he said with a grin. Janice twitched.

"I'll have to see how many excuses I can find to send her down to Sales today," I said. They all looked at me with a combination of pity and scorn, making me feel like I'd have to stretch to reach a grasshopper's knees. I didn't expect them to stand up for me in front of Mimi, but I'd hoped they'd acknowledge the value of my idea behind her back. No such luck.

I dreaded the rest of the day. Mimi was already ticked at me for reminding her that she'd okayed the meeting she was ready to grill April about; I'd put my foot in my mouth by daring to offer a suggestion; and then Joel had set her off. I'd be stuck with Evil Mimi for an indefinite period of time. When I got back to my cube, I noticed her office door was shut. With any luck, she'd spend the next half hour on the phone with Werner, sobbing about how horrible her day had been so far and how her terrible staff was so mean and nasty to her.

I put my notepad next to my computer and sank into my desk

chair, trying to remember why I put up with this job. At first it hadn't seemed so bad. Mimi had greeted me like a long-lost sister and gave every impression that she would be a mentor who would ease my way into the business world, as well as a best friend and soul mate. Then I made the mistake of correcting the horrendous spelling and grammar on a memo she'd written and running it back by her to approve my changes. That was the first time I saw Evil Mimi. Since then I found that on good days she was as friendly as I could hope. But the moment she was revealed to be less than perfect, she went nuts. I learned to just correct the memos before sending them and not let her know I was cleaning up her mess.

Why did I want this job? Oh yeah, that six hundred bucks a month for my share of the rent on a one-bedroom apartment that three of us shared. Not to mention several levels of income taxes, my share of utilities, food, transportation, and all the other little expenses that added up to consume my meager paycheck. I was barely getting by on my salary. Without a salary, my roommates were sure to get rid of me, even if we had been friends since college, and I'd have to go home to Texas, proving to my parents that I couldn't make it in the big city after all.

There were even days—like today—when I had to remind myself why that would be so bad. It wasn't as though I'd been unhappy at home. I'd just felt like I wanted something more. I didn't know what, not yet. I hoped there was something big out there with my name on it that would never have found me while I stayed in that little town. If I went back to Texas on anything other than my own terms, with some kind of business or personal success under my belt, I'd look like a failure. Worse, I'd feel like a failure.

Mimi was a small price to pay to avoid that. But it wouldn't hurt to start looking for another job, now that I had some non-feed-and-seed experience under my belt. It would be easier to hide my roots at the next job because they wouldn't have known me when I was straight out of Texas. That would have to make things better.

The new mail indicator was blinking on my computer. I clicked on my e-mail program and saw a message saying, "Job opportunity." I knew it was probably spam, offering me the chance to work at home stuffing envelopes or something lame like that, but given the day I'd already had, I opened it.

"Dear Kathleen Chandler," it said, "Your experience and work ethic have come to our attention, and we believe you would be the perfect fit for our firm. This is a once-in-a-lifetime opportunity you can't afford to pass up. I can promise you'll never receive a comparable offer, in New York City or anywhere else. Please reply via e-mail or call at your earliest convenience to schedule an interview."

It was signed, "Rodney A. Gwaltney, director of personnel, MSI, Inc." A Manhattan phone number was under his name.

I stared at the e-mail for a good, long time. It was very, very tempting, and it might not hurt to find out more, but one thing I'd learned in my small-town business experience was that if things sound too good to be true, they probably are. I couldn't think of any reason anyone outside my company would have the slightest idea who I was to know anything about my experience and work ethic.

With a disappointed sigh, I deleted the e-mail. The last thing I needed was for Mimi to accidentally see a job offer open on my computer screen. I promised myself that I'd borrow my roommate Marcia's computer that evening to search the online job listings and get myself out of this loony bin as soon as humanly possible.

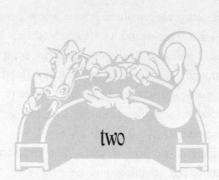

two

I would have walked home from work that day even if I hadn't been desperately trying to save money. On bad days the long walk up Broadway lets me blow off some steam, while the varied sights, sounds, and smells provide enough transition between work and home that work seems like it belongs to another lifetime by the time I get home. If I just go belowground after leaving the office and emerge aboveground at home, I'm still in work mode when I get home, and I hate subjecting my roommates to that. Cringing isn't a good look for me, and I didn't want them knowing just how bad things were. The last thing I needed was them sending me home because they were worried about me not being cut out for New York after all.

I was still muttering curses at Mimi under my breath as I changed shoes in the building lobby. Then I stepped outside, cut across to Broadway and began the long hike. The day had only gone downhill after the staff meeting, and more than once I'd been tempted to re-trieve that job offer from deleted mail, even if I knew it had to be a scam. A nineteenth-century sweatshop seemed like a saner working environment than laboring under La Diva Mimi.

I'd calmed down a lot by the time I crossed Houston Street. Now I could see the spire of Grace Church ahead of me and I knew I was almost home. I cut across to Fourth Avenue one street before the church because there was sometimes a gargoyle on that church that really wigged me out. It wasn't the gargoyle itself that gave me the creeps. It was the "sometimes" part that unnerved me. Gargoyles are carved of stone and should be part of the building. If one is there, you should see it all the time, not just on an occasional basis.

This church didn't usually have gargoyles at all, just carved faces. But every so often there was a classic winged, clawed gargoyle sitting over a doorway or on a roof ridge, and I always felt like it was looking at me. I knew that wasn't one of those weird New York things that everyone talks about, so I preferred to avoid the situation entirely.

A couple of blocks up Fourth, I noticed a costume shop next to a magic and fantasy shop, and I had to laugh at myself. That explained the girl with the wings. She must have been an employee, doing a lit-tle advertising by showing the wares around town. It didn't explain why she seemed to know those two men on the train, but then again, Mr. Right had got on at the same station, so maybe he lived in the neighborhood. They must have been neighbors.

And the magic shop may have had something to do with the gargoyle. It was an illusion, or maybe a prop, put on the church as a practical joke and removed before anyone in authority caught on.

I felt much less like I was going crazy when I reached my build-ing and unlocked the front door. By the time I made it up the stairs to my apartment, I'd managed to put both work and the weirdness of the day out of my mind. I'd barely had time to get the windows open so the place could air out when my roommate Gemma came home. She worked longer hours than I did, but she'd never do anything so crazy as walk home from work. Not in the shoes she usually wore.

She kicked off her high-heeled sandals inside the front door and stretched out her calves. "Is that what you're wearing?" she asked.

"Huh?"

"You must not have seen the e-mail I sent."

"Nope, sorry. Every time I tried to log on, Mimi stuck her head in my cube to demand something." I used a Web-based e-mail service for personal mail at work, since I knew getting personal e-mail on the company system would be asking for trouble from Mimi. Better safe than give her an excuse to yell.

"You have got to get another job."

"I know," I moaned as she went into the kitchen and took a bottle of water out of the refrigerator. For a moment I considered telling her about the e-mailed job offer, but I knew she'd just laugh at me. "So, what's going on and what should I be wearing?"

She came back into the living room and curled up on the other end of the sofa, tucking her bare feet up under her. "Dinner out, the three of us and Connie." Connie was our other friend from school who'd moved up here with Gemma and Marcia. When she got married and moved out, the other two invited me to come to New York.

"What's the special occasion?"

"I have news." Her expression remained enigmatic, and I knew Gemma well enough to know that I wouldn't get any more than that out of her until she was ready to spill. My stomach tightened up into a knot. I wondered if my worst fears were about to come true. She wasn't dating anyone seriously, so I doubted she was getting married and moving out, but maybe she'd been promoted and was moving to a loft in SoHo or someplace infinitely more fashionable than our dingy little apartment.

"Is there a reason I need to dress up?" I asked. It was hard enough to choose one outfit a day.

"It never hurts to make every outing into an occasion. You never know who you'll run into." Gemma was our self-declared social director, determined to make the rest of us experience life in New York to the fullest. Otherwise, she insisted, we might as well have just found jobs in Dallas or Houston.

She was right, though. You never knew who you'd run into, like movie stars or musicians. Or Mr. Right from the subway, who might live nearby, even if he was a little weird. I got up and headed back to the bedroom. "Any suggestions?"

She bounced to her feet. This was her area of expertise. After all, she did work in the fashion industry.

By the time Marcia got home we were both dressed to kill. Wearing a borrowed sweater of Gemma's, I felt almost glamorous, even though I knew I was a total plain Jane next to the rest of the crowd. I certainly wasn't unattractive, but I was extremely ordinary. I wasn't short enough to be delicate and petite like Connie, and I wasn't tall enough to be striking like Gemma. My hair was somewhere between blond and brunette, not short, but not long, and my eyes weren't quite green, but not quite blue, either. On the bright side, if I ever staged an armed robbery, witnesses would have a hard time giving an accurate description that didn't sound like half the city.

While Marcia changed clothes, Connie showed up. She was all a-bubble, which made me suspect that whatever Gemma was up to, Connie was in on it. That made me relax ever so slightly. It probably had something to do with setting all of us up on blind dates. That wasn't my idea of fun, but it was better than suddenly having to come up with an extra couple of hundred bucks a month because Gemma was moving out.

We got a sidewalk table at a little café on St. Mark's Place in the East Village. Gemma ordered the first round of drinks. "This round's on me," she insisted. That meant she was really up to something.

Once we'd all drunk enough to have any edges taken off, Gemma and Connie exchanged a look, then Gemma turned to us. "I have great news!" she said.

Now Marcia and I exchanged a look. "What is it?" Marcia asked suspiciously.

"We all have dates for this weekend."

"We do?" I asked. We all had dates almost every weekend, not because we were particularly popular, but because Gemma loved playing matchmaker. She was always setting us up on blind dates, and she'd accept any setup offer for herself that came her way.

"They're friends of Jim's," Connie explained, referring to her financial whiz husband. "That way, Jim and I can come along, and the guys will all know each other like we all know each other. It'll be fun."

It sounded like dating in junior high to me, but I kept my mouth shut. At least this way I'd still have someone to talk to, even if the date bombed.

Before Marcia had a chance to react, the waiter appeared with a tray of drinks. "We haven't ordered another round yet," Gemma protested.

"These are compliments of that gentleman over there," the waiter said as he set the drinks in front of us. We all turned to see a man sitting by himself at another table on the sidewalk. I almost fell out of my chair, for it was Slick from the subway.

I turned back to my friends, who were practically drooling on the table, even Connie, the married one. "Well, hello," Gemma murmured, crossing her long legs so her miniskirt crept a little higher. Marcia leaned forward against the table, enhancing her cleavage. Connie smiled and played with her hair. I looked back at him, but he was just as oily as I remembered from the subway. There was obviously something I wasn't getting.

I leaned closer to the others and whispered, "Is he someone I should know?"

"Why do you ask?" Marcia asked, not taking her eyes off Slick.

"Because y'all are staring at him like he's Johnny Depp."

"Mmm, Johnny Depp would be an accurate comparison," Gemma said. "You don't think it is Johnny Depp, do you?"

"Doesn't he live in Paris?" Connie asked.

I looked back at the guy, just to make sure I wasn't crazy, but it looked like I wasn't the one with mental health issues here. "Are you crazy?" I asked. "He doesn't look anything like Johnny Depp, not even when he gets all icky-looking for a role."

"Honey, you need your eyes checked," Gemma said.

I really did not get the appeal of this guy, who'd had the women on the subway and now my friends falling at his feet. I also didn't like the idea of him just happening to show up where I was having dinner. New York might be small geographically speaking, but there are thousands of restaurants, and the odds of him just happening to choose this one were slim. Oh goody, my first stalker. If one of the men on the subway was going to follow me, why couldn't it be the cute one?

I leaned forward again and whispered, "I think maybe he's following me. He was sitting next to me on the subway this morning."

"You lucky thing," Marcia purred. "If you don't want him, can I have him?" She winked at him and licked her lips.

"Oh look, he's coming over here!" Connie squeaked. They all set about arranging themselves attractively as he approached.

"Good evening, ladies," he said in the same oily voice he'd used with me on the subway. "Are you enjoying your drinks?"

They lost all pretense of New York sophistication as they dissolved in giggles. I just crossed my arms over my chest and raised an eyebrow.

He studied me intently, then, with his eyes still on me, said, "My name's Rod Gwaltney."

That was the name on the job offer e-mail. I was too stunned to respond. Fortunately—or not—Gemma was still on the ball. "I'm Gemma, and this is Marcia, Connie, and Katie."

"Pleased to meet you," he said.

I still couldn't respond. Now I was absolutely sure this wasn't a coincidence. But which had come first, the following or the job offer? Had he already been following me when I saw him on the train? Now I was even more sure that the offer was a scam. I'd never heard of stalking used as a job recruitment tactic. He probably ran some kind of sex slavery ring, but it had to be a pretty low-rent ring if they were resorting to someone like me, unless they specialized in procuring women for men with unhealthy girl-next-door fantasies.

While I'd been lost in shock, my friends were busy chatting flirtatiously with him. "It's been nice meeting you ladies," he said at last.

"And nice to meet you," Marcia said.

"Thanks for the drinks. That was sweet of you," Gemma added.

He glanced around the table, then looked directly at me as he said, "I hope I'll see you again, soon." Then he left.

As soon as he was gone, they all burst into giggles again. "I think he likes you, Katie," Gemma said. "Maybe we should cancel your date for the weekend. Looks like you're going to be busy."

I still felt sick and too stunned to speak. Connie must have noticed this, for she said, "Katie, hon, what's wrong?"

"I told you I saw him on the subway this morning, right? Well, he also sent me an e-mail today offering me a job. Three e-mails, come to think of it."

"What kind of job?" Marcia asked.

"I don't know. He didn't say. That's why I was so suspicious and just deleted them. I thought it was spam, one of those 'great opportunity' things where you can make a fortune working at home. He did say something about knowing my experience and work ethic, but how could he? I'm pretty sure I never saw him before this morning. And then to run into him again tonight . . ." I shuddered.

The others now looked a lot more serious. "What company was he with?" Marcia asked.

"Something like MSI, Inc."

She shook her head. "Never heard of it."

"You don't think it's a real job offer, do you?"

"I don't know, but I doubt it. Headhunters do contact people out of the blue, and sometimes they're vague about what company they're representing, but they usually tell you how they heard about you, and they usually recruit more in the, um, executive ranks." In other words, they wouldn't be out trying to steal a glorified secretary. "I wonder if this company is a search firm. It is possible that it was someone in your company who recommended you, maybe someone who's accepted another job but who hasn't given notice yet and who's recommended names of other people to steal."

That was certainly possible. Anyone on the marketing staff at my company could very easily be jumping ship, and they'd be sure to do anything they could to get back at Mimi on their way out, like having her assistant recruited. I liked to think that in spite of the difficult conditions and my unfortunate lack of city sophistication, I'd done a good enough job that my coworkers would be willing to recommend me. Still, the fact that the guy had shown up tonight made me nervous.

As if echoing my thoughts, Marcia added, "What is weird is that you've been seeing him around town. Recruiters don't usually work that way. They set up meetings rather than ambushing you and your friends with free drinks. And if a coworker recommended you, how did he know what you look like and how to find you away from work? This morning on the subway, was there any way he could have got your name or where you work? Did he follow you out of the subway?"

I shook my head. "No. He got off a few stops before I did."

"You don't have an ID badge or a luggage tag on your briefcase with your business card visible, do you?"

"No. I know better than that."

"Hmm. Weird."

The mood around the table was a lot gloomier than it had been before I confessed to the weirdness, and I hated being the wet blanket, so I said, "Well, if you thought he was hot, you should have seen the other guy who was on the subway this morning." They pressed me for details, and soon we were back in the swing of an evening out with friends.

I didn't sleep well that night, as visions of fairies, gargoyles, Mimi, and Rod danced through my head. The sleepless night meant I was out of bed early enough to walk to work, which I hoped diminished my chances of running into the same trio on the subway. I knew that the odds of randomly seeing the same three people on any one subway car were slim, but after yesterday, I wasn't taking any chances.

I sipped from a travel mug of coffee and ate a bagel as I walked and tried to think of what I should do. There wasn't much I could do. It wasn't like I'd respond to that shady job offer. I'd just keep deleting Rod's e-mails. If he continued to show up around me, I supposed I could get a restraining order, but until he was stealing my underwear and sending me threatening letters, I doubted the police would care all that much.

Nope, all I could do was focus my attention on surviving Mimi. Today, I got to work before she did, so I had a chance to catch my breath before I had to deal with her. She must have had a busy night with Werner, as she hadn't left me her usual half-dozen e-mails from home telling me things she needed me to do first thing in the morning. As I'd expected, there was also another message from good old Rodney Gwaltney. I couldn't resist opening it.

This one was addressed to "Katie" instead of "Kathleen." "It was a pleasure to see you again last night and to meet all of your delightful friends," it said. "I know I must have startled you, but please believe that I mean you no harm. Quite the contrary. My offer is truly one you can't afford to pass up. You are more valuable than you realize. Please contact me at your earliest convenience."

I was tempted to write back and tell him that if his offer was so good and so aboveboard, he shouldn't have a problem telling me what it was. My mama didn't raise any dummies, and even in a small town I'd know better than to contact a strange man who was so vague about his intentions. With a great sense of satisfaction, I hit the delete key.

Since Mimi still wasn't in, I took advantage of the opportunity to check my personal e-mail. There was the message from Gemma about dinner. And there was yet another message from Rodney. I added his address to the spam filter and deleted the message, unread, along with all the messages telling me I could lose weight, increase my breast size, make money at home, grow a bigger penis, buy herbal Viagra without a prescription, and get a lower mortgage rate. If all those messages were true, everyone would be slim, attractive, wealthy love machines. Obviously, that wasn't the case, so odds were, the job offer was no more real than all the other junk mail.

Mimi was her usual charming self when she arrived, meaning that she really was acting charming, and anyone who hadn't seen her evil incarnation would think she was just the coolest boss ever. Maybe ol' Werner had bought some of that herbal Viagra stuff. She remained that way all morning, but the daggers made an appearance at lunchtime.

I was sitting at my desk, trying to salvage one of her memos into something readable by English speakers, when she stuck her head into my cube. "Are you going to lunch?" she asked.

"Not right now, thanks," I said absently, still focusing on my computer screen. "I need to finish this, and I brought a sandwich."

"You know, it wouldn't hurt you to be more sociable around the office. Eating lunch at your desk every day isn't good for office unity. I'd prefer for you to go out with the rest of the staff."

I had to bite my tongue to hold back all of the responses that popped into my head, like telling her that she was the main problem with office unity and that I'd go out to lunch with her at the pricey bistros she preferred when she paid me enough money to be able to afford it. I certainly wasn't going to waste my precious entertainment dollars on socializing with her.

Fortunately, this was just one of her drive-by shootings and she didn't seem to want a response. Before I could think of anything to say that wouldn't get me fired on the spot, she was gone. Feeling lower than a snake's belly in a wheel rut, as my grandma used to say, I went back to work on the memo. My one spark of rebellious revenge was to leave a grammatical error. She'd never know the difference—obviously, since she was the one who'd written it—and since it was her name on the memo, anyone who did know the difference would get at least a whiff of incompetence from her.

Then I got my sack lunch, changed into my walking shoes, and headed out to Battery Park. There was something about looking at the water, with the Statue of Liberty looming not too far in the distance, that helped calm me down.

Plenty of other people were out enjoying the gorgeous early fall day. There were a couple of busloads of tourists toting cameras, a few classes of schoolkids waiting for the ferry to the Statue of Liberty, and a lot of lower Manhattan business types enjoying the same kind of office escape I was.

A guy roller-skated past me, and I wouldn't have given him a second thought if it weren't for the elf ears he wore. I watched as he skated down the sidewalk and met up with a girl wearing fairy wings. I wasn't sure if it was the same Miss Airy Fairy I'd seen the day before or if I was wrong about those things not being a fashion trend. The elf and the fairy gave each other an enthusiastic kiss. Nobody else in the park seemed to notice them.

Then I wondered what I found so weird about the situation. It wasn't like there really was a roller-skating elf kissing a fairy, given that neither elves nor fairies actually existed. It was just two people in costume, and that shouldn't faze me at all. I'd known people in college who'd gone to class for weeks in their live-action role-playing game costumes when they were in the middle of a major campaign, and that wasn't even in the weirdness of New York.

I turned my head and noticed a man in silver skin paint and a metallic jumpsuit doing robot mime for a crowd of tourists. I didn't think that was particularly strange, so why did all this other stuff bother me so much? I guess I wasn't as sophisticated as I wanted to be.

With a sigh, I shook the crumbs out of my sandwich bag, folded it up, and put it back in my paper lunch sack, which I then folded neatly and stuck in my purse. I dropped my apple core in a garbage can as I passed it and headed back to my office with a heavy heart. Every time I went out for lunch, it grew more and more difficult to force myself back inside. That was yet another reason I usually ate at my desk.

Mimi must not have found a group to go out to lunch with, for she was already back in the office when I returned. "Where have you been?" she shrieked, loud enough for the whole floor to hear. Dogs in Battery Park City whimpered and put their paws over their ears.

"At lunch," I said as calmly as I could. Getting mad back at Mimi only escalated the situation.

"I thought you said you weren't going to lunch," she accused.

"I said I'd brought my lunch. I just took it out of my office to eat it."

By now people were staring, heads peeping up over the top of cubicle walls like prairie dogs peering out of their holes. "You should tell me when you're leaving the office."

"You were at lunch." I frowned in fake concern and tried to keep my voice from shaking. "Am I supposed to get permission to take a lunch break? I wasn't aware of that policy."

There wasn't anything she could say to that, not with so many witnesses. She'd never get a reprimand about daring to leave the office for lunch while she herself was gone to stick. Unfortunately, she knew she was powerless, and she hated that more than anything. "I needed the draft of that news release from PR before I could go to the executive meeting," she snapped. "I tried calling you from the executive conference room to bring it to me, but you weren't at your desk."

"I put it in your in-box this morning, as soon as I got it from Leah."

Now she was really angry. Most bosses would be glad to find that their employees were competent, but not Mimi. Competent employees made her look bad and took away all of her excuses. She must have shown up at the executive meeting without the release, then tried to blame me, saying I hadn't given it to her. With glaring, bugging Evil Mimi eyes, she whirled back to her office, snatched the release out of her in-box and stalked off toward the elevators. Her body language said, "I'm not through with you yet, missy."

I was almost in tears as I slunk into my cubicle, fell into my desk chair, and changed back into my office shoes. She made me so angry, and since I couldn't do anything about her, my frustration came out in tears. The last thing I wanted was for her to think she'd made me cry, so I sat blinking furiously in my cubicle.

My hands shook as I raised them to my computer keyboard and hit a key to bring the screen back to life. The message-waiting indicator was blinking, and there at the top of my e-mail in-box was a message from Rodney Gwaltney. I opened it. It was the usual stuff talking about what a great opportunity he had for me.

I knew it had to be a scam, but I couldn't take much more of this job, so I had to either find another one or admit defeat and go back home. Maybe a nice Texas girl like me wasn't cut out for life in the big city. But before I gave up, I thought I ought to give it one more shot. I'd have to do whatever it took to find another job.

Before I realized what I was doing, I'd hit Reply and typed out, "When would you like to meet? My schedule is pretty busy, so it will have to be at lunchtime or after work." No matter what he was offering me, it had to be better than this. Then, before I could change my mind, I hit Send.

three

As soon as I sent the message, I regretted it. What had I gotten myself into? I knew they only opened the firewall to let e-mail come and go every few minutes, so there was still a chance that I could call IT and ask them to kill it, but that would mean admitting I'd responded to a job offer. I was sure the computer guys wouldn't tell on me. They'd sympathize, since they had to help an ungrateful Mimi with one kind of computer problem or another on a daily basis. The longer I hesitated, the lower my chances were of taking it back.

But I couldn't bring myself to make that call. Worst-case scenario, aside from the sex slavery possibility, was that Rodney might leave me alone if I met with him and still turned him down. There was always the possibility that the offer was everything he said it was, but I knew that really good things usually came with a catch.

I forced myself to concentrate on my work instead of thinking about the job, but every time I heard the ding that announced new mail, I quickly clicked over. They were pretty much all from people needing to get on Mimi's calendar or asking if she'd yet looked at something that she had asked for last week and said was urgent.

Maybe Rodney hadn't been serious after all. It was just a game he played with innocent young women on the subway. In addition to doing whatever he did to make women drool over him like they did, he also liked to pretend he had power over their lives. But that still didn't answer the question of how he knew who I was and how to find me to send the job offer. I really shouldn't have responded.

Then there was an e-mail ding, and Rodney's reply appeared in my in-box. It took me two tries to open it, for my hands were shaking so much that I couldn't hold the mouse steady. "I'm glad you decided to hear us out, Katie," the message read. "Five fifteen today, the coffee shop on Broadway near Rector. You won't regret it."

I wrote the information in my planner, replied that I would meet him at the designated place and time, then deleted the e-mail. Out of sheer paranoia, I went into my sent items folder and deleted both my initial response and my confirmation. I knew Mimi wasn't nearly computer literate enough to know there even was a sent items folder, but I wasn't taking any chances. I wanted the next job firmly lined up before I left this one, willingly or otherwise.

After her outburst earlier in the afternoon, Mimi was strangely quiet the rest of the day. That only made me nervous, for it was likely just the calm before the storm. She was probably in her office plotting ways to make me look bad without making herself look stupid. I kept my fingers crossed most of the day, hoping she didn't pull one of her "Oh, before you leave today" routines of dropping something on my desk at five minutes to five.

At four thirty I took a casual stroll to the bathroom to touch up my hair and makeup. I wasn't dressed quite the way I'd like to be for a job interview, but this didn't sound like it would be a conventional job interview. It wasn't like I was begging Rod to hire me. Instead, I was asking him why I should even listen to him. He should be the one dressing up.

When I'd put a call through to Mimi that I knew would keep her occupied for a while, I printed out my résumé, then sprinted to the printer room to collect it the moment it came off the printer. I got it into my briefcase just as Mimi hung up the phone, but she still didn't come into my cube, which was a relief.

The second my computer clock said it was five, I shut it down, then gathered my purse and briefcase. I didn't change into my walking shoes, but that wasn't unusual, as I most often changed in the lobby. I liked to look professional the entire time I was in the office, ever since the day Mimi caught me with an assignment as I came through the door and I had to spend most of the morning in the wrong shoes.

My heart beat faster as I neared the coffee shop. Why was I doing this? Oh yeah, I was stuck in a dead-end job working for a complete psycho. The city sanitation workers had a more pleasant working environment than I did.

Rodney was waiting at a table by the window, just inside the doorway. With him was Mr. Right, the cute guy I'd seen on the subway. I hadn't been imagining that they knew each other. They both stood as I entered. "Katie!" Rodney greeted me, his tone warm and friendly, with none of the smarmy oil he'd had in our previous encounters. "Good to see you. And I'd like you to meet Owen Palmer, one of my colleagues."

Owen, who was just as cute as I'd remembered, actually blushed as he shook my hand. He didn't quite meet my eyes, ducking his head a little bit instead. Most guys who look that good are pretty confident about it, but his shyness was absolutely adorable. If he was part of this company, this job was looking better and better.

"Please have a seat," Rodney said. "Can I get you something to drink?"

"A cappuccino, please," I said. I normally didn't let myself buy the pricier coffee beverages, but it looked like he was paying, so I might as well indulge myself.

He headed off to the counter, which left me alone with Owen. It looked like conversation was up to me, for he seemed to be trying to read his fortune in the nutmeg sprinkles on the top of his own cappuccino. "So, do you live around Union Square?" I asked. "I noticed you yesterday at the subway station."

He blushed again, then looked up at me with a shy smile, almost meeting my eyes this time. "Yes, I do," he said, the first words I'd heard him speak. He had a pleasant voice.

"It's a great area, isn't it? I've lived around there a year, and I don't think I've even begun to explore it." I laughed. "Boy, I sound like a tourist, don't I? No native would gush this much."

Still blushing, he smiled. In spite of his dark, almost black, hair, his skin was fair, so the blushes really showed. Poor guy. I wondered how he survived in business. Maybe he was a real demon in writing. He couldn't cope with meetings, but his memos were killers.

Rodney returned to the table and placed a small swimming pool of cappuccino in front of me. Seriously, I could have used it as a hot tub. I promised myself I wouldn't drink all of it, not if I wanted to sleep that week.

He took his seat, waited for me to take a sip, then said, "I'm sure you have a lot of questions."

"Yeah, about a zillion. All of them, in fact. Your e-mails weren't very informative. You didn't even tell me what kind of company you're with."

The two men exchanged a look I couldn't read, then Rod turned back to me and said, "It's hard to fit that kind of information into an e-mail."

"It's also difficult to describe our business in a way that doesn't sound alarming," Owen added, in the first full sentence I'd heard him speak. It seemed he did okay when he was on a business footing. Maybe he just didn't know how to talk to women.

Then I realized what he'd said about the business sounding alarming. Sex slavery, I knew it. I cleared my throat so my voice wouldn't crack and said, "Um, what business are you in?"

They looked at each other again. Owen said, still in business mode, "We research and develop products that facilitate convenience for a specific population, as well as monitor and supervise the use of our products in the public marketplace."

That didn't tell me much, other than that it didn't sound like I was going to be shipped off to some South Seas isle to be a tribal ruler's love slave, unless that was the population they provided convenience for. A sex slave could be a convenience. But I didn't get that vibe here. No one would use business buzzwords to describe sex slavery. "Like software?" I asked, hoping I was in the right ballpark.

Owen smiled and blushed. "Yes, very much like software, but our business predates the computer industry by many decades."

"I see," I said, even though I didn't, not really. But I didn't care much what business they were in as long as it wasn't immoral, illegal, or dangerous to me. I barely knew what the company I currently worked for did. "And what would my role in all this be?"

Rod leaned forward, made eye contact with me and held it for a second before he said, "You'd be more in the administration end of things. You wouldn't have to concern yourself with the actual products, just the running of the business itself. You'd function in an advisory capacity to our executives."

I wasn't sure what I could advise anyone about, unless it was which fertilizer to use on which kind of plant, how to know just when to pay the bills to maximize bank interest while not making a late payment, or where to put commas in a memo, but I knew the business code phrases as well as anyone did. "In other words, I'd be an administrative assistant, like I am now."

Owen looked down at the table and shredded his paper napkin with his fingers. "Sort of, but not really," he said.

"This particular position is unique to our company," Rod said smoothly as he flashed a smile at a tall blonde entering the coffee shop. She eyed him appreciatively in return. I suspected he'd have her phone number before she left. He returned his attention to me. "It's difficult to describe this position, although it does involve some of the usual administrative functions. But believe me, this is a job you were born for. You'll never find another job that so uniquely suits your abilities."

"But how do you even know what my abilities are?" Only then did I remember the résumé in my briefcase. This wasn't going like any other job interview I'd ever been on. "I do have a résumé with me," I said as I bent to retrieve it. "Sorry, but I only made one copy."

Rod took it from me, skimmed over it absently, then handed it to Owen, who studied it more intently. "You certainly have an impressive record," Rod said, "but that's not why we want you. We've already thoroughly screened you and determined that you have the attributes we need for this position."

"Oh, so that's why you've been stalking me." Out of the corner of my eye I saw Owen grin, a totally unself-conscious grin that said, "You are so busted." If he was adorable with his blushes and shy smiles, now he was downright gorgeous. I would have been willing to scrub toilets to work in the same building with this man, but I tried to get my libido under check. That was no way to go about finding a job, even if men had been using that method to hire secretaries for ages.

"Testing you," Rod corrected.

I pondered that. Maybe it had been an emperor's new clothes deal, where the fact that I didn't join the crowds to swoon over Rod counted as something. I'd proven that I wasn't easily swayed by peer pressure, but I'd also proven that appearances did apparently count with me—although it was more Rod's smugness and oily manner that had turned me off.

"But why me?" I asked after a while. "I'm just so . . . so ordinary. There are probably hundreds—thousands, even—of people in this city with exactly the same qualifications. Okay, maybe not who have worked in a feed-and-seed store, but you see what I mean."

"You'd be surprised how rare the truly ordinary is," Owen said softly. It was the kind of thing Yogi Berra would have said, but Owen made it sound profound and mysterious. I squinted at him in confusion, and he continued. "You have a unique perspective, a way of looking at things, that we find valuable."

"Oh, I get it," I said with great relief. "You're looking for a reality check."

His face lit up, and I fell just the least bit in love with him. "Yes! Exactly."

Now everything made a lot more sense. Some big corporation actually wanted my small-town honesty and common sense, instead of looking down on me because I grew up west of the Hudson River. I still wasn't sure how they'd found me in the first place, but I was sure big companies had all the resources they needed to find the right people.

"So, would you like to pursue this further?" Rod asked. "Things can get a little complicated from this point. Our executive team would have to interview you, and of course we'd tell you more about who we are. We would expect some discretion on your part, in return. We operate out of the public spotlight, so we'd ask that you not discuss our business matters with anyone else."

There was still something just the least bit odd about all of this, but by now I was intrigued. I wanted to know who these people were, and I couldn't resist the idea of working for someone who might actually respect me a little bit, who had made such an effort to recruit me, out of all the people in New York. The more cautious part of my brain warned me that they could be playing to my ego, but curiosity overruled caution. "Sure," I said, hoping my voice didn't shake quite as much as it felt like it did.

He smiled, a real smile instead of a fake one calculated to charm, and for a second he actually looked good, proving that I'd been right about him. A less oily personality and a little effort made a big difference. "Great! If you'll excuse me for a second, I can try to line up the next step."

He got up and went outside, which left me alone with Owen, and the moment the situation turned from business to social, he got shy again and clammed up. We both sipped our cappuccinos in silence, darting little glances at each other. I'd have to get advice from Gemma on how to get a shy guy to relax and speak.

Rod came back inside, and I dabbed at my lips with a napkin, hoping I didn't have a foam mustache. "Is there any way you can get away during the day on Thursday?" he asked. "That's about the only time I can get together the people who need to meet you."

I didn't want to risk losing this. I wasn't quite sure if I was desperate to escape from Mimi or excited about this job, but I knew I'd do just about anything to pursue the opportunity. "I can take a sick day," I said, then I suddenly worried that being so willing to admit that would dim my image of small-town honesty. "I haven't taken one yet," I hurried to explain. "And if you knew my boss, you'd know they owe me a mental health day or two." Oops, I'd just committed another job interview sin, complaining about my current boss. But they didn't seem to care.

"Great. We're set, then. We'll see you at ten Thursday morning." He handed me a business card that had *MSI, Inc.* printed on it in Gothic lettering, along with his name and the usual contact information. "The address is on here, but it can be a little hard to find, so let me draw you a map." He took the card back, turned it over, and sketched in a few streets and landmarks. "Just ask for me at the front desk," he said as he handed the card back to me.

I tucked it carefully into my purse as we all stood to leave. Rod was the first to shake my hand. "I'm glad you finally decided to meet with us," he said.

"I figured it was either that or you would have driven me crazy."

"You're not wrong about that," he said, and he wasn't laughing or smiling. "You have no idea how much my bosses want me to get you on board."

Owen came around the table and shook my hand. "I look forward to having you on the team," he said softly, meeting my eyes for the first time, and then immediately blushing from his collar to the roots of his hair. He had the prettiest dark blue eyes, but they didn't do him any good if he didn't let anyone see them. He and Rod made quite a team. Rod acted like he looked like Owen, and Owen acted like he looked like Rod. Maybe there had been a science experiment gone wrong somewhere in their past.

"I'll see y'all on Thursday," I said, so flustered that I forgot not to talk Texan. Then, with my head still spinning, I turned to walk up Broadway toward home, pausing to change into my walking shoes when I was well out of sight of the coffee shop.

This was another occasion when I was glad of the nearly hour-long walk home. I needed to think. For one thing, I needed to find a way to explain to my roommates that I was pursuing that job offer after all, but I figured I'd wait until I had the job sewn up. In the meantime I needed a reason I was getting home so late, but in New York that was easy.

Even Marcia, the workaholic, was home by the time I got there. She and Gemma looked up at me from where they sat on the sofa eating Chinese takeout. "You're home late," Marcia commented. "Bad Mimi day?"

"The worst," I said, kicking off my shoes and dropping my purse and briefcase. "I did some window shopping on the way home to help me recover."

"And you didn't buy anything?" Gemma asked with a raised eyebrow. "I admire your restraint." I refrained from telling her that it was easy to be restrained when you had no money to spend. She patted the sofa cushion next to her. "Take a load off. We've got plenty of kung pao."

The next person I had to fool was Mimi, but I knew that shouldn't be too difficult. I didn't wear any makeup the next morning, so I'd look pale and sickly. As I walked into lower Manhattan, I kept an eye out for the building that supposedly housed MSI, Inc. According to Rod's map, it was across from City Hall Park and down a side street.

I tripped over my own feet and had to steady myself against the side of a building when I saw it. It looked like a turreted medieval castle looming over the more Victorian storefronts. Why hadn't I seen that before? I was usually too busy trying to look into the lobby of the Woolworth Building when I walked that stretch of sidewalk, now that I thought about of it.

That whole day at work, I played the "I'm coming down with something" game. I looked as listless as possible, coughed every so often, and made my voice hoarser as the day progressed. By the time the day ended, most of my coworkers were telling me I should stay home the next day. Even Mimi had commented on my illness, but without much sympathy. She seemed more worried that I'd spread the germs to her.

That meant no one would be the least bit suspicious when I called in sick the next morning. As I walked home that evening I wondered if I'd managed to convince myself that I was sick. I had a headache, my legs felt heavy, and every time I heard a subway train pass beneath a sidewalk grating I envied the people who weren't walking. It would be so nice not to have to worry about every little dollar, to be able to ride whenever I felt like it. I reminded myself that they were crammed up close to one another, while I was aboveground, enjoying fresh air and exercise, but this time the mind games weren't very effective. It wasn't that I wanted to have a ride to and from work every day. I just wanted the option without feeling guilty about it. I wanted not to have to keep a running cash register tape in my head so I'd know where every penny went. Rod and Owen hadn't discussed money when talking to me about the job, but if they were recruiting that heavily, there had to be some perks involved. Even a few hundred extra a month would be nice. It would make the difference between getting by and really living.

I didn't have to explain anything to my roommates to keep them from getting suspicious. I just declared that evening that I was going to take a mental health day, and they cheered, saying it was about time. Gemma even commented that I looked tired and needed a break to keep from getting sick. That gave me an excuse to go to bed early.

While Gemma and Marcia watched TV in the living room, I tried to compare the little map on the back of Rod's business card to my stash of New York guidebooks. You'd think a building as striking as the one I'd seen would be listed, but there was no mention of it. The street it was on didn't appear on any maps I could find. I knew there were all sorts of twisty little side streets in that part of town, mostly from having been lost on them, but I would have thought that all of them would be on the map. That just made this whole situation even more interesting.

I called in and left a hoarse message on the answering system the next morning before the office opened, then stayed in bed while Gemma and Marcia got ready for work. As soon as they were gone, I printed a few copies of my résumé from Marcia's home computer, put on my interview suit, and put my hair up before taking it back down.

They wanted me for my girl-next-door values, so there was no point in giving them a city girl.

This time, I let myself take the subway. I didn't want to have to carry extra shoes, and I didn't want to arrive at the interview tired and sweaty. I got off at City Hall and crossed the park, pausing to flip a penny in the fountain for good luck. Then, following Rod's instructions, I crossed Park Row and headed down a narrow side street that apparently did exist, even if it wasn't on any map. Again I saw what looked like a medieval castle, with an entrance that looked more like it belonged on a cathedral than on an office building. But the shield on the wall next to the giant wooden doors bore the same logo as Rod's business card, so I knew this must be the place.

There was a gargoyle perched on the portico that sheltered the door, and I could have sworn I saw it wink at me as I gathered my nerves and stepped toward the door. I reached to push the door open, but before I touched it, it swung open on its own.

The interior was dim, most of the light coming through stained-glass windows set high in the walls. Once my eyes adjusted, I saw a security guard seated at a raised desk in the middle of the lobby. Instead of the polyester rent-a-cop uniforms you usually saw on building security guards, he looked like he was wearing royal livery, with the company logo embroidered on his sleeves at the wrists.

I stepped up to the desk and said, "I'm Kathleen Chandler. I have a ten o'clock appointment with Rodney Gwaltney of Personnel."

He ran a thumb down a giant book that lay open on his desk and said, "Ah, yes, Miss Chandler. We've been expecting you." He placed his palm on a crystal ball that sat on his desk and said softly, "Rod, your visitor is here." Now, that was an unusual intercom system. The crystal ball was held by a pewter dragon sculpture that looked like something I'd once seen on sale at a Renaissance festival. The crystal glowed, then the guard looked back at me, smiled, and said, "He'll be with you in a moment."

It didn't take Rod long at all to come down the sweeping staircase at the back of the lobby. "Katie, good to see you," he said. "Right this way." He escorted me toward the stairs, saying as he walked, "Unfortunately, we don't have elevators in this building. I hope you don't mind the stairs."

"My apartment's a walk-up. I think I'll manage," I said as I followed him.

If I'd been intrigued before, now I was downright curious. What kind of company would be based in a building like this? It was a pretty safe bet that I could rule out anything in the high-tech industry. I remembered what Owen had said the other day about predating computers. Something financial, maybe? That wouldn't be out of the ordinary around here. "Curiouser and curiouser," I muttered under my breath.

"What was that?" Rod asked.

"Nothing. Just feeling a bit like Alice."

We'd reached the top of the stairs and now faced a pair of doors almost as impressive as the front doors. "Well, Alice, welcome to Wonderland," he said as the doors swung open.

I'm not sure even Alice would have believed what I saw inside that room.

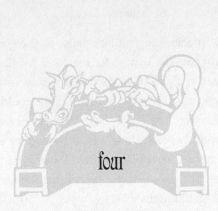

four

I felt like I'd stumbled into a Broadway-caliber production of *Camelot*. This was no conference room. It was a great hall, with soaring, Gothic-arched windows—complete with stained-glass crest insets—along one wall, banners hanging from a wood-beamed ceiling, and a giant round table in the middle of the room.

Seated around that table was an example of just about every weird type of person I'd seen in New York—the kind of weird that others didn't seem to notice. There were a few women with fairy wings, several people with pointed elf ears, and some tiny gnomes like the figures I'd seen in parks around town and assumed were a bizarre form of animatronic lawn decor. The gnomes sat on pillows piled high in their chairs so they could reach the conference table, while the fairies floated inches above their seats.

Either the company was celebrating Halloween a month early and

I'd interrupted an elaborate costume party, or there was something very, very weird going on. I voted for the latter. While I knew it was possible to strap on a pair of wings or add points to your ears with plastic tips, there was no way a normal person could shrink into a gnome, and these were very clearly living beings, not lawn ornaments.

Mixed in with the freak show were a number of people in ordinary business attire. I recognized Owen, looking particularly handsome in a pin-striped navy suit. He flashed me a smile, then ducked his head and blushed furiously.

Rod cleared his throat and gestured toward me with a flourish. "Ladies and gentlebeings, may I present to you Miss Kathleen Chandler. Katie, to her friends."

I felt about twenty pairs of eyes on me as every person in the room turned to look. Feeling self-conscious, I gave them as big a smile as I could muster and fluttered my fingers at them in an awkward wave. Rod stepped forward to pull a chair out for me. I sat down, then he helped me scoot up to the table before taking the seat next to me.

He clasped his hands together on top of the table, and suddenly he was a polished business executive rather than a sleazy pickup artist. "As you're all aware," he began, "we've increased our recruitment efforts substantially in recent weeks. Unfortunately, immunes are few and far between, and they don't last long in this city. The new varieties of antipsychotic drugs aren't helping matters, because those apparently undo the immunity and make people susceptible again. That reduces the pool even further."

"We're working to find ways to counter that," Owen put in, clearly in business mode, for he spoke strongly and clearly, and his skin tone remained even.

"In the meantime," Rod continued, "it leaves us at something of a loss. We need immunes now more than ever, and there aren't as many to be found. That's what makes Miss Chandler here such a rare find. Not only is she entirely immune—according to every test we've put her through—but she seems to have held on well to her sanity and common sense."

He might have spoken too soon about the sanity. I felt like I'd left it behind somewhere out on the street. I must have looked as confused as I felt, for an elderly man seated across the table from me remarked, "Obviously, she hasn't yet been briefed."

Rod snapped to attention, and I assumed this must be the head honcho. He was a distinguished-looking gentleman with silver hair and a neatly trimmed silver beard and mustache. It was hard to tell just how old he was, other than that he was quite old. "No, sir," Rod stammered, having now lost all pretense of swagger. "I thought it was best to wait until—"

The boss cut him off. "Until she'd lost that precious sanity you were so proud of?" he asked, his voice stern but not unkind. He turned to me. "My dear, I believe we owe you an explanation or two." His voice was deep and rich, with a hint of roughness, as though he'd recently gone a long time without talking. I thought I detected a trace of an accent, but I couldn't identify it. When it came to accents, I was only good at figuring out which part of Texas someone came from.

"Do you believe in magic?" he asked. That's not on the list of likely job interview questions, so I didn't have an answer for him. It seemed to be a rhetorical question anyway, which was good, because I couldn't get my chin off the table so I could answer. "What about elves or fairies? Are these real to you, or are they stories?"

I finally got my brain in gear. "Well, up until a few minutes ago, I would have said they weren't real. But something tells me I would have been wrong. I'm not sure yet about magic."

The boss looked toward Rod with a smile. "You did say she had common sense." He turned back to me. "Magic is real. Unfortunately, the very qualities that make you valuable to us make it difficult for us to prove it to you. You see, you are one of the rare human beings without the slightest hint of magic in you."

That didn't sound like such a good thing to me. After all, doesn't everyone wish for a little magic from time to time? That's the reason Harry Potter books fly off the shelves, little girls try to wiggle their noses after watching *Bewitched* on TV Land, and audiences clap their hands to cure Tinker Bell, no matter how silly that makes them feel. Being told that magic does exist but that I had no part of it was a huge disappointment, whether or not I was ready to believe they were telling me the truth about magic.

My distress must have shown on my face, for Owen, who was seated at the boss's right hand, leaned toward me across the table. "That's actually valuable to us," he said softly, as though he and I were the only two people in the room. His words had the confident ring of his business persona, but his manner was shy. "Most people have only enough magic in them to make magic work on them. They can be influenced by spells or fooled by illusions. Meanwhile, those of us who are magical, who have the power to do magic for ourselves, also can be influenced by magic." I wasn't sure what to make of the fact that he'd used the words "we" and "us." Did that mean Owen was a wizard?

"You, however," he continued, "are of the rare breed who can neither do magic nor be influenced by magic. You see the world as it is. You see through the illusions we use to shield the magic from the rest of the world. Surely you've noticed things you can't explain?"

Oh, boy, had I. I supposed I should have been freaking out about all these revelations, but they came as something of a relief to me. This meant I wasn't going crazy after all. That, or I'd suffered a total psychotic break. "I'd just always heard New York was kind of weird," I said at last. "I guess we don't have magic back in Texas."

There was laughter around the table. "No, you don't," a man about ninety degrees around the table said. "Just a few isolated pockets. For the most part, settlement in that area is too recent to have a fully developed magical culture, except among the native groups."

That actually made a strange sort of sense. All of this did. "Okay, that explains a lot. But it doesn't explain who you are or why you need me."

All heads turned to the big boss. "We are Magic, Spells, and Illusions, Inc.," he said. "Magic is our business—and I don't mean the card tricks and fake wands that your people think of as magic. We create the spells that magical folk use to get through their daily lives."

This made less sense. I shook my head. "But don't you people have spell books handed down through generations? Or have I seen too many movies?"

Owen picked up the explanation. I wondered what his job here was. "While it is true that there are some timeless spells, we also need spells that keep up with the pace of modern life. None of the ancient spells passed down from our forefathers would be of much help in summoning a subway train, for example."

"I thought that's what you were doing," I said. "Well, no, I didn't think you were really calling the train, but I did think that's what it looked like you were doing."

He gave me a wry grin. "I didn't even try to mask that spell—not that it would have mattered to you. Nearly everyone stands on the subway platform, urging a train to come soon. I'm just more effective at it than most people."

I felt sick and dizzy. Maybe this was one of those dreams you have the night before a big event that you're anxious about, where you dream the whole event but it's gone horribly bizarre. At any minute I'd wake up and realize I'd dreamed the wildest job interview ever. I pinched my thigh under the table, but I was still there at the round table in the great hall.

"A lot of what we do also involves illusion to hide the nature of who we are or what we do," Rod said, apparently not noticing that I was on the verge of a total meltdown. "That's why you see so many things others don't. One rule we have about magic is that nonmagical folk can't see what we're doing—although that does no good with people like you. Most people see only ordinary humans when they encounter fairies, elves, and other magical creatures. They see what we want them to see when we do magic."

I nodded like I understood. I did, in a way. In fact, all of this made too much sense, and I knew I shouldn't be buying such outlandish explanations so easily. I needed proof, but they'd built themselves an easy out if I asked for it. They could just say I couldn't see what they were doing. Then I looked at the fairies floating above their seats and the gnomes seated on the piles of cushions. I didn't know what to believe anymore.

"It was your immunity to illusion that helped us find you," Rod said. "Owen noticed you a couple of weeks ago, staring at something you shouldn't have seen, and reported it to me." I tried to remember what I might have seen a couple of weeks ago, but that seemed like a century and a half ago now. Then my brain zeroed in on the fact that it was Owen who'd noticed me from afar, and I felt my cheeks grow warm in a blush worthy of Owen himself. I reminded myself that it was my magic immunity Owen had noticed, not my great legs or bouncy, shiny hair, as Rod continued.

"So we began observing you, and you did appear to react to things that should have been veiled to you, but you weren't extremely obvious about your reactions, so we weren't sure. We'd noticed that you were most likely to take the subway on Monday mornings, so we set up the test for you. Owen made sure that the train I was already on arrived at the right time, and then we were able to measure your reaction to me."

If I'd felt sick and dizzy before, I felt worse now. I didn't like the idea of these freaks spending a week or so watching me. "How was I supposed to react?" I asked.

He gave me a sheepish smile. "What do you see when you look at me?" he asked. All the women in the room leaned forward with great interest, but I couldn't think of a diplomatic way to phrase it. He must have noticed my discomfort, for he said, "Don't worry, I know. You won't hurt my feelings."

"Well, um, well, your nose is a little big, and you could use a good skin-care routine," I said with a wince. The other women in the room stared at him, then looked at each other with raised eyebrows. "But it wasn't the way you looked that put me off that morning," I hurried to add. "It was more your personality. You were kind of sleazy, and you acted like you thought you were hot stuff, which is never attractive."

"All part of the test," he said, as one of the fairies on the other side of the room rolled her eyes and a business-suited woman snorted.

"So, what was that supposed to prove, that I have good taste in men?"

"What you see isn't what other people see. Let's just say that the face I show the world is a far cry from the way you see me. I was also using a fairly intense attraction spell, both in the subway and with your friends. Your reaction to my appearance could have been just your personal preference, but believe me, if you could be influenced in any way by magic, you would have been affected by the attraction spell, no matter what your personal tastes might be."

I remembered my roommates comparing him to Johnny Depp and wondered if that was the illusion he wore or the effects of his spell. Then I realized that I was taking all of this seriously. I'd yet to see any proof that magic really existed. I'd just seen that some rather unusual people could apparently walk the streets of New York without drawing unwanted attention. "That's all very interesting," I said, "but it's not as effective a proof as you might think. I mean, there have been a lot of men everyone else seems to think are gorgeous while I'm not impressed. Take George Clooney. I don't find him appealing at all, but everyone gushes over him."

"Would you like something to drink?" Owen asked in what

seemed like a major non sequitur or evasive action, until a small silver tray bearing a crystal goblet of water appeared in front of me with a poof and a flash of light that lingered for a second. I looked up at Owen, then he waved his hand and a red rose appeared on the tray next to the goblet. "Or would you prefer coffee, perhaps?" The goblet disappeared and was replaced by a steaming mug. "Cream or sugar?" he asked with a mischievous smile that was almost as cute as the grin I'd seen Tuesday.

I tried to think of a way this could be a trick. I was sure there was some way he could have staged that. Maybe there was something in the table that could spring up at the touch of the right button. That might explain the initial appearance of the tray when I hadn't been looking, but I wasn't sure how the coffee could have just appeared. I tried to keep my hands from trembling as I reached to pick up the coffee mug. I brought it to my lips, but I could tell as it got near that the coffee would be too hot to drink.

"Too hot for you?" Owen asked, then waved his hand, and I felt a puff of cool air sweep past me. Now the coffee was just the right drinking temperature. I would have dropped the mug in shock, but the coffee smelled too good to waste just for the sake of a dramatic gesture.

"I don't suppose you can conjure up some Valium?" I asked, trying to keep my voice steady.

"Does this mean you believe us?" the head honcho asked.

I thought about his question. I knew that the more I considered things, the more excuses I could come up with to explain everything away, but I'd reached the point that any explanation I could come up with would only be hideously complicated, something worthy of Agent Scully. I'd spent my college years yelling at the television and complaining about how someone so supposedly smart could be so dense and insist on disregarding evidence that was so obvious.

The only noncomplicated way I could think of to explain people with fairy wings, the unreasonable attraction of every woman in sight to a man I found repulsive at the time, and the sudden appearance of refreshments out of thin air was that I was the victim of the latest television reality show. There could be hidden cameras recording my reactions. But then I remembered that I'd seen weird stuff from the moment I got to New York. They couldn't have been following me all that time.

No, chances were very good that this was real. "Yeah, I do think I believe you," I said at last. "But where do I fit into all this?"

"It's like Owen said the other day," Rod put in. "We need a reality check. We need someone who can tell us what's really there. Imagine if someone wrote a clause into a contract, then veiled it so we couldn't see it. But you could. If we compare what we see to what you see, we have a better chance of getting to the truth."

"So what you're saying is that my superpower is that I'm totally ordinary and unmagical?"

"That's pretty much it," Rod said with a grin. "What do you think?"

"I don't know yet what to think." Any decision I made in this room, surrounded by strange people and with that red rose on the tray in front of me, was bound to be a bad one. "Can I get back to you?"

"Take all the time you need," the boss said kindly. "I'm sure this has been a lot for you to take in and understand in such a short time. Believe me, I understand."

"I'll get back to you on Monday, after I've had the weekend to consider."

"You have my contact information on my business card," Rod said. "We can set up another meeting to talk specifics. But we'd like to get a firm statement of interest from you before we get into issues like salary and benefits. You'll still be free to turn us down if we can't come to an agreement there, but we'd like to be sure you're joining us because you find the prospect interesting rather than because of the amount of money we'll be throwing your way."

I liked the way the idea of throwing money at me sounded, but I still wanted to think about this. Part of me still wasn't sure I was awake yet. The real job interview that happened when I woke up would involve stuff like filling out long applications that managed to reduce everything on my résumé to boring inadequacy.

I thanked the room in general for taking the time to meet with me, then Rod escorted me out and down the stairs. "I'm sorry if that was overwhelming for you. We haven't yet found an easy way to say 'Oh, by the way, magic's real. Do you want a job?'"

"I can imagine," I said. And I could. I couldn't think of a way they could have explained it to me without causing a little bit of a freak-out.

We reached the front door and Rod shook my hand. "Thank you again for coming in and hearing us out. I do hope you choose to join us. We need you, and I think you'd enjoy working here."

The doors swung open and I stepped back into the bustle of lower Manhattan, feeling like I'd moved forward centuries in time. "Hey sweetheart, I take it things went well for you," a voice near me said.

I looked around for a bum who might be on the sidewalk nearby, watching comings and goings, but I didn't see another living being. There was a sharp whistle and the voice said, "Hey, up here." I craned my neck to see the gargoyle perched on the awning over the door. If I wasn't mistaken, it was the same gargoyle I sometimes saw at Grace Church, the one whose occasional presence disturbed me so.

"Let me guess, you're real, too, but most people don't see you at all," I said.

"Got it in one," he said, and this time I saw his grotesque mouth move, so I knew he was the one talking to me. "Sam's the name, building security's my game. This here's the day job. I sometimes fill in at other spots around town."

"Well, nice to meet you, Sam," I said, feeling like Alice must have when she found herself in a conversation with a white rabbit and a deck of playing cards.

"I coulda told 'em long before pretty boy spotted you that you were special. In fact, it was looking at me that got you noticed by him. He was gonna stop and say hello to me, but you were doing a big double take as you passed by. So, anyway, doll, what's it gonna be? You joinin' us?"

"I don't know yet. I have to think about it." Then I realized that I was standing on the sidewalk having a conversation with a gargoyle. "Uh, Sam, what do people see when I'm standing here talking to you?"

"Don't worry, babe, since I'm interactin' with you, you're safe inside my 'don't notice me' field. Unless, of course, someone like you happens along."

"That's good to know," I said, nodding. "Well, Sam, it was nice meeting you. I suppose I'll see you around town, even if I don't take the job."

"Oh, you'll take it, all right. I can tell."

I wished I was that certain, but I wasn't sure that someone who had conversations with stone gargoyles should be allowed to make potentially life-altering decisions.

I knew this would get a lot easier if I'd just wake up. Otherwise, I was sure I'd be late for my job interview. Unfortunately, I showed no signs of waking. On those nights when I dreamed worst-case scenarios and bizarre twists on the next day's big events, I usually woke every half hour to look at the clock and make sure I wasn't oversleeping, but if I was still asleep, I was resting better than usual.

That meant this must be real. For a change, I wished I could walk home. I needed the thinking time. And, to be perfectly honest, I wanted the chance to look at New York with the knowledge I'd just gained. I wanted another look at all the weird stuff that had been bothering me all along. I didn't have to worry about the Grace Church sometime-gargoyle anymore, now that I'd met him, but I was sure there were other things I'd tried to excuse in my head that should now make perfect sense.

But there was no way I was walking home in my good shoes. If I didn't ruin them, I'd ruin my feet. I caught the M103 bus on Park Row. It would cost just as much as the subway, but it offered some of the same mental transition benefits as walking. I got off the bus at Fourteenth Street and headed home. Glancing at my watch as I entered the building, I was surprised to find that it was just past noon. I'd felt like I was in that conference room all day, but it had been little more than an hour.

It felt weird being at home alone during the day, but I was too restless to sit around the apartment. I changed into jeans, tennis shoes, and a sweatshirt, then went downstairs and headed over to Union Square. The market in the heart of the city made me homesick at times, but it also felt like a reassuring piece of home. I could talk to the farmers who sold their produce there and actually sound like I knew what I was talking about. This, I knew, was real, and the only magic involved was the miracle that turned sun, water, seed, and soil into fruits and vegetables. I'd never been there on a weekday before, and I noticed that the market was smaller than usual, without any of the vendors I knew. I picked up a few things I could turn into dinner that night, some apples for a pie, and a small bunch of flowers to brighten up the apartment.

Today the market had made me homesick. I'd consulted my family on every major decision I'd made in my life, but this was one decision I had to make by myself. My parents had been opposed to me going to New York, trying first guilt and then scare tactics to change my mind. But even if I hadn't ultimately gone along with their advice, I had consulted them. I couldn't begin to imagine what they'd say if I told them I'd been offered a job at Magic, Inc.

Then again, they'd never had a conversation with a gargoyle, so what advice could they offer?

I went home, opened the windows, put some music on, and sat down at the kitchen table to peel apples while I thought about everything that had happened this week. It was easier to think about magic while doing something so mundane.

My parents were far enough away that I could get away with just telling them I'd changed jobs, but what about my roommates? They'd expect to be in on the decision. They'd helped me find my current job, and they were constantly on the lookout for something better for me. I'd mentioned Rod's e-mails to them. They were going to think I was stark raving insane.

Or would they? I might have been tempted to tell them about all the magic stuff if Rod hadn't already warned me that it had to be a secret. They were pretty open-minded. They might actually believe it. Or else they'd ship me back home for medical help. I wished I could find a way to get their input on the decision, though. Sharing the burden would make it easier on me.

My pie was just coming out of the oven when Gemma got home. "Don't tell me you spent your day off cooking," she said.

"Not the whole day. But they had some gorgeous apples at the market, and I couldn't resist."

"I thought the market was closed Thursdays."

A shiver went down my spine as I remembered that the vendors had been different. Did that mean it was a magic market? It would be just my luck if the place I went to ground myself turned out to be magical. This new job was looking more and more inevitable. "Oh, it was just a sidewalk vendor," I said, hoping my voice didn't sound as shaky as it felt.

Gemma didn't seem to notice anything odd about the way I was acting. "It smells like heaven," she said, opening the oven door and taking a whiff.

"It should be ready to eat about the time Marcia gets here."

She put on the teakettle, then sat down at the kitchen table. "What else did you do today?"

I hated lying to her, but this wasn't my secret to share. I wasn't even ready to talk about changing jobs. "Oh, I mostly just took it easy and walked around. I really did try to use this as a de-stress day."

Marcia came home a few minutes later. "Mmm, something smells good."

"Katie baked a pie," Gemma said.

Soon, we were sitting around the table together, chatting about life in general while eating apple pie. I felt the years of friendship surrounding me like a warm blanket, and I wondered if maybe I should share some of what was going on. It might make the decision easier.

To be honest, though, I knew what I wanted to do. I wanted to give this a try, to learn all about magic. I wanted to be valuable to a wizard who was capable of making incredible things happen with a wave of his hand. I wanted to get away from Mimi. It was a no-brainer, really.

But I also knew I was getting carried away with the idea and needed to get back to reality before I could decide for sure. One more day in the office, I told myself. Then a normal weekend. Maybe a little research to see if what I knew of the story checked out. And then I could decide with a clear head.

Or else I'd wake up in the loony bin.

five

Going back to work the next morning was one of the most difficult things I'd ever done. It was astounding how different I'd felt during my day off. Even with that huge decision hanging over my head, I'd felt lighter. But today the weight was back on my shoulders as I trudged down Broadway.

I was granted a minor reprieve in that Mimi wasn't at the office yet when I got there. I answered the expected inquiries from my coworkers about my health and only then remembered that I was supposed to have been sick. That gave me enough warning to look weak and to throw in the occasional cough when Mimi got there. She tended to be suspicious of people who took sick leave, along with people who suddenly wore interview-appropriate clothes. It never seemed to dawn on her that she wouldn't have to worry about losing her staff if she wasn't such a bitch.

And speak of the devil, I heard her coming down the hallway, already complaining about something. I tried to look diligent at my desk and hoped she passed me by. No such luck. "Oh, you're back," she purred as she paused in front of my cubicle door. "Feeling better?" Her tone implied that she thought my illness was fake. The fact that it was didn't make me like it any more.

I gave her a weak smile. "Yes, thank you." I punctuated it with a little cough before turning back to my computer.

But that was only her opening act. She called me to her office every five minutes, loading me with enough work that someone who really had been sick would be sure to collapse under the weight. I wasn't holding up too well as it was. "You have a lot to make up for," Mimi chirped as she handed me the most recent stack of documents to sort and staple. I restrained myself from asking why she hadn't had the copier collate the stack because I knew her answer would be that if I had been there the day before, I could have handled the copying myself.

I spent the afternoon in the conference room putting together copies of multipage reports for a board meeting. I'd almost finished, incurring multiple paper cuts in the process, when Mimi came into the room. "What are you doing?" she asked.

It took all the patience I could muster to say, "I'm putting together the reports, like you asked me to."

In that instant she turned into Evil Mimi, complete with glowing eyes. I wondered if she really was a monster, but then I, of all people, would see her monster form when she changed. No, she was just a nasty human. "I made a major change an hour ago, and now you don't have time to get the right reports ready in time for the meeting."

There was no point in telling her that if she'd told me she changed the report, I would have had time. Human logic didn't apply to her. I was supposed to read her mind and pick up the new version just as she made it. I was tempted to tell her I was incapable of reading minds or doing any other magic tricks, so she'd just have to communicate with me the normal way.

Then again, why not? I already had the next job lined up, and as long as they paid me a living wage, it had to be better than this. I stared her down. "Mimi, I am sick of you blaming your lack of organization on me. Why didn't you give me the report when you changed it? How was I supposed to know you'd changed it if you didn't tell me? I can't read your mind—really. Believe it or not, I don't have ESP. I don't have a shred of magical talent in me, and I've actually had that verified. There is no way I can win with you, and I'm sick of trying. I quit. Staple your own damn report."

And with that I put the stapler down on the conference table and walked out. She didn't say a word. Either she was shocked that her meek little assistant had finally stood up to her, or a blood vessel in her brain had exploded and she was having a stroke.

It must have been the former, because I heard her behind me even before I got to my cubicle. "You can't quit," she said.

"Watch me," I replied. "Just give me a second to write up a formal letter of resignation. I could give the standard two weeks notice, but I think we'd both agree that it's better if I don't. If I'm this saucy now, just think what I'd be like if you couldn't fire me because I'd already resigned."

"That report—the new version—had better be copied, stapled, and on my desk before you leave today or you're fired."

"You're not paying attention, are you? I already quit."

She stalked back to her office. The prairie dog heads were once again in evidence, shocked faces peering above cubicle walls. I sat down at my desk, found Rod's business card and dialed his number. While I waited for an answer, I typed a two-line letter of resignation. I couldn't remember the last time I'd felt this good.

When Rod answered, I said simply, "It's Katie. Let's talk turkey."

"So you are interested? I thought you were going to take the weekend to think it over."

"It didn't take a weekend."

Smooth operator that he was, it didn't take him long to recover and get right to business. "Okay, here's the package we have to offer you. Everything is, of course, negotiable." He named a salary figure that made my head spin. It wasn't astronomically high, but it meant I wouldn't have to be so careful about my pennies anymore. I might even be able to afford to buy my friends some rounds of drinks, to make up for all those they'd bought me. "Full medical and dental. We do have on-site healers, but they might not be effective on you. We offer a full pension plan, as well as life insurance. Ten days sick leave per year, and you accumulate a day of vacation per month, which you can start taking after six months of service. Is there anything you'd like to negotiate?"

It all sounded good to me, and better than what I currently had, but I didn't want to sound so desperate that I'd agree right away. I tried to think of something to ask for, then had a brainstorm. "I want a monthly unlimited MetroCard, provided by the company. And if I have to work late at night, I want a company-provided cab ride home."

"Sounds reasonable to me, and I suspect we can do better than a cab ride." I could only begin to imagine what that company might use for transportation. I had a mental image of arriving home from work in Cinderella's pumpkin coach. "So, do we have a deal?"

"We have a deal."

"Glad to have you aboard. Now, when do you want to start?"

"How's Monday?"

"So soon?"

"I, um, already resigned from my current job." I figured it was safe to tell him, now that I'd officially accepted.

He laughed. "That bad, huh?"

"You have no idea."

"Why don't you take Monday to rest and recharge, and we'll make it Tuesday? You should have some transition time."

That sounded reasonable to me. "Okay, Tuesday it is."

"We'll see you then. Welcome aboard."

It was only after I hung up that I thought of one more thing I should have asked for: having Mimi turned into a frog. It wasn't even like they'd have to change that much. Oh well. It didn't matter so much as long as I'd no longer have to deal with her. I printed my resignation letter, retrieved it from the printer, signed it, and dropped it on Mimi's desk.

She looked at it, then up at me. "You're serious?"

"As a funeral."

"What will you do?" She almost sounded concerned, but I suspected she was more worried about not having an assistant than about me ending up on the streets.

"I've already got another job, paying a thousand dollars a month more than this one, and with better benefits. Now, my office is fairly well organized, so you should be able to find everything you need. I don't have any projects pending, other than that report you didn't give me in time." I unclipped my employee ID badge and handed it over, along with my office key. "So, anyway, have fun!"

Applause came from somewhere in the office as I walked back to my cubicle to collect my belongings, but it died down pretty quickly. Those left behind couldn't afford to further antagonize the monster.

I didn't have many personal items in my cube, so all I had to do was put my coffee mug and Dilbert calendar in my briefcase, then grab my purse and go. I had a sense of what the fairies must feel like as I walked out of that building for the last time, for my feet didn't seem to touch the ground. I hadn't realized how badly that job had worn me down.

Ironically, although I would now be earning a larger salary and had just negotiated unlimited use of the public transportation system as part of my compensation, I chose to walk home. It was hard to feel weightless on the subway, and I was enjoying the feeling. The only thing I had to worry about now was explaining things to Gemma and Marcia.

They wouldn't be at all surprised or upset that I'd quit my job. There had been many times over the past year when they'd even offered to cover my share of the rent for a month or so until I could find a new job if I needed to quit immediately for my own sanity, but I couldn't bring myself to accept their charity after they'd already given me a free ride for my first month in the city. But explaining to them that I had met with and accepted a job from the guy I'd been complaining about would be more difficult. Given Rod's apparent propensity for popping up around town, I knew I'd better tell at least a version of the truth.

By the time I reached Houston Street, I had a plan. I'd just say that he'd followed up after the uncomfortable encounter at the café with an apology and a much more professional job offer, one I'd considered worth exploring. The next challenge would be explaining what kind of company it was and what my job would be. I wondered if MSI had a standard cover story they gave their nonmagical employees. I supposed I could just say it was another admin position but with more responsibility, and I could try to remember the way Owen described the company in that first meeting, which seemed like it had happened at least a year ago. So much had changed since then.

This time I didn't veer off before Grace Church. Now that I knew the gargoyle was supposed to come and go, it wasn't nearly as disturbing. I think part of me also wanted to see if he'd be there, to see if it had all been real. Or had I just quit my job for nothing?

No, there was a gargoyle perched on the chapel roof. As I approached, he waved a wing at me. "Hey doll, welcome to the club."

I stepped into the churchyard and craned my neck to look up at him. "Hi, Sam. And thanks. I'm looking forward to it. I think."

"Oh, don't worry about it. You'll do great. They're good people, and they need you, so they'll treat you right. You picked a good time to join, too. Things are about to get interesting."

"Interesting?" I asked, the nervousness returning.

"Oh, it's always interesting, but with the big boss back from retirement, this is a particularly good time."

I wondered if he meant that distinguished gentleman who had been at the interview, but I decided to wait and learn the ropes at the office rather than quizzing a gargoyle. "It was nice to see you again, Sam," I said, turning to head back out to the street. "See you Tuesday."

"Not if I see you first."

It was a measure of just how much my life had changed this week that I didn't feel the least bit odd about having a conversation with a gargoyle. It felt a lot less odd than avoiding that stretch of street because the gargoyle was inexplicably coming and going.

When I got home, my roommates were already there, which was unusual, even for a Friday. I knew I'd have to tell them my news right away, or else they'd accuse me of holding out on them when they found out. "You'll never believe what I just did," I said as soon as I got through the front door.

"You quit your job," Gemma said without looking up from her magazine. She sat with her feet out in front of her, cotton between her toes, like she'd just polished her toenails.

I put my purse and briefcase on the dining table and joined her on the sofa, feeling a little limp now that she'd taken the wind out of my sails. "How'd you know?"

"The answering machine was full of messages for you when we got home," Marcia said from the bedroom, sticking a head covered in hot rollers into the living room. "Your coworkers were worried about you, and Mimi didn't think you were serious. She wants you to come in over the weekend to finish a project." She disappeared back into the bedroom.

"I put it in writing," I said with a sigh. "I don't know how much more serious I could be."

"You quit, just like that?" Gemma asked.

"Yeah, angry snit and all."

"She finally pushed you too far."

"That, and I already had another job lined up. I'd planned to give notice, but Evil Mimi persuaded me otherwise."

Marcia came into the room, wearing her bathrobe, her hair still in curlers. "What other job?"

I launched into the story I'd concocted about Rod getting back in touch with me and apologizing. "So it turned out it was for real, and it was a good opportunity," I concluded.

"That's why you called in sick yesterday!" Marcia said, sounding like Sherlock Holmes when he's just solved the case. "You were out interviewing. But why didn't you say anything?"

Fortunately, I had a story ready for that, too. "It was a decision I had to make for myself." Even as I said it, I realized it was the truth. "I lean too heavily on you guys to help me figure out what I should do, and I needed to figure this out on my own."

"Well, congratulations," Gemma said. "Now, hurry and get dressed. You're going to be late."

"Late for what?"

"Our big blind date."

My heart sank. "Oh, that." I supposed it was too late to call it off, but I was so drained that all I wanted to do was curl up on the sofa with some ice cream and watch an old movie. But if I'd managed to tell off my boss and stalk out of the office, I could face a blind date. "What should I wear?"

Apparently, I'd said the magic words. Okay, so it wasn't real magic, but it worked almost as well as anything Owen had demonstrated. Gemma was off the couch in a heartbeat. "I've already got something picked out for you."

We met Connie and Jim at a cozy Italian restaurant in the Village. With Jim were three uncomfortable-looking guys. I wondered if he'd had to bribe his friends to show up. He'd shown time and again that he was willing to do just about anything for Connie, so I wouldn't put it past him.

Jim made the awkward introductions as we stood on the sidewalk in front of the restaurant. Marcia's date, introduced as Ethan Wainwright, was tall and lanky, with wavy brown hair and glasses that hid his eyes. He not only looked like he wanted to be anywhere but there, he looked like he wasn't entirely there. Maybe he really was invisible and only I could tell that his physical form wasn't entirely solid. Gemma's date, Will Ericson, basically looked like the male version of Gemma—sleek and elegant. It looked like Jim had done a good job with that match. My date was named Pat, and I forgot his last name almost as soon as Jim said it. Not only was my mind mostly elsewhere, but he wasn't a very memorable person. He looked like he didn't want to be there, and when we were introduced, he didn't even try to fake interest in me. Jim must have managed to get Yankees playoff tickets to get him to come tonight. Was I so hard to match up that the best he could do was a fairly blank man?

We all went into the restaurant, where they had a long table set up for us. Connie took care of the seating arrangements, putting us in boy-girl order with each of us sitting across from our date for the evening. I was on the end, with Pat across from me and Ethan to my left. This was going to be a long evening.

Once Jim had ordered a bottle of wine for the table, I put on a smile and attempted to make conversation with Pat. "So, Pat," I began, "what do you do?"

"I work in finance." Wow, a complete sentence. Then again, that was better than Owen had managed in our first attempt at conversation.

"Really? You work with Jim, then."

"Yes."

One-word answers weren't especially helpful for keeping the conversation flowing, but I plugged on. "Are you from New York originally?"

"No."

"There don't seem to be many people who are," I said with an attempt at a laugh. "I guess all the natives move away, and they're replaced by the newcomers."

No response. Gee, would it kill him to ask me a question or two? I felt like I was running an interrogation. I'd have to break out the lead pipes to get him to talk. In desperation, I turned toward Marcia and Ethan, hoping I could flow into their conversation. That might bring Pat out of his shell. What was it with me and shy guys lately? Except there was a big difference between someone who was shy like Owen and someone who just plain didn't want to communicate.

Marcia was already arguing with Ethan. Apparently, they hadn't even made it to the "What do you do?" part of the conversation before he made a statement that she challenged, and then he questioned her facts, setting off a good debate. It was hard to tell whether that was a good sign. Marcia didn't mind a good argument, but she had issues about having to be the smartest one in the room. Gemma should try setting her up with a himbo sometime. That would probably work better than the brainy types people usually picked for Marcia.

On the other side of Ethan and Marcia, Jim and Connie gazed at each other adoringly across the table, seemingly oblivious to the chaos caused by their matchmaking. At the end of the table, Gemma seemed to have fallen in lust at first sight with Will. That wasn't unusual. She liked all men who had an appropriate level of admiration for her.

With a sigh, I turned back to Pat. "What do you enjoy when you're not at work?" I asked.

He shrugged. "I watch sports." Bingo. Jim had definitely bribed him with tickets to some big event.

The argument next to me died down as Marcia and Ethan studied their menus. I glanced at my own menu and decided to order lasagna. It was the easiest of the pasta dishes to eat because it didn't involve twirling spaghetti around on a fork and then trying to get it all in your mouth at once, something that's just asking for a disaster on a date.

As I closed my menu, Marcia put on her best fake smile and asked, "So, Ethan, what do you do?"

He frowned at his menu, then looked up at her. "I'm an intellectual property attorney."

Her fake smile remained in place. "Oh. Interesting."

Desperate for conversation, I asked, "What does that mean, exactly?"

"A lot of what I do involves employment cases and patent infringement."

"Employment? Are you saying that people are considered intellectual property?"

He shook his head, and for once he looked solid, like he was really there. "No, but some of what people have in their heads is considered company property." He picked up the saltshaker in front of him. "Say you've got this employee here. His job is inventing a gizmo for company A. But then company B offers him a job." He moved the saltshaker from the candle to the floral arrangement. "Then he invents a newer, better version of the gizmo for company B—based on what he invented for company A. That could be considered a theft of intellectual property because he took work he'd done for one company and essentially gave it to another company."

I nodded. Normally, I didn't much like talking about work, but this was fairly interesting. Well, more interesting than Pat's sullen silence. "But it's usually more complicated than that," Ethan continued. He was now talking directly to me, as Marcia had turned to chat with Jim and Connie. "What if the gizmo at company B isn't based directly on the gizmo from company A, but the employee does use things he learned from inventing the gizmo for company A to invent the new gizmo, and because of that they can get a better gizmo to market sooner?"

"I don't know," I said. "It's not like you can wipe your employees' brains when they leave a company. Everyone learns things at one job that they go on to use in the next job." I had a mental image of Mimi with a giant vacuum cleaner, trying to suck out my brains, and I shuddered.

Ethan's eyes lit up, and I could see behind his glasses that they were a silvery gray. He was fairly cute, in a reserved, conservative way. "Exactly! That's where it gets tricky. Where do you draw the line between using work you've done at one company in your next job, and merely applying the experience you've gained?"

"But haven't employers taken too strict an interpretation of that?" Marcia asked, her attention back to us now that her date was paying attention to me. I left them to their argument, glad that I had nothing of value to take from my last job. I'd only learned a lot about what not to do. Even though no one in New York was impressed with that particular item on my résumé, my lifetime of handling the business side of the feed-and-seed store was still the most valuable real-world experience I had. I wondered if my parents could accuse me of intellectual property theft.

I'd run out of questions to ask Pat, and he hadn't bothered asking me anything, which was probably for the best, given that I didn't yet have a good explanation for my new job. Talking about work could get me in trouble. His eyes were focused on something in the distance behind me. I glanced over my shoulder and saw a TV set mounted above the bar. Good. At least he'd be entertained. Meanwhile, I could enjoy my meal in peace and think about everything that had happened to me this week.

By the time the salads came, Ethan and Marcia were debating something to do with the economy, and it wasn't a foreplay debate loaded with sexual tension. They clearly weren't hitting it off well and had given up trying to make a good impression on each other. Meanwhile, Gemma and Will would be on the floor under the table before we got to dessert, at the rate they were going. I ate my salad in silence as I tried to decide which was worse, a date who wouldn't shut up or a date who wouldn't talk at all.

A group of women with wings came through the door. Out of habit, I turned to see if anyone else noticed them and saw that Ethan was frowning. For a second I thought he must have noticed the fairies, too, but then he took off his glasses, polished them, and put them back on. Nothing more magical than a smudged lens, then. And I could tell from the foot that kept accidentally bumping against mine under the table that he was, indeed, solid and real. I decided his mind was just clearly elsewhere and that was what gave him such a vague look.

It felt like we were going to break the New York record for longest dinner ever by the time we got dessert and coffee. I couldn't take any more of Pat's silence and retreated to the restroom while the others finished their dessert. Armed with fresh lipstick, I returned to the table just in time to hear Pat talking to Jim. "It'd be like dating my sister," he said. It was a safe guess who he was talking about. I got that reaction from men all the time. I could understand it in a small town where most of the boys were my brothers' friends, but how did it transfer to New York, where nobody even knew my family?

Finally, everyone finished their coffee and we made our way out of the restaurant. I wasn't at all surprised when Gemma and Will announced that they were going to hit a nearby jazz club. They invited the rest of us, but clearly didn't want us to take them up on the offer. I didn't expect Gemma to make it home tonight. The rest of us said insincere things about how nice it was to meet each other, then said good night for the evening without bothering to exchange contact information. You know your blind date hasn't gone well when nobody even asks for a phone number.

Jim and Connie hailed a cab, and Marcia linked her arm through mine. "Want to walk home?" she asked. "I need to work off that dinner."

I wasn't wearing the best shoes for walking, and I'd already had two long walks that day, but walking through the Village at night is almost magical—but not in the real magic way, with spells and illusions and all that. Though come to think of it, I'd seen more than the expected amount of weirdness in the Village at night and written it off as just another New York thing. It would be interesting to see how much of it really was magical.

Marcia and I headed off down Bleecker toward our side of the island. The whole time we walked, Marcia complained about her date. "Could you believe him? All he could talk about was work."

"Y'all talked about more than work. You were arguing a lot."

"About work. He questioned everything I said."

"He's a lawyer. He's used to having to analyze and interpret everything."

"Don't tell me you're defending him," she said with a laugh.

"No, not really. He was just more interesting than my date. At least he actually spoke."

"You do have a point there."

"And he didn't think of you as an annoying little sister."

She winced. "So, you heard that."

"I came back from the bathroom at a very good time."

"If it makes you feel better, he did say you were okay, cute, even."

"But he's just not interested in that way." I couldn't fight back a sigh. Was it too much to ask to make a man's heart beat faster, just once?

She gave my arm a squeeze. "Don't worry about it. Your time will come. You just have to meet the right guy who appreciates you for what you are."

"Marce, I'm your age, remember. You don't have to treat me like your kid sister."

"Sorry about that. But look on the bright side. A few years from now you'll be glad for people to think you're younger. And like I said, you have to find the right guy. You're the kind of girl men go for when they're ready to settle down."

"So I'm not the kind of girl they want to go out with when they want a good time?"

"Is that so bad?"

"I don't know." To be honest with myself, I wasn't anyone's idea of a good-time girl. I was the kind of woman who made people think of things like apple pie and picket fences. That didn't make me very popular in a place like New York, where people came to get away from picket fences.

"I guess those are two guys we can cross off our lists of Mr. Right potentials," Marcia said, interrupting my musings.

"How many million does that leave in the city?"

"It can't be a million, not if we exclude men who are gay, married, or seriously involved, or that we've gone out with before. We've got to be down to the thousands."

I had another category to add to that: men who weren't quite human, and I wasn't sure where men who could make things appear and disappear at will fit on the scale of eligibility. I was pretty sure that apple pie and picket fences weren't what they were looking for in a woman. If my degree of ordinary was boring for normal men, I'd send magical men straight into a coma.

six

Tuesday morning came a lot more quickly than I expected. After dressing in my second-best suit, I took the subway to work, and I was relieved to see Owen standing on the platform at the Union Square station. It meant I wouldn't have to walk into the building by myself. "Hi there!" I greeted him.

He turned his usual shade of pink before responding. "Good morning, Katie. I'm glad you're joining us."

"So am I. I'm excited about it. And a little nervous." I figured that he, of all people, should be able to understand some nervousness about a new situation.

He gave me one of his mischievous grins, and my knees went just a bit weak. "Want to get to work early?"

"Oh, why not?"

Still smiling, he did something with his left hand, and sure enough, a train hurtled out of the tunnel to stop in front of us. "After you," he said with a gallant gesture. There weren't any empty seats, but we found an empty pole to cling to. "Want to make it an express trip?" he whispered to me.

"I don't think that's necessary," I whispered back. "Let's not inconvenience everyone else."

He turned crimson. "I did summon another train right behind ours so they weren't inconvenienced that much."

"That was awfully sweet of you." I wondered what he'd do if I kissed him on the cheek, but I was rusty on CPR, and I doubted it would be an appropriate way to interact with a coworker even if he didn't have a heart attack.

It was bad enough that at every station, the momentum from the train stopping threw me up against him. He might not be a big man, but he was solid and sturdy. "Now I remember why I usually walk to and from work," I said after one particularly abrupt stop. "It's much less violent."

We finally reached the City Hall station and left the train together. Owen wasn't particularly tall, but he walked quickly enough that I had to work to keep up with him as he went through the park. He crossed Park Row against the light and away from the crosswalk, but there wasn't any traffic at the time. I wondered if that was a fluke or something he did. In spite of all his bashfulness, I began to get the impression that he was a very powerful person who cleared a path for himself through all of life's little inconveniences without even a second thought. The contrast was disconcerting.

Summoning subway cars and making coffee appear out of thin air seemed rather benign, almost like the parlor tricks one of my uncles liked to do at family gatherings, only much more useful. But this was a business, and apparently a rather large one, so I knew there had to be more to magic than that. It had to affect your way of looking at the world to know that you could control the elements like that. Would you expect to have that kind of control over everything? I decided I'd be safer if I focused on the impression of power instead of the bashfulness when I dealt with Owen. If I only let myself see the cute, shy guy, I'd underestimate him, possibly even to a dangerous degree. It was like dealing with the sales reps who used to come to our store. The nicest, most friendly good ole boys were the ones you really had to look out for.

As if reinforcing my mental lecture, as soon as Owen stepped through the doorway into the building he almost became another person, very confident and professional and matching that impression of power I'd just had from him. "Good morning, Hughes," he said to the lobby's security guard. "You remember that Miss Chandler is joining us?"

"Of course, sir. Welcome, Miss Chandler."

"Katie, please," I insisted.

"I'll take her up to Personnel," Owen said.

"Very good, sir. Have a good day, sir, Katie."

"You, too," I called over my shoulder as Owen led me toward the stairs.

"Rod will take care of your orientation," he explained, winding his way through corridors. I wished I'd thought to bring some bread crumbs so I wouldn't get lost, but I didn't have time to worry about that now. Everyone we passed greeted him with some deference. Now I couldn't help but wonder just who this guy was. He couldn't be much more than thirty, yet they treated him like he was the top brass. I should see past any illusion he used to make himself look younger. Maybe he wasn't human at all and was some human-looking species that lived a very long time, so he could still look around thirty while actually being three hundred.

We reached a doorway and he came to a stop. "This is Rod's office," he said. "I'll leave you to him, but I'm sure I'll see you around."

"Thanks for leading the way."

He turned a little bit pink, looked like he was about to say something, then turned and went back down the hallway. I steeled myself before stepping through the doorway into what appeared to be an outer office. The largest woman I'd ever seen sat at a desk with the newest model of iMac, along with a crystal ball thingy like the one on the desk in the lobby and an ordinary office phone. She wasn't fat, just big all around. She could play linebacker for the Dallas Cowboys. Before I could open my mouth to say who I was and what my business was, she stood up, towering over me, and gave me a huge smile. "Katie! Sweetheart! You're here!"

I had relatives who didn't greet me that warmly at family reunions, and I'd never met this woman before in my life. "Hi," I said. "Apparently I'm supposed to meet with Rod Gwaltney here."

"Of course you are. Rod's not in yet, but I expect him soon. Please, have a seat. Can I get you some coffee? A bagel?" Somehow, I'd expected something stranger than this, but this was the way I'd expect to be treated at any particularly friendly firm. "Some coffee would be nice," I said, sitting down in one of the room's overstuffed chairs.

"Cream and sugar, right?" she asked.

"Yes, please."

When the coffee mug appeared in my hand, I remembered that this wasn't just any firm. "Oh!" I gasped, then tried to steady myself before I spilled coffee all over myself.

"Sorry about that," the woman said. "I should have warned you if you're not used to this sort of thing."

"I imagine it will take some getting used to."

"By the way, I'm Isabel, Rod's assistant."

"Nice to meet you, Isabel."

"We are so glad to have you." She glanced toward the doorway, then turned back to me and said in a conspiratorial tone, "That was young Owen Palmer who brought you here, right?"

"Yes, it was."

She fanned herself with a piece of paper from her desk. "Oh my. Now, he would be quite the catch. Brilliant and gorgeous. That boy is going to go places. If only you could get him to talk to you when he's not talking business." Now, this felt like the kind of gossip session you'd find at any other company. As different as things promised to be when working at a business that was essentially Magic, Inc., so far there wasn't anything different at all.

"He seems nice," I said, trying to keep my tone neutral. The last thing I needed was to start a new job as the subject of office gossip. If I agreed he was gorgeous, there was a good chance that by noon word would have spread throughout the company that I was interested in him. Businesses were a lot like small towns in that respect. "In fact, everyone here seems nice, so far," I added.

"We are a good bunch, though we do have a few skeletons in our closets." I had a sick feeling she meant that literally. "And what workplace doesn't have a monster or two?" She probably meant that literally as well. But I'd worked for Mimi, so as long as the monster didn't try to eat me, I'd still be better off than in my old job.

Rod came through the doorway then in a snazzy suit right off the fashion runways. It didn't go well with his otherwise sloppy personal appearance. I wondered what illusion he wore. Whatever it was, he used it as a disguise and didn't even bother with his real appearance. The illusion must not have covered clothes. Otherwise, he wouldn't have bothered with the nice suit. I decided I was grateful for that. If magical people could dress themselves with illusion, I'd have been exposed to more nudity than I really cared to see. I also would have probably turned around and left New York as soon as I got here. One of my mother's scare stories involved naked people freely roaming the streets.

"Katie, you're here already!" Rod said when he saw me.

"I didn't want to be late on my first day."

"Come on back to my office and we'll get you started."

I picked up my briefcase and followed him. He got settled at his desk and gestured me toward yet another overstuffed chair. I had to give these people credit for having decent office furniture. A mug of coffee appeared on his desk, and he took it between both hands.

"We just have a little paperwork to do—IRS forms, health insurance, and the like—and then we'll do an orientation so you'll have a better understanding of how all this works. After that, we'll get you set up in your office."

I nodded while I tried to process the unlikely juxtaposition of tax forms and learning how a magical firm operated. "You deal with the IRS?"

"Of course. The IRS has their own set of wizards, and they never let us get away with anything." It had never crossed my mind that I might not have to file taxes, so that wasn't a big letdown, even if the idea of taxes and magic still didn't go together in my brain. I was even more unnerved about the idea of the IRS having wizards working for them.

He had me fill out all the paperwork, then handed me a packet on the health plans. "Just look that over later, fill out the forms, and get them to Isabel," he instructed. Then he grinned, opened a desk drawer, and pulled something out. "And here's your MetroCard."

I took it from him and tucked it into my purse. Now I had transportation freedom without having to think about the balance on my card. It was almost as good as having my own car again. That had been one of the biggest adjustments for me in moving from Texas to New York.

Rod settled back into his chair and said, "Now, do you have any questions?"

"About what?"

"About anything."

"To be honest, I'm not even sure where to begin."

"Then let's take a tour. You can leave your things here."

I followed him to the outer office and out into the hallway. He talked as he walked. "We do everything here from researching, developing, and testing new spells to distribution and monitoring of the spells."

I felt like I was struggling to keep up, even if the struggle was more mental than physical. "How do you distribute your spells?" I asked. "In other words, how do you make money?"

"We sell them in magic shops, of course, as well as at other retail outlets."

I came to a halt. "Magic shops? You mean those places that sell card tricks and top hats?"

He raised an eyebrow at me. "Have you ever gone into one?"

"No. I've never been all that interested in magic, to be honest."

"That makes sense. You see reality instead of illusion, so it's no fun for you. But you'd be surprised at what you'd notice in a magic shop. The props are for the general public, but if you know what you're looking for, you can also buy any spell you might need. You'd see the spells for sale, while most people just in there looking for a trick deck of cards wouldn't."

"Not that the spells would do me much good," I muttered.

"They also can't be used against you. Although, none of our spells can be used to cause harm. Minor inconvenience, at the most. We're very strict on quality control."

"So, people can just go into a store and buy a spell? How do they pay for something like that?"

"We set our prices based on what went into developing the spell, how useful it is, and how many people are likely to need it. A simple spell that's likely to be used just about every day to make life a little simpler may run about twenty dollars. A more complex spell for a specialized purpose might run into the hundreds. We do some custom work, but usually more for businesses than individuals."

"Dollars?"

"Of course. What did you expect, wizard's gold?"

Actually, I expected something along those lines. That must have shown on my face, for he laughed and said, "You've read too many books. We just have our own business, not our own economy. Now, here's the sales department."

We stepped into a suite of offices opening onto a central room. In those offices, the sales force sat talking on phones or into those crystal ball things. I noticed two who looked like ordinary humans—well, probably not entirely ordinary—two elves, and a gnome, who sat on top of his desk to talk into the crystal ball.

Rod waved his hand, which apparently sent a signal into the crystal balls, so that all the sales guys looked up at us. Those who were talking through whichever communications device wrapped up their conversations. "Everyone, I'd like you to meet Katie Chandler. She's joining the verification department. After today, feel free to call on her when you have a contract or need to go on a call to check out a vendor." They all smiled and waved, then returned to their sales work. Rod turned to me and explained, "You'll spend most of your time dealing with Sales. You may go with them from time to time to check on their accounts and make sure the sellers are being honest, and you'll review all contracts before they're signed."

"I'm not a lawyer," I pointed out.

"You don't have to be. They know what should and shouldn't be in the contracts. You just read them out loud, and they'll know if something was added and hidden, or removed and replaced with an illusion."

"Are magical people that devious?" I asked, almost afraid of his reaction to the question.

"People in general tend to be, don't you think? True, the majority of the population is honest, but there's always someone looking for a loophole. We just have more ways of creating loopholes."

He led me out of the sales department and up a flight of stairs.

We went into a large, dimly lit room. Various monitors, both the computer and the crystal variety, rimmed the room. "This is the monitoring department," Rod said before introducing me to this group of people. "They make sure all our spells are being used properly. Unauthorized use can result in spell privileges being revoked. You may be asked to take a shift here occasionally. We generally have at least one verifier in here at all times. It's a specialized verification job, but we sometimes need someone from the pool to fill in."

We left that room and went up another flight of stairs. "What would be considered unauthorized?" I asked.

"The big one is using a spell to cause harm. Our spells are designed with fail-safes to prevent harm, but if you try hard enough, it is possible to work around them. There's also not supposed to be any sharing of spells. Only the purchaser is able to use them, but there are those who try to come up with ways to get around that."

"And if privileges are revoked?"

"You can't use that spell again without repurchasing it. If it's used for harm, you aren't allowed to repurchase it at all. You may even be banned from other uses of our products."

"Is that a big problem?" I didn't like the idea of hundreds of magic users held back only by what sounded like the fine print on the back of the box and a pretty small group of monitors.

"Not really. The wicked enchanter driven mad in his lust for power is yet another thing that you mostly just find in books and movies. It happens, but for the most part, if your life is already pretty good, there's not much reason to go around hurting others. People with real psychological disorders are screened out early in life, so they don't get their hands on spells to begin with, or else they're rehabilitated."

"That's good to know."

The next door didn't just open for Rod. He had to press his hand against a metal plate and say something under his breath in what sounded like Latin before the lock clicked and the door opened. "This is R and D, Owen's domain," Rod said.

The area looked like something out of a Frankenstein movie, or something else involving mad scientists. A corridor ran between glass-walled labs, some full of bubbling bottles, others looking more like libraries. People wearing white lab coats walked around with clipboards, making notes. The occasional popping sound and flash of light came from labs as we passed.

"This is where the magic happens, literally," Rod said.

We reached a final, larger lab. This one could have existed in any major university without anyone thinking anything of it, aside from the rather odd things written on the whiteboards that rimmed the walls. Owen stood in front of one of the boards, holding an old book in one hand and writing on the board with his other hand. Rod waited until he finished what he was writing before he said, "Owen."

Owen blinked, then turned to see us and smiled. "So, you're getting the grand tour?" he said to me, pink spreading up his face toward his hairline.

"Looks like it. It's fascinating."

"Owen heads our theoretical magic division," Rod said.

"We try to determine what is and isn't possible using magic," Owen explained. "A lot of it is going back to the ancient texts and seeing if there's a way to update the spells for the times, or finding out if the spells ever worked at all. Some of the ancient wizards elaborated a bit too much in what they recorded."

"We also have a practical magic division that takes what Owen discovers and fine-tunes the spells for mass distribution," Rod added.

Just then a young man with spiked hair came limping into the room. His pants leg was shredded from the knee down. "For the record, that dog-soothing spell you translated doesn't work," he said to Owen. "I don't know if it's the translation or the spell itself, but . . ." He gestured toward his tattered pant leg.

Owen winced. "Sorry about that, Jake." He made a note on his whiteboard. "I'll look into it. You'd better go see a healer."

Jake limped away. "Dangerous line of work," I commented.

"That wasn't an authorized test," Owen said. "Some of us can't resist trying out something we've read about. Most of us are more careful, though." He grinned abruptly. "But when you're in a tricky situation, the last thing you've read is generally what comes to mind. That's the risky part about working in theory. You never know if it's going to work when you need it."

Rod laughed. "Yeah, remember that time when you—" He shut up immediately when Owen shot him a glare. "Anyway, what they do here isn't without its risks, but fortunately for you, you won't need to work much with R and D."

"You're welcome to visit anytime, though," Owen said. "We'd be happy to answer any questions you might have about magic, and this is where the resident experts are."

"I'll start a list of questions, once I know enough to even know what I should be asking."

"Well, we have a tour to finish," Rod said, taking my arm and guiding me away with what almost seemed to be a hint of jealousy, which struck me as odd. For one thing, I'm not the kind of woman who inspires jealousy. I've never had anyone fight over me. For another, it wasn't like Owen had said or done anything to inspire jealousy. It was probably my imagination.

After a second Owen came after us. "Oh, I almost forgot. Mr. Mervyn wants to see Katie when you're through with the tour, and then he's called a lunch meeting for the usual suspects."

Rod groaned. "Nice of him to give me advance warning. We're not all precogs, you know. Good thing my calendar's clear."

"He cleared everyone's calendar last week, as usual."

I was still puzzling over that exchange as Rod led me out of the R&D department. I noticed as we passed through the corridor that every woman made a point of giving Rod a smile and a come-hither look. I wished I could see what they saw. He smiled back, but it looked like he did it more out of habit than out of any actual interest. He was still frowning, apparently from what Owen had said.

I finally got up the nerve to ask, "What was that about?"

He shook his head. "Nothing. Just office politics. The boss has a pretty small group of people he trusts entirely and relies upon, and I'm on the fringes. He includes me often enough, but never seems to communicate with me directly. It always comes through someone else, most often Owen."

Ah, that explained the apparent jealousy. It wasn't about me, it was about the job. "Personnel is always on the fringes," I said. "Even in nonmagic companies. It's essential, or else you wouldn't have employees at all, but it's not a direct profit center, so it's often forgotten by the executive ranks."

He brightened considerably. "Really?"

"Yes, really. The people who bring in the money are the ones who get the attention. Marketing works the same way. You wouldn't sell anything without marketing, but because it doesn't make money on its own, the department gets ignored and is the first thing to be cut when there are budget problems."

"It also doesn't help that Owen is being groomed for bigger, better things, while I'm never getting beyond what I do. Don't get me wrong, I love my job, but I know I'll never be running this company, and one day Owen will be. He'll be good at it, too."

"He just needs a little confidence."

Rod shook his head. "No, he's better off as he is. In fact, I think they brought him up to be shy on purpose. As powerful as he is, you don't want him to be bold."

That sent a shiver down my spine, but before I could ask Rod to clarify, we'd reached another doorway. "This is P and L, the Prophets and Lost department," he said as the door opened.

"Profits and loss?" I asked. That sounded more like a spreadsheet than a department.

"No, Prophets and Lost. This is where we predict the market trends or trace things that seem to have disappeared."

"Like Elvis!" I quipped.

"Exactly!" He didn't sound like he was joking. He ushered me into the office suite, which was decorated like something out of a Gypsy's tent at an old-fashioned carnival. "Hi, everyone!" he said to the dreamy-looking bunch of people who sat around on the velvet cushions. "This is Katie, she's new in Verification."

An elegant woman dressed right out of a fashion magazine—next year's fashion magazine, or what I imagined next fall's clothes would look like if current trends progressed—looked up at me. "Take the bus home this evening," she said.

I blinked. "Huh? Oh, yeah, sure. Thanks. Nice meeting you." I'm sure the bus warning was important, but couldn't she have clued me in to hemlines as well? I'd hate to hem all my skirts, only to find out we'd be wearing them longer next season. Gemma would kill for that kind of foresight.

Rod ushered me back outside. "Don't let them get to you. It's company policy that you're not supposed to ask them about things like lottery numbers or the outcomes of sporting events, but if they tell you something spontaneously, it's generally a good idea to take them at their word."

"Okay. I'll take the bus, then."

He paused in the middle of the hallway, rubbing his hands together while he frowned in thought. "Let's see, you've already met Sam in Security—he's been talking about you for days. I think he has a bit of a crush. What else do I need to show you?"

I tried not to think about a stone gargoyle having a crush on me. How scary would it be if it turned out that was the type I attracted? Instead, I focused on Rod's question. "How about my office? And all that important little stuff like the coffee room, the bathroom, and such?"

"We'll deal with that this afternoon. Unless you need the bathroom now?" I shook my head. "Okay, then we'd better get you up to see the boss."

"That's Mr. Mervyn, right?" I asked, remembering the name Owen had used. "He was the one at the interview?"

"Yep, that's the one. And let me tell you, you made quite an impression on him." We reached what appeared to be one of the building's turrets, with a long spiral staircase leading upward. I'd barely had a chance to start dreading climbing those stairs when Rod tapped the staircase's center post and the stairs began moving upward, like an escalator.

"Magic?" I asked.

He shook his head. "No, mechanics. This is new. The boss likes to tinker, and he hates climbing stairs. He thought this was far more interesting than an elevator. I suspect there was some magic involved in the invention, however."

We stepped onto the spiraling escalator, which deposited us in a lush office suite. There was a reception area with a fairy hovering over a chair behind a giant mahogany desk. Behind her was a pair of ornate wooden doors, and off to the side there appeared to be another office. "Oh, good, you're here," she said as we approached. "He's been expecting her."

The doors swung open and we stepped into the boss's office. It looked like pretty much every CEO's office I'd ever seen—not that I'd seen a lot—with fancy furniture, thick carpets, and elegant artwork on the walls. I got the impression, however, that this furniture was really antique and not a modern reproduction. The far wall was all windows overlooking City Hall and the park, while the adjacent wall had a nice view of the Brooklyn Bridge.

I shouldn't have felt intimidated about meeting the boss, but I did. My dad was CEO at the store, but he was just Dad. I'd never met the CEO at my last job. The newspapers painted portraits of extremely wealthy, powerful men who'd never notice a low-level flunky like me. I suddenly felt like a kid called into the principal's office. I wondered if I should bow or curtsy. From what I'd heard about some chief executives, falling on my face on the floor and chanting "I'm not worthy" wouldn't be out of the question.

The distinguished gentleman who'd held court during my job interview came around his desk to greet us. "My dear Miss Chandler," he said, taking both my hands in his. He then looked up at Rod. "Thank you, Rodney, for bringing her here. I'll see you at lunch." Rod looked stung by the dismissal, but he nodded and left. The doors shut behind him. "Please, have a seat." He led me toward a sofa that was angled to have a nice view through either window.

"I'm glad you decided to join us, although I knew you would," he said. There was a ring of certainty to his voice that said he really had known I'd take the job, not because he'd guessed it or because he knew how I'd react, but because he'd seen it. Now I remembered what Rod had said about precogs.

"The offer came along just at the time I needed it," I said.

"And you came along at just the time we needed you. It worked out for everybody." His smile was warm and genuine, which made him less intimidating to me. "I must apologize for the rather abrupt way in which we've introduced you to our company, and I hope to rectify that with you this morning. First of all, I've been remiss in not introducing myself. My name in modern English is Ambrose Mervyn, and I'm the chief executive officer of Magic, Spells, and Illusions, Inc. I held that position a very long time ago, then retired. Recently, I came out of retirement to take up my old position and help steer the company through some challenging times."

"I guess the economy sucked even for magical people," I said with a knowing nod, even as I tried to figure out what he might have meant in making a point of saying that his name was the modern English version.

"Yes, I suppose it has," he said, sounding like he'd just realized that. Now I wondered what he'd really meant.

"As a result, I'm getting reacquainted with the company, just at the same time you're learning about it. Things have changed a great deal since my day." His voice grew distant and wistful. I imagined he had a vacation house in Vermont that he'd had to abandon. "The company's grown considerably and moved its operations to the New World, which is something of an adjustment for me." Strike the vacation house in Vermont, move it to the Cotswolds. But this operation didn't look recent. It had been in New York for at least a century, from the looks of things. I decided not to think too much about it, for it was enough to give me a headache.

"My role has changed as well," he continued. "In my day, we weren't quite so businesslike. Our focus was more on what they call research and development now." Which explained his apparent fondness for Owen. He knew and understood what Owen did, while personnel would be a foreign concept to him. How old was he anyway?

"As a result, I'm not sure how many of your questions I'll be able to answer, but feel free to ask them at any time. In the meantime, I'd like to learn more about you."

"What would you like to know?"

"Just tell me about yourself."

"Okay, well, I'm from Texas, which you already knew, since we talked about it during the interview." I wondered for a second if I should explain where Texas was, but he was bound to know that much, even if he wasn't American. At least, he could look it up. "I lived in a small town, way out in the middle of nowhere. My family runs a business there for farmers, selling farm supplies like seed, fertilizer, and food for the farm animals." He smiled, and it looked like he truly understood what I was talking about.

"I worked in the store from the time I was little bitty, and as my folks didn't have much of a head for business, no matter how much they knew about farming, I ended up more or less running the place. Then I went to college to study business so I'd really know what I was doing, and I came back home to get things in order. All my friends from school came up to New York. It was something they'd been planning for a while. They figured that it was the best time to do something like that, before they got settled in anywhere else. But I knew my folks needed me."

"You're a very dutiful daughter," he said with a solemn nod.

"Sort of. Last year, one of my friends got married, so they had an empty spot in their apartment. I came up for the wedding, and they talked me into moving here for good. My parents weren't crazy about that, but I had the systems all in place to run the store. It just felt like my last chance to get out of there and really make something of myself, so I did it. And, here I am."

"I imagine it was an adjustment for you."

"Oh, in a big way. It would have been, no matter what, but then there were all those weird things I kept seeing. To tell you the truth, I just thought that was New York, but nobody else seemed to notice, so I figured I was still a small-town hick."

"No, you have a very special perspective on the world. Don't lose that perspective, Katie. Now, how do you like New York?"

"I love it. I get homesick sometimes, but here I feel alive. There's so much going on, it makes my life seem fuller, somehow. I feel like I'm getting more living into each day than I ever could have back home."

"You don't find it frightening and noisy?"

"Noisy yes, but not really frightening."

He gave me a smile that reminded me of Owen in his more bashful mode and said softly, "Sometimes I find it frightening. It's been difficult for me to adjust, even with the spells Owen prepared for me."

"You just need someone to show you around, get you settled in. That's what my friends did for me."

He nodded. "That is a very wise suggestion, Katie Chandler."

I didn't know if it would count as sucking up to the boss, but I took a deep breath and said, "If you like, I could show you around some. Maybe we could go out to lunch one day and walk around."

He looked genuinely pleased. "Yes, I would like that. Now, we have an appointment for lunch. You need to meet the rest of the executive staff."

I got the impression that it hadn't just been the usual recruitment talk when they told me that I was important. At my last job I'd been introduced to my coworkers, and that was it. But here I'd been introduced to everyone but my coworkers. Maybe it had something to do with me learning about how magic worked and what the company did. If I was going to help them figure out what was for real, I'd need that. It was still odd.

He stood and extended a hand to help me up, then tucked my arm through his and escorted me out of the office. We went back down the spiral escalator—he seemed pleased when I complimented him about it—and down more stairs and more hallways until we were back at the big conference room where they'd interviewed me. I'd have to invest in a GPS tracker to find my way around this place.

The same people who'd been at my interview were there, gathered around the table. There was an empty place setting in front of each seat. Mr. Mervyn sat me at his left hand. Owen sat at his right. Food appeared from thin air, and as everyone ate, Mr. Mervyn introduced me. I had to alternate eating with answering questions about myself. It was more strenuous than the job interview.

After the meeting, Rod walked me out of the conference room. "Don't worry about that interrogation," he said. "They just need to get comfortable with you so they'll know you for verification jobs. Now we'll get more into the day-to-day stuff. Let's get your things, then we'll go to your new office."

I got my purse and briefcase, then we went up another flight of stairs and down a hallway to a suite marked VERIFICATION.

"I don't suppose you've got a map," I asked. I wasn't sure I'd be able to find my office without help the next morning.

"Don't worry, we'll take care of you," he said as the doors opened into the verification department, my new home away from home.

For the first time that day, I wondered if I'd made the right decision.

seven

As magical as everything else I'd seen so far at MSI was, this department was about as drab as any office I'd ever been in. It was an open-plan office, without even the privacy of a cubicle, just desks lined up in rows. The cube in my old office looked palatial in comparison.

The desks were almost bare, with just phones on them, no computers. I couldn't remember the last time I'd seen a desk without a computer on it. There was a larger desk at the head of the room, and that desk held a computer, a phone, and one of those crystal ball thingies that seemed to serve as a company intercom. Behind that desk sat a balding man with a bristly mustache.

"Gregor, here's your fresh face," Rod called out. Gregor looked up from his crystal ball and glowered at us.

"About time," he muttered.

"She was meeting with the big boss. You know how that goes." Rod turned to me. "Gregor manages the verification department. You'll be working under him."

Gregor got up and came around his desk to shake my hand. He wasn't much taller than I was, and he had a spare tire around his middle. He didn't look particularly thrilled to see me, but I couldn't tell if that was just his usual personality or if he had taken a dislike to me already. "We needed another person in here," he said gruffly. "We're up to our eyeballs these days."

The other people in the office didn't seem all that overworked. A middle-aged man who looked like the sort of person you meet at a Star Trek convention—not that I'd know that firsthand—sat at the desk to the far right, reading a paperback thriller. A girl who looked like the sitcom stereotype of a Long Island girl sat at the desk nearest the door, painting her fingernails a bright metallic blue. The rest of the desks were empty. I supposed the other people must be out verifying.

"This'll be your desk," Gregor said, pointing to the one behind the nail polish girl. "The drill is, you wait here until someone calls for verification. We send out whoever's up next, unless they request someone. First few days, we'll send you out with some of the others until you know what's going on, then you'll be on your own. You might want to bring a book or something to do while you're waiting." He turned to the girl painting her nails. "Angie, show her around the office." Then he stomped back to his desk and sat with a grunt.

"I'll leave you to get settled in," Rod said. "Just let me know if you need anything. You can reach me by phone, or come down if you have the time."

"Thanks," I said. "I'll see you around." He waved at me and left. I turned to see Angie with a scrunched-up look of distaste on her face.

"Who let the dogs out?" she said in a nasal Long Island voice. Even though I thought her remark was rude, it was nice to have my view of Rod's looks validated, after seeing so many others swooning at his feet.

"He's actually pretty nice," I said, putting my purse and briefcase down at the desk Gregor had pointed out. I'd almost forgotten how unattractive Rod could be, the more time I spent with him. When he wasn't trying so hard to play the charmer, he was much more appealing.

Angie finished her nails, then closed her bottle of nail polish. "Okay, I guess I'd better show you around," she said, waving her hands in front of her face. She held them out, her fingers spread wide, as she got out of her chair and headed to the far side of the office. "Over here's the coffee room. The pot with the orange handle's decaf. When you finish a pot, make a fresh one, and by finish we mean anything less than a full cup left in the pot. No leaving a tablespoon and claiming you didn't empty the pot, like certain people do." She raised her voice and said, "Gary!" apparently addressing the guy who still had his nose stuck in his book. "Creamer and sugar are in the cabinet, and there's also tea. Hot water comes out of that spout on the coffee machine."

We walked farther into the coffee room, and I noticed that the sink was full of empty coffee mugs. "You'll want to bring your own mug, and you're supposed to wash up after yourself. Refrigerator is community property, but if you want to keep your lunch, put your name on it. Sodas are free. If there's something you like that we don't have, let Gregor know. He'll kvetch about it, but he'll order it. He's also supposed to get us lunch if we want it, but that just wigs out most of us, so we brown bag. Sometimes we all go out together."

She walked past me, still waving her fingers in the air to dry her nail polish, and headed down a short hallway. "Supply room's in there—pens, paper, what have you. Not that we really need it." She didn't pause as she passed the open doorway. "And here are the bathrooms. Any questions?"

"I think that covers it." I felt queasy as I went back to my desk. This wasn't what I'd had in mind. They'd made me feel so important, so special, and here I was in a low-rent version of the secretarial pool. With any luck, I'd stay so busy that I didn't have to spend much time in this depressing office. If verifiers were so important to the company, I couldn't help but wonder why they didn't have better working conditions.

I sat at my desk and, for lack of anything better to do, started opening drawers to see what was in there. I'd just found a stash of multicolored sticky notes when the office door opened and a frazzled-looking woman came in. She was slender to the point of being skinny, with a halo of frizzy hair surrounding her face. I couldn't tell if she was middle-aged or if it was just the effect of her skinniness combined with the obvious degree of stress she was under that made her look that old. She crossed the room without acknowledging me and sat at the desk across from Gary.

Angie leaned back in her chair. "Don't let her get you worried. They didn't catch Rowena before she nearly went around the bend. It's not the job. She's just that freaked out all the time." She then turned back to her desk and started on a second coat of nail polish.

I'd been heading around the bend myself before I found out I wasn't imagining things, so I could sympathize with Rowena. I got up and went over to her desk. "Hi, I'm Katie," I said to her.

She looked up at me, then blinked like she expected me to disappear. Then she squinted, and at last she said, "I'm Rowena." There was something vague about her voice, like she lived in her imagination most of the time. If she really was the dreamy sort, then I could see where being able to see magic all around her would be enough to send her right over the edge.

Gregor's phone rang, and he grunted a few times while taking down some info. Then he bellowed, "Angie!"

"Just a sec, boss," she said, still painting her nails. "I need to finish this hand."

He came out of his seat, his face turning red. "I don't remember the last time we had a personal grooming emergency around here, but we've had plenty of verification emergencies!" he bellowed. He looked a lot like Mimi did before she turned evil. Angie ignored him, continuing to apply polish to her nails. He grew even redder. And then he turned green.

I blinked like Rowena had, but he was still green, and his eyes were red. It was almost like the Incredible Hulk, but he didn't get bigger, just scalier and greener, and horns sprouted out of the sides of his head. I'd heard about having monster bosses. I'd had monster bosses. But this was ridiculous.

Angie painted the nail of her pinkie, then screwed the lid shut on her bottle of polish and stood up. "Okay, Gregor, what is it?" she asked.

"They need you down in Sales. You need to see Hertwick. Take the new girl."

"C'mon, Katie." I got up to follow her. "You mind getting the door for me? My nails are wet."

I was eager to get out of there, so I rushed ahead of her to get the door open. Once it shut behind us, she said, "Don't worry about Gregor. He's all bark, no bite. He may roar and turn green, but he's cast a spell on the office that keeps him from being able to hurt any of us when he's in monster mode."

"What is he, exactly?" I hadn't seen anyone like Gregor in the city, and with the rate that people fly off the handle, you'd think I'd have seen at least one person turn green.

"Oh, he's human. Used to work in R and D, and then there was an accident. Rumor has it he was working after hours, trying to find a way to make himself look more fierce, and this is what happened. They moved him where he couldn't do any harm, and that cutie Owen got promoted into his old job." She gave me a sidelong look. "Did you get to meet Owen on the grand tour?"

I knew it was tacky of me, but I couldn't resist playing this particular card. "Yeah, but I knew him before. He was the one who spotted me in the first place. He was in on my testing, and then he was with Rod when they first told me about the job." I tried to sound casual, like the whole thing was no big deal.

"Whoa, you are so lucky. I just love it when I get called to R and D, which doesn't happen often, or to some big executive meeting. He's a total hottie. Too bad he can't talk, but he's cute when he turns red."

"He is kind of cute," I admitted, but I didn't want to get into a drool session any more than I'd wanted to rag on poor Rod. I felt it was time to change the subject. "Do you get called in on executive meetings often?"

"I don't. There's this stuck-up bitch Kim they usually request for executive stuff. Apparently, I don't project the proper image. Whatever." I couldn't argue that point, so I kept my mouth shut. "Anyway, like I was saying, don't worry about Gregor. Even when he turns green, he can't hurt you, and he can't fire you. Only the big boss can fire you, and they need people like us so bad that you're not gonna get fired unless you do something truly evil—and I do mean evil, not just walking out with some office supplies in your purse."

We reached the sales department, and although I'd tried to keep track of where we were going, I'd let myself get distracted by Angie's monologue. I was going to need a guide to leave the building at the end of the workday. Angie waved a hand at the door, and I opened it for her. The door had opened automatically for Rod that morning, but it looked like that had been a magic thing and nonmagical people like us had to do it the hard way.

Inside the office suite, Angie headed straight for the office where the gnome sat on his desk. "Yo, Hertwick, need something verified?" she asked.

"No, I just called up there because I wanted to see your face again," he snapped in a gruff voice.

"New contract, huh?" she said, flopping down into the chair that sat behind his desk. "Lemme have a look."

He shoved a piece of parchment at her. "And make it snappy. The customer's waiting." I looked out into the outer office and noticed a tall, slender man wearing a loud bowling shirt sitting on a sofa, drinking a Coke.

Angie frowned at the contract. "Well, looks like you got seven clauses here. That sound right to you?"

Hertwick growled. "There were supposed to be six."

I leaned over her shoulder to look at the document. I wouldn't have been entirely surprised if she had the count wrong, but there were seven clauses in the contract. I skimmed over the headers, avoiding the legal mumbo jumbo buried within. "Looks like number six is the problem one," I said, forgetting myself and thinking out loud. "They've got a clause in here about being able to return the merchandise for cash if it doesn't sell in thirty days."

Hertwick snatched the contract back. "Let me see that!" He squinted as he studied the page, then climbed down the side of the desk, using pulled-out drawers as a staircase, and ran into the outer office, his arms waving as he shouted at the visitor.

"You're not supposed to interpret, just tell them what's there," Angie said, sounding bored as she inspected her nails. "Then they figure out what shouldn't be there after you read it to them."

"This one was pretty obvious," I said. "I used to run a store, so I'm used to vendor contracts. That clause looked different from the rest, and thirty days is a pretty short period if you're selling on consignment."

She looked up at me, and I could tell I'd already been labeled as the wannabe teacher's pet, the one who was going to ruin things for the rest of them by going above and beyond the call of duty. It wouldn't be too long before I became "that stuck-up bitch Katie, the one who thinks she's hot stuff because Owen found her."

It wasn't a position I liked being in, but I also felt it was important to do a good job. I reminded myself that I didn't have to find friends at work. I already had a lot of friends, good friends. Besides, if Angie had time to sit around the office painting her nails, chances were good that she wasn't necessarily the cream of the crop in Verification. Maybe the rest of my new coworkers were different.

We helped Hertwick double-check his contract, once he finished yelling at his customer, then we went back to our office. There were more people in there now, including a prim-looking thirtysomething woman in a business suit. That had to be Kim. Sure enough, she stood to greet me when we came through the door. "Hi, you must be Katie. I'm Kim. Sorry I wasn't here when you arrived, but I had executive business to contend with."

I heard a snort from Angie, and as much as I hated to agree with her, I did get the impression that Kim was stuck-up, at the very least. I'd have to wait to determine the "bitch" part. I forced a smile. "Hi, Kim, nice to meet you. Have you worked here long?"

"Two years. I'm the senior member of this department. I'm your best bet if you have any questions." She said this with a disdainful glance at Angie, who snorted again.

"I'll keep that in mind," I said as I sat at my desk. Angie pulled a bottle of clear top coat out of her desk drawer and went to work on her manicure.

Now I wished I'd thought to bring a book with me, if my job was going to involve sitting around and waiting until I was needed. There had been plenty of books in Owen's lab area, and I wondered if any of them were worth reading. There was a company roster in the top desk drawer. I found Owen's name, then picked up the phone. This felt awkward to do surrounded by my coworkers, but none of them seemed to be paying attention to me, so I dialed.

Owen answered his phone himself, and fairly quickly. "Katie!" he said, before I had a chance to identify myself. For a second I wondered if he was a precog of some sort, then I noticed that the phone had caller ID on it.

"Hi," I said, deliberately not saying his name. "I was wondering if y'all had any books there that might be a good intro to magic. I didn't bring anything with me, and it looks like I might have time to kill, so I thought maybe I should just start studying up."

"That's a good idea. I'm sure I have something around here. When I find it, I'll have it sent over."

"Thanks so much," I said. I hung up the phone to find most of the office staring at me. Was it so odd to take initiative around here? Kim narrowed her eyes at me, as if she saw me as a threat. Angie just rolled her eyes and went back to blowing on her fingernails. Gary looked up from his book, shook his head, and went back to reading. Rowena glared at me for a second, then went back to spinning around in her chair.

I reminded myself that even though these weren't ideal working conditions, it wasn't Mimi. Boredom was better than frustration. Then there was a flash of light and a popping sound and a stack of books appeared on my desk. That was handy. I wondered what else could be teleported like that.

The books were all old, with rich leather covers embossed in gold. The top one's title was *A History of Magic*. I opened it and found a note stuck to the inside cover. "Let me know if you have any questions." It was signed "O.P." I was glad he'd put the note where it wasn't immediately visible, then realized he had to be aware of the interest shown in him. Knowing him, I suspected he hated it.

History had always been one of my favorite subjects, so I dove right in. It went all the way back to prehistoric times, covering ancient sects and discussing the difference between religious magic and the kind of magic that was an inherited skill. Some of this stuff would have made a great novel, and it was hard to believe that people around here considered it real history.

I'd just reached the part about the role of magic in the rise of King Arthur when another call came through. This one rang straight to Kim's desk. She answered with an overkill of brisk professionalism and took a page full of notes before she hung up the phone and turned to me. "I need to sit in on an important meeting. Katie, you should come with me."

Although I'd reached a really interesting spot in my book, I eagerly followed her out of the office. She carried a notepad and pen with her, and I wondered if I should have brought something. As we walked she gave me her own version of life in the verification department. "I would discourage you from emulating Angie," she said, her lips curling in disapproval. "The fact that our kind is too rare for them to fire us is no excuse for slacking off. A person can rise within this company from our department. All the executives want a verifier as a personal assistant. Play your cards right and impress the right people, and you may just make your way out of the pool."

"You've been here two years, right?" I asked, and then realized that was the wrong thing to say. As professional as she tried to act, Kim was still in the pool. "You must really know your way around," I added, hurrying to cover up my foot-in-mouth episode.

"I pay attention, and I keep my eyes and ears open. If you do the same, you could move into my position when I leave."

"You're planning to leave?"

"There's a new chief executive. He's going to need an assistant, and the best assistants for executives are immunes. Who else from Verification is he going to choose?"

I had to admit she had a point. I couldn't imagine flighty Rowena, lazy Angie, or whatever Gary was when he wasn't reading working with Mr. Mervyn. Then again, I wasn't sure I could see Kim at his side, either.

We reached the conference room where I'd been spending a lot of time lately. Kim took a seat not at the table, but in a chair set against the back wall. I sat next to her. She got out her pen and notepad and whispered to me, "I outline the gist of the meeting—who's sitting where, what they look like, then each major point of action and what everybody's agreed upon. Before the meeting ends, I hand my notes over to the meeting leaders, then they check for any discrepancies before adjourning the meeting. The other side has their own verifier. If there's a discrepancy on either side, they hash things out before they leave."

It sounded complicated, and more than a little paranoid. I'd have to ask someone how often people tried to use illusion in a business deal. It must happen often enough, considering that I'd already caught someone trying to fudge a contract and I hadn't even been on the job a whole day.

Some of the MSI people were already at the table, and then the doors opened to admit a new group of people, all wearing dark business suits. "This is a corporate client," Kim whispered. "We're doing some custom spell work for them."

I recognized a few of the MSI people from lunch. One of them flashed me a quick smile, and I felt a lot less out of place. I noticed that none of them acknowledged Kim.

The meeting began, and it was pretty much like every other business meeting I'd ever sat through. There was the usual amount of hot air being blown around, only sometimes literally in this case. It seemed that they felt the need to show off by adjusting the room's temperature to their personal preferences, summoning food and beverages, and generally doing a lot of arm waving. Kim's pen moved constantly.

I didn't have to compare notes with a magical person to tell who was trying to pull something. Their body language was a good enough clue. It was just like being able to tell when someone was lying to you and thought they were getting away with it—shifty eyes, ill-concealed smirks, body twitches. Both sides seemed to be playing the game, but the visitors were more flamboyant about it. I didn't get the impression that they really were trying to cheat, just trying to test the waters. The MSI guys were doing just enough for gamesmanship. It was almost like watching a congressional debate on C-SPAN, only a lot more interesting.

Finally, all the blather came to a stop and both sides called their verifiers over. Kim handed her notebook to the head of the MSI faction, and I watched his reactions carefully. "The guy in the red tie was trying to pull something," I said, more musing out loud to myself than actually saying anything, but the MSI executive, someone who'd been introduced to me as "Ryker, Corporate Accounts," looked up sharply.

"That is what it looks like," he said. "But how did you know if you didn't see the illusion that masked it?"

I shrugged. "He looked shifty. And he was saying things I was pretty sure you wouldn't agree to."

Ryker nodded and continued reading Kim's notes, cross-referencing with his own notes from time to time. At last both sides reconvened and hashed out the details. They checked notes one last time to make sure everyone was still being honest, and then the deal was sealed. By the time we got out of the conference room, the workday was almost over. I dreaded going back to the verification pool, even for just a few minutes. As long as I was out of the office, the job didn't seem so bad, but there was something soul-sucking about the verification room.

It didn't help matters that I'd managed to seriously piss off Kim, who seemed to think I'd deliberately stolen her thunder in the meeting. Great, now I was seen as a threat by the ambitious person who thought I was out to steal her promotion, while the lazy people saw me as a threat to their cushy jobs. I'd get to be universally hated in the office, and I'd only just started. Maybe I should have learned to keep my mouth shut, at least for a while. My old job had taught me plenty about how unwelcome a simple, common-sense observation could be. Too many people liked things complicated and difficult. I guess it made them feel more important.

"That doesn't seem like a very efficient way to handle things," I commented to Kim as we walked. Maybe if I gave her an idea for an improvement she could suggest to the boss, she'd see that I wasn't so bad. Or was that naive of me? Back home, I'd found that if I could figure out what someone else wanted and find a way of helping them get it, they'd be easier to deal with. So far, that hadn't been very effective in the New York business world.

"What do you mean?" she snapped, proving the point I'd just made to myself.

"Well, if you wait until the end of the meeting to make sure nobody pulled a fast one, you almost have to start all over again because you don't know how much was affected by the trick."

"This is the way it's been done for years. I think we'd know if there were a better idea." She punctuated her sentence by shoving the door to our office open. Okay, then, maybe she wasn't open to filling the suggestion box as a way of getting executive attention.

I wanted to continue reading the books Owen had sent me, but I didn't think it would be a good idea to take books that treated magic as reality home, so I put them in a desk drawer for the night and wearily gathered my purse and briefcase to head home. The others— except for Kim, of course—were out the door the instant it hit five, a moment punctuated by a bell. Kim stayed around looking busy, but I couldn't imagine what she could be doing. I didn't worry about it. I just wanted to get home and process this day. I also wasn't sure I could get to the front door without following someone, so I hurried to keep the others in sight.

My way out of the building became easier when I ran into Rod. This time I forced myself to pay attention to each turn along the way so I wouldn't feel so lost.

"How'd the first day go?" he asked.

I hesitated, then decided there was no benefit to anyone in telling a white lie. "We need to talk. You've got a serious issue in that department."

He blinked in surprise. "Gregor never said anything."

"You think he would?"

"Well, no, I guess not." We reached the front door. "Come by my office tomorrow, and we'll talk."

These people might have had the powers of the universe at their disposal, but they didn't seem to know a lot about business. Now that I thought about it, it made sense. After all, it wasn't like they could just call in a corporate consulting firm to help them establish more effective practices. Magic and MBAs don't seem to go together. I had a vivid mental image of a group of consultants checking themselves into rehab because they thought their latest client had told them their business was magic. Not to mention the fact that when you can work your will with a flip of the wrist, efficiency becomes meaningless. These people were way too used to taking the easy way. They could stand to listen to someone who was stuck with the hard way.

I might be able to contribute more in that area than in being able to see what was really going on. They trusted my word enough to listen when I pointed out that something they didn't see was really there. Maybe they'd trust me to tell them about other things I saw that they didn't. The thought made me feel marginally better about my new job.

The sky was threatening rain, and I had that shiny new Metro-

Card in my purse, so I started to head for the subway. Then I remembered the warning from Prophets and Lost and hesitated. Was the problem with the subway, or was there some reason I was supposed to be on the bus?

Just then the M103 pulled to a stop almost in front of me. It seemed to be a pretty good sign, so I climbed on board.

eight

Before the bus could get going, it lurched back to a stop and the doors opened. An out-of-breath Owen thanked the driver as he climbed on board, although I suspected the driver had nothing to do with the bus waiting for him. Owen saw me, smiled—more with relief than with greeting—and dropped into the seat next to me.

A series of little shivers ran up and down my spine, but not because of his proximity, even if he did look especially cute with his hair all rumpled and windblown. Taking into account what I'd seen of Owen's abilities and the fact that he usually seemed to take the subway, along with the warning I'd been given, there was a pretty good chance that a disaster was ensuing below the streets of Manhattan.

"How was the first day?" Owen asked, turning only a little bit pink.

"Kind of weird," I admitted. I didn't want to get into the specifics of the weirdness on a city bus, even though it wouldn't necessarily be the strangest conversation ever held on one.

"I can imagine," he said with a knowing nod.

"Oddly enough, I think the verification department was the weirdest group of people I've met in the entire company."

He nodded again. "That's been an ongoing problem. Unfortunately, people of that nature seem to be affected that way." He appeared to be measuring his words for public consumption as well. "That's what makes you so special. You're not like the others." He turned pinker and suddenly took great interest in inspecting his watch.

I gave him a moment or two to collect himself, then said, "Thanks for the books, by the way. I think they'll be helpful."

"If you need anything else, just ask." It didn't sound like the kind of flippant, insincere offer you usually hear from new coworkers. He sounded deeply sincere, and he held my gaze with those deep, dark blue eyes of his until I almost forgot what we'd been talking about. I got the impression that he truly meant it, that I could call him at any time and he'd come rushing to my rescue. It was kind of cool to have a friend with superpowers, even if he did seem more like Clark Kent than Superman.

For a moment I let myself ponder just how useful that could be. No more being nervous about walking home alone late at night or being one of the few noninsane people on a subway car. No more worries about dogs that got away from their owners in the park— assuming he had a dog-calming spell that actually worked. He could probably even help if I got locked out of the apartment. It was a real shame I couldn't tell my folks about this, but I wasn't sure if it would make them feel better to know their daughter was well protected or make them worry that I was associating with someone who had that kind of power.

Now that I thought about it that way, it was unnerving, considering what else I'd learned about Owen. I remembered what Rod had said about him being encouraged to be shy so his power wouldn't be dangerous. Did that mean he was more powerful than the others? He certainly seemed to have their respect, even though it didn't seem to me that he did anything to demand it.

I steered the conversation to small talk before I let myself get wigged out and he blushed himself to death. He probably didn't mean his offer of help in such an intense way anyway. He just sounded so sincere because he wasn't a flippant person. We got off at the same bus stop, but walked in opposite directions after saying good-bye. I got to my building, climbed the stairs, and turned on the evening news before heading to the bedroom to change out of my work clothes.

I had one leg out of my panty hose when something I heard from the TV sent me hobbling back to the living room. "A body across the tracks at the Canal Street station has brought subway traffic on the N and R lines to a standstill, with at least one train stuck between stations. Authorities don't yet know if the incident was accidental or a deliberate suicide or homicide," the announcer said.

I all but fell onto the sofa, one leg of my panty hose dangling limply to the floor. Oh . . . My . . . God. It was real. It was all really real. Up to that point I'd been treating it as a game. I hadn't really let myself believe in magic. But this brought it all home to me.

If I hadn't had that warning, I'd have been stuck belowground for who knew how long. And the woman in Prophets and Lost had known. Owen had known—though would it have killed him to say something? Or did he already know that I knew?

Back home, I knew plenty of people who could predict the weather without even looking at a newspaper or a TV weathercast. They just looked at the sky, smelled the air and determined the wind direction, and could tell you with a great deal of accuracy whether it would rain and how hot it would get that afternoon. This was different, though. What would it be like to know what was going to happen before it happened? And how much did they know? Was it just a flash of insight, or did they get the full picture? Could they tell beyond the shadow of a doubt that it was real foresight, as opposed to wishful thinking or fears? I had plenty of images of the future in my head all the time, but none of them ever came true—which, for the most part, was fortunate. I was working with people who dealt in very powerful forces I couldn't begin to understand. This wasn't like magic in books or movies. It was something that had the power to affect people's lives.

I was still sitting on the sofa, holding my panty hose, when Gemma came home. "How was the new job?"

There was no way to convey what my day had been like without sounding absolutely insane, so I just said, "It was interesting." That was the understatement of the century.

"Do you think you're going to like it?"

"It's too soon to tell, but yeah, I think so."

"Must have been a tiring day," she said, and then I remembered that I was still dressed in my second-best suit, holding my panty hose.

"Just a little draining," I said, forcing myself off the sofa to finish changing clothes. Both Gemma and I had changed out of our work clothes and ordered pizza when Marcia finally came dragging in.

"God, that commute was a nightmare," she said, dropping her briefcase just inside the door. "I got stuck in the subway for what seemed like forever. You don't want to spend that long in a crowded subway car with wall-to-wall people, not all of whom uphold ideal personal hygiene standards."

"I heard about that on the news," I said, getting up to pour her a glass of wine. It was the only thing I could think of to do to ease my guilt. I could have warned her so she wouldn't have been stuck. But how? She'd have laughed at me if I called her at work and told her not to take the subway home that evening. I couldn't have explained how or why I knew, and she might not have believed me if I did.

I'd just have to accept this as one of the perks of my job, I supposed. She couldn't share insider stock tips from her brokerage firm, and I couldn't share portents of the future from my magic company.

The subway disaster the day before changed the subway platform dynamics the next morning. Commuters who normally tried to pretend that nobody else actually existed were swapping war stories of the previous day's adventures. The week before, I'd felt like an outsider because I reacted to things no one else seemed to see. Today, I felt like an outsider in a different way. Or maybe I was the ultimate insider because I'd known something no one else did. Yeah, that was it. For once in my life I was the person in the know. I had to fight back a smile as I eavesdropped on conversations about sitting for an hour in the subway tunnel. It was like finding a great deal at the Neiman Marcus outlet and feeling smugly superior that there were people out there wearing the same thing who'd paid the full price. I'd felt guilty about Marcia being stuck, but I didn't owe these people anything.

The access to insider information made me feel somewhat better about heading to the dreary verification office. My specific office might be miserable, but there were definite benefits to working for a company like this.

Kim was already in the office when I arrived. She glared at me before returning to whatever it was she was working on. Since our job didn't appear to require extra work while we were in the office, I wondered what she was up to. There had to be something in place to keep people from writing tell-all books about a magical company. Not that anyone would believe anything she wrote. She could possibly hit the best-seller list if she sold it as a novel, though.

I went to the kitchen area and put my lunch in the refrigerator, poured coffee into the cup I'd brought from home, and added cream and sugar before returning to my desk and getting Owen's books out of the drawer. I'd just started reading about the use of magic during Arthur's reign when Gregor arrived. He grunted at us and went to his desk. Angie, Gary, and Rowena drifted in a few minutes later, along with two other people I hadn't met the day before. They didn't seem to notice that there was a new person in the office, and I didn't feel perky enough to initiate the introductions. The ones I'd met already thought I was an apple polisher, and I didn't want to add to my reputation.

Unfortunately, my reputation got added to without me doing anything. "Katie, good call on that meeting yesterday," Gregor called from his desk.

The others all turned to look at me, and none of them looked happy. I was particularly glad that Kim couldn't use magic, whether or not it was kosher to do harm with an MSI spell. "Thank you," I said to Gregor before burying my head in the book. I decided to put off my talk with Rod, for fear I'd look even more like I was coming in to shake things up, no matter how badly they needed to be shaken.

Fortunately, calls for verification started coming in, and the staff was sent off to various parts of the company, which meant I had fewer people glaring at me. Gregor didn't send me to shadow anyone, for which I was grateful. I wasn't sure I wanted much one-on-one time with these people. Finally, he called my name. "You can go out on your own today, given how well you handled yourself yesterday," he said grudgingly. Angie looked up from changing her nail polish to a hot-pink shade and rolled her eyes. "We need you to take a sales call. Head down to the sales department."

I put a slip of paper in my book to mark my place and hurried out of the office. I wasn't sure how I'd find Sales, but my memory was better than I thought, for I found myself there without any false turns.

Once inside the suite, I called out, "Hi, did anyone call for verification?"

A tall elf who looked incongruous wearing a business suit stuck his head out of his office door and said, "Be with you in a sec." It looked like Tolkien's version of elves was the accurate one. That was nice to know. I liked the idea of tall, elegant creatures far more than I liked the short, cute little things that appear in animated Christmas specials or Keebler commercials.

He reappeared a few seconds later and stuck a hand out at me. "Hi, Selwyn Morningbloom, MSI Outside Sales." After shaking my hand, he gave me a business card.

"Katie Chandler, Verification," I said, but I didn't have a business card to give him. It was somewhat disconcerting to see an elf acting like a high-end car salesman. Legolas wasn't supposed to sell cars.

"Okay, Katie, shall we?" He ushered me toward the door, which flew open at our approach. "We're doing a check on one of our retail outlets. I need you to let me know what the place really looks like, in case they've got merchandise hidden."

"What should I look for?"

"You tell me what you see, and I'll decide if it should or shouldn't be there." We reached the lobby, where Selwyn called out to the security guard/butler, "Hughes, we're gonna need transport."

"Very well, sir," Hughes said. He did something with his crystal ball, and when we stepped outside there was a flying carpet waiting for us.

That beat the pumpkin coach I'd imagined. "It's a nice enough day for a convertible, and this gets us past traffic better than some of the other options," Selwyn explained. "Hop on."

The flying rug hovered a few feet off the ground, so getting on board while wearing a skirt wasn't going to be easy. I had a flashback to my high school years, when I had to find a way to get into my dates' pickup trucks while wearing date-appropriate clothes. As I did back then, I stood with my back to the rug and boosted myself up so I was sitting on the edge, then swung my legs around. Next I had to figure out how to sit politely, since flying carpets don't have bucket seats. My skirt was slim and knee-length, so I couldn't sit Indian style. I settled for sitting with my legs folded to the side.

Selwyn hopped on easily, with the grace I expected from his species, even if most of what I guessed about him I'd got from books and movies. He "drove" by gesturing with his hands, and the rug took off, rising above the traffic as it flew uptown. I was glad I wasn't afraid of heights, for there weren't any seat belts on this thing. I wondered if it had any safety measures built into it, like maybe a field to keep us from being thrown off. There wasn't even anything to hold onto. Selwyn seemed to be a pro at this, but he was also the kind of guy who tries to take corners on two wheels in his sports car to scare and impress his date.

"You'd think I would have noticed one of these things," I said as we swooped up Broadway.

"How often do you look up?" he asked. He had a point. That had been part of the safety lecture Marcia and Gemma gave me when I first moved here, and since I knew they weren't trying to scare me away from the city, I'd listened. Staring up at the skyscrapers was a sure way to brand yourself as a tourist and was an open invitation to pickpockets. No matter how much I wanted to gawk at all the tall buildings, I forced myself to keep my eyes straight ahead.

"We also have designated routes to take," he continued. "That lowers the chances of anyone seeing us." Once I got him started by asking a question, he talked nonstop through the rest of the journey, telling me about all the retailers who'd tried to pull one over on him. The way he talked, you'd think he didn't even need a verifier. We came to a stop on the Upper East Side, in a neighborhood that looked pretty ritzy. Once we'd both climbed off the carpet, Selwyn rolled it up, tucked it under his arm, and led the way to a gift store.

It was the kind of place that sells cards for every occasion, gift wrap, and things classified as "gifts" because they had no other discernible purpose. But this store had a rack labeled "Special Occasion Cards" in which there were items that didn't quite look like greeting cards.

They were shrink-wrapped booklets with labels on the front, grouped under headings like Household Spells, Transportation, Workplace Convenience, and Masking Illusions. So, that's what a spell looked like on the market. Selwyn had me read all the headers off to him, and he nodded. "Okay, looks like they're in good shape. There isn't anything else?"

"Like what?"

"Oh, just anything different. Anything that doesn't look like it belongs." He didn't look me in the eye as he said this, which made me wonder what was going on.

I shook my head. "I don't think so. Everything has a similar look to it, like it's all from the same company."

"Good. Good." He looked more relieved than seemed reasonable in that situation, but after a moment he got the same blandly pleasant salesman's look on his face and pulled a notepad and pen out of his pocket. "Give me a count of what's in each category."

I noticed that the pen wrote the numbers without any help from him, and that made me lose count in the Household Spells category. Just as I was finishing the last category, a woman came from around the cash register and said, "Selwyn! What brings you here?"

"Madeline, you're lovelier than ever," he said, bowing to kiss her hand. "I'm just making sure you have everything you need."

"Oh, I don't know about everything," she said with a saucy wink, "but I'm well stocked on spells. The subway summoner is doing particularly well. I may need a restock on that one soon."

While they talked I looked around the store to see if there was anything else that should be out of place in a small gift shop, but it all looked pretty normal to me, mostly ceramic cat sculptures and candle holders shaped like angels. Once Selwyn and I were back outside, he shook the rug out until it hovered in place and we climbed on for the trip back to the office.

"Do you really get cheated that often, or are you people just paranoid by nature?" I couldn't resist asking.

"It happens often enough that it's wise to take measures."

"So, even though you have this no harm decree, magical people like to see what they can get away with?"

He pointed a finger at me like he was firing a gun. "Bingo. Otherwise, what's the fun of having this kind of power?"

I had to admit that he had a point. If I were magical, what would I try to do? I might be tempted to adjust the expiration date on a grocery coupon or tinker with the bank's computers so my rent check wouldn't clear as quickly. There were times when I'd wished I could turn someone into a frog—like Mimi—or give the snooty popular girls a bad acne attack, but that probably fell into the category of doing harm. I winced at the thought. Did it make me a bad person that one of the few things I could think of using magic to do involved hurting someone else? Maybe it wouldn't count if it was just a practical joke, something that wasn't real, such as an illusion that would wear off in a few hours.

Otherwise, there wasn't much I could think of. I might get away with something, but my own conscience wouldn't let me rest. I'd probably even run back to the grocery store to pay them the thirty cents I'd had taken off with the expired coupon so I could sleep at night. Unfortunately, I knew there were far too many normal people always out to see if they could beat the system. Why should it be that different for people who could do magic? The degree of paranoia certainly wasn't a good sign. I've found that the most paranoid people are that way because they know what they'd do to others, given the chance.

It was lunchtime when we made it back to the office. I got my lunch out of the refrigerator and ate while reading, making sure not to get crumbs on Owen's books. The Camelot story was fascinating. I'd seen many versions of King Arthur's story, but this was different. It was history rather than fable, supposedly, and instead of focusing on the feats of Arthur and his knights, it focused on the activities of Merlin, the king's magician.

While Arthur was forming his round table, Merlin was forming his own society, an organization of magicians dedicated to advancing and policing their craft. A footnote said this was the beginning of what was now known as the corporation Magic, Spells, and Illusions, Inc. That was cool. To think, I was working at a company founded by Merlin himself.

With that revelation, I decided to put the history of magic on hold and read the company history Owen had sent. It picked up the story from Merlin's time, telling how once the organization was established, he had gone into a deep sleep in a cave of crystal as a form of retirement. He was to be awakened when Arthur returned to lead a victorious Britain, or when the organization he founded had dire need of him.

That triggered a memory in my brain. They'd talked about the big boss coming out of retirement because the company needed him. But that couldn't be the same thing, could it? I switched over to the magical biography book and looked up Merlin. The book gave many forms of his name. The Welsh form was Myrddyn Emrys, which meant Emrys from Myrddyn. And that translated into modern English as Ambrose Mervyn. The name "Merlin" seemed to have something to do either with Latin or a mistranscription of the Welsh.

"Holy cow," I whispered to myself. It couldn't be. He'd have to be more than a thousand years old, but I supposed it was possible that he didn't age while he was in that cave. I remembered bits and pieces of conversations, his stating what his name was in modern English, as if that meant something, talking about the New World, adjusting to the bustle of the city.

If Mr. Mervyn really was Merlin, it was a miracle he was coping as well as he was. I couldn't imagine the difference between Britain in the Dark Ages and New York City today. Had they at least let him wake up in England before bringing him here, or had he awakened in the middle of Manhattan and found himself suddenly at the helm of a multinational corporation that bore little resemblance to the organization he'd founded?

It was a measure of how my last couple of weeks had gone that I was more concerned with how he must be coping than I was startled by the revelation that I was working for the real Merlin.

I read the rest of his biography. The last paragraph said, "Merlin was recently brought out of his cave to steer the company he founded through a challenging situation that threatens the very fabric of the magical community." That sounded ominous, and far worse than dealing with a bad economy. You brought your founder and CEO out of retirement from his cottage in the Cotswolds or his cabin in Vermont for a bad economy or a corporate scandal. What would be so desperate that you'd revive an ancient and legendary enchanter from more than a millennium of magical slumber and bring him across an ocean to a world that must be as foreign to him as another planet? Whatever it was had to be bad, and that could be the reason they were so paranoid and so badly in need of verifiers like me.

I felt dizzy. I'd have breathed into my paper lunch sack if I didn't think it would draw unnecessary attention from my coworkers. I couldn't resist pinching my thigh under my table. Maybe I was stuck in a long, elaborately detailed dream. This sort of thing didn't happen to me, Katie Chandler. My life had been so very, very normal—boring even—up to this point. I'd managed to make even a magical job seem ordinary, with the drab verification office that was as bad as any secretarial pool I'd seen during the desperate days of temping I'd gone through when I first got to New York. Only I could turn working at Magic Inc. into a dull nine-to-five job.

They'd said repeatedly that verifiers were important to them, but what could someone like me possibly do in a situation bad enough to bring Merlin—*the* Merlin—out of a magical coma? I could run a small business and track the details of launching a marketing campaign. That was the extent of my skill base. If they were counting on my help, they were in bigger trouble than they realized.

After the confusion came anger. They'd left out that minor detail about the challenging situation during the hiring process. It would be like getting a job and then finding out on your second day that the company and its executives were under federal investigation, the company had just filed for bankruptcy, and its pension fund had been drained.

I needed to get to the bottom of this. I went back to the company history and flipped to the end. There were several blank pages at the back of the book. The last page with printing on it was only halfway complete. It mentioned the revival of Merlin and the challenging situation, but didn't give a lot of details. I flipped a few pages before that and was just starting to read when Gregor called my name.

"She's on lunch," Angie said before I could respond.

I ignored her and said, "Yes, Gregor?" She stuck her tongue out at me and went back to eating her lunch.

"Got a verification request for you, from R and D. They asked for you personally. You'll be seeing Mr. Palmer."

Owen. I needed to have some words with him. I could see Rod trying to pull the wool over my eyes, but I expected more out of Owen. He'd acted so concerned about my well-being. How could he have let me take this job, knowing there was something going on, without telling me there might be trouble?

I closed my book and stood up. "I'm on my way." I noticed as I headed for the door that both Kim and Angie were glaring at me. Kim was probably jealous of me getting so close to someone whose star was clearly on the rise, while Angie envied my chance to cozy up to the hottie. I just hoped I had the chance to ask him about my discovery and get an explanation.

I was worried about how I'd get through the door once I made it to R&D, since Rod had needed a code to get through it, but the door swung open as I approached. I headed back to Owen's lair in Theoretical Magic. He wasn't in the lab where I'd seen him before. Instead, I found him in his office, which was a snug room lined with books. It looked like the study out of an old English manor house. I had a sudden craving for hot tea and a good mystery novel.

Owen sat behind the big wooden desk. Across from him sat a small, thin, nervous-looking man. Both men were intently studying a book that lay open on Owen's desk. I rapped lightly on the doorframe, and both heads turned to look at me. Owen smiled immediately. Just the tips of his ears turned red, and he was cute enough to defuse some of my anger. "Katie! Come in. Have a seat."

I entered the office and perched on the edge of the big leather chair next to Owen's guest. "What can I do for you today?" I asked.

"Katie, I'd like you to meet Wiggram Bookbinder. He's a rare book dealer who finds me most of my more esoteric resources. Wig, this is Katie Chandler, from our verification department. She's an immune."

I shook the man's hand, being careful not to squeeze too hard. His hand felt fragile, like the bones were barely held together. The man himself looked frail, swallowed by a faded black trench coat. Wisps of grizzled hair dotted his mostly bald head. There was more hair coming out of his ears than on his entire scalp. "Pleased to meet you," I said.

"Likewise," he replied, but his voice shook and he'd gone an ashy shade of pale. He certainly didn't look like he was pleased to meet me.

Owen folded his hands on top of his desk and said in a pleasant tone with a hint of ice behind it, "Now, Wig, is there anything you want to say to me before I ask Katie a question?"

The little man went even paler. His lips were now a ghostly shade of blue. He shook his head vigorously, causing his ear hair to flutter.

Owen then turned to me. "Katie, please take a look at the book on my desk and tell me what you see."

I stood up and moved over to his desk. The book was a giant tome, but it wasn't like the obviously ancient, leather-bound books on the shelves that lined Owen's office. It looked more like a modern hardcover. I closed the cover and found that it was just what I'd thought, only without the paper outer cover books are usually sold with. Then I checked the spine and couldn't hold back a grin.

"It's a Tom Clancy novel, not his latest, but one from a few years back. I gave this one to my dad for Christmas that year." I opened the book again and checked the copyright page. "It's not even a first edition. You could get it used for about five bucks."

"Thank you, Katie." Owen's voice was frosty, and he didn't take his eyes off Wig, who visibly trembled as he cowered in his chair. I suspected my task was complete, but since no one had dismissed me, I sat back in my chair to see what happened next. "That's a very interesting assessment, considering that Mr. Bookbinder here just told me it was one of three remaining copies of a sixteenth-century Welsh codex, worth a lot more than five dollars. Very nice illusion, Wig. You certainly had me fooled. Fortunately, I had Katie here to help."

Owen's voice remained pleasant and conversational, but it was the kind of pleasant that sounds menacing because it's too calm for the situation. I could practically taste Wig's fear, without me having a shred of magical talent. I could also sense the power behind Owen, and now I knew why he was considered such a rising star. It was a little scary, and also rather hot, even though I've never gone for the dangerous kind. He definitely didn't fit the typical bad-boy mold that usually turns me off, not in those nice suits, though with his coloring

I imagined he could work up a good scruffy look just by skipping a day of shaving. Did someone actually have to do bad things to be a bad boy, or was it all about the potential? If it was the potential that counted, then maybe it was the restraint that was so sexy, knowing that he could do something dangerous and powerful but had the restraint not to. If he had that kind of control in that area, then maybe it applied to other areas as well. I squirmed in my seat and hoped to high heaven that mind reading wasn't one of his gifts. If it was, they could put the pair of us on the roof and use our red faces as beacons to warn off approaching aircraft.

Owen shook his head in pity, and it looked like real pity, not the mock pity you show to someone you're about to destroy. "You must be really desperate to take that risk. Surely you knew you'd be found out?"

Wig opened his mouth to respond, but all that came out were gasps and stammers. I couldn't make a single word out of all he said.

"Now, what I find interesting is the fact that you were able to do such a solid, detailed illusion," Owen continued. "That has to mean that you've actually seen a copy of this codex. Otherwise, you wouldn't have been able to make this up so well. You wouldn't still happen to have that copy around, would you?"

"Y-Y-Yes. I-I-I do."

Owen smiled. "I thought so. Otherwise, you wouldn't have risked offering it to me. You know how much I need it, and you know I've been looking everywhere for it. You must have thought you could sell this illusion to me, then when the spell wore off, I'd be so eager to get my hands on the real book that I'd pay extra to get it. But thanks to Katie, we can skip that part. Give me the real book, Wiggram." There was a hard edge to his last sentence that scared me, and I wasn't the one he was mad at.

Wiggram bent to the bulky canvas satchel at his feet and pulled out a book that was roughly the size and shape of the Tom Clancy book, but otherwise bore no resemblance. The cover was dark leather, worn smooth with the years, and the title was embossed in gold on the cover. I couldn't read the lettering, for it was in a language I'd never seen before. He laid the book down on Owen's desk, and Owen opened it and flipped through it, a look of awe on his face.

The pages of this book were thick and uneven. It was obviously not a book made in mass quantities on a machine. It looked like it had been made by hand. Even the lettering looked like it was written by hand. The room already had a faint scent of old books, but this one had a stronger, older scent to it.

"I think it's the real deal," I said to Owen softly, so I didn't interrupt his inspection. "It's obviously old, the cover is leather, and the pages are handwritten on uneven paper. I don't know if it's what you're looking for, but it's not a Tom Clancy novel."

He nodded in acknowledgment, then said, "I'll pay your asking price, minus a thousand for trying to cheat me."

Wig nodded enthusiastically. "Y-Yes, sir, very good, sir, thank you. And please keep the novel as a gift. It's a very good book."

"My dad liked it," I put in.

Owen nodded, not taking his eyes off his new toy. "Go down to Accounting. They'll cut you a check. And, no, we won't pay you in cash. For a transaction this large, we need a paper trail."

"Of course, sir, thank you." Wiggram stood, collected his bag, then bowed to me and handed me a card. "Please keep me in mind for your rare book needs. I've also got a wide selection of nonmagical books." I took the card, even though I doubted he'd have copies of any of the out-of-print romance novels I was looking for. He hurried out of the office like someone had set his coat on fire.

Owen still sat poring over the book. He seemed to have forgotten I was there. "So, that's why you need people like me," I said.

He looked up, blinking. "Oh. Yes, yes, that's why we need people like you. Thank you. You were brilliant. There's more to verification than just telling the truth, you know. If you present the truth in the right way, it can be quite effective."

"I guess it's showbiz, as much as anything." I glanced toward the doorway where Wiggram had disappeared. "You're letting him wander free like that in the building?"

"He's being monitored. And I have his book already, so he's going to want his money. Speaking of which, excuse me for a second." He put his hand on the crystal ball thingy that sat on his desk, but he didn't speak. After a second or two he withdrew his hand and turned back toward me.

I knew he wanted to look through his new book, but I also wanted some answers. "Thanks again for the books you sent me. They're really interesting. I do have a question, though."

He smiled. "Yes, he is."

I shook my head. "You don't know what I was going to ask."

"Yes, I do."

"How?" I hoped it wasn't mind reading, not after the mental image I'd had a few minutes ago.

He shrugged. "I just do. Besides, you're smart enough. I was sure you'd eventually see the connection."

"Would it have killed you to tell me up front? It can't be too big a secret, not if you were willing to give me those books that made it so obvious."

He looked enigmatic, which must have been a real trick for him, given that his emotions were usually so visible on his face. "Let's just say that it's not a secret if you've got the initiative to do research and the brains to figure it out, but it is a secret if someone has to tell you."

"So we're working for the real Merlin, as in Camelot, and all that?"

"Not quite like in *Camelot*. That was highly fictionalized. But yes, he's the real thing."

"Why was he brought here now? It would have to be something pretty big, right?"

"That, I can't tell you."

"Because you don't know, or because I'm not supposed to know?" He continued to look enigmatic. "Okay, I get it. Company secret. Fine. But I want it on record that I'm not happy that you hid the possibility of a crisis from me when you were hiring me."

"Would it have changed your decision?"

I sighed. "Probably not. You guys did a great sales job."

"Don't worry. You'll find out eventually."

"Or I'll figure it out." I tapped my forehead. "Smart, remember? Now I'd better head back to the pit of despair." I got out of my chair and headed toward the doorway.

"Thanks again for your help," he called after me, but before I was out the door he was already buried in his book.

The laboratories were busy, but the hallway leading to the exit was nearly empty. I noticed a man coming toward me, not wearing the white lab coat that seemed de rigueur in these parts. As he approached, I smiled and nodded, but he didn't respond at all. He acted like he couldn't see me—or like he thought I couldn't see him. I didn't recognize him, but I didn't know most of the people in this department.

"Hi," I said to him. His eyes cut my way, then he went back to looking right past me. Either I'd come across the least friendly employee in the whole company or there was something fishy going on here. "Hey!" I called out. He flattened himself against a wall, like he was trying to look invisible. I noticed he had something hidden beneath his jacket. That was definitely not right.

He tried to ease past me, but I got directly in his way. He sidestepped me, and now I was sure he wasn't supposed to be there and that he thought no one could see him. "You aren't invisible, you know," I said, rolling my eyes. "I can see you."

He looked startled, glancing around to either side like he was looking for an exit or for verification that he was more visible than he thought he was. That proved something was wrong.

"Hey!" I yelled again, this time to anyone within earshot rather than to him. "Security! Intruder! Help!"

nine

The guy looked like he was going to run for it. I grabbed his jacket and held on. He muttered something in Latin and I felt a charge in the air, but nothing happened. That startled him, and I took advantage of the opportunity to reach for his arm. If he was going to get out of here, he was going to have to drag me with him. I tried to dig my heels into the floor, but the tile didn't give me much traction. All this time I was screaming at the top of my lungs. "Hello! Help! Security! Somebody!" Finally, in desperation, I yelled, "Owen!" He better have meant it when he said to just ask if I needed help.

The intruder then gave up on magic and went for physical force, shoving me roughly away from him. He was bigger than I was, so the force carried me across the hallway to hit the opposite wall. There was an audible thunk as my temple smacked into the wall. I slumped to the ground, dazed.

Why wasn't anyone coming? I thought I'd shouted loud enough to wake the dead. But then the interloper flew back against the other wall, as though someone had thrown him. He remained pinned there, his feet several inches off the floor. He no longer looked like he thought no one could see him.

I turned to see Owen standing in the corridor, his face flushed and his hair mussed, like he'd run the moment he heard my shout. Good old superhero friend Owen. But he wasn't the sweet, shy guy I'd come to know in the past week. He looked like someone I wouldn't want to mess with. If I'd thought the hint of restrained danger he'd shown earlier was sexy, now he was downright hot. I understood why heroines in superhero movies were always swooning into their unitard-wearing heartthrobs' arms after being rescued. It wasn't that they were shrinking violets or weak girly-girls. It was just that seeing a man do something so extraordinary and supernatural to save you has a way of making your knees go weak in a very pleasant way. I'd always heard power was an aphrodisiac, but I hadn't considered the possible implications of that when working for a magical company.

The guy pinned to the wall seemed to try to do something to counter whatever it was Owen had done to him. He muttered something in a foreign language, waved his hands, and even twitched his nose, and I felt the tingle of energy that came with magic use, but it didn't do him much good. He remained stuck there.

"Who are you?" Owen asked him in a voice that was soft, yet full of power.

The man opened his mouth to speak, as if compelled to do so, but then he struggled to clamp his mouth shut again. Owen held out his hand, and the packet of papers that had been under the guy's jacket flew to him. The guy continued to struggle. Owen waved his hand casually, and the man slumped to the ground in a daze.

Now I thought I understood what Rod had meant about keeping Owen shy for safety. The intruder was panting and sweating with effort, while Owen didn't have so much as a bead of moisture on his forehead. I could see where you wouldn't want someone with that kind of power to have a big ego or a sense that anyone owed him anything. If he got it into his head that he wanted to take over the world, it wouldn't be easy to stop him.

Wouldn't you know it, I'd go and develop a thing for a guy who was way out of my league, in so very many ways. A super powerful wizard didn't really fit into my lifestyle. I could just imagine taking him home to meet my folks. I'd have enough trouble explaining my job to them. What could Owen possibly say about his job that wouldn't send my dad off to get his shotgun to scare this weirdo away from his daughter? It would be even worse if I'd inherited my magical immunity from my parents. Then the last thing I needed to do was let anyone magical into my nonwork life. Not that Owen would have the slightest interest in going to Texas and meeting my folks. Hadn't they said during my interview that I came from a very nonmagical place?

The department door opened and Sam flew inside, followed by a crew of large men. "Took you long enough," Owen said, sounding more like his usual self.

"Aw, I knew you had things under control, boss," Sam said as he landed in front of the intruder. "Take him away, boys."

"Hold him in Security. We'll have someone talk to him later," Owen directed.

Sam saluted with one wing, then flew off after the security group that was levitating the petrified body down the hallway. Once they were gone, the sense of power and energy that had filled the hallway faded away. I tried to get up, but a hand on my shoulder pushed me back down. I looked up to see Owen leaning over me, his face full of concern. Then he turned around and said, "Everyone, back to work." I noticed people disappearing into labs up and down the corridor.

"Are you okay?" he asked me softly.

"I'm fine, really."

He shook his head. "No, I don't think you are. We need to get someone to take a look at you. And I suspect the boss will want to talk to you."

"The boss. You mean Merlin?"

"Yes, Merlin."

The fact that I was talking like I'd had a couple of glasses of champagne on an empty stomach was a pretty good sign I wasn't okay, but I wasn't sure I wanted to deal with Merlin in this state, and I was definitely sure I didn't want to deal with Owen right now. Dealing with Owen without making a total fool of myself required the ability to think straight, something I didn't have at the moment.

"Okay, I'm not so fine. Just a bit dizzy. There's a hospital down the street, though."

He got an arm around me and helped me to my feet. "That's not necessary. Mr. Mervyn is a healer. He can see to you while we talk about what happened here."

"I'm not magical, remember? Immune. Magic healing won't work on me."

He chuckled as he draped my left arm across his shoulders and circled my waist with his right arm. That felt really nice, a little too nice. When was the last time a man had put his arm around me like that, whether or not it was for romantic reasons? "Not all healing is magical. Mr. Mervyn was a Renaissance man long before the Renaissance."

"I'm about to find out what's going on here, why they brought him back, aren't I?" I asked as we made our way slowly to the turret escalator.

"Yes, I imagine you are."

Merlin/Mr. Mervyn met us at the top of the stairs. "Is she hurt?" he asked.

"I think so," Owen responded. "She hit her head."

"Get her to my office. The suspect's in custody?"

"Security has him."

Soon I was deposited on a soft sofa. There were more voices in the room now, but all I noticed was Owen's hand gripping mine. "I don't know how he got in, but if Katie hadn't spotted him . . ."

"What was he trying to steal?" Merlin's voice came from across the room.

"Our research on the Idris situation."

"Then he's definitely worried, or he suspects we are." This time, Merlin's voice came from nearby. Something cool touched my forehead. It smelled good, minty and flowery. "Here, rest this against the lump. It should take down the swelling."

I opened my eyes to see Merlin kneeling beside me. Take away the business suit and put him in robes studded with stars, then grow his beard out to be long and pointy instead of neatly trimmed, and he was right out of a picture book about King Arthur I'd had as a child. "Merlin," I said. I thought I'd been musing silently, but I must have spoken out loud. "Mind if I call you Merlin?"

"Not at all, dear. Now, tell me what you're seeing."

"I see you, and Owen. And your office."

He held a hand in front of my face. "How many fingers am I holding up?"

I squinted at the wavering image. "Two. I think."

He exchanged a look with Owen, then the two of them helped me lie down on the sofa. Merlin put a pillow under my head, while Owen took off my shoes and covered me with a light blanket that I didn't remember being there.

Merlin knelt beside me again. "Katie, I believe you have a mild concussion. You need to rest awhile. I'll give you a cordial that should prevent a very bad headache, and the poultice will keep you from swelling and bruising too badly."

He went away for a moment, then came back and lifted my head gently as he put a small glass to my lips. "Now, drink." I obeyed, and a tangy, sweet liquid flowed down my throat. I sank gratefully back against the pillows.

I didn't fall asleep, but I let myself drift as the voices in the room began speaking to each other, apparently ignoring my presence. They sounded like they were having an emergency meeting. It had to be a meeting about the intruder, which must have had something to do with whatever was threatening the company enough that they'd brought Merlin out of retirement to deal with it. I tried to listen, even though I kept drifting away.

A voice I didn't recognize asked, "How did an intruder get in anyway? I thought that area was secured."

"It is secured," Owen protested. "All I can think is that the intruder tailed someone else into the building and into the department, using an invisibility spell." He groaned and added, "I'd just had Wiggram Bookbinder in, selling me a rare codex. The intruder probably followed him. Or, as desperate as Wig seemed to be, it's entirely possible that the whole thing was a setup to get the spy inside. If Katie hadn't been there to see past that spell, we'd be in big trouble."

"Maybe you'd better meet with your shady sources somewhere other than in a highly secured department," the other voice said, but then he seemed to swallow his argument before he got really wound up.

I soon learned why. "Gentlemen, I believe the real issue at hand is that Mr. Idris has been reduced to espionage," Merlin said, his voice sounding grim. I could only imagine what his face must have looked like. It would be enough to shut anyone up.

"But why?" one of the other voices asked.

"He wants to know what we're planning to do about him," Owen said.

"What are we planning?" another voice asked.

"That's the problem," Owen said with a sigh. "We don't have much to go on. If he'd managed to get his hands on these notes, he would have laughed at how ineffectual we are. All we know is what he was working on when we dismissed him. There's no way of telling what he's doing now until we find a copy of a spell. Even then, we don't have any control over what he does. All we can do is find a way to counter it."

"It's a little late to worry about that, isn't it?" the other voice asked. "We've heard he's already got some spells out there. They're not mass market, but he's got customers. Whatever he's doing has been unleashed on the world, and we don't know what damage will be done before we can develop a counterspell."

"Perhaps some of our panic is premature," Merlin said softly. "We don't know who might buy or use these spells. All we know is what he wanted to market through us, and that our corporate leadership found his ideas distasteful. There's a very good chance that the general magical population will find his ideas equally distasteful."

"But what do we do if people buy and use these spells? Judging by what we saw him doing here, we know his work is dangerous. I can't begin to imagine his work would be any less dangerous without our constraints."

"We need more time," Owen said softly, his voice full of despair. "We're doing everything we can, but it's not enough."

I couldn't help but feel sorry for him. As powerful as he was, it had to be hard to acknowledge that doing everything he could wasn't good enough. I also didn't like the idea of a rogue sorcerer selling bootleg spells, or whatever this guy was doing. Unfortunately, I knew next to nothing about magic, so there wasn't much I could do to help.

Or was there? I did know a thing or two about business, and this seemed to be as much a business problem as it was a magic problem. In fact, although this business seemed like it belonged to another universe, it wasn't that different from a situation I recalled from my days at the feed-and-seed. Our family had been running that business for nearly a century, as long as the town had been around. Not only had we been supplying the current generation of farmers and ranchers, but we'd supplied their fathers and grandfathers. A few years ago a national chain store had opened in a nearby town, offering lower prices. Farming is a low-margin business at the best of times, so those low prices were tempting to our customers. We just had to remind them why they'd been coming to us all those years, and why that new store wasn't the same.

Holding the poultice pack against my head, I sat up very carefully and waited for the room to steady itself before I said, "It seems to me that your main problem at this point is that you have competition, regardless of what your competition is offering. Make him compete on your level, and you can reduce the impact he might have."

All the men in the room turned to look at me, and I felt suddenly very self-conscious. Maybe I should have kept my mouth shut and continued to play dead, but it was too late for regrets, so I plunged on while they were too stunned to say anything. "I don't really know the situation, so maybe I'm missing something, but from what y'all have said, it sounds like one of your former employees went into business for himself and now may be offering some less pleasant alternatives to your products."

"That's a very acute and concise summation of the situation, Katie," Merlin said.

"Okay, good. Thanks. Well, anyway, until you've got a way to stop the less pleasant effects of what he's doing, it seems to me that what you need to do is get people to choose your spells over his."

They all looked at one another and nodded. Merlin and Owen both smiled. "How do we do that?" one of the others asked me.

"Have you ever tried marketing?" Most of them looked blank, but one of the men grinned.

"Marketing is basically letting people know what you have to sell and getting that product to the right people," he said.

Merlin still looked blank, but he was new to this century. "Surely you've seen ads," I said. "Have you ever watched TV?"

Faces lit up all the way around the table, and I could see comprehension dawning in their eyes. "Those ads tell you why you're better off buying this car or shampoo or soap than you would be if you bought the other kind. That's based on market research, which is finding out what your customers are like—what do they need, what concerns them, what do they prefer? Then you create an ad that addresses those things, letting your customers know that what you're offering them is exactly what they need, that it will solve their problems, and that you're the only one who can do so."

"So we tell our customers why they should choose our spells?" Merlin asked. He looked like a little kid who's just figured out how the multiplication table works and can't wait to multiply everything in sight. If I wasn't careful, MSI would be running a Super Bowl ad soon.

"Exactly! You might not want to come right out and say that your competitor is evil and his spells will do harm, but you do want to let people know why what you're selling is their best bet."

"If we can put a big dent in his sales, make it harder for him to get his spells into the market, we may be able to buy enough time to come up with a counterspell," Owen mused. "I like it. Great idea, Katie."

"So, we'll try marketing," Merlin said, rubbing his hands together. "How do we do that?"

"Let me guess, you don't have a marketing department," I said. Of course they didn't, not if I'd had to define the concept of marketing for them. "How have you made sales in the past? How have you let customers know what's available?"

They all looked at one another. "We have a sales department," the man who'd defined marketing said. He looked like a sales guy, not the kind wearing a plaid sport coat, but the kind who could convince someone to spend several thousand dollars on a diamond ring because otherwise they wouldn't be investing properly in their relationship. He was as good-looking as Owen, but in a slick, plastic way that I didn't find attractive. Come to think of it, he looked like a Ken doll brought to life. At this company, I wouldn't rule out the possibility. "The salesbeings work with the retailers to let them know what we have available, and the retailers let their customers know. There's been no alternative to our commercially produced spells, so we haven't needed to do much in the way of marketing."

"Not on a widespread level," Owen added. "There are a few niche products, and there's always been kitchen witchery, homemade spells people develop to suit their individual needs, but for centuries magical people have known that MSI spells are the best way to go. We take care of all that necessary and sometimes messy and dangerous trial and error."

"Could you do this marketing for us, Katie?" Merlin asked.

Oh boy. Now I was in over my head. I'd been responsible for marketing the family store, but even in our worst crises with competition, that had amounted to putting ads in the local weekly paper and mailing the occasional flyer to our customer list. My job as a corporate marketing assistant had taught me very little aside from the process of getting brochures produced. But I had taken some marketing courses for my degree, and it seemed I was better qualified than anyone else in this crazy company. Magic immunity or not, I appeared to have my own brand of sorcery. Maybe I wasn't so far out of Owen's league after all.

"I guess so," I said. "It's not going to be a major campaign, but anything is better than what you have—or haven't—been doing up to this point. The way I see it, the main thing you'll want to get across is what Owen said, that you've been the source for spells for centuries. How can anyone else compare? You can brag about how safe your spells are, and how they're extensively tested for effectiveness. Get in a subtle message that no newcomer can offer that, so naturally everyone will want to go with the tried-and-true provider instead of the upstart."

"Wonderful!" Merlin said. "You'll work with Mr. Hartwell here. He heads up our sales department." The plastic man stepped forward and shook my hand.

"But you'll start tomorrow. For now, Katie must rest," Merlin continued. "Back to your offices." He all but chased the others away. Owen looked like he was about to put up a fuss, but a glare from Merlin apparently changed his mind. Once they were gone, Merlin returned to the sofa where I sat and took my chin in his fingers. He studied me for a long moment, then smiled. "You'll be fine. How is your headache?"

I'd forgotten I was supposed to have a headache. "It's gone, I think. It's just a bit sore where I bumped it."

"Excellent. We can't thank you enough for stopping that intruder."

"I take it he was supposed to be invisible."

"So we were very fortunate that you were there. We don't often have need for verification services in the research department, though I believe we should start incorporating immunes into our security force to guard against future intrusions."

"Who is this Idris guy, anyway?" I asked.

He sat next to me on the sofa and clasped his hands together over his knees. "I've never met the gentleman. It was because of him that I was brought back. But from what I understand, he was on Owen's staff. Quite brilliant, but not entirely ethical. He'd unearthed some ancient spells and was working to modernize them, but they were dark spells, spells to use for harm. We don't allow that, so we certainly wouldn't want to market spells specifically designed to cause harm. He conducted unauthorized tests of these spells, so he was let go. Then we got word that he was continuing his work on his own and intended to provide dangerous spells to the magical community. It was one of the biggest threats we've faced in centuries, so the board saw fit to bring me back to face it."

"Do you really think he could cause serious trouble?"

"That, we don't know. Our people haven't been tested like this for a long time, although problems have arisen every so often. I'd like to think that most folks will ignore his spells because they have no need of them. But it's also possible that this will encourage the less noble elements of society to be bolder, and that's a potential problem left over from the last time we faced a test like this. Our people removed the leadership of that challenge, but the more restive elements are still out there. I'm afraid the outcome this time could be an all-out magical war."

I shuddered and tried to swallow the lump that had developed in my throat. Suddenly, as a way of stopping a major magical war, my little marketing idea seemed awfully weak. If marketing was the key to saving the world, then we were in big trouble, considering the marketing people I'd worked with. I had a frightening mental image of Mimi wearing a brass bra and a helmet with horns as she faced down the rampaging hordes by flinging brochures at them. No, that would never work. I reminded myself that I was just buying time for Owen and his people to come up with a way to defeat these evil spells. I wasn't being asked to save the world.

Merlin reached over and squeezed my hand. "We are fortunate to have you with us," he said. "Your idea may be what saves us." Great, and just when I'd convinced myself that what I was doing wasn't such a big deal. I didn't need to be reminded of the pressure.

I fought back a groan. "I hope it works. I've never run an entire marketing campaign before. I've only been an assistant." And the campaigns I'd been involved in hadn't been particularly good. It didn't help that I knew so little about the magical community. Did they have their own media? How did they get their magical news? They were certainly connected, but was it just gossip or was there a more organized dissemination of information? I had a lot of questions for Mr. Hartwell. I doubted Merlin was the best source for information on modern magical life. He was probably nearly as lost there as I was.

"You'll do fine," Merlin assured me. He had that same creepy confidence in his eyes that I'd seen in Owen at times, and I suspected he wasn't just trying to make me feel better. He was telling me something he knew for a fact. I wondered how that precognition thing worked, but that was a question for another time and place. I had so many questions, and it never seemed to be the right time to ask them. For instance, there was a lot I wanted to know about Merlin, but neither of us could go into that right now.

"I'd better get back to my office," I said, handing him the cloth with the poultice on it. "Thanks for patching me up."

"It was the least I could do, given the service you've rendered us."

Only then did it really hit me that I'd actually saved the day, in more ways than one. I'd nabbed the intruder and I'd come up with the big idea. Not bad for a day's work. While I was still feeling confident, I made a detour by Rod's office, thinking I might as well have that talk with him now. It would minimize the amount of time I had to spend in the verification hellhole.

Isabel greeted me like a whirlwind when I entered the outer office. "Oh, you poor dear! Are you all right?" she asked, enveloping me in a suffocating hug.

"I'm fine. Or I will be. Is Rod in? I need to talk to him."

Just then Rod's office door opened and he stuck his head out. His face brightened when he saw me. "Katie! I heard about what happened. Good show!"

"Yeah, thanks. Have you got a minute?"

"Of course, come in." He ushered me into his office, shut the door, and steered me toward the big overstuffed chair I'd sat in the last time. Was it only yesterday? "What did you need to talk about?"

"Well, the verifiers and other immunes are pretty important to you people, especially now, right?"

"Of course!"

"Then why do you have them working in such a pit? Not to mention making them have the boss who tends to turn green and grow horns when he's angry. What genius thought of putting him with the one group of people who can actually see what he's like?"

"You mean Gregor still has that anger problem? He said he got that treated."

"Anger problem? So, that's what they call it. Well, he's got it in a big way. Fortunately, nobody seems to care much, but it still doesn't make for a pleasant working environment. What is he anyway? Angie swore he was human, but I'm not sure I believe that."

"Oh, he's human. There was a bad lab accident. He used to run Theoretical Magic until he accidentally turned himself into an ogre. I'm not sure what he was trying to do that had that particular side effect. It wasn't entirely reversible, but they were able to cure him enough so he could lead a normal life. It must not have worked as well as they thought. Owen got his job when he was transferred."

"Well, anyway, morale down there sucks. Nobody except Kim seems to care enough to try, and I'd keep an eye on Kim. She's ambitious, but I'm not sure her priority is the good of the company. All of those people are bored. If you want to keep them or get anything productive out of them, you're going to have to do better." Then I had a burst of inspiration based on my earlier conversation with Merlin. "Hey, I know, maybe you could assign the verifiers to offices in various departments. That way, they'd be around to spot people trying to play invisible while they wait for assignments. They wouldn't feel quite so useless or bored, and they'd get more of a chance to interact with the company. That might make them feel like part of the big picture, so they'd care more about what they do."

"That's a great idea. I'll talk to Gregor. Meanwhile, I understand you have a project of your own to work on."

This place had the fastest office grapevine I'd ever seen, including the one in my family-owned store where most of the employees were related and lived under the same roof. "Yeah. Seems like it. I guess that takes me out of the pool for a while."

"It doesn't sound like you mind all that much," he said with a wry grin.

"Not in the least. Those people are weird, and around here, that's really saying something." I started to get up, then had an idea and sat back down. "Maybe you can help me with this."

"Of course. What do you need?"

"I don't know enough about the magical world to know how to market to it. How do you all get your news?"

"Most of us have cable."

I shook my head. "What about magical news? You don't have something like the cable magic channel or anything like that, do you? How do you find out about news in the magical world?"

"Well, there are a few good Web sites out there, but most of us get the major bulletins from the crystal network." He waved toward that thingy that sat on his desk.

"Yeah, I've noticed those things. They seem to be a combination office phone and e-mail system."

"More or less. Like e-mail, you can communicate directly to a particular individual, or you can receive a message sent to many people. If there's anything major that everyone in the magical community needs to know, that's how it's sent."

"And how do you decide what's major enough for everyone to get it?"

"There's a group of people who manage mass communications for the network. If you have an announcement, you send it through them. If they think it's worthy, they pass it on. An individual can't do a mass message."

I sighed. "That makes things difficult for me, if you can't get advertising out there. This would be so much easier if we could buy air time on TV, or the magical equivalent, and do a really good image ad."

"Sorry I couldn't be more helpful."

"You were very helpful. I'm just going to have to be more creative. And I have to get back to my own office." I forced myself out of the chair before I got too comfortable and drifted off. Maybe that concussion was worse than I thought. Rod stood and came around his desk to open his office door for me.

"Let me know if you have any other questions," he said.

"Don't worry, I will. You may get tired of me."

He laughed. "I don't think there's much danger of that. And thank you for your suggestion. I'll think about it."

After the exciting afternoon I'd had, I hated going back to the dreary verification pool. As soon as I saw my coworkers, I couldn't help but wonder if my great idea about relocating the verifiers was so smart after all. The rest of the group seemed to enjoy their leisure on company time. How would they react to being asked to work harder? Would they really feel more like a part of the company? Thinking about it made my head hurt.

Speaking of my head, I made a stop at the bathroom before going to my desk and took a look at myself in the mirror. There was a knot forming on my temple where I'd hit the wall. It was currently red, but it was the kind of red that turns black and blue by morning. I wasn't sure how I'd explain a goose egg like that to my roommates. I tried pulling my hair across my face, but that made it look worse by drawing attention to it. I needed to come up with an excuse.

Fortunately, I wasn't dating anyone, so they couldn't jump to the conclusion that any lame excuse I gave them was a cover-up for an abusive boyfriend. They might think I had an abusive boss, but since

I'd survived a year with Mimi, they had to know it couldn't get much worse. I supposed I'd just have to tell them I'd bumped into a wall, which was the truth, more or less.

It wasn't fair. Marcia came home with stories about big deals she'd had a part in, and Gemma was always telling us about the famous designers and models she ran into in the course of her job. Until now I'd never had anything more exciting than tales of Mimi's latest outburst. They'd listened politely and had done a pretty good job of faking interest, but I couldn't help but wish I had a job where I could do something important or interesting. Now I finally had something worth talking about, and I couldn't tell anyone about it.

The closing-time stampede struck just as I returned to my desk. Still deep in thought, I gathered my things and left the building. "That was some catch, sweetheart," Sam said as I stepped onto the sidewalk.

"Yeah, not bad for a day's work, huh?"

"Are you kidding? That was spectacular. I'd try to get you transferred to Security if I thought I could get away with it."

"All it took was a good eye and a strong set of lungs. Owen did all the work."

"Yeah, but he wouldn't have known what to do if you hadn't been there, pointing the way."

That was something to think about. Owen might be one of the most powerful wizards around, but that intruder could have got away with stealing stuff from his department if I hadn't been there. "It's nice to be needed," I said with a smile.

"And it sounds like you have even more on your plate now. At the rate you're going, you'll be running the place by Christmas." He saluted me with one wing. "Now, go home and get some rest. You've got a busy day ahead of you tomorrow."

He was right about that. I had a marketing plan to put together and a magical war to fight. This company and these people needed me. More important, they knew they needed me, and they were willing to listen to me. It was enough to make me want to call Mimi just to blow a big raspberry in her ear. Look out, world. Little Katie Chandler wasn't quite so ordinary anymore.

My head was still hurting and I was tired when I got home, so I should have been glad to be the first one there. It would give me a chance to rest and recover a little before I had to face Gemma and Marcia. But I was about to explode from nervous, restless energy. Even if I couldn't talk about what had happened, I needed to talk to someone. I could at least tell them I had an important new project. That sure beat having nothing better to say about work than "I typed another memo today."

Fortunately, Gemma and Marcia got home within a few minutes of each other so I didn't have to decide between holding myself back or telling the same story twice. As soon as we'd all changed out of our work clothes and opened the take-out containers they'd brought in, I blurted, "You won't believe what happened at work today."

ten

My audience lacked the look of rapt anticipation I'd hoped for. Instead, they looked concerned. "Does it have something to do with that lump on your head?" Marcia asked.

Actually, I'd been planning to talk about being assigned a big project by the CEO, but the moment she asked the question, all my good intentions about telling a boring cover story to explain the knot flew right out the window. I couldn't keep one of the most exciting days in my life entirely to myself. It wouldn't hurt to tell a teensy little part of the story, would it? I could talk about the adventure without getting into magic. "Yeah, it does."

"Oh, Katie, you don't have another bad boss, do you?" Gemma asked. "I know Mimi was awful, but at least she wasn't physically abusive."

"No, I don't have a bad boss. Well, okay, he's not perfect. He has anger management issues." And that was putting it mildly. "But the head honcho is great, and anyway, that has nothing to do with this. We had a little adventure at the office today. Some guy got in and was looking to steal some stuff, and I was the one who caught him."

Marcia nodded. "I've heard about that happening, people wandering around offices, trying to look like they belong and stealing laptops when no one is looking. You caught him?"

"I don't know about catching, but I saw him and yelled for help, so he was caught."

Gemma gave me a friendly punch on the shoulder. "Way to go, Katie. How'd you know he didn't belong, since you're so new?"

Oops. Maybe I should have thought this through before I blurted anything out. "He really looked like he didn't belong, and he looked like he didn't expect anyone to see him there." And that would be because he was invisible to everyone but me, but I definitely needed to leave that part out. I shrugged. "He just looked suspicious, and my instincts kicked in."

"How'd you get that lump, then?" Marcia asked, her eyes full of concern. "Did he hurt you?"

"He tried to take off when I yelled, so I grabbed onto him until Security got there, but he shook me off and I hit a wall. But I'm okay. They had someone take care of me at the office."

Marcia frowned. "This place you're working isn't dangerous, is it?"

That one was going to be a challenge to answer with any degree of honesty because you need a pretty good idea of the truth before you can come up with a good cover, and I didn't really know the truth. "I don't know that it's any more dangerous than any other place." That is, any other place that wasn't in the middle of a magical war against an evil rogue wizard.

"You win the prize for most interesting second day on the job," Gemma said with a grin.

"It gets better. Well, maybe not better, but there is more."

"The security guard who came to your rescue was incredibly buff and handsome, and he wants to take you out to dinner this weekend?" Gemma asked hopefully.

"Not exactly." The person who'd come to my rescue was incredibly handsome, and when he'd been helping me up to Merlin's office, I'd noticed that he had some decent muscles. On the other hand, the security guard who'd shown up was made of stone and had wings. As far as I knew, neither of them wanted to take me out to dinner this weekend. I didn't want to delve too deeply into this particular topic. "Actually, these two things aren't directly related. I got assigned to a pretty important new project."

"That's better than a studly security guard, especially if it gets you some executive attention," Marcia said. "It could be your first step on your way to the top."

Gemma rolled her eyes. "Don't sneeze at studly security guards. If one was cute, maybe you should ask him to dinner to thank him for coming to your rescue."

"We're talking about Katie's career," Marcia said. "That's the priority."

"That's coming from someone who hasn't experienced a studly security guard who's feeling like a hero. Otherwise, you'd have a totally different opinion."

I held up my hands in the T-shaped time-out signal. "Whoa, guys, hang on here a second. Can I finish telling my story before you decide whether my career or my love life is more important?"

"Sorry," they said in unison. Then Marcia asked, "What kind of project is it?"

"They haven't done much marketing at this company, so they want my input on a marketing plan."

"That's terrific!" Marcia said. "Just watch, you'll have a private office and a title before you know it."

The funny thing was, as exciting as my news was to them, I'd left out the most interesting parts of the story, like the invisible man, the powerful (and gorgeous) young wizard, and the fact that I was working for Merlin. It was frustrating that I had to keep the most exciting aspects of my life such a secret, even from my closest friends. I knew I'd have to be careful not to let anything slip in a rush of enthusiasm.

"What are you two doing Friday night?" Gemma asked, changing the subject before I was tempted to say more.

"I don't know. Why?"

"I may have another setup for us."

Marcia groaned. "I don't think I've recovered from the last one. Are you sure that guy wasn't a carrier of African sleeping sickness?"

"He wasn't so bad. And he was good-looking. He's also pretty rich. What about you, Katie?"

I tried not to groan. What with having to come up with the plan that would buy some powerful wizards time to save the world from magical evil, I didn't feel like dealing with a blind date. "I'll have to get back to you on that," I said. "With this project, I may be working late."

"Not on a Friday, silly. Just let me know when you're sure."

For the first time in my life I hoped I'd be working late on a Friday.

The next morning I did my hair in a style that left a curtain of bangs falling across one side of my forehead. It hid the bruise and made me look like a movie star, but I had a feeling that having my hair in my face would drive me stark raving mad before I even got to work.

Once again Owen was at the subway platform when I got there. I halfway suspected him of doing that on purpose, and I wondered if he was able to do it because I was so predictable or because he was using some of his more unique abilities. I was tempted to test him, to switch to a different subway line or leave earlier or later in the morning to see what happened. On the other hand, what was so bad about commuting every morning with a nice, good-looking guy who could keep me safe from any criminals or lunatics that might cross my path? I'd have to be insane to look for a way not to run into him every morning. Then I remembered the look on his face as he'd held that intruder pinned to the wall, and I couldn't help but shudder. In my world, a weird, scary guy was one who didn't get the hint when you told him three times in a row that you couldn't go out with him because you were busy washing your hair. A guy who could fling people around with his mind was a whole new level of weird and scary.

He smiled when he saw me, then immediately frowned and looked worried. "Your head, is it okay?" He looked so sweet and cute that I couldn't help reminding myself that as powerful as he was, I was immune to his magic. I didn't have to worry about him flinging me around. Obviously, however, I wasn't immune to his charm, for I immediately got a warm, yet shivery feeling in the pit of my stomach when I saw his smile. He was the boy next door, a heroic rescuer, and a dangerous potential bad boy all rolled into one. I knew if he made any effort at all to woo me, I'd be as helpless as the victims of Rod's love spells. It was a good thing he was too shy to make the first move—that is, if he had any interest in me whatsoever.

"I'm fine," I insisted, hoping I wasn't blushing enough to give away what I'd been thinking about him. "Just a nasty bruise, and thus the attempted cosmetic cover-up."

"It looks nice." He turned a particularly interesting shade of pink before adding, "I'm sorry."

"For what? It wasn't your fault."

"Yes, it was. If I'd made it to you sooner, I might have been able to help you before you got hurt." He ducked his head and studied the platform floor. "I finished reading the paragraph I was on before I got up and ran."

I laughed, which made him turn even pinker. "That's okay, really. I still don't think you'd have made it before he shoved me into the wall. I should have known better than to try to tackle an intruder by myself."

Before he could respond, a train came rumbling out of the tunnel. "You did us all a big favor," he said as he ushered me onto the train. "You were very brave." Now I was the one who was blushing.

The train was too crowded for conversation, especially the kind of conversation we'd be most likely to have, so we didn't try to talk during the journey. We walked together across the park to the office building, greeted Sam at the entrance, then parted ways at the top of the lobby stairs. I went into the verification pool just long enough to inform them that I'd be out on an assignment most of the day, then headed to the sales department.

I asked Hertwick where to find Mr. Hartwell, and he directed me to a pair of giant double doors at the far end of the corridor. Mr. Hartwell was apparently quite the bigwig. Just as I was about to knock, the doors creaked open. He sat behind a wooden desk almost as large as the one in Merlin's office. "Good morning," I said.

He looked up from his work to smile at me. "Ah, Miss Chandler. Good morning."

"I thought we ought to get started right away."

"Most definitely. Please have a seat. Would you like some coffee?"

"Yes, please," I said, settling myself in the armchair in front of his desk. I braced myself for the mug to pop into my hands. This time, I didn't jump or spill any of the coffee. With the hand that wasn't holding coffee, I flipped open my spiral notebook to the notes I'd made the night before.

"The first thing I need to do is get a better idea of how you get your products into the marketplace and promote them," I said.

He looked puzzled by my question. "We send them to the stores and put information on what the spells do on the packaging."

"That's it?"

"It's all we've ever needed to do."

"You're going to need to do more than that now. Assuming your competition isn't quite ready for the mass market, we have a slight head start. It's best if we can get our messages into the market before the competition gets there, so we don't look so much like we're reacting to the competition. How fast can you get your packaging changed?"

"Instantly."

I took a deep breath. Too bad I hadn't had access to magic in any of the other marketing campaigns I'd done. In the real world, it would take months. Here, we might be in gear before the end of the day.

"That makes life easier," I said. "What we need to do is incorporate some key messages into everything you do to communicate about your company and your products. A line or two on the packaging and in the material you send out to announce a new product should do it."

"Oh, that's quite doable."

"Now, is Merlin's presence here a big secret, or is that something you can promote? He should be a real celebrity in the magical community, and you may be able to play on that."

He frowned and clasped his hands together on top of his desk. "That can work both ways. Most people know he'd only be brought back if there was trouble, so they'd assume something was wrong if they saw him."

"Good point. Okay, we scratch Merlin as a celebrity endorser." I crossed that idea off of my notebook. It struck me that I was very possibly in way over my head. I wasn't up to running a major campaign like this for a normal company, but here I was trying to market something I didn't fully understand, and the stakes were a lot higher than they would be for launching something like a soft drink. The way they talked, this sounded like a life-or-death issue. "But we can change the packaging, add some additional corporate messaging to the spell release information, and get some information out to the various magic-specific Web sites, right?"

He nodded enthusiastically, and I got the sinking feeling that he understood about as much of what I'd said as I understood when they talked magic. We were all clueless together, in our own individual areas. "Sounds like a great plan! You'll just need to talk to the design department."

"You have a design department?"

"Of course. Someone has to design the packaging."

Design was one of my comfort zones. Not that I knew that much about how to design, but I understood a lot about the process. That department had been one of my hiding places on Mimi's bad days. They hated her as much as I did, so I found any excuse I could to tarry when I was sent there on an errand.

Mr. Hartwell thanked me again and gave me directions to Design. The department was tucked away into a basement room, and the word "department" was something of an overstatement. It was more like an individual. He was quite young, young enough to make me feel old, and so tall and lanky that at first I thought he must be an elf. He sat slumped on a beat-up old sofa in the corner of the office, his long legs stretched halfway across the room. He appeared to be playing with a Gameboy, but I was sure it was something far more magical than that. I didn't see any of the usual design department trappings in here, such as a drafting table or a super powerful Macintosh computer. Maybe this was just the break room.

I waited until he finished a game—judging by the muttered curse and sigh of disgust when he lowered the gadget for a second—then cleared my throat and asked, "Are you the designer?"

He looked up at me like I'd just materialized out of nothing. "Yeah, you must be Katie." News really did travel fast around here. "I'm Ralph."

"Hi, Ralph. I need to talk to you about the packaging design."

"Cool. I've been trying to get them to jazz it up for ages." He showed no signs of even thinking about unfolding himself and getting off the sofa to head to his office, so I assumed we would conduct the meeting where we were.

"I don't know how much we'll be able to jazz things up, but we will add more corporate messaging."

"Aw, hell, we might as well give 'em a makeover while we're at it." He put down his Gameboy—now I was pretty sure that's what it was—and waved his hand in the air. A packaged spell fell into my hands. It startled me enough that I had to juggle for a second to keep from dropping it. "What do you think?"

Once I managed to get a good grasp on the package, I took a look at it. Then I had to blink, and I wished I had some sunglasses handy. It certainly was different. The packaging I'd seen on the previous day's visit to the store had been basic and straightforward, just stating the spell and its possible uses in an attractive layout. This used wild graphics and bright colors that blinked at me. "It's very eye-catching," I said, trying to think of a diplomatic way to say, "Hell, no!"

"See the scrolling text?" He pointed to a spot on the packaging where information rolled across like a news ticker in Times Square.

"Yeah. That's . . . interesting."

He beamed. "I figured out how to do that a while ago. We can have it say whatever we want, like putting things on sale or announcing a special offer—buy that spell, get another at half price."

I had to admire his initiative, even if I couldn't admire his design. It was giving me a headache. "That's a great idea," I began. "I'm just worried that it'll be a little confusing to our customers. If they have to wait for information to scroll past at the right time, they might miss something." That always happened to me when I watched the morning news shows that used the scrolling tickers. I usually caught the tail end of a headline and had no idea what the story was about, then didn't have time to wait until it scrolled around again.

"But it's cool!" he insisted. "I bet the competition won't have it."

I restrained myself from suggesting that we give the idea to our competition as a form of sabotage. Was it possible to perform a spell with a splitting headache? If we could inflict pain on anyone who bought one of the bad spells, we'd be able to nip this problem in the bud. "It might be too much for us to do at this stage, but keep working on the idea."

He did something with his hand, and the scrolling ticker disappeared. I felt the muscles around my eyes relax. "What about the rest of it?" he asked.

"It's certainly bright and colorful, but I'm not sure it conveys the message we want."

He glared up at me through bangs that fell across his eyes. "What do you want?"

"I'm sure you know about the situation we're in. We need to make sure people know we're the only tried-and-true source for reliable, safe, well-tested spells, and we have been for more than a millennium. You can't trust anyone else to give you the results you want."

"Okay, so more boring-like. Got it." He waved his hand, and the package I held changed. Now it looked positively corporate, with the information I'd given him included as a tagline under the logo on the package cover. Better still, it didn't give me a headache to look at it.

"Perfect! I'll just run this by Mr. Mervyn and see what he thinks, and then we can roll it out. How long will it take to get this in production and out in the market?"

"Say the word, and it's out there."

I stared at him for a second, not sure what he meant. "You mean, you can change what's already on the shelf?"

He shrugged. "Sure. Why not? You want posters, too?"

"Yes, of course. Thanks. This is great." There had been many times when I'd wished that it was this quick and easy. I'd be spoiled for working at any company that didn't have a designer who could make retroactive changes to materials that had already been produced. Then again, someone like Mimi would abuse that power to keep changing her mind indefinitely.

I left the dungeon and headed toward the turret. Merlin's receptionist looked up from her work as I reached the top of the stairs. "Go right in, he's expecting you," she said. I wondered just how much he knew, and how he knew it. The explanation could be as simple as Ralph calling ahead, but just as I was pretty sure Owen didn't stand around all morning on the subway platform, waiting for me, I was pretty sure Merlin didn't need a phone call.

He greeted me as soon as I stepped through the doors. "Katie! How are you?" He brushed my hair away from my face and studied my bruise. "That's ugly, but it's already on the mend. Please, have a seat. I was just making some tea. Would you care for some?"

"Yes, please," I said as I took a seat on the sofa and waited for the cup to appear in my hands. Then I noticed him standing over by a counter tucked into a corner of the office, fussing with an electric teakettle. He was really making tea.

As he worked he talked. "Tea is quite a remarkable beverage. We had nothing like it in my day, as the British had barely journeyed beyond our own kingdom at the time. We had to settle for herbal infusions. Every day I seem to discover something new."

"I imagine you do." I felt almost overwhelmed when I considered what he must be going through. His intellectual curiosity was probably what kept him sane.

"Milk or lemon?"

"Milk, please."

He brought two cups and a sugar bowl over on a tray. "There, now we can talk."

I handed him the revised packaging design. "What do you think?"

He studied it carefully, then handed it back to me with a sad smile. "It does seem to say what we want it to, but I must confess I don't know enough to know if this is good or not."

"It's good, really."

"Then by all means, please carry out your plan."

"I'll let Ralph know, and then apparently everything will be changed automatically. The sales department is also gearing up to make a big splash with their next release, which is scheduled this week."

"Good, good." Then he looked grave. "Do you think this will save us?"

I looked down at the mock-up packaging I held. "I don't know. I don't think it can hurt. The object does seem to be to shrink the impact your competitor can have just long enough to come up with a way of fighting him. This may do it."

"Then I am most grateful." He chuckled. "Here they brought an ancient sorcerer out of hibernation, and our problems are solved by a clever girl without an ounce of magic in her."

"Hey, I didn't say anything about solving this. That part's up to you guys." I took a sip of my tea and thought for a moment, then plunged ahead with the question I wanted to ask. "How bad is this Idris guy, anyway?"

"Phelan Idris is a great danger, and not just because he's angry at us. He's dangerous because he believes in using his power to its fullest extent, without regard for the consequences and with no thought for the people who might get in his way. He would have left eventually, for he chafed under our rules, but we sent him away angry."

"And everyone's in danger, not just magical people?"

"I'd say the nonmagical people are in greater danger, not because he has any particular enmity toward them, but because they lack the resources to protect themselves."

"And is he really all that powerful?"

"I don't think he can counter the combined might of our best people. But in order to counter a spell, one must first understand it. Unfortunately, understanding it may involve some risk, as would testing any countermeasures we might devise."

"You'd have to be on the receiving end of it," I guessed.

"Or very nearby."

I didn't like to think about that. It meant Owen was out looking to be hit by one of those spells, and as powerful as I knew him to be, I still thought of him as that sweet, shy, harmless-seeming guy. "All this"—I indicated the package—"may just rile him up for you."

"Then your plan will have unexpected benefits." He rose from the sofa. "Now, what about your offer to go out to lunch with me and show me the area?"

"It's still good. I just need to give Ralph the go-ahead on the packaging."

"We'll go see him together. Is there anything I'll need with me?"

"It's a bit nippy, so you may need your jacket. And you'll need money." I certainly couldn't afford to buy lunch for both of us at too many places around here.

He took his jacket from a coat tree, then went into the outer office and asked his assistant for some of the local currency. He waited in the hallway outside the verification department while I grabbed my jacket and purse, then we went down to the basement together. Ralph jumped to attention when he saw the big boss enter his den.

"Very good work, son. Please implement it immediately," Merlin said.

"Yes, sir, boss, right away."

As we left the building I said, "I haven't really explored this part of town, other than walking through it, but I think there are some restaurants over on Broadway."

"Lead on, then. You're more of an expert than I am." He held his arm out for me to take as we walked toward Park Row. Anyone we passed on the streets probably thought I was out for a stroll with my grandfather.

In a way, Merlin did remind me of my long-dead granddad. My real grandfather had been a Texas farmer, and not very much like a Dark Ages wizard, but both of them had the same curiosity and good humor. If they'd met, they probably would have been friends.

Along Park Row was a string of computer, music, and electronics stores. Merlin slowed to look through the windows. I imagined this stuff would be fascinating for someone like him. "Do you mind if we go inside?" he asked.

"Not at all."

The store was crowded with lunchtime browsers. Merlin headed straight to the DVD section, which astonished me. I wouldn't have thought he'd know where to go in a store like this. "Do you have a DVD player?" I asked him.

He raised an eyebrow at me. "Of course. Otherwise, my evenings would be lonely. I find it a fascinating way to learn about this place and time. Owen taught me how to operate it and loaned me some films about New York."

I moved closer to him and dropped my voice so the other shoppers couldn't hear me. "You do know it's not real, the stuff on the DVDs, right? Unless it's a documentary. Otherwise, it's fake, with actors and scripts."

"I came to that conclusion when I saw the one about the giant gorilla," he said dryly.

"Yeah, that would tend to do it."

He apparently found whatever he was looking for. "Ah, yes, this is the one."

I leaned over his shoulder to see what he was holding. "*Camelot*?"

"Yes. I'm curious as to how the story has been portrayed."

"It's a musical. The characters burst into song from time to time."

"Then that is certainly different from the actual events." He smiled. "What kinds of songs does a certain wizard sing?"

I hadn't seen *Camelot* since the drama club put on a production when I was in high school. "I don't think you—I mean, Merlin, has any songs. It's mostly about what happens to Arthur after Merlin goes away."

"I've read the historical accounts, of course. Very sad."

I guided him to the checkout counter, but just as we got there, a teenager in a coat way too heavy for the temperature stepped forward and pulled out a gun. "Gimme whatever you got in the cash register," he said to the clerk.

The clerk shrieked and stepped backward, her hands in the air. I clapped my hands over my mouth to stifle my own scream. The last thing I needed was for the robber to notice me. All I had in my purse that he might want was about ten dollars, my MetroCard, and a credit card with a laughably low spending limit, but to me that was a lot to lose. Not to mention all that nice blood I had coursing through my body, that I really wanted to stay inside my body. What if this guy didn't want to leave any witnesses? That was the way it always went in the movies, the robber freaking out and shooting everyone in sight so no one could identify him. Or what if he took us all hostage and this turned into an all-day standoff?

The really scary thing was that my mother was right about something. She'd warned me about how I was sure to be mugged and robbed in the big city, and here I was, being robbed. Okay, so technically I wasn't the one being robbed, but there was a man with a gun not five feet away from me. Forget the fight or flight response. I was frozen to the floor. All I knew was that I didn't want to die. I needed to live long enough to have something vaguely interesting to look at when my life passed before my eyes.

Then I remembered that I wasn't alone. I was with one of the most powerful wizards in all history. A teenage thug robber wasn't going to take out Merlin. That made me feel marginally better. I glanced at Merlin to see what he would do, but he didn't look at all alarmed, which made me nervous again. Surely all those movies he'd watched would have shown him that a gun was a weapon. Could you even make a movie in the United States that didn't have a gun in it? But then I noticed that nobody had moved—not the clerk, not the robber, not anyone else in the store. It was like time had stopped, and Merlin and I were the only ones still moving.

"Neat trick," I said, letting the breath I'd been holding out in a long sigh. "Now what?"

"You should summon emergency help, and I'll make sure no one can be harmed."

I went to the phone next to the cash register and dialed 911. Out of the corner of my eye I saw Merlin take the thug's gun, empty it of bullets, then put the gun back in the thug's hand. On the other end of the phone line, a recorded voice told me to please stay on the line if this was an emergency. "Put the phone in the clerk's hand," Merlin instructed me. I did as he said. "Now, we should go. I have legal papers establishing my residence here, but it's best that I not be questioned by the police."

That seemed like a good idea to me. I wasn't sure how long he could sustain whatever cover he'd established before he said something that would get him locked up for psychological evaluation. We headed for the door, but before we got there I took the *Camelot* DVD out of his hand. "You can't take this out without paying."

"Ah, good point. I shall have to come back here another time."

I put the DVD on a nearby display, then hurried to catch up with Merlin, who was holding the door. As the door closed behind us the store came back to life. I thought I heard the clerk say, "We're being robbed."

"We're near City Hall, so I'm sure there'll be police here soon," I said, more to make myself feel better than to reassure Merlin. Then a thought crossed my mind and I gasped. "What if they have security cameras? It'll show up on tape that we were there, that we tinkered with the scene, and then that we left before the cops got there."

"Don't worry, that was taken care of as part of my spell."

"You know about security cameras?"

"I know about a great many things. My focus in the first few months after I was brought back was intensive study of your world. Now, some lunch would be nice, don't you think?"

Merlin spotted a pizza stand on a side street and said, "I want to try this food. I've seen it in the movies, and it looks interesting." So, we got a couple of slices to go and took them to a nearby plaza to sit and eat. He struggled with the strings of mozzarella that came off his pizza, and it became easier once more to think of him as a kindly old man who was a little out of his element, not as someone who could freeze the world around him.

We had just finished lunch when Sam swooped in and settled onto a nearby bench. "Good, I found you," he said, sounding about as out-of-breath as a stone creature could.

"What is it, Sam?" Merlin asked.

"You need to get back to the office right away, boss."

eleven

I glanced around to see if any of the other people in the park were
staring at us. Even though I knew there was magic in place to keep
people from seeing Sam or us interacting with Sam, it still felt
funny to talk to a gargoyle in public.

But everyone continued eating and talking, paying us very little
attention as we got up and walked away, Sam flying just ahead of us.

"Sam, what's going on?" I asked. I couldn't help but worry.
Maybe I was in trouble for taking Merlin outside.

"They got their hands on one of that guy's spells. Palmer's about
to check it out. He thought you'd want to be there, boss. Katie-bug,
too." He glanced over his shoulder with a smirk. "Apparently, we need
a professional opinion on the marketing and packaging. And we need
to make sure there's nothing hidden in it." It was nice to have an excuse to tag along without having to come up with one on my own.

Merlin moved pretty quickly for a man more than a thousand years old. In fact, I was the one lagging behind him and Sam. With his wings, Sam had an unfair advantage. We reached the building, and Sam took his usual post on the awning. Merlin and I went inside and straight to the R&D department.

Owen and Jake—this time without a shredded pants leg—were in Owen's lab, both their heads bent over something that lay between them on a table. They looked up as we entered. "Mr. Mervyn, Katie," Owen greeted us.

"So, this is it," Merlin said, leaning over to look at the booklet on the table.

"Yeah, found it in that hole-in-the-wall dive charm-and-record shop in the East Village," Jake said.

"I'm afraid to ask what he was doing there during office hours," Owen said dryly. I thought the fact that Jake was wearing a New York Dolls T-shirt was a pretty good clue, but Owen didn't strike me as a punk fan. I only knew because of a college roommate who was the reason I ended up moving off campus with Marcia, Gemma, and Connie, which eventually led to me moving to New York. I owed a lot to the punk movement.

Merlin made "Hmmm" sounds as he flipped through the spell book. "Well, then," he said as he closed it and handed it to me. "What do you think, Katie?"

I assumed he meant the packaging, as I couldn't tell him the first thing about magic. I turned it over in my hands. "Well, for starters, this Idris guy doesn't have a marketing department. He must have done this with his home computer and an ink-jet printer." It didn't even look like he was trying to market his products. Then again, the contents would sell itself to the kind of person who'd be interested in this sort of thing.

"Let others do your dirty work for you," the package said on the front in big letters. In another font, in smaller letters, it added, "Use unsuspecting normals as your personal slaves. They won't even remember what they've done for you. Always have an alibi, for you were nowhere near."

I looked at the others and smirked. "You have to admit, they have a compelling message. You don't need a lot of flash when you've got a proposition like that." Although I tried to keep my tone flippant, the thought of it sent chills down my spine. I knew I was safe because I was immune, but there were too many people I cared about who weren't immune. "A personal slave sounds pretty appealing. I could get someone to do my laundry and wash the dishes."

"Or carry out a robbery while you were somewhere else, with plenty of witnesses to verify your alibi," Owen remarked.

That made me think of the robbery Merlin had just foiled. I wondered if that thug was operating under his own will or someone else's. "That, too." The crime implications alone were staggering. I imagined a rash of bank robberies carried out by people who were somewhere else at the time. "I'm not sure our marketing campaign can beat this," I said. "If someone's interested in this kind of thing, they won't care about all that quality and testing stuff."

"But your marketing may keep many stores from stocking these spells," Owen said, not looking directly at me. I mentally kicked myself for not having thought of that for myself. I was supposed to be the marketing expert here, even if Owen was an all-purpose genius.

"That's true," Jake added. "This was the first one I found, and that shop isn't too picky."

"We'll just have to keep an eye on the stores where most people shop. Maybe we should do a brochure and really hit the stores with our next big push," I said.

"Good idea," Merlin said, and I got the impression he actually knew what I was talking about. Another genius. I was surrounded by them.

"Our best bet is to make these things as hard as possible to find," I added, trying to make myself sound more authoritative than I felt.

"What do you think of the spell itself?" Merlin asked Owen.

"It's along the lines of what he was working on when he was here. His project started as a fairly simple influence spell, one that can make anyone more likable. To be honest, I wasn't entirely comfortable with that, but Gregor thought there was a real market for it, and it wouldn't cause any real harm because there would be limits built in. But Phelan took it beyond that, and that's when we put an end to it. I don't know if he ever got it to work. I suppose we'll have to find out."

Jake groaned. "Don't make me do anything stupid or embarrassing, okay?"

"No, you don't make me do anything embarrassing." At Jake's blank, shocked look Owen added, "I need to feel the effects of the spell to get a better sense of what I'll have to come up with to counter it."

Jake grinned, showing crooked teeth in his freckled face. He looked like Jimmy Olsen in a lab coat and a punk rock T-shirt. "Sure thing, boss."

"Don't get too excited," Owen said. "Remember, even if I'm not supposed to remember what you made me do, I have witnesses."

"Geeze, take all the fun out of it. I was only going to make you cluck like a chicken."

Owen looked alarmed. "No chickens!" I imagined it was difficult for someone like him to put himself in such a helpless role. It didn't help matters that he was so easily embarrassed. He blushed when he spoke to someone. I couldn't imagine how he'd feel if someone made him cluck like a chicken or take his clothes off. "First, though, we'd better make sure there's nothing hidden in there. Katie?"

I flipped the book open. "What do you want me to do?"

"If you don't mind me reading over your shoulder, I'd like you to read what you see out loud to me, word for word."

"Isn't that dangerous?"

"You're immune. You couldn't do magic if you tried. In fact, you're the only one who's safe reading it out loud. Anyway, there's more to magic than saying some words."

"Okay, here goes." I was curious what a spell looked like, and this was my first chance. In a way, it was like reading a cookbook, with a list of ingredients, then some directions, and the incantation itself. Most of the words made no sense whatsoever to me. It was hard to concentrate on the details with Owen leaning over my shoulder. I felt his breath on my neck, right under my ear. I reminded myself that he was powerful, potentially dangerous, and probably not interested in me. When I got to the end, I turned to look at him. "Is it what you expected?"

"It's clean. The spell may not be what we'd approve of, but he's not trying to sneak anything in."

"What did you think he'd do?"

"Who knows? Make it so that there was an implied contract where if you actually used the spell, you'd owe him something. That kind of thing."

"He could do that?"

"I wouldn't put it past him." Owen took the book from me and handed it to Jake. "And remember, no chickens. No bats. No clucking. No removal of clothing."

"You're no fun."

"Yeah, but I'm your boss."

"Okay, everyone stand back," Jake said after he'd flipped through the booklet. Merlin and I moved to the side of the lab. I felt like I ought to put on safety goggles.

Owen moved to the other end of the room and took a few deep breaths, like he was trying to steady himself. Instead of turning his usual ten shades of red, he'd gone very pale. Even his lips were bloodless. Jake didn't look much better. He'd turned a grayish shade be-

neath his freckles. As often as I'd fantasized about zapping my boss
with a curse, it would be another thing entirely to be asked to do it,
especially when you had no idea how it would actually work.

"Would you get a move on?" Owen snapped through clenched
teeth. "You should already know how this works from hearing Katie
read it."

"Just making sure," Jake said. His voice shook. I glanced at Merlin and noticed that a muscle was jumping in his jaw. This was, apparently, a very big deal.

"Okay," Jake said at last. "I need something of yours. It doesn't
have to be much." Owen pulled a pen from the pocket of his lab coat
and tossed it at Jake, who caught it easily with one hand. "Great. That
should do it. Okay." He took a deep breath, then held the pen out in
front of himself in the palm of his left hand. He held his right palm
over the pen. Then he took a deep breath and began speaking the
nonsense words I'd read earlier.

I might have been immune to magic, but I was sure I sensed a
buildup of energy, like when it's winter and there's so much static
electricity that you get a jolt every time you touch something metal. I
felt like if I touched anything, there would be a spark. The air seemed
heavy, like it does just before a bad thunderstorm, the kind that brings
tornadoes. When the air felt like this back home, my parents turned
on the weather radio, just to be sure.

Jake then turned his right palm face out, toward Owen, and said
some more nonsense words. All the crackle, pressure, and tension in
the air caved in on itself and disappeared, all at once. I glanced at
Owen to see if he was okay. It couldn't possibly be healthy to be hit
with something like that. He seemed fine, more or less, although he
was still deathly pale and there was a blank look in his eyes.

Jake nibbled on his lower lip, looking like he was lost in thought.
After a moment he made a subtle gesture with his right hand. Owen
then went to the whiteboard and picked up a marker. He moved per-

fectly naturally. He certainly didn't look like a mind-controlled zombie. No one who didn't know Owen would think anything at all was wrong. Even someone who knew Owen well wouldn't notice a difference unless they got a good look in his eyes. JAKE DESERVES A RAISE, he wrote in large capital letters. I didn't know his handwriting well enough to recognize it, but this writing looked very different from the textbook-perfect script that filled the rest of the board. After he finished, he capped the marker and stepped away from the board.

A smaller dose of the crackle and pressure in the air returned as Jake clasped the pen in his right hand, then it was all over. Owen swayed, and as I was closest to him, I ran to steady him. He must have been in a pretty bad way, for he was shaking and he didn't even try to pretend he was okay and didn't need help. "Owen?" I asked him.

"I need to sit down," he whispered. Now I got to return the favor he'd done for me yesterday. I draped his left arm over my shoulders, put my right arm around his waist and walked him to the nearest chair. Once he was seated, he bent over, his elbows braced on his knees and his head between his legs, like they tell you to do when you feel faint.

Merlin and Jake joined us. "Boss?" Jake asked, his voice shaking even worse than it had when he'd done the spell. "You okay?"

"Just give me a minute." Owen's voice was muffled, coming from down around his knees. Jake shot a worried look at Merlin, who took one of Owen's wrists to check his pulse.

"Maybe I should go get some tea," I said. "Strong, sweet tea is just the thing in this kind of situation." But before I could start to look for the nearest coffee room, Jake had a steaming mug of tea in his hand. Oh yeah, I kept forgetting about that.

Merlin rubbed Owen's back. "Deep breaths, that's a boy," he soothed. He looked so worried that I had to fight back panic. I wondered if this was a typical reaction to a spell, or if this was just a particularly nasty one. Either way, I was very glad I was immune. Any remaining disappointment in my absolute lack of magic dissipated.

After a few minutes Owen pulled himself into an upright position, with a visible effort. Even though he'd spent a while with his head upside down, his face was still ashen. "Wow," he said. "That was unpleasant. I don't think he's tested that." In spite of his apparent attempt to sound flippant, his voice quavered.

"Something tells me he doesn't really care," I said.

Jake handed Owen the tea, but Owen's hands shook so badly he couldn't get the mug to his mouth. I reached to help him steady the mug. He took a few sips, then took a few more deep breaths. The next time he spoke, he sounded more like himself. "What did you make me do? I feel like I've just run a marathon."

"You don't remember at all?" Jake asked.

Owen shook his head. "Nothing. I remember you starting the spell, and then the next thing I knew, I felt like I was about to faint."

Jake pointed toward the whiteboard. "See that?"

Owen looked at the board, then one corner of his mouth crooked upward. "I wrote that? Well, I know I wouldn't have written that of my own accord." Then he frowned. "That's not even my handwriting." He turned to Jake. "It's yours."

"You wrote it," I assured him. "I watched you."

"You did write it," Merlin agreed. "Most interesting."

Owen took a long swallow of tea. Some color was coming back into his face. If he blushed now, he'd almost look human. "Interesting, but possibly a flaw in the spell." He looked up at Jake. "You didn't do that on purpose, did you?"

Jake shook his head. "No. I didn't specify what handwriting I wanted, just what I wanted you to write."

"Then he really didn't test this thoroughly. If you were going to do such a thing, that's not the way you'd want it to work."

"What do you mean?" I asked.

"It would make this entirely useless for forgery. If you wanted someone to purchase something for you, their signature would be wrong for a check or credit card. You couldn't make someone sign a legal document, because it would be your handwriting if you were the one dictating what to write. If the authorities got a handwriting sample, it would be your handwriting they'd be able to trace, even if you didn't leave your own fingerprints."

All three of us stared at him. Who would have thought sweet little Owen had a mind devious enough to think so fully about the implications of something like this? "Boss, sometimes you scare me," Jake said after a long moment of silence. I was glad he'd said it before I did.

"Just thinking logically," Owen said with a shrug, but his color returned to normal quite suddenly, which made me think he was probably blushing furiously. "Anyway, that's not the only weakness in the spell. Your victim would certainly know something was wrong, whether or not he remembered what he'd done. It doesn't work as advertised."

"Can you fight it?" Merlin asked.

"That, I don't know. We have to do more tests in a controlled environment. I can't think of anything offhand that I know would work. I didn't try to fight it this time, and I'd prefer to wait a while before going through that again." He shuddered, and Merlin patted him on the shoulder.

"Don't worry about it, son," Merlin said. "This is enough, for now."

"But it's not." The blush had faded, so Owen looked pale once more, and there was a worried crease between his eyes. "Whether or not it works properly, this spell is very, very dangerous. Used by the wrong person who didn't have a tight control on the amount of power he was applying, this could kill its victim. It's not enough for our people to learn a way of fighting back. We have to stop it. He can't put dangerous, untested things like this out on the market."

"There should be negative word of mouth from anyone who tried it and didn't get the results they hoped for," I said, even though it didn't sound very encouraging.

"We'll distribute this to our forces and have them be on the look-out," Merlin said. That caught my attention. Forces? What forces? Every time I thought I knew what was going on, I learned one more detail that threw the balance off again. But before I could question that, Merlin gave me a tight smile. "I mean, our sales forces, as well as our monitoring team. We should have an idea if anyone is using this in great numbers." Somehow, I doubted that was what he meant, but I didn't press the point.

"I should get back to my office," Merlin said. "I'll send down a cordial that should help you recover."

"Thanks," Owen said. He looked and sounded better every minute, but I still thought he should be at home, in bed, bundled up in blankets and with someone bringing him chicken soup. I wasn't volunteering, no matter how tempting a picture it made.

I knew I ought to be getting back to my office, too, but I didn't want to. I wanted to know more about what was going on, and I wanted to make sure Owen would be okay. "What you need right now is some chocolate," I said once Merlin had gone. I dug around in my purse and found a square of Dove dark. "Here you go."

"I don't think this is one of those spells that chocolate is a counter to," he said.

"Chocolate makes everything better. And you could use the sugar."

"Then thank you." He unfolded the foil, then popped the choco-late in his mouth.

"You carry chocolate in your purse?" Jake asked.

"Hey, not everyone can snap their fingers or wave their hand or do whatever it is you people do when you want a snack. I never go out without an emergency supply of chocolate."

"That's a very wise policy," Owen said, giving me a smile that made my knees grow weak, no matter how hard I tried to resist him.

"Are you going to be okay?" I asked him.

He took a long, deep breath that he let out as a shaky sigh. "I think so. Eventually. I don't think I'll go to the gym tonight, though. I'll just go to bed early and sleep it off."

"If it makes you feel any better, I have a headache now," Jake said, rubbing his temples. I handed him a square of chocolate.

"This is unusual, isn't it? You don't normally get all woozy when someone does a spell on you, do you?" I asked.

"Not our spells," Owen said. "We work very had to ensure there are no ill effects."

"Yeah, by the time one of our spells gets out there, we've figured out everything that could go wrong," Jake added. "Now, this kind of thing isn't too uncommon for us in this department."

"Occupational hazard," Owen said dryly, then winced. He looked like he had a headache, too.

"What would happen to a nonmagical person if someone used this spell on them?" I asked, thinking of my friends.

"Probably the same, very likely worse effects."

"I didn't keep him under long at all," Jake said. "But I'm not sure how long anyone could keep someone under, if that short amount of time makes you feel like I do now. It's a big energy drain. We try to make our spells more efficient."

Still thinking of my friends, I asked, "Is there anything anyone could do to protect themselves?"

"That's what we're working on," Owen said. He sounded tired, both from what he'd just gone through and what he had ahead of him. "It would be safest to avoid dropping anything or loaning a personal object to anyone else. We don't know how substantial the object needs to be, but obviously, a pen is enough."

I tried to think of a credible-sounding story I could tell my friends to explain why it wouldn't be a good idea to loan a pen to the stranger in line behind them at the bank. Maybe it was time for another good anthrax scare. Or was a new strain of Ebola going around?

Unfortunately, I doubted they'd believe me unless it showed up in the news. I hoped my friends didn't run into any evil magical people who wanted to use them for nefarious activity.

"Word will spread if the spell doesn't work as well as it's supposed to, and if it gives you a killer headache when you use it, right?" I asked, hoping they'd reassure me.

"We can only hope so," Owen said. He sounded not just tired, but defeated.

"You should go home and get some rest," I told him. "In the meantime, I'd better get back to my office before Gregor wonders where I am."

"If he's concerned about it, he could find out where you've been easily enough," Owen said. "Don't worry about him."

"I'm not worried about him. I just don't want to deal with him." I turned to Jake. "Make sure he gets home okay."

"I'll take care of him. C'mon, boss. Let me get you home. I feel responsible."

"You are responsible." But Owen was grinning at his assistant, so I felt better about his condition. "And I can get home by myself."

"You shouldn't go on the subway in that condition," Jake insisted. "You're just asking to be mugged."

"Let them try." There was that edge to his voice again that sent a chill down my spine. I left him and Jake still arguing and headed to Verification.

The moment I stepped through the door into the office, the green color began to rise in Gregor's face. By the time I made it to my desk, he was in full monster mode. "Where have you been?" he snarled. "That was a particularly long lunch."

"I've been with Mr. Mervyn the entire time," I said, draping my jacket over the back of my chair. "A situation came up where he needed my help. You can ask him about it, if you like." I almost surprised myself with my calm tone, but I hadn't survived a year with Mimi without learning how to deal with a boss in the midst of an outburst, and there I didn't have the CEO on my side.

Gregor changed back into his human form so rapidly he looked like someone had stuck a pin in him and let all the hot air out. Then just as rapidly, he swelled up again. The change was so sudden that it was more funny than scary. "And what's this I hear about you making recommendations about my department to Personnel?"

Oh, that. It crossed my mind that maybe I should have at least pretended to follow the chain of command when I'd suggested having verifiers placed in other offices, but as it had grown out of my comment about having the monster boss in the one place where the employees could see the green skin, I hadn't really thought of talking to Gregor first.

But I was in no mood to deal with someone desperately trying to hold onto whatever power base he could after what must have been a devastating demotion. "It grew out of a conversation I was having with Rod about other matters," I informed him with as much ice in my voice as I could muster. For a moment I allowed myself a fantasy of suggesting him as a test subject for that new spell.

"You have a complaint to make, you make it to me."

I faced him directly and said, "I've only been here three days, and I've seen enough already to know that this has to be the worst-managed department in the entire company. You're treating extremely rare and valuable people like cattle, and it's a miracle you haven't lost your entire staff by now. There, now I've complained to you. And now I'm going to talk to Personnel again."

Actually, I was going to bitch to Rod about the way he must have broken the news to Gregor to piss him off like that, but Gregor didn't have to know that. He could stew about what I was going to report. I imagined he'd gotten in some trouble for lying about having his anger-management problem under control.

I gathered my belongings and stalked out of the office in a beautifully dramatic exit, if I do say so myself. I just wished the big-picture stakes weren't too high for me to threaten to quit, but I couldn't get the image of a faint and shaken Owen out of my mind.

For once, I felt like I had a real mission that I had to help carry out, no matter what the inconvenience to me might be. And if I could do something about that inconvenience, well, so much the better.

I hoped Rod was ready for Hurricane Katie.

twelve

I still had a good head of steam going when I reached the personnel office. "Is Rod in?" I asked before Isabel had a chance to greet me. "He's in a meeting—an employee review up in P and L—but he should be back any minute if you want to have a seat."

She didn't have to ask me twice. I sank wearily into the over-stuffed chair in front of her desk.

"Can I get you some coffee?" she asked.

"How about a margarita?"

She grimaced. "Ouch. Let me guess, Gregor?"

I nodded. "How do people work under him?"

"Don't ask me, sweetie. I just know there was a resounding sigh of relief when he was reassigned after his 'accident.'" She made air quote marks with her fingers and smirked. Then she perked up. "I can't give you a margarita on company time, but a group of us are getting together for a girls' night out tomorrow. You should come. You'd get to know some of the other women who work here. Let's face it, there are times when this place is positively medieval when it comes to women in the workplace. It helps for us to all pull together."

"It sounds like fun," I said. The more people I knew inside the company, the better I could do my job. There was a nagging thought in my head that there was something I was supposed to remember about that night, but I flipped through my day planner and found nothing written in. "Sure, I'll come along. The others won't mind me being there, will they?"

"They'd love to have you along." She winked at me. "You can tell us if any guys we spot are really cute or just using a cute illusion."

As if on cue, Rod walked through the door. I hoped he hadn't heard Isabel's last comment. Then I wondered if Isabel even knew about his illusion. I tried to imagine how other people saw him. "Katie!" he greeted me, sounding surprised.

"Can I have a word with you?"

"Of course. Come in." I gathered my jacket, briefcase, and purse and followed him into his office. "How's your head?" he asked as I settled into a chair.

I touched my temple, just then remembering what had happened the day before. Had it only been one day? It was hard to believe. So much had happened to me in such a short span of time. "It's fine. I'd even forgotten about it. It's not all black and blue, is it?"

"It looks pretty nasty. Want me to mask it for you?"

"I thought magic didn't work on me."

"An illusion doesn't have to work on the person who wears it. It's a spell that follows you around and works on other people."

"My roommates have already seen it, so it would raise questions if I came home with no lump on my head at all, but thanks for the offer."

"Oh. Good point." He sounded truly disappointed. He probably wanted to show off for me, and here I'd gone and dashed his hopes. "I could just make it look not so bad, so they won't worry too much."

I couldn't see much harm in that, so I shrugged and said, "Sure, why not?"

He grinned, a truly delighted smile breaking out across his face in such a way that he looked truly attractive, even with his flaws and lack of grooming. Now I was glad I'd agreed. He rubbed his hands together, then placed one hand just above the knot on my forehead, closed his eyes, and muttered something under his breath. I felt the same charge and sense of pressure in the air that I'd noticed in Owen's lab, but on a much smaller scale. A second later he opened his eyes and backed away, a satisfied smile on his face. "There you go," he said. "I set it so it would wear off as the bruise fades away."

"Thank you," I said, even though I felt like a character in the fable of the emperor's new clothes. I wouldn't be able to tell whether he'd really done anything, so I just had to go along with it and act like he'd done me a favor.

He went around his desk, opened a drawer, and brought out a small hand mirror. "Here, take a look."

"Remember, immune. I can't see it."

He shook his head as he handed the mirror to me. "You can with this. It's an image checker, so you can see how well your illusion works. Even you should be able to see with this."

I brought the mirror up to my face, and sure enough, the ugly lump on my head had faded to just a bit of blue and yellow, like a bruise that's about to go away. Catching a glimpse of Rod peering over my shoulder, I finally had a chance to see him as others did.

Johnny Depp wasn't a bad comparison. He wasn't quite as classically handsome as Owen, but he had a slightly dangerous bad-boy allure to him, like he should be wearing a leather jacket and hanging out at a disreputable nightclub, where he'd have to fend off the women throwing themselves at him. He still wasn't someone who would draw my attention for more than a passing, appreciative glance, but I could see where some women might find him intensely attractive, especially when he threw in a love spell.

Then I turned around, and he was just the Rod I knew, who wouldn't be half bad if he put the same effort into taking care of himself as he put into his illusions. "Thanks, it does look better. I bet that comes in really handy for covering zits," I said. Then I couldn't resist asking, "Does this mean you don't see your own illusion when you look in an ordinary mirror?"

He shook his head, and there was a dejected look in his eyes. "Unfortunately not. You can see other people's illusions in a mirror, but not your own. It has something to do with the reflection or refraction of the spell, or something like that. I was never very good with the physics of magic." Now I had to wonder at his self-esteem. How could he go around acting like he knew he was God's gift to women when he saw something else entirely in the mirror? Or did he ever look in the mirror at all? I didn't see how anyone could bear to go through life wearing an entirely different face. It would be weird to me. I'd rather just get my hair done and have plastic surgery, or else find a way to learn to live with myself the way I was. That would be a lot less confusing. Magic might come in handy, but I was starting to see that there were places where it caused more problems than it solved.

"One of those image checkers might be helpful in my line of work, for comparing what really is there against the illusion," I said, when I realized I'd been silent too long.

"We've tried, but haven't had much luck getting it to work. There's something about the mirror image that's distorting when it comes to in-depth image versus reality comparisons."

"Still, I'd like to get one and tinker with it."

"I'll requisition one for you." He put his mirror back in its drawer and sat behind his desk. "Now, what was it you came to see me about?"

I'd almost forgotten. What with talking to Isabel about a girls' night out, getting an illusion cast on my bruise, and seeing Rod's illusion, my anger had faded. But as soon as I thought about it, it came rushing back. "It wouldn't hurt for you to use a little discretion when dealing with Gregor. He went all ogre on me, and he was seriously ticked that I'd gone behind his back."

Rod winced. "Sorry about that. I keep forgetting that he's masking his anger issues, and I can't get a verifier into any meetings I have with him without having to talk to him in front of his staff. In the future I'll borrow a verifier from monitoring. He seemed perfectly fine when I was talking to him."

"Well, I just got an earful, complete with fangs. I don't want to sound like a diva, but I'm not sure I can keep going back in there. I like it here, really, and I can see where what we're doing—what I'm doing—is important. But I don't want to dread this place."

"Don't worry, you won't have to go back there—not as a permanent office location. You'll still need to report in from time to time. We decided to use your idea and spread verifiers out to keep an eye out for intruders. You'll be officing in R and D."

That made me feel better. I even felt kind of mean for having been so angry. "That should be a nice change of pace," I said.

"You'll report to Verification in the morning. It'll be best for Gregor to be the one to send you up to R and D. Pretend to be surprised."

I smiled. "Don't worry. It'll be an Oscar-winning performance. I'll try not to jump up and down with glee when he gives me the news."

"I'd appreciate that."

I put on my jacket, gathered my purse and tote bag, and went into the outer office. "See you tomorrow," Isabel said. "We'll meet here after work."

"Okay, see you then."

I looked around for Owen when I got to the subway station, but he wasn't there. I was surprised how much I missed him. I hadn't admitted it to myself, but the sight of him on the subway platform gave me a thrill every time. It looked like I'd developed myself a nice little crush. A pointless crush, from what I could tell.

It was my night to cook, so I changed into jeans and a sweatshirt when I got home and headed to the kitchen to think of something interesting to do with hamburger meat. I was stirring a simple meat and tomato sauce and trying very hard not to daydream about Owen when Gemma came home.

"Mmm, something smells good," she said. Then she took a second look at me and frowned. "What's wrong?"

"Wrong?" I wondered if Rod's illusion had slipped or gone horribly askew. I didn't look like I had leprous lesions coming off my forehead, did I?

"I don't know. You look worried. Don't tell me you've got job problems already."

I decided against sharing my adventures with armed robbery. If I told that story the day after telling about stopping an intruder, my friends would think I didn't have a job at all, that I just spent my days on a park bench, then came home and made up wild, imaginative stories about what went on at work. Besides, there was no way I could think of to explain how we'd dealt with the robbery without bringing up magic and Merlin. "No, no job problems. Everything's going fine at work."

"Good, because that's Marcia's department. Man problems?"

"No."

"Yep, definitely man problems. That, I can handle. Just let me change clothes. Pour me some wine, could you?"

"Sure." I poured two glasses of wine and gave my sauce a stir. She came back a few minutes later dressed in low-slung yoga pants and a cropped sweatshirt.

"So, what's the deal, someone at the new job?" she asked as she sat at the dining table and took a sip of wine. I turned the burner down on the stove and joined her.

"That's what I've been trying to figure out." I suddenly felt like we were back in school, discussing the guys from our classes. "There's a guy at work I've been thinking about a lot since I met him."

"And you've got a thing for him."

"It's just a crush, I think," I said with a shrug. "He's good-looking and he's nice to me. He lives near here, so we go to and from work together. When I get used to him, it'll probably fade. And I don't think it'll go anywhere. He isn't interested in me, I don't think."

"What makes you say that?"

"He's really shy, the kind of guy who doesn't talk easily to anyone, let alone someone he's interested in, and he talks to me."

"You are easy to talk to."

I rolled my eyes. "It's my curse. But it's not like he talks to me about anything other than business, not even when we're on the subway. I couldn't begin to tell you what he does away from work."

"Yeah, it doesn't sound like sparks are flying." She must have seen my face fall, for she frowned.

I drank some wine, then laughed. "Isn't that how it always seems to go? The ones you like just want to be friends. Why can't I seem to break out of high school dating patterns?"

"Because men never really mature." She put her wineglass down on the table and crossed her arms over her chest. "Okay, here's how I see it. Don't give up on him. Even if nothing else happens, friends are good to have, and you never know what friendship can grow into. Now, I know just the way to distract you from your problems. Are you going to be able to make it tomorrow night?"

"Tomorrow night?" Then I remembered what I was supposed to be doing. "God, Gem, I'm sorry, I totally forgot about it and said I'd go out with some of the women at work. I knew there was something I was forgetting."

"Don't worry about it. I'm not sure he was right for you anyway. Go out with the work people. But after that, you could use some masculine distraction. When was your last boyfriend?"

I got up to check my sauce so I wouldn't have to look her in the eye. "Steve Sprague," I said softly.

"Steve? Junior year Steve? You haven't had a serious relationship since then?"

I white-knuckled the wooden spoon as I fought to keep my composure. "Well, we made that no boyfriends, no entanglements that will hold us back from taking on the world vow our senior year before y'all left for New York. Then I was stuck in Hicksville for a few years, and there's no big singles' scene there. All the guys got married while I was off at college. Since I've been in New York, I haven't dated anyone more than once or twice. I just seem to go on blind dates that don't go anywhere." As soon as I said it, I regretted it. She'd worked hard to help me fit in after I got to New York, and I didn't want her to think I was criticizing her efforts. "The 'like a sister' thing has a double effect here," I added with an attempt at a laugh.

"Okay, no more blind dates just to be dating. We're looking for a real boyfriend for you."

A boyfriend, huh? It sounded nice. I'd never been the kind of girl or woman who needed a man in my life to make me feel complete. I was perfectly happy on my own. But I liked the idea of trading dressing up, going out, and meeting guy after guy for having that one special guy. I had a sudden craving for a quiet evening at home, wearing sweats and snuggling on the sofa together, eating takeout and watching an old movie. That wasn't something you could do on a blind date. It was a definite boyfriend activity.

"That sounds good. Just pick a good one for me."

"I'll have to look around. Until now, I haven't been thinking about long-term prospects when I've been arranging things."

The front door opened and Marcia came in. "Mmm, dinner smells good. Katie must be cooking tonight."

"Hey!" Gemma protested, but she was grinning. She'd be the first to admit that her favorite recipe was a Chinese delivery menu.

"What's going on?" Marcia asked as she tucked her briefcase into the end table that also served as her nightstand.

"We're getting Katie a boyfriend."

"We are? What brought this on?"

"I'm tired of all the dating," I said before Gemma could say anything. "I'd like the chance to really get to know someone."

"You do realize you'll have to date some in order to find a boyfriend, don't you?" Gemma teased.

"Does this mean you are or aren't joining us tomorrow night?" Marcia asked, peering into the pot of tomato sauce and giving it a stir.

"I'm not. But not because of the boyfriend thing. I'm going out with some people from work. I figured it would be a good chance to get the real scoop on the office politics."

Marcia poured herself a glass of wine. "That's a very sound strategy."

I got up and put some water on to boil for the pasta. I felt all warm inside, and not just because the tiny kitchen was hot from the cooking and all the bodies. It felt good to have my friends here and to remember how much they cared for me. That was something I never wanted to lose, no matter how deep I got myself into the magical world.

The next morning, Owen was in his usual spot on the subway platform. I felt a flutter in my stomach when I saw him, then reminded myself to forget about it. He appeared tired and haggard, with dark circles under his eyes, but otherwise he looked much better than the last time I'd seen him.

"How are you feeling?" I asked when I got near him.

"Better, thanks. I'm not looking forward to going through that again."

"You have to do it again? Can't someone else?"

"I wouldn't ask anyone else," he said solemnly as a train screeched to a stop.

We didn't talk on the way to work. He looked lost in thought, and I was lost in thought, so neither of us minded the relative silence. The subway during rush hour isn't a prime conversational zone anyway, especially when the topic of conversation involves magic.

I headed straight to the verification office, which took every ounce of will I had in me. I made a show of putting down my bags and draping my jacket across the back of my chair, then was just about to go put my lunch in the refrigerator when Gregor shouted at me. "Yes?" I asked innocently.

"You'll be officing up in R and D. We'll send your assignments there."

"Oh, okay." I kept my face as blank as I could while I picked my bags and jacket up and left the office. Only when I was safely out in the corridor did I smile in relief. It was going to be a lot easier to come to work from now on.

As it had at my last visit, the R&D door swung open when I approached. Once inside, I wondered where I should go, but I soon heard a flutter of wings and a fairy approached. Those wings might look insubstantial, but it seemed that a fairy could move pretty quickly when she wanted to. I recognized her as the fairy I'd seen on the subway that day last week that had changed my life.

"Hi!" she said cheerfully. "You must be Katie. I'm Ari. They sent me to show you your office."

"Oh, good. I was wondering where to go."

"It isn't far. They want you just inside the entrance so you can spot the bad guys. Good work the other day, by the way."

"Thanks."

"And here we are!" She hovered just inside the doorway to a small office with glass walls that overlooked the main corridor. It wasn't palatial, but it beat the verification pool, and it beat my cubicle at my last job. It even had a door. "We've already got the phone set up, and your computer will be delivered this afternoon."

"A computer?" That was something I hadn't had back in the pool.

"Yeah, special orders from the boss. Bathroom's around the corner. We don't have a coffee room or kitchen, but if you need anything, just grab someone and ask for whatever you want. I'm in the lab across the hall, so yell if you want something. Oh, and yell if you see someone who doesn't look like they belong, but that goes without saying. Any questions?"

"Not right now. Thanks."

"Great. Then I'll see you tonight."

"Tonight?"

"You're going out with the girls, aren't you?"

"Oh, yeah, that. You're coming, too?"

"Sure thing. It'll be fun. Welcome to R and D."

As she fluttered away I pondered the idea of a girls' night out that included a winged fairy. It looked like this would be an interesting evening, to say the least.

I'd just wrapped up my work for the day when Ari appeared at my door. "You ready to hit the town?" she asked.

"Sure, just give me a second to shut down."

"Grab me across the hall when you're ready to go and we can head to Isabel's office together."

I shut down my newly arrived computer and packed my things,

then made a quick dash to the bathroom to freshen up before stepping into Ari's lab. It was all chrome and white surfaces, with several large computers. "There you are," Ari said as I arrived. "Welcome to my domain, the last step in Practical Magic."

"What do you do here?"

"Final testing before a spell is released—make sure there aren't any typos, make sure it works as advertised, any necessary editing to get it down to the tightest, most concise spell you can get. Some of those theoretical guys get a little wordy. They read too many old books. Archaic language may make a spell look impressive, but it doesn't make it work any better." She picked up her purse and said, "Looks like it's the weekend."

Isabel greeted us in her usual effusive manner when we got to her office. "Trix just called down and said she'd be a few more minutes," she said.

"So it's just the four of us?" Ari asked.

"Yeah, some of the others had dates."

"Traitors!" Isabel laughed at Ari's outburst, but I wasn't sure if Ari was serious or not. She wasn't laughing, but maybe she had a dry sense of humor.

"How was your first week on the job, Katie?" Isabel asked.

"It was interesting, to put it mildly."

"You're coping very well with all the excitement, though. We lose more verifiers the first week than you'd imagine."

Actually, I didn't find that hard to imagine. Either the depressing working conditions or the craziness and fear that maybe all of this was the result of a total psychotic breakdown would get to you. Then again, I'd managed to get myself into more than my fair share of trouble. I doubted most verifiers had first weeks like mine.

I looked up to see a man coming into the office. "He in?" he asked Isabel, who nodded. She looked like she was having a hard time forming words. Then I looked at him again and found myself more than a little stunned. It was Owen, but I'd never have recognized him at first glance. Instead of his usual business suits or lab coats, he wore jeans, a baseball jersey, and a Yankees cap. He looked entirely different, and utterly adorable.

He saw me, blinked, blushed, and said, "Hi, Katie. What are you doing here?"

"I was about to ask you the same question."

He turned even pinker. "Playoff game. Rod thinks he has a spell to get us in."

Isabel groaned. "He's not trying that again, is he? Didn't you two almost get in trouble last year?"

Rod's office door opened and he stuck his head out into Isabel's office. "I've got it figured out now, though," he said. Then he got a good look at Owen and frowned. "Are you sure you're up to this?" he asked. Owen did look pretty much like Death with a hangover, even with the baseball cap pulled low over his eyes. He must have spent the day testing that horrible spell.

"I could use a night out," Owen said. "I'll be fine." I thought he'd be better off home in bed, but a night at a baseball game might be good for him.

Just then another fairy, whom I recognized as Merlin's receptionist, showed up. That had to be Trix. "You girls ready to par-tay?" she whooped.

"Girls' night out?" Rod asked, raising an eyebrow.

"Yes, and you two are not invited," Isabel said.

Owen narrowed his eyes. He didn't exactly frown, but he didn't look happy, either. I glanced at the other women and saw that Ari was giving him a look of raw, undisguised hunger. That must have made him uncomfortable.

Isabel took her purse out of her desk drawer. "Well, you boys be good, and don't call me if you need someone to bail you out."

"We'll be fine," Rod said with a laugh. "Owen can get us out of any tricky situation. You girls have fun, and be careful."

"Don't get Katie into any trouble," Owen added softly. The two fairies laughed, a tinkling, musical sound like little bells. The four of us headed out, leaving the men behind.

Isabel was apparently our cruise director for the evening. "I thought we'd warm up by hitting happy hour near here—all those cute Wall Street guys getting off work. Then who knows?"

We settled into a dark, noisy downtown bar and ordered a round of cosmopolitans. If I hadn't been with two women who had wings on their backs and hovered slightly above their chairs, I'd have felt like I was back in my old life, on one of the rare occasions when my coworkers convinced me to join them for a drink-and-bitch session after work.

As soon as we had our drinks, Isabel said, "Okay, first item on the agenda is Trix's breakup."

"I am never dating an elf again," Trix muttered.

"This may be a stupid question, but are there guy fairies?" I asked.

"Sure there are," Ari said. "They just don't like to be called that."

"They prefer the term 'sprite,'" Isabel said, putting air quotes around the word "sprite."

Ari snorted. "Yeah, like that sounds any less gay."

"I don't think I've seen any of them around the company."

"There aren't too many who work at MSI," Isabel explained. "They prefer outdoor jobs. You'll find a lot of sprites working as messengers or as gardeners. Anyway, back to the agenda. What does the dirty, cheating elf deserve?"

"Cheating?" I asked.

Trix rolled her eyes. "Yeah, it seems like he had a weakness for anything in wings."

"Then hit him with a love spell that makes him fall desperately for a butterfly," Ari suggested. We all laughed at that. I might not be magical, but I had to appreciate the mental image of a man in love with a butterfly.

"Are you really going to do that?" I asked, suddenly wondering if this was just girls' night out talk or if it was more literal in the magical world. My friends and I had wished all sorts of horrible things on men who'd done us wrong, but we didn't have the power to actually do anything about it.

"Of course not," Isabel said.

"But it would be funny," Ari added.

"It would serve him right," Trix said, "but it falls into a gray area. It's not outright harm, but it's also not a good idea to manipulate another person's free will. No, I'll just have to satisfy myself with the knowledge that I'm better off without him. I guess I'll have to hang out in the park more often, since I'm off elves and humans don't do much for me."

"I like human men," Ari said with a lascivious smile.

"But what's the point? You can't have children with them."

"Who says I want children? I just want fun, and human men are a lot more substantial than sprites. I like a guy I'm not worried about breaking. Besides, if I had kids, I'd just piss off my parents by not giving my kids some sappy fairy name."

"You have a perfectly nice name," Isabel said.

"Yeah, until they came out with *The Little Mermaid,* and suddenly every human girl is naming her cat Ariel." She turned to me. "It totally ruined the name."

"You shouldn't complain," Trix said. "I have a cousin who got stuck with the name Tinker Bell because her parents thought it was cute. She goes by Belle. Unfortunately, there's not a lot you can do with Trixie. Half the Westies in New York are named Trixie. It's embarrassing when you hear your name, turn around, and then find out they're talking to their dog."

"Looks like we've wrapped up that agenda item," Isabel said, signaling to the waiter for another round. "Item two: surveying and possibly selecting male companionship."

I took a sip of my new drink as I took in my surroundings. I couldn't remember the last time I'd gone out on the prowl with friends. With Gemma's unofficial dating service, that usually wasn't necessary. The bar was full of suited Financial District types. Some of them were quite attractive, but they were all a little too intense for me.

"What do you think, Katie?" Isabel asked. "Anything that isn't what it appears to be?"

"I don't know. Remember, I don't see what you see. Point someone out to me, and I'll tell you what I see."

Ari pointed to someone who looked like a taller, slightly older, much slicker version of Owen. She definitely had a type. "What about him?"

"Tall, dark, and handsome. No pointed ears, horns, fangs, or wings."

"Hmmm." She cast her eyes in his direction, caught his eye, then glanced away. Gemma had tried to teach me that game, but I was hopeless at it. I either stared too long and made my target uncomfortable or not long enough and never caught his attention.

As I watched the flirting I asked, "What do others see when they look at you guys?"

"You mean fairies?" Trix asked.

"Yeah."

"Basically, just us with no wings and no hovering. Human men find us incredibly cute. Personally, I'm not so thrilled with human men."

"All men are trouble, whether or not they have wings, or how their

194 | Shanna Swendson

ears are shaped, or how tall they are," Isabel said. She sounded like what Gemma called the Bitter Single Woman—the kind who pretends to hate men to cover up her hurt about men not being interested in her. Isabel was attractive enough, in a striking Amazonian way. I wondered if she was fully human or if there was something else in there, like maybe a trace of giant blood. Still, it would take either a very large or a very confident man to cope with her. We needed to find a professional football player, maybe an offensive lineman. I considered putting Gemma on the job.

"Men are okay," I said. "I like them well enough." I hated to dampen a good bitch session, but I'd never had a guy really screw me over. They had to be interested enough in me to give me any hope in order to cause much damage, and I hadn't had many get that close. Gemma was right, I needed a boyfriend.

"You're single, though, aren't you?" Trix asked.

"Yeah. But my roommate's working to fix that. She's set me up with half of Manhattan."

"And nothing right for you yet?" Isabel asked.

"Not yet. But if you kiss enough frogs, you're bound to stumble upon a prince."

Trix slammed her palm against the tabletop. "Brilliant idea, Katie. Isabel, I propose a change of agenda. Let's find ourselves some princes."

"Where? The pond in Central Park?"

"That's where I have the best luck."

I had to interrupt. "Whoa, you mean there really are men who've been turned into frogs?"

Isabel shrugged. "Sure. But what they don't tell you in the storybooks is that only the real assholes get punished that way, and being a frog doesn't have quite the personality reforming effect you'd expect."

"But they do tend to be very, very grateful about being rescued, and that's good for at least one night of fun," Ari argued.

"I was being figurative about kissing frogs, in case you were wondering," I said, wondering if this conversation was really taking place or if I was drunker than I realized. "In my world, that just means you go out with a lot of people, even if they don't seem to meet your criteria on the surface, because you never know which one might be right for you."

"That's boring. Wise, but boring. Our way's more fun," Trix said.

"And I bet our chances of finding someone are better than they are in here," Ari added.

We paid our tab, then stumbled out of the bar. I'd lost track of time while we were in there, and now it was dark. I wasn't sure wandering around Central Park at night in the condition we were in was a great idea. Maybe they didn't metabolize alcohol the same way normal-sized humans did, but I was only just sober enough to be aware of how drunk I was. Unfortunately, I was drunk enough to let myself get swept along with the group.

Isabel hailed a cab—she had a rather effective method that involved blocking the street with her body. If a cab wanted to avoid serious damage, it stopped. We piled inside, Isabel in the front passenger seat and the rest of us in back. This wasn't quite what I'd had in mind when I agreed to an evening out with the girls, and the cab ride up to Central Park was long enough for me to sober up enough to be self-conscious about doing something so crazy. As often as I'd used the expression about kissing frogs, I'd never had any desire to carry it out literally.

We all fumbled for purses as the cab came to a stop near the Plaza Hotel, but Isabel said, "Don't worry, I've got it." Then we piled out, crossed Fifty-ninth Street, and followed the path down to the pond.

"You're really going to kiss frogs?" I asked as we made our way down to the edge of the water. "This time of year, you may not see many. It's getting too chilly for amphibians."

"That actually makes our chances better," Trix said. "It's the enchanted frogs that'll still be around. They don't want to give up on the hope that someone will break the spell until they can't tolerate the cold anymore."

"How many of these are there? We don't have a lot of princes in this part of the world, you know."

"Prince is a figure of speech," Isabel said. "It can apply to anyone in a position of power or wealth who needs to be taken down a peg. Oh, look, here's one!" She lunged at a little tree frog sitting on a rock. It took her a couple of tries to grab it, then she held it trapped in her hands and brought it up to her face. I wanted to look away as she puckered up and kissed it, but morbid fascination made me stare. Nothing happened. She sighed and released the frog, which hopped away with an affronted-sounding "ribbit."

I heard sirens on the street above. "We're gonna get arrested for molesting frogs," I moaned. I could imagine explaining that to my folks.

"Don't worry so much," Ari scolded as she lunged for a frog. Her fairy grace and speed gave her an advantage, so she caught it on the first try. Or maybe the frog just thought she was a giant fly and it had scored a super-size meal. "Nobody can see us, even if they look right at us. We're safe." Then she addressed her frog. "Now, handsome, make my dreams come true." She kissed it, and then I almost fell over in my hurry to step backward.

The frog glowed. The glowing aura around it grew bigger and bigger, until Ari released the frog. Instead of falling to the ground, it hung at eye level. Soon, the aura spread into the rough outline of a human form. When the glow faded, what remained was a handsome young man in an old-fashioned suit. Men's dress clothing hasn't changed much over the past hundred or so years, so it was hard to date his out-

fit, but he wore his hair in a flowing, Byronic style. He also looked utterly terrified. I put myself in his shoes—coming out of a froglike state
to find himself facing a giantess and a couple of chicks with wings—
and had to sympathize.

"Wow," I said. "So it's real?"

Ari shot me a glare. "You doubted us?"

"Not really, but you have to admit, it is weird, especially for someone like me."

"Who are you?" the man asked. "You have no right!"

"Get over yourself," Ari snapped. "I broke the spell that made you
a frog for God knows how long, so the least you could do is show me
some gratitude."

He jolted, looking almost like he'd been shot, then gave Ari a
courtly little bow. "I sincerely apologize. I beg you to forgive my poor
behavior. I am most grateful, in spite of my churlishness." When he
rose from his bow, the panicked look returned to his eyes. "Now, if
you ladies will excuse me, I must be leaving. Terribly busy. Somewhere
else I must be. It was a pleasure to make your acquaintance."

He then took off in an all-out run. I could have tripped him as he
passed me, but I felt sorry for the guy. Besides, Ari had wings. If she
wanted to catch him, she probably could.

But she didn't. She just folded her arms across her chest and said,
"You're welcome."

Isabel patted her on the shoulder. "Like I said, it's the assholes
who get that done to them. Not to mention out-of-date assholes.
Casting frogging spells was outlawed decades ago. He'd want you to
do his laundry and cook for him."

"You could try another one," Trix suggested.

"No, it's Katie's turn. An old-fashioned guy would be just right
for her."

I had no intention of actually kissing a frog, but I didn't want
them to think I was a stick-in-the-mud. It could just take me all night

to catch a frog, if I worked hard enough at it. They didn't have to know I was a country girl who knew all about catching frogs, bugs, and other critters. With my brothers, I either had to learn to get used to them or spend my life screaming. "I want to look for a good one," I said as I headed toward a stand of bushes on the other end of the pond. I could hide in there, pretending to look for frogs, until they sobered up or got bored.

I parted the bushes, stuck my head inside, and then shrieked at what I saw.

thirteen

There was a naked man crouching on a rock behind the bushes. Fortunately, the way he crouched kept me from seeing more of him than was really appropriate on such short acquaintance. He looked up at me and said, "Ribbit."

"Um, news flash, but you aren't a frog," I told him.

The others then reached me. Ari and Trix got there first, their wings flying them over any obstacles. A crashing sound behind them told me that Isabel was on her way, flattening anything in her path. "What is it, Katie?" Trix asked.

I pointed to the naked man. Words failed me.

"It's a frog," Ari said.

Isabel arrived, breathing heavily. "Are you okay? What happened?"

"Katie found a frog," Trix explained.

"No, I didn't. I found a naked guy who seems to think he's a frog. With that other guy, I saw a frog before Ari kissed him. This is different."

"Ribbit!" Naked Frog Guy said, with great enthusiasm.

I knew there were a lot of less than mentally stable people who lived in the streets and parks of New York, and a guy who thought he was a frog wasn't out of the realm of possibility, but the fact that everyone else also thought he was a frog made me suspect that something else was going on here. It must have been the results of an illusion spell rather than an exhibitionist crazy homeless guy or a real enchanted frog prince.

"It's probably a practical joke or a fraternity prank," Ari said. "If you see him as human, that must mean someone cast an illusion on him to make him and everyone else think he's a frog. You don't see the frog because of your magical immunity."

"What do we do about it?" I asked. "We can't leave him out here like this. He'll die of hypothermia. It's cold at night, not to mention the fact that he's naked and around water."

"Ribbit?" he said in a pleading tone of voice.

I snapped my fingers in front of his face. "You're. Not. A. Frog," I told him firmly.

"You'll have to kiss him to make him snap out of it," Isabel said.

"Kiss him?"

Ari rolled her eyes. "How else do you break a frog enchantment?" She left off the "duh" at the end of the sentence, but her tone implied it.

"But why me? Why do I have to be the one to kiss him?"

Trix ticked off reasons on her fingers. "A: You found him. B: At least you'd be kissing a human. If one of us kissed him, we'd be kissing a frog. Kissing any human is better than kissing any frog."

Naked Frog Guy said, "Ribbit, ribbit, ribbit!" He was practically hopping with excitement.

"Whoa, chill, okay?" I told him. I wasn't entirely opposed to the idea of kissing naked men, but it depended heavily on the circumstances. For starters, I strongly preferred to actually know the guy and to have established a relationship. I didn't think it was asking too much for me to really like the guy, even to believe that I loved him (though I knew that being with a naked man tended to cloud your judgment in that area). Call me a prude, but I also preferred an indoor location or, at the very least, some privacy.

In short, kissing a naked man who had said nothing more than "ribbit" to me, while surrounded by friends in Central Park, was not high on my list of turn-ons.

But what I'd said earlier was true. He probably would die if we left him out there, and if I kissed him, it might get me off the hook for any other frog kissing that night. "Well, here goes nothing," I muttered as I knelt next to him. This would be easier if I was drunker. Maybe we could go to a bar, then come back and finish this. But I was already here, so I might as well get it over with. It wasn't like I had to tongue-kiss him. That was fortunate. What if he'd been eating flies? Ewww.

I screwed my eyes shut, then leaned in and gave him a quick peck on the lips that landed slightly off center. Before I could back away, he grabbed my head and pulled me back for a rather more thorough kiss. After thinking about flies, I very determinedly kept my lips sealed together.

Finally, he let me go, and I couldn't stop myself from wiping my mouth with the back of my hand. Almost immediately he grabbed my hand and lavished kisses on the back of it. "Oh, thank you, thank you, thank you," he said, which was an improvement over "ribbit," even if he hadn't added much variety to his vocabulary. "I owe you big-time."

"Don't mention it," I said, freeing my hand and wiping it on my skirt as I backed away from him and stood up.

He made as if to stand up, too, then glanced down at himself and noticed he was naked. "Um, well, I'm going to have to stand up now, but I'd like you all to take into consideration the fact that it's pretty cold before anyone makes any snap judgments," he said.

Isabel took off her cardigan and tossed it to him. He wrapped it around his waist, then adjusted it carefully as he stood up. It covered him completely from waist to knees. When he stepped out of the bushes and into a better lit area, I saw that he wasn't bad-looking. He was about my age, which made him a little old for a fraternity prank, and his body was nicely defined. He had shaggy blondish hair and a tattoo on one well-sculpted bicep. He looked more like a California surfer dude than like someone you'd meet in New York. Ari gave a low whistle, then elbowed Isabel. "Why'd you have to give him the sweater?" she hissed.

"Now that you're all disenchanted, you should go home and warm up," I said brusquely. I didn't want him to think I'd kissed him for any reason other than to release him from the spell. If I'd run into him anywhere else, I might have been interested in a little flirtation, but meeting him when he thought he was a frog was just too weird for me. I vowed never again to use that old saying about kissing frogs, not now that I knew I wouldn't want anyone who used to be a frog, even if he was a prince.

"Is there a problem, ladies?" a voice asked. I whirled in shock. We hadn't been caught red-handed while molesting frogs, but standing around in the dark in the park with a seminaked man wasn't the most innocent activity. The speaker turned out to be a park ranger—a park ranger who had wings on his back and slightly pointed ears. This must be a sprite.

"This gentleman has just been disenchanted," Trix said. She and the sprite had locked eyes in a way that was entirely familiar to me, a look of intense, instant attraction. Not that I'd experienced it personally, but I'd watched it happen to friends.

"We'd better get him inside and taken care of, then," the sprite ranger said.

"I'll come with you," Trix said, fluttering her fingers at us as she took Naked Frog Guy by the arm and joined the ranger.

"It's a rebound. It'll never last," Ari opined as they disappeared into the darkness.

"You're letting him go like that?" Isabel asked me.

"Uh, yeah, looks like I am," I said.

"Why? You actually found a prince. It turns out you were right about kissing frogs."

I shuddered. "No, no, I wasn't. This is a worse way to meet men than singles' bars."

Isabel brightened. "We could go to a singles' bar."

"Not tonight," I said with a sigh. "I hate to be a wet blanket, but I'd rather just go home now."

"You're not having fun?" Isabel asked, looking and sounding worried.

"I had lots of fun, really. But it's been a long week, and it all caught up with me at once. I'm glad I came, though. Thanks for inviting me."

I must have sounded convincing, for she looked more like her usual cheerful self. "I'm glad you had fun. We'll have to do this again sometime."

"Next time, we can skip the frogs."

She and Ari laughed. "It was your idea," Isabel said. I didn't try to argue that when I brought it up, I hadn't expected them to take me literally. I gave them a halfhearted wave and hurried up to Fifth Avenue to see if I could catch the M1 bus. One of Marcia's city safety rules was that the bus was better than the subway when you were alone at night because you could sit near the driver and you were less likely to be stuck underground with crazy people. I glanced at my watch and was surprised at how early it was. I felt like I was crawling home in the wee hours after a night of debauchery, but I'd probably beat my room-mates home.

A bus showed up before long, and I climbed on board. For the first time in my life I felt like the oddball surrounded by normal people, instead of the other way around. No matter what anyone else on the bus had done that evening, it couldn't possibly be any weirder than what I'd just done.

In the space of about a week's time, I'd gone from being perhaps the most ordinary person on this island to being one of the weirdos. I wasn't sure yet if that was an improvement.

I was rudely awakened the next morning by all the lights coming on in my bedroom and the window shade going up to let in the feeble sunlight that ventured into the air shaft. "Wake up, sleepyhead!" Gemma called out.

I pulled the covers over my head, but she pulled them back. "You don't want to sleep all day, do you?" she asked. "I've already been for a run."

I pried my eyes open to see that she was dressed in a high-fashion velour jogging suit, very similar to one Madonna had been wearing in a photo in last week's *People*. "Since when do you run?" She had the kind of body that stayed fabulous without exercise. If I didn't love her so much, I'd have to hate her.

"Since I heard that Saturday morning in the park is a great place to meet buff guys." She perched on the edge of my bed. "Not that I actually bothered running. The trick is to always look like you're about to run, or like you've just finished running. It's hard to hook up with someone while you're in the process of running."

"Did it work?"

She grinned. "Yep. I met a really hot guy, very nice, too. He had old-fashioned manners like I haven't seen since I left Texas. I don't think he was there for running, but hey, it's the results that count, not the process."

"Did you get his number?"

"Not exactly. But I did tell him where my friends and I always hang out on Saturday nights, and I invited him to drop by and join us."

I frowned. "Where do we always hang out on Saturday nights?"

"I found this cute little bar. You'll come with me tonight, won't you, Katie? Maybe he'll bring a friend."

I groaned. "I'm not sure I'm up to it."

"Oh, come on, you were already in bed when we got home. You're not hungover, are you? How much did you have to drink last night?"

"Not that much," I said, mentally calculating. Oh God, I'd been persuaded to go kissing frogs in Central Park on only three cosmos. I was such a lightweight. But my hangover was more emotional than physical. I was still freaked out by the whole frog-kissing incident.

"Did you have a good time? What did you do?"

"Oh, the usual girls' night out stuff, looking for guys. Like they say, you have to kiss a few frogs—"

"Before you find a prince," she completed the saying for me. "Did you find any?"

"A prince is in the eye of the beholder." Let her interpret that any way she wanted to.

I wasn't sure I was ready to cope with the bar scene again, but I let Gemma drag me out that night anyway. Marcia begged off, saying she had work to do. That almost made me change my mind. If Gemma hooked up with her guy, that would leave me the odd one out. I supposed I could always beat a strategic exit if it came to that.

The bar she'd found was a comfortable neighborhood place, the kind where we might hang out regularly, if we were so inclined. By the time we'd been there about five minutes, she'd managed to turn herself into a regular who knew the names of every waiter and bartender in the place. I still couldn't figure out how she did it.

I ordered a glass of wine because cosmos made me think of frogs. Gemma tried to make casual conversation about how my week had gone while her eyes scanned the room, looking for her guy. Fortunately, her attention was too focused on looking for the guy for her to notice much of what I said. My week didn't really bear deep examination.

Finally, she lit up. "There he is!" she said. I turned to see a tall man with dark, Byronic hair enter the room. He wore dark gray slacks and a flowing white shirt with suspenders. He looked vaguely uncomfortable and out of place. He also looked familiar. "Philip!" Gemma called to him, standing and waving a hand in the air. He smiled and some of the unease left his posture when he saw her.

She pulled out a chair for him at our table. "Philip, this is my friend Katie. Katie, Philip." He took my hand and bowed over it when we were introduced. I hoped he didn't kiss it. That would only remind me of Naked Frog Guy. Then he placed his hands on the back of the chair she'd pulled out and waited expectantly. When she plopped into the chair she'd been sitting in instead of the one he was holding for her, he frowned and looked confused, then rushed to help seat her and scoot her up to the table before taking his own seat.

That was when I realized who he was. He was the frog prince from the night before, the one Ari had disenchanted with a kiss. He didn't seem to have recognized me, but considering he'd been surrounded by a giantess and two fairies, he probably hadn't noticed the plain vanilla girl. I wondered if he was magical himself or if he'd just been the victim of a cruel spell.

Either way, I wasn't sure I wanted my roommate dating him. But what could I say? It wasn't like I could suggest to Gemma that it was time for a trip to the restroom, then warn her that her new guy used to be a frog. So far he'd been very polite and had given me no excuse to take such a strong dislike to him that I'd use a roommate veto. Those had to be saved for very special circumstances, such as when you recognized your roommate's date from the artist's rendering of a serial killer on the news and she refused to acknowledge that fact. I wasn't sure the former frog status was quite that bad.

They seemed to be nicely at ease with each other. In any other circumstances this would have been time for me to come up with someplace I needed to be so I could leave them alone. But I couldn't leave Gemma alone with a former frog. A fly buzzed through the bar, and I watched with a sick feeling in my stomach as Philip's eyes tracked it hungrily. When he licked his lips while watching it, I'd had enough.

I waited until Gemma turned to talk to the waiter, then leaned over to Philip. "Look, I know what you used to be, and I hear that's not something that happens to nice guys. So I want to make it very, very clear to you that if you give my friend anything to complain about, I know people who can turn you right back into a frog. Are we clear?"

His eyes grew wide as he nodded. I doubted I could really get one of the guys at MSI to turn him into a frog, considering that the girls had said frogging spells had been outlawed, but he didn't have to know that.

Just as Gemma returned her attention to us, a waiter came over and put a glass of champagne in front of me. "Compliments of that gentleman over there," he said.

I turned, my heart in my throat. I didn't know what to hope for. I'd never had that sort of thing happen to me, so I steeled myself for disappointment. It was something Rod might do if he ran into me in public.

But it wasn't Rod who smiled at me from across the room. It was Naked Frog Guy, now fully dressed. "Wow, Katie, an admirer!" Gemma said. "Go talk to him." In other words, leave her alone with her frog—er, guy.

Oh, I definitely wanted to talk to him, but not for flirtation purposes. I stood—Philip rose slightly from his chair as I did so, proving that he was from more than a decade or so ago, since few modern men did that sort of thing—picked up my drink, and made my way over to Naked Frog Guy's table. He stood to greet me. "My dearest Katie, I can't begin to thank you for what you did for me," he said, sounding like a surfer dude attempting to perform Shakespeare. It didn't quite work.

"How do you know who I am? How did you find me?"

"Your fairy friend told me who you are. Finding you wasn't difficult. I'm Jeff, by the way."

I wanted to pluck off Trix's wings and feed them to her. "Thank you for the drink. But it was no big deal, really." I leaned closer to him. "I'm not sure you realize this, but you weren't really a frog. It was just an illusion. I didn't do anything."

"You freed me. You saved my life. And you're the most beautiful thing I've seen in a long time."

I got the impression that it might not have taken a spell to get him to sit naked in the park and ribbit at people. His mama must have dropped him on his head one too many times when he was a baby. "We're even now. You bought me a drink, so all's square. Now, have a nice life, and stay away from strange lily pads. What happened to you, anyway? Did you lose a bet?"

He looked sheepish. "Something like that. But now I feel like the winner, for it brought you to me." He twitched his wrist, and a red rose appeared in his hand. He then presented the rose to me with much ceremony. Great. Now I had a crazy stalker who had magical powers. "Please take this as a token of my devotion."

"Wow. Thanks. But really, this is too much. We're completely even now, okay? You don't have to do anything else. Now, I have to go. 'Bye." I dashed out of the bar before he could do anything else. After this weekend, going to work Monday morning was going to feel practically humdrum, even at Magic, Inc.

* * *

Owen was already on the platform, leaning against a pillar, when I got to the subway station Monday morning. He looked much better than he had the last time I'd seen him. The dark shadows were gone from beneath his blue eyes, and his skin had a healthy color to it. Baseball must have agreed with him.

"How was the game?" I asked. "I hear the Yankees won."

He studied the toes of his shoes and turned pink. "What makes you think I had anything to do with that?"

"Sounds like someone has a guilty conscience. I didn't say anything about how the Yankees seem to have won. But you know, it does explain a lot."

"I take it you don't approve."

I shrugged. "I'm a Texas Rangers fan, and they used to be the Senators—you know, from *Damn Yankees*—so you get the picture."

"Sorry about that. And it wasn't like we did anything major. We just improved the umpire's eyesight a little bit."

"Yeah, sure." He grinned at my teasing tone, and as the train pulled into the station I realized it was the first time we'd talked about something other than work. He was still breathing, he wasn't any pinker than normal, and he hadn't passed out during a whole conversation that had nothing to do with business. He was even looking me in the eye. That pretty much proved that his interest in me didn't extend beyond friendship. Pity.

As we clung to a pole together on the train, I asked, "Are you a big baseball fan?"

"I don't know if I'd call myself a big fan, but I like it. It's so—" He groped for words. "—normal, and that's not something I feel often."

His eyes looked troubled, and I wondered if magical ability might be as much curse as it was blessing. Hoping to make him smile again,

I stood on tiptoe and whispered in his ear, "I guess that's when you're not casting spells on the umpires." It worked. He grinned and turned a rather becoming shade of pink.

That evening, I hovered around my office a little past quitting time, hoping to causally step out into the hallway just as Owen walked by so we could go home together. Maybe I'd learn another personal detail about him. Unfortunately, he didn't show. He must have been back to work on finding a counterspell. Reluctantly, I headed home alone.

When I came aboveground at the Union Square station, I was glad he wasn't with me. At first I didn't pay much attention to the guy standing by the station entrance, playing a guitar and singing. Then I heard my name. He was singing Barry Manilow's "Mandy," but just saying, "Oh, Katie" over and over again in tune with the music, or rather, out of tune with the music. Afraid of what I'd see, I turned to find Jeff, the Naked Frog Guy, beaming at me. Still strumming and singing, he lowered himself until he was down on one knee. *Please, don't let him propose,* I prayed.

He had a look of utter devotion on his face that reminded me of Cletus, the not so bright but incredibly friendly black Lab we'd had when I was a kid. Unfortunately, Cletus wasn't too discriminating. He'd give that same look of devotion to family members or burglars, whoever was willing to rub his tummy. I suspected this guy was much the same way. It had to be a result of the spell. I tried to remember how the frog prince spell went in fairy tales. Did my breaking the spell mean he was doomed to be in love with me forever? This would be a whole lot more fun if he just had to grant three wishes for me.

I figured I had a couple of options. I could ignore him and keep walking, running the risk that he'd follow me. Or I could stop and tell him to give it a break, which might or might not do any good if he was under a spell. I decided that having a short conversation here was better than having my own personal troubadour following me through the streets of New York.

I got as close to him as I dared, then hissed, "What do you think you're doing?"

"I'm serenading my maiden fair, the one whose gentle kiss saved my life." He was back in Shakespearean surfer mode.

"Well, knock it off. I don't want to be serenaded."

"My humble offering doesn't please you?"

"It embarrasses me." It should have embarrassed him, but once you've sat naked in Central Park, everything else is only minor humiliation. Then I got an idea. "You know, absence makes the heart grow fonder."

Within a heartbeat his guitar was back in its case and he was gone. I should have thought of that sooner. With a great sense of relief, I headed home.

Thus began my second week at MSI. This week was a little more ordinary than the last one had been—or as ordinary as things were likely to get at a magical company. There weren't any intruders—at least, not that I spotted—and I wasn't called upon to help check out any new, potentially dangerous spells. I met with Mr. Hartwell a few times to talk about marketing, but I didn't see Merlin at all.

Presumably, Owen and his team were still testing the spell and trying to find a counterspell, for he went back to looking pale and tired most of the time. After another week with apparently no good news, he developed a worried crease in his forehead. We still rode to work together most mornings, but that was all I saw of him.

I got in the habit of regularly eating lunch with Ari and occasionally with Isabel, and through them I got a better orientation about life in the magical world. During the next couple of weeks I also got a better sense of what my job really was all about. I went on sales calls, always checking for any of Idris's spells that might have been hidden away and making sure that the shop owners were on board with our marketing messages. I also sat in on a few meetings and fine-tuned my ideas for a more effective way to do real-time, live verification.

Settling into my job made it easier for me at home. Things went back to normal with my friends, except for the fact that I wasn't being set up with a different guy every weekend. Gemma swore she was working on Project Boyfriend but hadn't found the right guy for me yet. I enjoyed the break and the chance to spend more quality time with my friends. Gemma was still dating Philip the Frog, and for her, sticking with the same guy for more than a week meant she was getting serious. My own frog guy, Jeff, hadn't shown up again, but I worried about what might be in store when he decided he'd been absent long enough for my heart to grow really fond of him.

By my fourth week on the job, I couldn't imagine working anywhere else. The strange old building felt like home, and there didn't seem to be anything odd about working with people who had wings. I'd learned to have my hands ready if someone offered me a cup of coffee, and I'd been spoiled by having whatever I wanted for lunch delivered instantly.

That Thursday morning, I got a verification call from the sales department. I entered the department to find Selwyn, the elf I'd gone with on my first call, waiting for me. "Hey, Katie, babe," he said, pointing his fingers at me like guns. "Ready for some action? I've got a few accounts I need to check on." He dropped his voice to a stage whisper and added, "Not to mention looking out for a few other things, wink-wink, nudge-nudge."

"How are sales?" I asked as we made our way to the building exit.

"We aren't seeing a lot of inroads from our so-called competition, but then the competition isn't selling anything that would affect what we sell. That marketing stuff seems to be working, though. Our sales are up, and that's made most of our distributors more eager to work with us and less eager to take risks by carrying anything less than kosher."

We stepped outside and climbed onto the flying carpet. I now almost felt comfortable riding these things. I felt far more comfortable with anyone but Selwyn driving, however. He was the worst kind of show-off, and I think I only encouraged him by looking nervous.

"So we're doing okay?" I asked, trying to mask my flying anxiety.

"Looks like it. They've only caught a few people using those spells, and they don't appear to be as effective as they're advertised to be. Word gets around about things like that." I'd been keeping an eye on the news, looking for signs of inexplicable crime sprees, but it just seemed to be normal New York crime levels. Maybe things weren't as bad as we'd feared, but then I doubted they'd have brought Merlin back for something so easy to solve.

We reached our first stop, a music shop in the East Village. I wondered if this was where Jake had bought that spell. It was a seedy place I wouldn't have gone into by myself, and I doubted they'd sell the kind of mainstream music I liked anyway.

"This is a surprise inspection, so make it look good," Selwyn whispered to me as he pushed the door open. "Hey, Marco!" he shouted.

It took me a few seconds to figure out whether the being that stepped from behind the beaded curtains at the back of the store was human, and even though I guessed he was, I still wasn't entirely sure. He was skinny enough to have been a male model in the days of heroin chic, and his arms and legs were long in proportion to his body, giving him an insectlike look. He had more metal hanging off his face than I'd had in my mouth with a particularly elaborate set of braces. He didn't look happy to see Selwyn. "I'm good. Don't need to restock."

Selwyn didn't let his customer's dour reaction dim his salesman's enthusiasm. "Just checking in. I like to keep my finger on the pulse of sales, keep it real down here on the streets." As Selwyn went into his pitch, I took it as my cue to scan the shelves. In addition to the records and CDs, there was an entire rack of spells. Most were MSI spells, in their new packaging, but there were a few copies of the spell Jake had found. I caught Selwyn's eye and nodded.

He instantly dropped the smooth salesman's air and grew cold. His eyes looked like chips of flint, and I was glad I wasn't the one he was mad at. "So, you're selling that trash," he said, looming over Marco. If I wasn't mistaken, he'd actually grown a few inches. Were elves stretchy?

Marco wasn't easily intimidated. In fact, he looked bored. "Yeah, so?"

"So, it violates every ethical standard our people live by."

"Hey, man, I don't make judgments. I just sell what the people want."

"And how badly do the people want it?"

"We've sold a few. Not so much lately. Word's out it doesn't work so well."

"Does that mean you knowingly sell shoddy merchandise?"

Marco shrugged. "Caveat emptor."

"Word gets out you're selling bad stuff, and soon no one is buying any stuff from you."

"I'm just the distributor."

"We could find another distributor in this area. You aren't making a lot of sales for us."

"And that means I'm not selling enough to miss you if you go. You're gonna have to shake things up to make my customers happy. This whole make-the-world-a-better-place routine is stale."

"I can think of one very quick, very easy way to improve the world," Selwyn said, with a layer of iron under his casual tone.

Marco snorted. "Yeah, like the good guys would do that."

"We have before. You've been around long enough to remember that. When it all comes down, you'll want to be on the right side." I wasn't sure what he meant, but Marco seemed to. He paled, but kept his defiant stance.

Selwyn gestured to me, and we left the store. "Fortunately, he's in the minority," he said as we climbed back on the flying carpet. "We'll need to keep an eye on shops like that. It looks like that's the primary distribution point."

"But it's good to hear sales aren't going so well."

"Just as long as he doesn't fix the bugs. If he gets it to work, we're in trouble."

fourteen

I got to work the next morning—after a rare subway ride without Owen at my side—to find an e-mail notifying me of a meeting in Merlin's office. I hurried upstairs. Owen was already there, looking shattered and uncharacteristically unkempt, his clothes wrinkled, his hair mussed, and a dark shadow on his jaw. I thought I recognized his tie from the day before. In a strange, almost disturbing way, that look was very appealing on him. Gemma needed to find me a prospect soon to jolt me out of this crazy crush.

"So, that's why you weren't on the subway," I remarked, trying not to pant or drool as I took a seat at Merlin's conference table.

He rubbed his eyes. "Yeah, I was here all night, working on a counterspell."

Mr. Hartwell and Gregor then joined us, along with a gnome I didn't recognize. He was introduced to me as Dortmund, head of Corporate Accounting.

Merlin had just taken his seat at the table when a plump woman bustled in. "Sorry I'm late," she said. "Guess I should have seen that delay coming, huh?" She turned to me and said, "Katie, I don't believe we've met. I'm Minerva Felps, head of P and L."

She wasn't what I expected of a seer. I was thinking more of a mysterious Gypsy woman like the fortune-teller at the county fair, or maybe someone ethereal and vague. But she looked more like a busybody aunt who made it a point to know everyone's business. Then again, I suppose that was basically her job.

Merlin called the meeting to order. He seemed to fit in this place and time better than the last time I'd seen him. He was losing a little of his lost quality. "Given that it's been a month since we started more specifically addressing the possible threat from our new competition, I felt it was an opportune time to regroup and see where we stand. Mr. Hartwell?"

"Sales are doing well, better than before we started Miss Chandler's marketing campaign. I don't know how it's affecting our competition's sales, but our bottom line is only being affected in a good way. We've seen a few of the competing products in stores where we have accounts, but none in any of our key accounts. They're mostly in out-of-the-way places that most proper magic folk wouldn't frequent."

"We're getting positive feedback from the store owners," I added. "Whether or not it directly addresses the threat, it might be good to keep the marketing campaign going. It certainly seems to have helped keep those spells out of the mainstream."

Owen massaged his temples with his thumbs. He looked so tired he didn't even blush before speaking. "What helps us there is that it isn't a very good spell. It's a big energy drain, and it doesn't work as well as you'd expect from a commercially produced spell. He was in a rush to get something into the market. But I know him well enough to know he won't stop there. He'll get it worked out, and then we'll have problems."

"How are you doing on the counterspell?" Merlin asked.

"I've got a counterspell for this one, as of about five this morning. I'll just have to get it to Practical Magic for distribution. But it's only good until he gets the problems corrected. Then I'll have to start all over again." He didn't sound like he looked forward to that.

"Is there any insight from Prophets and Lost?"

Minerva shook her head. "Sorry, but this one's a big blur. There aren't any signs at all, let alone clear ones. Anything could happen. Now, we're not picking up on any major disasters, and civilization does seem to be more or less intact for the foreseeable future, so I doubt we've got a major apocalypse on our hands that will change life as we know it. But I can't tell if the good guys or the bad guys are going to win this one." She shrugged. "That makes us about as useless as a screen door on a submarine, but there you go."

Merlin laced his fingers together on top of the table. "There we have it. We seem to have stood our ground well enough to avert an immediate crisis, but the danger certainly hasn't passed. Mr. Palmer, could you anticipate what might be done to correct the spell?"

"I could try to correct it myself. I doubt he'd take a vastly different approach than I would. We were trained by the same people, after all. I'm just not sure I'm comfortable doing so. It gets into an area of magic I'd rather not delve into very deeply." If I wasn't mistaken, there was fear in his eyes, but he quickly cast his gaze down to the table, so I couldn't see for sure.

Merlin's eyes grew gentle. "Perhaps you can set this task for your staff, then supervise them closely."

Owen nodded without saying anything or even looking up. I remembered Rod mentioning that they were sometimes concerned about what Owen was capable of. It looked like Owen was concerned as well. Did that mean he was afraid he'd become evil if he played with darker magic? I couldn't imagine him being capable of harming anyone, but there was a lot I didn't know about magic or about Owen. I reminded myself that I'd known him for more than a month now, and all I knew about him as a person was that he liked baseball.

"What can Sales do to anticipate a future crisis?" Merlin asked.

Mr. Hartwell looked grim. "We're continuing to put pressure on store owners, make them aware of the quality differences, but we can't keep singing that tune if he fixes the spell. Meanwhile, there's the risk they'll call our bluff if we threaten to pull out of their stores. As long as we have spells in those stores, we have an excuse to investigate them. Once we pull out, we won't be able to track what he's selling. At least now we know where to go to get our hands on anything the moment it hits the market."

Merlin turned to Dortmund, the accounting gnome. "This may require additional budget. How are we set for funding?"

"We've got plenty of gold reserves. Our stocks hadn't been doing so well, but thanks to a hot tip from Minerva's folks, we're on an up-swing. Bottom line is, we've got the money to do what we need to do. If we don't spend it now, it may not matter much in the future. Like Hartwell said, sales are good. We're not hurting."

"Very well, then. It looks as though we're as prepared as we're likely to be."

I noticed then that he hadn't yet called on Gregor. I'd thought he must be there because of some verification project, like maybe to report on how things were going with using verifiers to sniff out intruders. But Merlin hadn't asked him anything, and Gregor hadn't volunteered anything. Now I wondered why he was even at this meeting. I certainly hadn't missed seeing his shiny red face—or his green, scaly one, either.

Merlin glanced around the table, then said, "There's one more item for today's agenda. As you all know, I've yet to select an assistant. I wanted the chance to get to know as many of the employees as possible before making my choice. With the crisis at hand, I feel it is crucial for me to have someone working with me whom I can trust utterly. And for that reason, I've selected Miss Chandler to be my executive assistant."

I had to give my head a little shake to clear it, just to make sure I'd heard what I thought I had. That was the job Kim had been counting on.

Merlin continued speaking. "Of course, that's if Miss Chandler is interested in the job."

"Yes, of course. Thank you." Although I hadn't even considered the possibility of getting that job, I didn't hesitate to take it. I knew from my last job that the top executives' assistants were the ones who really held the power in the company. This was definitely a vote of confidence in me.

He smiled. "Good. I know I'm taking one of Gregor's staff away from him, but I feel that my having verification abilities at hand is extremely important at this time. And Miss Chandler will be able to continue her other corporate functions as well. She will continue to head our marketing efforts, which have been so successful."

Gregor didn't look pleased, but he wasn't turning green or growing fangs, either. He was probably glad to get rid of me. Kim wasn't going to be happy, but that wasn't really my problem. I hadn't even seen Kim since I'd been working out of R&D.

Owen grinned at me. "Congratulations," he said. I wondered if he'd known in advance.

"Thanks. Wow. I don't know what to say."

"You've earned it, Katie. I can't imagine anyone I'd rather have working at my side," Merlin said with a warm, grandfatherly smile.

A bottle of champagne appeared on the table, followed by glasses for all of us. Minerva opened the bottle and poured, passing the glasses around. "You know it's a good day at the office when you're drinking before noon," Gregor muttered. I couldn't believe he'd actually made a joke. At least, I hoped it was a joke.

Merlin raised his glass. "To my new assistant. May she continue to provide me with wise counsel."

The others raised their glasses and echoed him. I felt proud and embarrassed, all at the same time. I'd toiled for a year in my previous job without so much as a raise. Now I'd been promoted barely a month into this job. It was a distinct improvement. Rod and Owen had been right when they told me at the beginning that I'd be valued here. I doubted even they had imagined I'd do this well. I wasn't sure I believed it yet.

The impromptu party broke up as the group returned to their offices. Owen pushed himself out of his chair with a visible effort, and Merlin stopped him with a hand on his arm before he could make it to the door. "You, go home now and rest. I don't want to see you again until Monday."

It was a sign of just how tired Owen was that he didn't protest. "Okay, then, I'll see you Monday. Have a good weekend, Katie, and congratulations again."

"Thanks. You, too. Get some rest."

"I should let you get settled, and then we'll talk about your new role," Merlin said. He walked with me to the outer office, where Trix sat at the reception desk. "Trixie, can you show Katie to her new office?"

"Right away, boss. And remember, you have a lunch meeting with Amalgamated Neuromancy."

"Ah, yes, that. I'll get back to you this afternoon, Katie."

Once he was gone down the escalator, Trix dropped her professional manners and squealed with delight. "Congratulations! I've known since yesterday, and I thought I'd burst from not being able to tell you. It'll be fun having you up here. Let me show you your new office."

She fluttered to a doorway opposite Merlin's office, and I followed. This office wasn't quite as big as Merlin's, but it was enormous, vastly superior to every other place I'd worked. For one thing, it had windows. The view was mostly of lower Manhattan, with the tall buildings getting in the way of anything truly scenic, but I was glad to have windows at all, no matter what the view was.

There was a large desk, with my computer already on it, a desk chair that might as well be a throne, a small conference table with chairs near one of the windows, and a big, overstuffed sofa along one wall. "Wow" was all I could say.

"Your stuff's already up here. The boss had me take care of that while you were in the meeting. If you need any books or decorations, let me know and I'll take care of it. I can also get you lunch, coffee, or whatever."

She then handed me a set of keys. "Here are your keys to the building, to this floor, and to your suite. Oh, and the bathroom's behind that door next to my desk." She gave me a mock pout. "Looks like I don't have a bathroom to myself anymore."

"I'll try not to hog it."

"Okay, then. I'll leave you to get settled in, and I'll let you know when Mr. Mervyn is ready to meet with you."

I had remarkably little to do for someone with such a supposedly important position, but I imagined that was likely to change soon enough. For now, I enjoyed having an office with windows and a door that closed. Even without much to do, the day passed relatively quickly. Merlin had to postpone our meeting until Monday when he got stuck in some tricky negotiations, so before I knew it, it was time to go home, and I had very little to show for my day, other than my new office. "Want to have a celebratory drink?" Trix asked when I passed her desk on my way out.

"I have to get home. I have my first Project Boyfriend date tonight, so my roommates need to make me over."

"Good luck with that."

"Thanks. I have a feeling I'll need it."

If I had to meet a guy Gemma was sure was the One—with a capital letter—today was as good a day as any. The day's events had left me feeling bold and confident, which was better than the nervous way I usually approached dates.

Gemma was already home when I got there. She must have taken off early, just for the occasion. "Are you excited about tonight?" she asked.

I didn't have to fake excitement. I just had to fake what I was excited about. "Yeah. It's already been a great day."

"Get in the shower, and then you can tell me all about it while I do your hair and makeup."

Half an hour later I sat in front of the dresser in our bedroom with my hair up in a towel while Gemma worked on my makeup. "I'm going for a fresh-faced girl-next-door look, so you just look nice, not like you've got a lot of makeup on," she said. "That should appeal to Keith."

"He's a guy. If he notices the nuances of my makeup job, he's probably not straight."

She acted like she didn't hear me. She was too busy taking the towel off my head and combing out the tangles. "I wish we'd had time to do highlights."

"If he hates me on sight because I don't have highlights, I don't want him."

Still ignoring my bad attitude, she asked, "So, what happened today that had you so excited?"

"I got a promotion at work. A big one."

"Congratulations! What's your new job?"

"I'm assistant to one of the top executives." I decided against saying I'd been promoted to be the top boss's assistant because that was so big it would raise too many questions. People just didn't rise from being an ordinary administrative assistant to being the CEO's right-hand person in the space of one month.

"That's super! See, I told you that last place you worked didn't appreciate you. Now, hold still."

I closed my eyes and tried to ignore the curling iron and goodness knew what else she was doing to my hair to make it look "natural." Then I reminded myself that I was going through this so I could get to a point where I wouldn't have to go through this as often. That fantasy of wearing sweats and watching an old movie was looking better and better.

Finally, I met with Gemma's approval. Marcia got home from work and gave her thumbs-up. "I still can't believe you're sending me out on my own like this," I complained before they shoved me out the door.

"When you meet in a group, it takes on a just-for-fun atmosphere," Gemma explained. "One-on-one is serious. Now go and be brilliant."

That was easy for her to say. Dating came naturally to her. I could talk easily to the guys at work, but put me across a table from a man in a situation where there were no legal pads or PowerPoint presentations involved and I froze. I couldn't remember the last real one-on-one date I'd been on. I was twenty-six years old, and there were high school freshmen with more dating experience than I had.

At least they'd picked a restaurant fairly close by, near Union Square. I could make an escape without having to hail a cab. As I walked to the restaurant, I noticed a gargoyle on top of a nearby building, and I'd never seen one there before. I didn't think it was Sam, though. This one had a different profile, more of a birdlike beak in-stead of Sam's grotesque humanlike face.

It was a chilly night, and a blast of hot air hit me in the face when I entered the restaurant. The place was already crowded, packed wall-to-wall with people waiting for a table. How was I supposed to find my date in this mob?

A tall, handsome man with wavy chestnut hair walked toward me. I automatically glanced behind me to see which supermodel he was approaching, but he looked me in the eye and said, "Katie Chan-dler?"

I gulped. Gemma didn't mess around when it came to looking for the One. "You're Keith?" I didn't mean it to sound like an incredulous question, but that's the way it came out. I never got set up with guys like this.

He gave me a smile that turned my insides to jelly and reached to shake my hand. "Nice to meet you."

"Uh-huh" was all I was capable of saying.

He didn't notice my awkwardness, or if he did, he was gentleman enough to pretend not to notice. "Let's see if our table's ready," he said.

I followed him to the host's stand, then nearly tripped over my own feet when I noticed a party of fairies and sprites come in. Damn. Why couldn't I escape from magic for one night? I hoped it wasn't anyone I knew and that they'd leave us alone. I wanted to make a good impression on this guy. Before I had a chance to see if I recog-nized anyone in the group, the host led us to our table.

Once the host was gone, Keith grinned at me. He had warm hazel eyes that lit up when he smiled. I could definitely imagine cuddling on the couch with him. "Gemma said you were cute, but I had no idea," he said.

I wondered if he meant cute as in attractive or cute as in "just like my little sister." I knew I was blushing, which probably increased the "like a little sister" impression. "Gemma didn't tell me anything about you," I admitted.

"Then it's very brave of you to take a chance on me in the blindest of blind dates."

Me, taking a chance on him? He had to be kidding. He was also way too good to be true. Maybe Gemma had hired him to go out with me, but that would defeat the whole point of Project Boyfriend. She knew I didn't need dates just to have someone to go out with.

We discussed the menu for a few minutes. He didn't have any weird food quirks that he felt the need to mention. He wasn't on any wacky diet, and he didn't reject menu items because they contained some food he hated. After too many blind dates with men who reminded me of toddlers on food jags, that was refreshing. I just hoped the conversation held up after we ordered.

The waiter came to take our orders and took away our menus, and we were left to work without a net. "So, what do you do, Katie?" he asked. It was the obligatory first question on any date. I wasn't sure why, when most people claim to hate talking about work.

"I'm just a secretary. Nothing interesting." I'd decided the best way around that tricky job question was to make my job sound so uninteresting that no one would want to ask more questions about it. "What about you?" I hoped turning the tables quickly would help move the conversation away from any possibility of me having to skirt the magic issue.

It didn't work. I'd found a guy who actually wanted to talk about me. "What company do you work for?" he asked.

"It's a small company. I'm sure you wouldn't have heard of it."

"Try me."

"It's called MSI Inc."

"You're right. I haven't heard of it. What do they do?"

I wished I could remember the way Owen had described it in that first meeting, which seemed so very long ago. "Oh, it's some kind of services stuff," I said at last, playing airhead. "I just type memos and make coffee. I don't pay much attention to what we actually do."

As boring as I tried to make it sound, he didn't look like he was about to fall asleep. If he wasn't truly interested, he was faking it well. For a moment I wanted to really wow him by telling him I was Merlin's assistant and I worked with wizards and magical people, but I had a feeling that would lead to the kind of commitment that involved padded cells rather than diamond rings. Ordinary Katie would have to do. I just hoped ordinary Katie would be enough.

As if to reinforce the weirdness of my life, the party of sprites and fairies walked past us on the way to their table and I recognized Ari. She winked at me as she passed. I forced my attention back to my date while I wondered how big a coincidence it was that one of my coworkers was at the same restaurant I was, especially given that Ari claimed not to like dating her own kind. Why did they have to pick this restaurant, tonight of all nights, the one time when I wanted to go back to at least looking normal again for a little while?

"Now, what do you do?" I asked again, but as interested as I really was, I couldn't stop my attention from wandering over to the table of fairies. They didn't seem to have noticed me, for which I was grateful.

He finished explaining his job to me, then opened his mouth to ask another question, but his water glass tipped over. He hurried to right it, then attempted to blot up the water with his cloth napkin before it could spill onto the floor. "Oops, sorry about that," he said. "I can be a real klutz." Fairy laughter tinkled in the background. I immediately suspected magical interference.

I tried to help him blot up the water and said, "They need to put a few more sugar packets under that table leg to keep it from wobbling."

He didn't seem to think anything too odd was going on, so I tried to calm down. A disastrous first date could be a real bonding experience if you handled it the right way. Fortunately, this place had good service, and we were quickly surrounded by waiters replacing napkins and water glasses. Soon, our salads arrived. Keith managed the delicate balancing act between eating and sustaining conversation. I wished I could do the same thing, but I was so sidetracked I couldn't help but wonder what Ari and her friends might do next. I soon found out.

One of the sprites came over to our table. Even though I knew it was a pretty good bet that Keith couldn't see the wings, it still felt weird having a conversation with someone like that around someone who was supposedly normal. "Sir, I understand you're having a problem with your table," the sprite said. Then I realized the sprite was posing as the restaurant manager. I wished there was a way for me to know when someone was using an illusion. Seeing reality was handy, but it would help to know when I was supposed to be fooled.

"It was nothing. Everything's okay now," Keith said.

"Sir, I must insist. We can't allow these things to occur, so please tell me what happened." I could hear Ari giggling in the background.

"Well, okay, I think the table may have a little wobble to it." Keith proceeded to demonstrate, trying to shake the table back and forth so it would wobble, but it remained steady. Peals of fairy laughter echoed through the room. Could everyone else hear that, or did they mask the sound, as well? That did it.

"Could you excuse me for a moment?" I asked, then grabbed my purse and headed for the restroom, hissing at Ari as I passed, "I need to talk to you." She got up and followed me back to the ladies' room.

"What are you doing with that loser, Katie?" she asked before I could get on to her about her meddling.

"Loser? I'll have you know this is the greatest date I've had in a very, very long time. He's got real potential, and I like him, so it would be very nice if you and your friends would quit interfering."

"But you don't want to be with someone like him."

"Why, is there something you know about him that I don't? I'd know if he were really an ogre in disguise."

She shrugged. "He's just boring. You can do better. We're doing you a favor."

"Believe me, I am perfectly capable of getting rid of a bad date without any help. But this isn't a bad date. At least, it wasn't until y'all started playing games. What are you doing here, anyway? You're not stalking me, are you?"

"Nah. Remember, I live around here, too. We just saw you and thought we'd have some fun." I noticed she didn't quite look me in the eye, but she also looked sheepish and ashamed of herself, so I couldn't tell if her evasion was because of embarrassment or because she was lying. "We're okay, aren't we? You know I wouldn't do anything to hurt you."

I sighed. "Yeah. We're okay. Just lay off it for the rest of the evening, okay?"

"Okay," she said grudgingly.

The fake waiter was gone by the time I got back to our table, and our food had been served. "Perfect timing," I said as I slid into my seat. Now that I no longer had to worry about magical interference, I could relax and enjoy the date.

"I hoped you weren't sneaking out on me," he quipped.

"There's no danger of that," I said, daring to meet his eyes. I wished I was a better flirt. I really wanted him to know I was interested. This was no time to play coy and risk sending mixed signals.

"Good, because I wasn't ready for this evening to be over so soon. I'd like to get to know you better."

"What would you like to know?" I asked, trying for some eyelash batting and hoping it didn't look like I had something stuck in my eye.

"It would be good to know what kinds of things you like doing. That might help me plan future dates."

I tried not to hyperventilate. He'd actually mentioned future dates. That implied he wanted to see more of me, and that he didn't think of me as a little sister. Things were looking very, very good.

There was a commotion at the front of the restaurant and I tried to ignore it. It was probably just the fairies, up to their usual hijinks. As long as it didn't affect me, I wasn't going to worry about it. But then a man in a tuxedo rushed to our table, thrust a bouquet of red roses at me and began singing something that vaguely resembled an opera aria, sung off-key and with my name sprinkled liberally throughout.

It was Jeff, the Naked Frog Guy. He had incredibly bad timing. I wanted to crawl under the table. And cry. Or maybe sit under the table and cry. This was so not fair. I chanced a glance at Keith, who was staring in shock at Jeff. After a while he turned to me. "Friend of yours?"

I wanted to play it cool and swear I'd never seen him before in my life, but I knew that wouldn't work. "My stalker," I admitted. "I thought I'd got rid of him."

"Apparently you didn't." He listened to Jeff's serenade for a while. "Stalker, huh?" He was taking this pretty calmly, and my hopes rose.

"Yeah. I did him a favor once, and he's extremely grateful."

"What kind of favor?" There was a tinge of suspicion in his voice.

"She disenchanted me," Jeff said helpfully. I wondered if there was a way to reenchant him. He'd be less of a bother if all he could say was "ribbit," and the restaurant would call the cops if he took his clothes off. "I was cursed to spend eternity as a frog, until she freed me with a kiss."

Keith turned to look at me, one eyebrow raised as if asking for an explanation. "He was lost in the park, and um, well, naked, and I got help for him." In essence, Jeff and I had told the same story. My version just sounded saner, even if his was more accurate.

"Do you do that sort of thing often?" Keith asked.

"No, just that one time." Jeff launched into another aria, one I recognized from a pasta commercial, even if I didn't know what opera it was from. I wondered what all the Italian words he put around my name meant.

I glanced toward Ari's table and saw that they were all staring— as was every other patron in the restaurant. I caught Ari's eye and mouthed the word "Help," but she gave me an innocent look, as if to say, "You told me to leave you alone." I narrowed my eyes at her, and with an exaggerated sigh she waved a hand. In midphrase the aria stopped and Jeff said, "Ribbit."

Had she put the frog illusion back on him? I wished I could see what my date saw. If a tuxedoed man singing arias to your date was weird, that man suddenly disappearing and a frog taking his place would be beyond strange.

The restaurant manager—the real one this time—came to our table and said, "Miss, is this person bothering you?"

"Yes. Yes, he is." The manager and one of the waiters each took Jeff by an arm and dragged him away. I assumed that meant they didn't think he was a frog, or they would have removed him from the restaurant in a different way.

Our waiter then stopped by and asked, "Would you like to see the dessert tray?"

Without hesitation, Keith said, "No thanks. Just the check, please." My heart sank. That was definitely a bad sign. When the waiter had gone, Keith turned to me and said, "I hope you don't mind if we call it a night. I have somewhere I have to be pretty early in the morning." In other words, I was being ditched. I couldn't blame him. In his shoes, I'd ditch me, too. But that didn't stop it from being a huge disappointment.

He paid in cash as soon as the waiter showed up with the check. Then he escorted me to the front door. "It was nice meeting you, Katie. It was an, um, well, interesting evening."

I winced. "Sorry about that." I wanted to say that sort of thing didn't happen to me often, but the problem was, it probably would, given my line of work. "Thanks for dinner, though."

"Yeah. Well, I'll call you." His tone made it the "you'll never hear from me again" version of "call you." The fact that he quickly disappeared around the corner underscored that impression. I was left standing on the sidewalk, holding the giant bouquet of roses Jeff had given me. It looked like I'd graduated from little sister to freak. Either way, it meant there wouldn't be a second date. With a deep sigh of regret, I began walking home.

As I walked I mulled over my situation. I was trapped between two worlds, not really belonging to either. I wasn't magical, and facing the reality of magical life—like kissing frogs—freaked me out. But I wasn't totally normal, either, for the magical world had a nasty habit of spilling over into the rest of my life. If I thought my social life was complicated before, now it was a tangled mess. I adjusted my grip on the roses, then gasped when I accidentally hit a thorn. I paused on the sidewalk to suck my injured finger, stepping out of the way so I wouldn't block the person I heard walking behind me. I froze when the sound of footsteps behind me also stopped.

My heart pounding in my chest, I moved forward again, walking faster. Now I didn't hear those other footsteps at all. Maybe I'd imagined them in the first place, or maybe the person behind me had turned off to step into a building or down a side street. The thought didn't calm me down much.

I had enough street smarts to know that if you think you're being followed, it's best to immediately head to a safe place, preferably one that's well lit and full of people. There was a Duane Reade ahead, open twenty-four hours, and usually with at least one cop in there buying snacks or antacid at all times. I'd just make it one more block, go into the store, and mill around enough to make sure I wasn't being followed. If I was still nervous and if there was a cop in there, I might be able to play Southern belle and sweet-talk him into walking me home, only a block or so away.

Having a plan made me feel better. I got a tighter grip on my purse and wondered if I could hit someone hard enough with the roses to make the thorns do any damage, then set off toward the drugstore with a purposeful stride.

I was halfway down the block when I felt the tingle and pressure in the air that meant someone was doing magic nearby. That made me nervous, even though I knew I'd be relatively safe. Magic couldn't affect me directly. Was someone trying to use that control spell on me, without realizing I was immune? I'd have to let Merlin and Owen know about this.

I forced myself to keep walking. I just had to get to the corner and cross the street, and I'd be safely at the drugstore.

Then I felt the tingle again, followed by a rush of wind and a loud pop. Something dark came out of nowhere and grabbed me hard around the waist, knocking the air out of my lungs so that I couldn't even scream for help.

fifteen

efore I moved to New York, I took a self-defense class at my
hometown's karate studio/tanning salon, mostly to make my
mother feel better about me going to the big bad city. This was
exactly the kind of situation the class had been designed to teach us
to deal with, but my mind had gone frighteningly blank. It was like
something out of a nightmare, being in danger but being so paralyzed
with fear that I couldn't scream or move.

It seemed like hours later, but it could only have been a second
or two before I thought of what to do. I shoved the roses into the
guy's face to distract him. He sneezed, but he didn't release his
grasp. Then I remembered something from the self-defense class
about kicking the guy in the knee. That was supposed to be a weak
spot. I was wearing pointy-toed heels, so I lifted my right leg and gave
my attacker a good wallop in the kneecap. The theory was that the

pain would distract him enough to loosen his grip on me so I could get free. He did loosen his grip, but it was so fast that my leg was still raised from kicking him, so I lost my balance and hit the pavement.

I hadn't been the best student in the class, needless to say.

Now I was in even bigger trouble because it would take time for me to get to my feet, and during that time he'd be able to grab me again. I'd dropped my purse when it fell, and I knew I was in real danger when instead of going after my purse, he came after me. He wasn't a garden-variety mugger, then. I pulled off one shoe and hurled it at his head. There was a thud and a curse, then he staggered. Got him! Those hours in the backyard with rocks and baseballs had paid off. I was getting my feet under me to make a run for it when I heard a rush of wings. I looked up to see Ari and her friends. They surrounded the dark figure, and I felt that magical tingle. This time there was an added charge in the air, as magic apparently flew back and forth between the fairies and my attacker.

A hand grasped my arm and I squeaked—which was an improvement over paralyzed silence, but still not very effective. "It's okay, Katie, it's me." I recognized Rod's voice and let him help me to my feet. "Are you hurt?"

"I don't think so. Only my dignity, I imagine." I found my shoe, put it back on and gave myself a quick survey, but from what I could tell, I hadn't even torn my stockings. "What's going on? What are you doing here?"

"We can talk about it later, but now I want to get you away from here. They've got it under control."

"Got what under control?"

Before he could answer, there was another whoosh of wings, and Sam was on the scene with some of his people, including the beaked gargoyle I'd seen earlier. "Okay, let's haul the perp away," Sam instructed.

Rod bent to pick up my purse, then put his arm around my waist and said, "Come on, let's get you somewhere safe."

"Safe would be nice."

"I don't live too far from here, if you'd rather go there and get yourself together, maybe talk some, before you go home." Under other circumstances I'd suspect that was a pickup line, coming from Rod, but he sounded genuinely concerned. If he was a big enough letch that he'd hit on a woman who'd just been mugged, then I might as well find out now instead of later.

"That sounds like a good idea," I said. It did. I wasn't sure I wanted to face my roommates until I'd calmed down considerably. Telling them about the date was going to be bad enough. Gemma would kill me for scaring off the perfect guy.

He walked me down a side street, then another side street, and then to a modern apartment building. We went through the lobby to a bank of elevators. "I didn't know you lived near here," I said when we were inside the elevator. It was a weak attempt at casual conversation, considering how badly my voice shook.

"There are a lot of us in this neighborhood."

"Any particular reason? It's not extra loaded with magic, or anything like that, is it?"

He smiled. "No, not really. There's just a lot to do around here, and some of the Village denizens are odd enough that nobody pays much attention to us." The elevator came to a stop, and he escorted me off. He unlocked a door, then pushed it open and said, "Welcome to my humble abode."

It wasn't all that humble. Magic must pay pretty well. It was the classic high-end bachelor pad—all sleek leather upholstery and blond wood furniture with glass insets. He had an entertainment center to die for and a view of the city lights. "Nice place," I said, admiring the framed classic movie posters.

"Thanks. Make yourself at home. Have a seat, or the bathroom's just down that hallway, if you want to freshen up. I'll make you some tea."

I wandered down the short hallway and found the bathroom. It was as small as most New York apartment bathrooms, and almost entirely devoid of grooming products, aside from basics like toothpaste. I supposed his idea of grooming was putting on that illusion.

In the light of the bathroom, I checked myself out. I had torn my stockings, after all, a small hole on the side of my right knee. I dampened a tissue and blotted the dirt off my skin. Otherwise, I seemed to be unscathed physically. Emotionally, I had a feeling I would be a total wreck as soon as the shock wore off. In fact, I was already shaking.

I took off my shoes before trying to walk back to the living room. My legs felt like rubber, and they wobbled in unpredictable directions. I barely made it to the sofa, where I collapsed into the soft leather cushions. Rod came into the living room, holding a steaming mug.

I took it from him, then fought to keep my hands steady. "Wait a second, you said you were making tea. You mean, you actually made this instead of zapping it into existence?"

"Believe it or not, we don't all go around just zapping things. For one thing, it's an energy drain. At the office, we have enhanced power circuits to draw on. Most of us don't have them at home."

I nodded. "That explains a lot. I was wondering why you bother going to restaurants or bars."

"It's the social factor. We need that as much as anyone else. And it never quite tastes the same. I wasn't sure I could get the tea just right without actually making it."

I tasted it, and it was very strong, and very sweet. If I wasn't mistaken, there was more than just tea and sugar in there. I drank a little more. "Thank you."

He sat next to me on the sofa. "Now, I imagine you're wondering what just happened."

"Yeah, I believe I recall asking you a couple of times. I don't think it was an ordinary mugging. He didn't even try to grab my purse."

"No, it wasn't an ordinary mugging. We'll know more once we talk to your attacker, but we think tonight's adventure came courtesy of our friend Idris. He must have figured out the role you've been playing, and he wants you out of the picture."

I shuddered, then gulped down more of the tea. "What role? I'm not magical. There are hundreds of people in this city who could have done exactly what I did. If he's going after people who are a threat, he should be going after Owen."

"Who said he isn't, on a daily basis?" Rod's tone sent shivers up my spine. "But you're also a key player in this, like it or not, and it would be just like Phelan Idris to want to know exactly what role you do play. His people have been stalking you for a while, and we've been watching them while we keep an eye on you."

"So you and Ari and her gang being there wasn't just a happy coincidence tonight?"

"Not in the least. Ari was supposed to be watching you in the restaurant, but you must have managed to get out of there before she had a chance to follow you."

"Disastrous date," I explained. "So they've been following me? I still don't get it. I'm not that important, really. I just have a few good ideas and some down-home common sense."

"Do you realize how rare that is? But I imagine the issue to Idris is that you're an unknown quantity. He doesn't know the role you play, and he wants to find out. He also wants to scare you."

I finished my tea. "Well, it worked. I'm scared. I've never been mugged before, and let me tell you, it's not fun."

He leaned toward me, putting one hand on my arm. "We'd understand if you wanted to walk away from all this. It's not your fight, so there's no reason you should be putting yourself in danger. We have ways of giving references that won't look suspicious, and I know people in other industries, so we could help you get another job. Don't feel at all obligated to us. I know when we offered you the job, we never mentioned the possibility of danger, so it's entirely our fault if you've had an unpleasant surprise."

I pondered that. Did I want to go back to living an ordinary life, working at a company where you actually had to brew coffee, having coworkers who might throw hissy fits but didn't turn into monsters, not really mattering in the grand scheme of things? True, it would simplify my life considerably. I would be able to talk about work with my friends, and I wouldn't have to worry about my dates being jinxed—literally.

But could I turn my back on what I knew was going on? If Idris thought I mattered enough that he wanted to stop me, then maybe I was more important than I thought. This thing was far bigger than I was, and now that I knew what the stakes were, I couldn't just walk away. Whether or not I had any magic powers, this was my fight, too, and I wanted to see it through.

I shook my head. "Nothing doing. Now they've just pissed me off."

He grinned. "I was hoping you'd say that. Don't worry, we'll continue to protect you. These days, we all need to look out for one another."

A realization struck me. "Is that why Owen's been coming to work with me every morning?"

"Yeah, he's part of your security detail, with the added benefit that you can spot anyone in disguise who might be after him."

"Oh." I couldn't help but feel a sting of disappointment to have it verified that his attention wasn't personal.

"More tea?" he asked.

I studied my empty cup and assessed my condition. I still wasn't ready to go home. I wasn't sure which would be worse, explaining why the perfect man Gemma had set me up with never wanted to see me again, or telling them that I'd been mugged. "Sure," I said, handing him the cup.

When he returned to the living room with a fresh cup of tea, I said, "Maybe you can help me with something."

"Anything you need. Just ask." His tone reminded me of Owen, that first day of work on the bus.

"Do you know anything about magical pranks?"

"A little. Why?"

I told him about the Naked Frog Guy, ending with his unwelcome appearance at my date that night. When he finished laughing and wiping the tears of mirth out of his eyes, he said, "Owen's the one you want to talk to about that."

Owen was the last person I wanted to talk to about either dating or about being serenaded by men who used to be frogs. "Why's that?"

"It sounds like one of his spells. The layering's the clue. Most prank spells are one-dimensional, but the beauty of this one is that 'breaking' the enchantment actually only makes it worse by making the victim become obsessed with the woman who breaks the frog part of the spell."

"I don't know him that well, but fraternity prank spells don't seem to be Owen's style."

"When we were in college, he made extra money by doing custom spell work. I'm surprised to hear that one's still going around, and that it's made it to the city." He shook his head. "He should have asked for royalties. That was one of his better ones. It really brought out his sense of humor."

"You mean all the bad poetry?"

"He was taking a Shakespeare class that semester."

"Don't tell me he's a Barry Manilow fan."

"No, that was the customer's request—they were looking for something really humiliating. The opera is pure Owen, though."

"So, how do I break this spell?"

"It's supposed to break when the victim meets someone he'd like even without a spell. Around the university, that meant it was usually over within a day or so."

"And if he doesn't? Or if he really does like the woman?"

"Then you'd have problems." He studied me for a while, and his gaze gave me shivers. I wasn't used to being looked at that way by men. The sweater Gemma loaned me must have been especially good with my coloring. "And I can see where that's a distinct possibility. Yeah, you should definitely talk to Owen if this guy keeps bugging you. He's probably got a back door built into the spell, so he could break it for you."

I wondered what Jeff's type would be. Dealing with the situation that way was far preferable to confessing my predicament to Owen. Whether or not he had any interest in me, I still had at least a minor crush on him, and the last thing any girl wants to do is talk about her dating woes to a man she's attracted to, especially when her dating woes are so weird.

I drained the last of my tea and said, "I'd better get home soon. My roommates will be dying to get the postdate debriefing."

He took my mug and carried it into the kitchen, then came back to the living room and helped me to my feet. "You okay now?"

"The shakes are pretty much gone. Thanks." I slipped my shoes back on and tested my balance in the high heels.

"Then I'll walk you home. You'll be safe there. The place is warded pretty well. Owen took care of that a while ago."

"Warded?"

"No one can magically attack you in your apartment."

"But no one can attack me magically at all."

"They can't attack you directly with a spell, but they can use magic to get access to you so they can attack you physically. That's what happened tonight. Your attacker transported himself magically to get to you so you wouldn't hear him approaching."

"But I did hear something."

"That was me."

"Why didn't you say something? You scared me to death."

"Sorry about that. Anyway, your building is secured so no one can use magic to damage it, open locks, or anything else like that. Someone can still get in using purely physical means, but if your locks are good enough to protect you from the usual criminal elements, you should be okay."

"That's nice to know."

We walked to my building in silence. I was too busy thinking of the story I would tell my roommates to make conversation. At my building, he waited for me to unlock the front door, then said, "Have a good weekend. And don't worry, we'll keep an eye out for you."

"Thanks for the help, and the tea. I'll have to thank Ari later for the lifesaving."

And now I had to make the transition from the magical to the mundane. The big news from my evening wasn't the date, but as usual, I couldn't talk about the really interesting stuff.

Gemma and Marcia mobbed me as soon as I got home. Then I noticed that Connie was there, too. "That was a nice long dinner," Gemma said. "Things must have gone well."

I fought to hold back tears as I collapsed on the sofa.

"I don't think things went well," Connie said softly. She sat next to me and took my hand. "What happened?"

Gemma perched next to me on the sofa's arm. "Didn't you like him? I thought he was perfect." She sounded hurt.

"He was perfect. I liked him. I just don't think he liked me."

"Are you sure about that?"

"He left skid marks getting away from me."

"But that was a pretty long date if he didn't like you," Marcia said.

"I ran into a friend from work on my way home, and we talked awhile," I said.

All their faces fell. "You at least got dessert, right?" Connie asked.

"He said no thanks to the dessert tray before I had a chance to say anything."

"Then it sounds like you're better off without him," Connie declared. "Any man who would deny you dessert isn't worth having." Connie has a rather strong sweet tooth, so skipping dessert deserves the death penalty in her book. She's the one who taught me to carry chocolate in my purse.

"Was it the sister thing again?" Gemma asked.

I couldn't lie—she was likely to hear Keith's side of the story. "No. It was just some weirdness that happened, and I think it scared him away." I didn't want to delve into the weirdness, and I hoped Keith was gentleman enough not to give details.

They all laughed. "If he thinks you're too weird, then he's never going to find anyone," Marcia declared. "You've got to be the most ordinary person in the world."

"Maybe I'm so ordinary, I'm weird." That was certainly the truth. I wouldn't have been in this weird mess if I hadn't been so ordinary. Little did they know, but my ordinary days were well and truly over.

Monday morning, I stepped out the front door to find Owen standing on the sidewalk. Owen was physically incapable of looking casual, so I suspected he was waiting for me. "You look better than you did the last time I saw you," I remarked as he fell into step beside me.

"You're the one we've been worried about."

"Me? I'm fine. Not a scratch." And I was fine, more or less. Only one teensy nightmare about being grabbed in the darkness. I wouldn't be walking home alone from anything after dark for the foreseeable future, but other than that I was A-okay. "But why didn't y'all tell me I might be in danger?"

"We didn't want to scare you." The sheepish look on his face showed that he knew just how stupid that sounded. "It didn't work so well."

"I'm alive to tell the tale, which is the most important thing."

I made a point of keeping my eyes peeled as we walked to the subway station, remembering what Rod had said about what I could do to help Owen.

"Other than being attacked, how was your weekend?"

"Not so bad. And yours?"

"I got some work done." That didn't tell me much, but now I knew from Rod that he liked opera in addition to baseball. He was unfolding like a flower.

The train arrived, and we shoved our way on board. It was particularly crowded this morning. Even standing room was hard to come by. Owen wasn't tall, but he was taller than I was, so he was able to grab an overhead handhold. Then he circled my waist with his arm and held me steady. I could think of worse ways to commute.

This morning we had to part ways at the doorway to R&D, then I went to the tower for my first day on the job as Merlin's assistant. "He wants to see you when you get a chance," Trix said as I topped the escalator.

"I'll be there in a sec." I checked my e-mail and sent a quick response to Rod's note asking how I was, then got a notepad and headed across the reception area to Merlin's office. Before I could knock on the door, he opened it.

"Katie, good morning, please come in." He ushered me in and shut the door behind me. "Have a seat," he said, gesturing toward the sofa. "I'm sorry to hear about your weekend adventure. You aren't suffering any lingering ill effects, I hope?"

I took a seat, and he joined me on the sofa. "Not really," I said. "I'm fine. Just mad."

"As are we all."

"I guess we could take it as a sign that this Idris guy is nervous, if he's desperate enough to try to take me out."

"He does seem to perceive our activities as a threat. I imagine he connected the timing of your arrival here with our increased efforts against him and wanted to find out what, exactly, your role was."

"He'd have been disappointed."

"I strongly doubt that. I understand you declined Mr. Gwaltney's offer of finding less hazardous employment."

"They just got me riled up. He'd better look out now."

He laughed. "That's the way I thought you'd respond. Now, I suppose I should let you know what I expect of you in your new position."

We spent the next half hour going over my duties, which seemed to be pretty much the same kinds of things I'd done in my last job, except with a far nicer boss. I was to read over every document he was given, only to look for hidden spells and illusions rather than for typos and grammatical errors. When necessary, I'd sit in on meetings along with Trix and compare notes with her to see if there was anything going on that shouldn't be. And I'd continue to head the marketing efforts. It sounded like I should stay pretty busy, which was okay by me.

"And don't hesitate to speak up if you have any ideas," he added. "I'm an old man who's been out of the world for far too long, and we need your fresh perspective."

I couldn't begin to express how good it was to have a boss who treated me like a human being with half a brain. In that long year working for Mimi, I'd started to let myself think I didn't know enough to be of use. "I'll try," I said. "I hope I don't let you down."

"You won't." Once again he had that eerie certainty about him that gave me a chill. One day, I thought, I'd get the nerve to ask him about it.

Late that afternoon, Trix tapped on my door. "There's an emergency meeting. He wants you in there."

I grabbed my pen and notepad, wondering what was going on. Would this be my first big meeting as Merlin's personal verifier?

When I saw who was gathered for the meeting, I doubted it. It was the same group as on Friday, minus Gregor and the accounting gnome. Owen looked grim and distracted, and he gave me only the slightest of nods as I entered. There was an aura of gloom and doom that hung over the room. I took my seat at the table silently.

Merlin kicked things off. "Owen, why don't you tell us what you've discovered today?"

"Idris has a new spell on the market, and it's quite dark. We're back to square one."

"What is the new spell?" Mr. Hartwell asked.

"It's basically the spell he was working on when we dismissed him. It seems he finally got it ready to sell."

"This could be a sign of panic on his part," I pointed out, "if the poor quality and whatever we were doing had an impact. He needed to get something on the market that he knew would work while he hurried to fix the other spell."

"That doesn't mean we don't have a problem," Owen said with a deep sigh. "This one works, and we don't have a way to counter it. It's good—no big energy drain, it's effective, it's everything he promises it to be. It's still all about influence, but not quite in the puppet-master way the other spell was—he was reaching too far with that one. This one just makes the victim incredibly open to suggestion. The victim still has some degree of free will, but he is strongly drawn to wanting to please the caster. In the wrong hands, it could be devastating. The victim won't ever realize anything's wrong, unlike with that other spell."

"And if it works as advertised, it means none of our marketing messages are going to be very effective," I said. "We can no longer stand on the position that our spells work and have been thoroughly tested." I think I was more upset about this development than I had been about being attacked. It made weeks of work practically useless.

They all turned to me, and I wished I hadn't spoken. "Katie, do you have any ideas?" Merlin asked.

I shook my head. "Sorry, but I can't think of anything right now. It seems like our real differentiator is that our spells can't be used to do harm. The people who don't want to do harm or use other people won't be interested anyway, and nothing we say will influence the people who do want to use others. 'Just say no' wasn't very effective for Nancy Reagan, and I doubt it will help us much."

I was sure I saw disappointment in Merlin's eyes, and I felt bad for letting him down. I'd let myself get a big head from my earlier successes and had managed to forget that I was a small-town girl with a business degree and a year working as a marketing assistant. "I'm sorry," I said after a while. "I'll have to think about it."

"Please do," Merlin said, and I fought to blink back tears. I turned away from Merlin to see Owen looking at me with compassion in his eyes. I realized he was in pretty much the same boat I was, where all his previous successes meant next to nothing now.

"How long until you have an effective counterspell that will render this one meaningless?" Merlin asked him.

"I don't know. I'm not sure we ever will. As I said, this was the spell he was working on when he left, and we've been looking for ways to counter it ever since then, yet we still haven't come up with anything. I've been over all of his source material. I've taken that spell apart and looked at it inside out and upside down. I'm afraid it's airtight."

"No spell is perfect. You can find a weakness." This was a whole new side to Merlin that I hadn't seen before. Until now, although I knew intellectually that this was *the* Merlin, it hadn't really sunk in that this was the man who had put Arthur on the throne, who had been instrumental in all those great deeds they still told stories about. I could see that legend in the man who sat at the head of the table now, and it was rather intimidating.

Owen flinched, a flush spreading upward from his collar, and he nodded. "I'll keep at it."

"Minerva?"

She shrugged. "Still nothing. I'm not getting any portents, one way or another, which means the situation is still in flux. We can influence the outcome."

"We'll get the sales force out on the streets, with verifiers to see where and how this stuff is selling," Mr. Hartwell said. "I can even call in some old debts and get customer names, so we know who to track." He must not have wanted Merlin coming down on him, so he was being proactive with the information.

"Good," Merlin said curtly. "If he succeeds here, then we know he'll continue trying. We can not allow this to succeed. We had these problems in my time, and it nearly tore Britain apart. I've read enough of the history I've missed to know the same thing has happened here, and fairly recently." That caught my attention. Had there been other magical wars the rest of the world didn't know about? Then maybe this situation wasn't as dire as I'd feared, since we'd all clearly survived. I made a mental note to go back to reading those books Owen had loaned me.

"But this is the first challenge we've faced that's come in business form," Merlin continued. "That gives it the slightest aura of legitimacy, which makes it appealing to those who might be wavering between light and dark. Few of those would sign up for the side of evil in a magical war, but give them a legitimate-looking product, and they'll be tempted. Corrupt them a little bit, and it's easy to corrupt them further. We must stop this now." I felt a surge of magical charge at his words and shivered. Okay, so maybe the situation was as dire as I feared.

I racked my brain for a way I could help, but I was getting nothing. I couldn't see a "Don't do bad magic" campaign going over too well. But what else could we do if we couldn't imply that the competition had shoddy spells? As I'd said, the people who'd be into this sort of thing already knew this was bad and didn't care.

I rewound the meeting to that point in my brain, searching for anything I might be able to use. Something Owen had said triggered a vague memory of something recent that hadn't been important or meaningful enough to think about at the time. But now it just might do the trick.

I was almost afraid to bring it up. What if they'd already considered, and then rejected, this idea long ago? Or worse, what if they'd considered and tried it, and it hadn't worked? It was so obvious, but I'd learned that what was obvious to me wasn't always obvious to people who for all intents and purposes lived in an entirely different world.

Oh hell, it was worth a shot. I cleared my throat. "I might have an idea."

sixteen

Every head in the room turned to stare at me, and for a second I thought I should have kept my mouth shut. "You may have already thought of this, but I haven't heard anyone bring it up yet." I licked my lips and wished I had a glass of water handy for wetting my suddenly dry throat. "My world has its own powers, you know. And like magic, some of them can be used for good or for evil. For example, lawyers."

I got a room full of blank looks. Surely I wasn't going to have to explain the concept of lawyers to them. "What do lawyers have to do with stopping the misuse of magic?" Mr. Hartwell asked.

"Lawyers can stop just about anything. Tie it up in court, and nobody gets anywhere for ages. That could buy you the time you need to come up with a better way of fighting this. I'm no expert, but you might have an intellectual property case."

"What's that?" Owen asked. The flicker of hope in his eyes gave me the courage to keep going.

"Anything an employee develops while working here belongs to the company, not to the employee. Surely you have some language to that effect in employment agreements."

Owen nodded. "Especially in R and D."

"The point of that is to keep an employee from developing something on company time, using company resources, then selling it himself. And that seems to be what Idris is doing. He's taking something he developed here and using it to create his own products. You might be able to make him stop that."

"How do we do that?" Merlin asked.

"I'm not sure, but I may know someone who would know. I'll have to check. It could take a couple of days." I was going out on a limb here, basing my grand idea for saving the world on a blind date my roommate had once had, but this situation sounded exactly like the one he'd described in his dinner table conversation.

"Please do check, then report as soon as possible."

The meeting broke up, and we all went back to our respective offices with our individual tasks. I'd felt exhilarated before, when my proposal for a marketing plan had been accepted, but now I was scared. What if it didn't work? These were awfully big stakes to hinge on something so vague.

I decided to wait until I got home to talk to Marcia. The three of us sat around the dinner table that night, still talking about the results of my Friday night date. "I don't know what you did to him, Katie, but he wouldn't even look at me today," Gemma said with a laugh.

"Oh, he's just worried she'll be hurt if she hears he doesn't want to call her again," Marcia said.

"Sorry that one didn't work out for you, hon. We'll have to try again," Gemma said, reaching over to pat me on the shoulder. "Maybe Philip has a friend."

Philip's friends were probably starting to hibernate—or whatever it is frogs do—for the winter. Or else they were all in retirement homes, if they dated from his prefrog days. "Actually, I may have an idea," I said, figuring this was as good an opening as I was likely to get. "Marce, you aren't going to call that Ethan guy you were matched up with a while back, are you?"

She frowned. "Which one was he?"

"Intellectual property attorney, tall, glasses, brainy. It was the night all of us went out with Connie and Jim."

She made a face. "Him? You want to go out with him?"

"I take that to mean that you wouldn't mind if I did."

"He's all yours, honey."

Gemma beamed. "So, you want me to call Jim and have him tell Ethan to call you if he's interested?"

"Yes, please. He seemed nice." This was too tenuous for my comfort. What would happen if he couldn't remember who I was, or if he didn't want to see me? The fate of the magical world—and maybe even of the nonmagical world, too—might rest on this date. I wasn't sure where I'd find an intellectual property attorney anywhere else, not one I could get to talk to me without me having to explain the situation up front and pay a hefty retainer. They'd think I was insane. I bit my tongue to keep from telling Gemma to tell him to hurry and call me because I didn't have a lot of time. That might be a subtle clue that I was after something other than a boyfriend.

The next afternoon I was surfing the Web in search of information on marketing campaigns for challenging situations when I got an e-mail from Gemma. "Jim said Ethan remembered you, thought you were cute. Jim gave him your number, and Ethan said he'd call sometime." That was good news, but I was worried about the "sometime" part of the equation. This was no time to deal with the typical male definition of the statement "I'll call you," which generally means "sometime before I die, if I think about it."

I felt as if I was back in high school, rushing home to check the answering machine to see if *he* had called, leaping for the phone whenever it rang, calling the machine several times throughout the day to check messages. My roommates must have thought I'd gone stark raving nuts. "I had no idea you were so taken with Ethan," Gemma remarked at one point. "You should have said something sooner."

He finally called on Thursday night. For once Gemma got to the phone before I could—by now Philip had learned to use a telephone, so there were two of us waiting for calls. Her face lit up when she answered, then she put her hand over the receiver and singsonged, "It's for you! Guess who!"

Still feeling like I'd reverted to my teens, I grabbed the cordless from her and retreated into the bedroom, shutting the door behind me. "Hi, Ethan," I said, fighting to keep my voice from shaking.

"Hi, Katie." He had a nice voice over the phone, soft and rich. "It's funny, but I was just about to ask Jim if he thought enough time had gone by so it would be okay for me to ask you out. I wouldn't want to cause any trouble among friends, but I did want to see you again."

Now I felt bad because I really only wanted him for his legal mind. Then again, he was cute. And as far as I knew, he wasn't prone to zapping things in or out of existence. He was probably the most normal man I knew right now. "I got permission from Marcia," I said, then wondered if that made it sound like Marcia had no interest in him whatsoever. But if he was wondering about me, it meant he had no interest in Marcia, so he wouldn't get his feelings hurt.

"Would you like to get together sometime?" he said.

I was tempted to be sarcastic and say I'd only asked him to call me so we could talk on the phone for hours, but this was no time for games. I had to be very, very clear. "Sure. When did you have in mind?"

"Is tomorrow night too soon?"

"Not at all." If he'd wanted me to, I would have thrown on a pair of shoes and run to meet him right then.

"What about dinner after work? I can get away about six. Where do you work?"

"I work downtown, near City Hall, but I live near Union Square, so anywhere in between could be good for me."

"I know this place on MacDougal, not too far from Washington Square. It's nothing fancy, but it's good, and it's a place we can just sit and talk."

"Sounds great."

He gave me the address, and we arranged to meet at six thirty. Now I just had to find a way to get him talking about work. Judging from the last time I'd seen him, I doubted that would be too difficult. The trick would be getting useful information, and then finding a way to use it. We'd have to hire a lawyer to really accomplish anything, and that might take confessing to the magic situation. I'd have to play it by ear to see if Ethan might be remotely receptive to the idea. At the very least, maybe I'd learn enough to know what steps to take next.

I reported to Merlin the next day that I'd be meeting with my source, then I left early to prepare myself. Since Ethan thought I was meeting him right after work, I had to strike a balance. I wanted to look nice, but not like I'd put in a lot of special effort. I had to look like I'd just come from work and still managed to look gorgeous. This was why I hated dating. Even the simplest, most casual date could be so very complicated.

I had a last minute burst of nerves as I rode the subway a short distance across town, then one stop downtown. Why did I think this would work? I might be bright, capable, and in possession of some degree of common sense, but I was lousy at dating. If the fate of the world rested on me having a semisuccessful date, we were in big trouble. I just hoped Jeff the Frog Guy kept his distance tonight.

Ethan had chosen a restaurant in a spot I couldn't get to directly via public transportation. This was the first time I'd walked alone after dark since the attack the previous week. I knew I wasn't really alone. There were very likely magical people nearby, watching my every move. In a way, that made me even more nervous. I didn't want an audience on a date. I really, really hoped Owen had more important things to do tonight than play bodyguard.

As I approached the restaurant I caught a glimpse of Sam perched on an awning and relaxed. Sam might tease me later, but he made a good bodyguard.

Ethan was waiting in front. He smiled when he saw me, which I took as a good sign, for it meant he really did remember which one I was. He was taller than I recalled. When I got closer to him and shook his hand, the top of my head barely reached his shoulder, and I was wearing heels. "I hope I didn't keep you waiting long," I said.

"You're right on time. I managed to get away earlier than I expected."

He was right that the place was nothing fancy, just a nice little casual restaurant, but it was warm and cozy, and we didn't have to wait for a table. He helped me out of my jacket, then hung it and his coat on the hook over our booth. We made the usual small talk while studying the menu, then ordered burgers and fries. I liked the idea of someone who didn't feel the need to put on the dog on a first date, who could just go someplace comfortable. Even if this didn't work out in a business sense, maybe there would be other benefits after all.

After we'd ordered, I decided it was time to get to work. "You said you worked in intellectual property law, right?"

He smiled. "Wow. You really were paying attention. I thought I'd bored everyone to tears. I was such an enthralling conversationalist that night that my date never wanted to see me again."

"You weren't that bad. I actually found it interesting. How often does that really happen, though, where an employee tries to take what they've done at a company somewhere else?" It was the best I could come up with to get him talking, short of trying to convince him that legal talk made me hot and bothered.

"It depends on the industry. We see it a lot in software. There's a lot of job-hopping, and people take bits of code with them. But then there's always the argument that they're just applying things they've learned, not using anything they actually developed. There've been attempts to come up with noncompete clauses, where people can't go to work for their company's direct competitor for a certain amount of time after leaving, but that often gets struck down as unfair restraint of trade."

The waitress brought our drinks, and he used that as an opportunity to change the subject. "Enough about me," he said. "What do you do? I don't think it came up that last time. I was too busy droning on about my work."

"My work isn't nearly as interesting as yours. I'm a secretary. That's about it." I stuck to my most boring job description, hoping he wouldn't ask me more questions.

"Oh, I don't know, I bet your life can get pretty interesting, depending on your boss."

"I have a good boss, so no real horror stories. Not even any funny ones. Sorry."

His eyes narrowed, and I wondered if I'd overplayed the boring angle. He probably felt much like I had with my date the night we'd met, desperately trying to keep the conversation going without much help. But then I realized he wasn't frowning at me. He was sitting facing the restaurant entrance, and he was frowning at the doorway.

"What is it?" I asked.

He shook his head like he was trying to clear it, frowned again, took off his glasses, rubbed his eyes, polished his glasses, then put them back on, blinked, and frowned once more. "Nothing. I just thought I saw something weird, out of the corner of my eye." He gave a nervous laugh. "It's been a long week. And I'd better stick to one beer tonight."

I turned around and saw Trix and her sprite park ranger—in civilian clothes tonight—standing in the doorway, waiting for a waiter to show them to a table. I turned back around to face him, a queasy feeling forming in my stomach. I'd never seen what their masking illusion looked like, but I'd never seen anyone else react this way to seeing them. Anyone, that is, but me. I remembered that he'd cleaned his glasses that first night when the fairies had come in to the restaurant. Could I have found another immune? "What did you think you saw?" I asked cautiously, trying to sound casually curious even though my heart had migrated to my throat.

"Nothing," he insisted, but I stared at him until he sighed and said, "There's a trick of the light that makes those people look like they've got wings. But I only saw it for a second." He sounded more like he was trying to convince himself than convince me.

Yep, I recognized that symptom. "Could you excuse me for a second?" I asked.

I slid out of the booth, then gave Trix a meaningful glance as I passed the table where she and her date had been seated. The restrooms were downstairs, which would make a quick powwow easier.

Trix joined me less than a minute later. "What's up?" she asked. "This date seems to be going better than your last one."

"The frog guy hasn't shown up, but the night is still young. And let me guess, you and Ranger Bob are my designated bodyguards for the evening."

She giggled, which sounded rather like jingle bells. "Ranger Pippin, actually."

"Are you two masked tonight—I mean, would most people see you as human?"

"Of course. It's second nature away from work."

"Well, then, I may have just found another immune. My date saw you. He thinks he's going crazy because he's seeing people with wings."

She gasped. "Oh, boy."

"So, what do I do? How do I handle this? He's that intellectual property attorney I mentioned. Do I just tell him right out that magic is real, or do I talk him into coming to the office for a consultation, and then let Mr. Mervyn and the others give him the orientation?"

She shook her head. "Don't tell him anything until we're sure what he is. We'll need to put him through a few tests, and then we can approach him." I remembered the weirdness that morning on the subway when they'd tested me, and had a sinking feeling that I was about to have the kind of evening where Naked Frog Guy showing up with his guitar would serve as a nice dose of comic relief.

She took a cell phone out of her purse, dialed, then said, "It's Trix. Katie needs to talk to you."

She handed the phone to me and a voice said in my ear, "Katie? It's Rod. What's up?"

"You know that attorney I was talking to tonight?" I hoped the office grapevine had done its usual tricks. "Well, I think he's an immune. He saw Trix's wings."

"Stay there. Try to keep him relaxed and talking. We'll be there in a moment." I found it more than a little unnerving that he didn't have to ask where we were.

I handed the phone back to Trix. "Looks like we're about to run some tests."

She grinned and giggled again. "Oh, good. That's always fun!"

Our meals had just arrived when I got back to the table. Ethan still looked twitchy, darting little glances toward Pippin, like he was trying to figure out what he was seeing. He smiled with great relief when he saw me. We ate and made small talk for a while, and I tried not to show any nervousness about what this testing would entail. If someone used a love spell on my date—even if he wasn't really a date—I'd be rather annoyed.

To keep the conversation flowing and to get back to business, I said, "Back to what we were talking about earlier, I'm curious about something. What about people coming up with something brilliant at one company, then taking it with them and starting their own company?"

"That's also something we see a lot of in software. People come up with something great, and instead of letting their employer get rich on the idea, they try to get rich for themselves. In those cases, a lot depends on whether the idea grew directly out of a work-related assignment or if it just happened to be something the employee came up with on his own while working for the company."

I frowned. This didn't look good. "What if it was something the employee came up with as part of a work assignment, but his employer wasn't happy with the direction he took it and declined to market it?"

"That's the kind of situation that pays my salary. It takes digging into documentation, doing interviews, that sort of thing, to determine what's going on. Generally, though, if the development work was done on company time using company resources, the company wins— especially if they have better lawyers."

"Is that the side you're usually on?"

"Yeah, I'm a tool of the evil corporation." He laughed. "And now you're just being polite. There is no way you're that interested in my work. Or are you planning on stealing something from your boss?"

"Only Post-it notes and pens," I said, mustering a laugh of my own. It did sound like we needed a lawyer to deal with this situation. The trick would be finding a way to hire one without him thinking we were insane. If he turned out to be immune and they brought him in on the secret, that might help. "But I really am interested. I haven't heard of this before. I once thought about law school, but I didn't know about this field of law." I crossed my fingers under the table to counteract the lie.

Out of the corner of my eye I saw a couple of men dressed like they'd just come from the gym enter the restaurant and take seats at the bar. That normally wouldn't have caught my attention—there were already several other similar men sitting at the bar, eating and watching a basketball game on the television suspended from the ceiling—but the two men were Rod and Owen. I wanted to bang my head on the table. It was bad enough faking a date with someone for business purposes without having the man I had a minor crush on be present. Now I felt doubly fake. Even worse, without Owen in the picture, I might manage to be interested in Ethan, and he was a lot closer to being somewhere in the general vicinity of my league. In fact, it looked like we might have more in common than I thought.

I forced my attention back to Ethan and gamely tried to continue the conversation, even as I dreaded what the magical dynamic duo might come up with as a test. "What happens if a company thinks their employee has stolen something and is using it to compete against them?"

"First step is we write a nice, official cease and desist letter. In a lot of cases, that scares them into stopping. Most people don't realize what they're doing or that it's wrong. They then just have to modify their product enough to make it be something that's truly their own. It gets more complicated if there's a lot of money involved, if the original employer really suffers damages, or if the ex-employee gets defiant."

I wondered if a letter would do the trick here. I wasn't sure how we'd get a case involving stolen magic into the court system. Would that even be a credible threat?

At that moment, Ethan's nearly untouched beer disappeared, to be replaced by a bottle of Coke. I suspected most people would still see and even taste the beer. Ethan blinked, went a little pale, picked up the bottle and studied it for a second, then laughed. "I forgot I'd ordered that. But I did say I was only going to have one beer tonight."

I wasn't sure whether to contradict him. He hadn't ordered it. The waitress had been nowhere near. He was in deep denial, but he'd definitely noticed the change.

I tried to glance as casually as possible toward the bar area. Rod raised an eyebrow at Owen in an "Okay, you try something" look. Owen bit his lip and frowned in thought, and my stomach knotted in dread. From my experience with his magical creativity, I suspected we were in for something interesting.

In the blink of an eye our nearly empty dinner dishes and glasses disappeared, to be replaced by a white linen tablecloth covering the previously bare Formica table. On top of the tablecloth were china dishes holding a sinfully rich chocolate dessert. We each had steaming mugs of cappuccino, and a crystal vase in the center of the table held a single red rosebud. I could certainly go for that kind of testing. I had to fight not to shoot a grateful glance in Owen's direction. He didn't know much more about me than I knew about him, but it looked like he'd been paying attention. During the first job interview, I'd ordered the cappuccino like it was a rare delicacy, and he knew I carried chocolate in my purse.

But I couldn't let myself go hug another man when I was on a date, not even a date generated on dubious pretenses. And speaking of that date, I studied him to see how he reacted. He stared at the table and gulped, then shook his head, took a deep breath, and said, "We must be the millionth customer, or something like that."

The waitress chose that moment to stop by and say, "Are you interested in dessert tonight?"

Ethan looked at her, then at the molten chocolate cake on our table, then back at her. "Uh, we're good. Thanks. This dessert should do it."

The waitress stared at him for a long moment, frowning, then shrugged, said, "Whatever," and left.

I turned my head with the pretense of watching the waitress leave so I could see Owen's and Rod's reactions. Both of them looked surprised, then Rod rolled his eyes and shook his head. Owen's eyes narrowed in a challenge. I braced myself.

Ethan reached for his cappuccino, but the cup scooted away from him. He tried again, and it darted sideways. I watched, wondering how he'd rationalize this one. "Boy, it's slippery," he said after a while. "I'm glad I stuck to one beer."

I put a bite of chocolate cake into my mouth—no sense wasting it, and it kept me from having to say anything—and glanced at the guys. Now Owen was grinning smugly while Rod looked frustrated. I got the feeling this was no longer about verifying Ethan's response to magic. Magical men appeared to be just as competitive as anyone else with a Y chromosome.

It then started snowing gently over our table. White flakes danced and spun in the air, then settled on us and on the table before vanishing without making us cold or damp. It was a truly spectacular sight, and no one else in the restaurant gave it a second look.

Ethan closed his eyes for nearly a full minute, then opened them again to see that it was in fact still snowing indoors. He then looked at me with a desperate plea in his eyes. "Tell me I'm not going crazy."

"Why would you think you're going crazy?"

"Either I'm having vivid hallucinations or some very strange things are happening here."

"Like what?"

"Well, first there were the people with wings. And by the way, they still have wings. It wasn't a trick of the light. And then my beer turned into a Coke. And then we got dessert worthy of the Ritz, but the waitress doesn't even notice and asks us if we want dessert. I can't catch my cup, and now it's snowing inside a restaurant. Water I could understand from a leaky ceiling, but snow?" He shook his head. "And now you're going to tell me that none of that happened, and you're mad at me for telling the waitress we didn't want dessert."

I glanced toward Owen and Rod. Owen, who looked just a wee bit smug, gave me a solemn "go ahead" nod. I turned my attention to Ethan and asked, "Do you see things like that often?"

He ran a hand through his hair, making it stand up on end. "Would it sound totally crazy if I said I did?"

"Try me."

"Okay, then. Yes, I do see things like that every so often, more often lately."

"How long have you lived in New York?"

"Just since law school."

"And where did you live before that?"

"A small town upstate."

"Did you see weird things before you moved to New York?"

He shrugged. "I probably wouldn't have noticed if I had. I never took my nose out of a book. I'm crazy, right? This is turning out to be a great date."

I leaned toward him across the table. "Have you ever considered the possibility that you really are seeing people with wings? Or that you've really seen elves and gnomes around town, or that gargoyles come and go from churches and buildings? Or that some people seem to be able to flick their wrists and get whatever they need?"

He stared at me like I'd grown wings myself. "How did you know?" he asked in a hoarse whisper.

"Because I see them, too, and I'm pretty sure I'm not crazy. In fact, I know that fairy at the other table. Her name's Trixie, but she prefers to be called Trix. I work with her."

His mouth hung open. "Huh?"

"Do you believe in magic?"

"Magic? You mean like pulling rabbits out of a hat and card tricks?"

"No, more like making things appear out of thin air—for real."

"I've read all the Harry Potter books, all the Lord of the Rings books, and the entire Narnia series, among others, but otherwise I haven't given it much thought."

It appeared that I'd found a real fantasy nerd. I wasn't sure if that would make this easier or more difficult. "Well, magic is real. It's different from the books, and to be honest, I don't know a lot about it, but a lot of those fantasy creatures you read about are real. There are people who really can do magic."

"Can you do magic?"

I shook my head. "Nope. I'm as nonmagical as you can get, to the point that magic doesn't work on me. And you're the same way. That's why you see the things you do. Most people have just enough magic in them to be influenced by it. They don't see weird things because the magical people have ways of masking them so they look normal. But we don't see the illusions. We see the truth. So we see the wings and the ears and the results of spells."

He took off his glasses and rubbed his eyes again. "Wow." He shook his head, then pinched his own arm, winced, and blinked. "Wow. Either I'm really and truly nuts or this explains a lot."

"Believe me, I know how you feel. I didn't get clued into all of this until very recently."

"I don't know what to think. I don't know whether to believe you or whether I should just start drinking heavily. There's no such thing as magic."

"You'd be surprised. Want me to introduce you to Trix?"

He shook his head violently. "I'm not sure I could deal with that right now."

"I do know some people who'd be better at helping you figure this out than I am. I work for a magical company. They need people like us to help them see through all the illusions. You could be an incredible asset to us. There was already the possibility we might retain you for some legal matters, if we thought you could deal with the truth, but you being an immune, well, that changes things. We're always looking for people like you."

"I just . . . I don't know."

"What will it hurt to talk? At worst, you'll get a better sense of whether or not you're crazy."

"Just talk?"

"And maybe a little legal advice. We really do need some help in an intellectual property matter." I decided I might as well come clean, through and through. "To be honest, that's mostly why I wanted to go out with you. I remembered our conversation, and it was particularly applicable to the situation we found ourselves in. You can understand how in our line of work, we can't just call the law firm of Dewey, Cheatem, and Howe and hire a lawyer."

"Yes, I can see where that wouldn't necessarily work so well."

"Not that I don't find you interesting," I hurried to add. "I just did have an ulterior motive. What's going on . . . well, it's big. And important."

He frowned in thought for a moment. "A new client is always good," he said after a while. "I have some time free at ten Monday. Would that work?"

I was pretty sure we'd make it work. Besides, Merlin would probably know already, in that weird way he had. "Ten would be fine."

I didn't have my own business cards, but I found the one Rod had given me in my purse. "Here's the address, and there's a map on the back. Let me write in my direct line for you." On the back of the card where the map was, I wrote my name and my office phone number. "Just ask for me at the front desk."

He took the card and studied it. "MSI, Inc., huh? What's that stand for?"

"Magic, Spells, and Illusions, Inc."

"Okay, then, I'll see you Monday. Do you mind if we call it a night? I'm not sure I'm up to dealing with anything else tonight."

"Not at all." I grabbed the check before he could. "I insist. After all, I lured you here under false pretexts for business purposes." He didn't put up a fight. He looked too drained to argue.

"At least let me make sure you get home okay. You said you live near Union Square?"

"Yeah, off Fourteenth. But I'll be fine." In the state he was in, I doubted he'd be much of a bodyguard.

"No, I can't leave a lady to get home by herself."

"Believe me, I'm well looked after. But you can walk me to the subway. I live very close to a stop, so I'll be fine." We left the restaurant, with Rod and Owen still sitting at the bar, and walked down the sidewalk toward the subway station. I saw Sam still on his perch from earlier in the evening and waved to him. "Hi, Sam!"

"Hey, sweetheart!" He left his perch and glided down to join us on the sidewalk.

I thought poor Ethan would have a stroke. "Okay, that's a gargoyle, and it's talking to us," he said.

"Ethan, I'd like you to meet Sam. Sam, this is Ethan. Ethan will be coming by the office Monday for a talk with the boss."

"Yeah, I can see why. Good call, doll face."

"Okay, I am definitely coming to your office," Ethan said, his face ashen. "If this isn't real, I need serious professional help."

I heard a voice singing my name, winced, and said, "Unless you don't think you've maxed out your weirdness quotient for the day, you should probably go now." He looked like he was about to ask a question, then changed his mind and took off.

seventeen

E than got away just in time, for as soon as he disappeared around
one corner, Jeff arrived around another corner, loudly serenading
me with his version of "Mandy." I didn't want to know how he
knew how to find me. There were way too many people following me
these days—Idris's henchmen, my MSI bodyguards, and my lovelorn
suitor. On the bright side, the more people who followed me around,
the harder it would be for Idris and his people to pull anything funny.

"Hi, Jeff," I said with a resigned sigh. "Want to make yourself useful?"

"Of course, my lady fair."

"Walk me home." He looked like I'd handed him the world on a
platter, and extended his elbow to me. I hesitated a second, then took
it. He extolled my beauty the entire way home, and by the time we got
there, I'd come to the conclusion that I could get used to that. It

would have been even better if he hadn't been under an enchantment that made him say those things, but I consoled myself with the idea that Owen was at least a little bit behind it all. Somehow, I didn't see him being quite so corny—or so eloquent—but it would be nice if he shared the same basic ideas about me.

I was hoping to sneak home and be in bed before the others got home so I wouldn't have to answer the ritual postdate interrogation, but my recent luck held, and Gemma and Marcia, with Philip on Gemma's arm, were just starting to unlock the front door as we approached. I hurried to disengage myself from Jeff's arm, which took elbowing him in the ribs, so I wouldn't have to explain why I'd gone out with one guy and come home arm in arm with another. I was about to send him away, but then I took another look at the trio at the door.

Philip and Gemma had that glow of new love. Marcia looked glum. I had a good idea what must have happened. Gemma had set Marcia up with someone so they could double date, and it had gone horribly wrong. I imagined another evening of arguing, as had happened when she'd been set up with Ethan. Then I took a look at Jeff. He was the opposite type from anyone Gemma ever set her up with, but that might be what she needed. He was good-looking, well built, and didn't seem like he'd give her much of a challenge. She'd like that, at least for a while.

I thought I might not need Owen's help to break this spell after all. "Come on, I'd like you to meet my friends," I said to Jeff. Then I shouted, "Hey, hold on a second!" to Marcia before she let the front door close. The three of them paused in the doorway as Jeff and I hurried to catch up.

Gemma and Marcia looked pointedly at Jeff, who was very clearly not Ethan. I gave them my best "I'll explain later" look and launched into introductions. "Everyone, I'd like you to meet Jeff. He's a friend I ran into on the way home. Jeff, this is Gemma, Philip, and Marcia."

Gemma gave him a dazzling smile. Philip gave him a proper hand-shake and said, "Pleased to make your acquaintance," then frowned and asked, "Do I know you? You look familiar." Marcia ate him up with her eyes, then glanced guiltily at me. I gave her a "go ahead" nod.

"Hi, Jeff," she said, her voice low and husky.

He took one good look at her, blinked, and shivered. Then he lost the silly love-struck expression he'd had since I'd kissed him and got a totally different silly love-struck expression, one that was much more suited to him. "Hey," he said, not taking his eyes off her face. "I know a great place just around the corner."

"Okay," she said, then said to us, "I'll catch you later," without taking her eyes off him. They took off down the street.

"And they say there's no such thing as love at first sight," Gemma remarked as she started up the stairs with Philip. I had a feeling the spell had been well and truly broken, with no magical help needed. And now both my roommates were dating former frogs. My life was so weird.

I got a brief reprieve from providing a date report since Marcia was out and Philip was around for most of the evening. Then, the next morn-ing as we sat around the table, eating breakfast and sharing sections of the *New York Times,* the focus was on Marcia and Jeff. Marcia was downright giddy, and she didn't usually do giddy, so this had to be something special. But I couldn't avoid the issue forever. Soon enough the topic of conversation turned to my social life. "You didn't say how your date went last night, Katie," Marcia said. "Was Ethan as boring as I remembered?"

"It couldn't have been too great if she came home with someone else," Gemma quipped.

"It wasn't bad, actually. He's a nice guy," I said. The date had been deeply strange, but he had been nice.

"Did he talk about anything other than work?"

I'd more or less planned it that way, so I couldn't blame him if he hadn't. "I found his work interesting, but we did get around to other subjects." Like my work and the existence of magic.

"Do you like him? Do you think you'll see him again?" Gemma asked.

"I have a feeling I'll see him again," I said in all honesty. "At least, I hope so. And I think I do like him." He was cute and smart, and he seemed to have a sense of humor. He was also as ordinary as I was. He didn't hide behind an illusion, and he couldn't work his will by waving his hand. That set him apart from all the other men in my life these days.

"He was pretty cute, in a nerdy sort of way," Marcia mused. "It was too bad he had no personality."

"I thought he had plenty of personality," I protested. "You just didn't like not being the smartest one in the room for a change."

"You may have a point there," she said. No one could say Marcia wasn't honest, even with herself. "But still, you're welcome to him. He's a better fit for you than he is for me anyway. Just as Jeff was definitely suited to me."

"Maybe we should swap dates more often."

By this time I was no longer surprised to find Owen waiting for me on the sidewalk each morning when I left for work. I was surprised neither of my roommates had commented on the gorgeous guy who made a habit of hovering in front of our building. This was Owen, though, who had a talent for making himself seem invisible, whether he used magic or not.

"That was quite a discovery you made this weekend," he said as we began the walk to the subway station. "You honestly had no idea you were dealing with an immune?"

"Not really, though I suppose there was a clue I missed. But it works out well for us if he is immune and he's a lawyer who may be able to help us. That's if he doesn't just go nuts."

"It must be difficult, to see things you know shouldn't be there and not understand why."

"You two didn't help with that. Were you trying to outdo each other in weirdness?"

He turned red. "How do you think he'll respond? Do you think he'll show up?"

"I certainly hope so. If he does, be gentle with him. He seems to have been on the verge of a breakdown for a while. He's been under a lot of stress, and that's why he thought he was losing it."

"Didn't we do a good job telling you the news?"

I tried to recall that day when my view of the world had been turned upside down. It seemed so long ago, I couldn't remember a time when I didn't know about magic. "I didn't go insane, and I seem to be functioning okay, so I suppose you didn't do so bad," I admitted.

He opened his mouth like he was going to say something else, then shut it abruptly, clenching his jaw like he was making a concerted effort not to say anything more. We didn't talk much the rest of the way to work. He looked pensive, totally lost in thought, and I let him think. We needed all the brainpower he could muster right now.

I let Sam and the lobby security guard know I was expecting a visitor, then went upstairs to check in with Merlin. "He's coming at ten this morning," I said. "I hope that's okay."

"It's wonderful. I can't believe you found us such a good resource."

"Let's not get carried away. He was really freaked, so I'm not sure how willing he'll be to cooperate. This might have been easier if we hadn't had to spring the truth about magic on him the way we did."

"I'm sure he'll be fine. We'll meet with him in my office."

"Okay, I'll let you know when he gets here."

It was hard to concentrate on my other work—going over some reports for Merlin—while I waited for ten to arrive. Then it was ten after ten, and I hadn't heard anything. I tried not to be disappointed. It was a lot to expect someone to deal with. I'm not even sure I would have shown up if I'd known ahead of time what I was facing.

Finally, at fifteen after, Hughes called me from the lobby to say my guest had arrived. I hurried downstairs and found a pale, sweaty Ethan standing there, looking dashing in a dark power suit. "I'm sorry I'm late," he said. "I almost didn't come at all. I walked around the block a few times before I made up my mind."

"That's okay. We understand. Come on up with me and you can meet my boss and some others who are better at explaining all this than I am."

His eyes roamed the ornate, cathedral-like lobby. "Interesting place you have here. I can't believe I never noticed it."

"It does sort of sneak up on you, doesn't it?"

The turret escalator took him aback, but I explained, "It's mechanical, not magical. Not everything here is weird. Just most things."

He did a double take when he saw Trix at her desk. "She's the one—"

"Yes, she's the one you saw the other night. Trix, this is Ethan. Ethan, this is Trix."

"Nice to see you again," she said. "The boss is expecting you. Go on in."

The big wooden doors opened before we got to them, and Ethan's eyes grew large. "Oh, boy," he breathed.

I patted him on the arm. "It's okay, really."

Rod and Owen were already in the office, sitting at Merlin's small conference table. They both stood as Merlin approached us. "Ah, so this is our new recruit," he said.

"Mr. Mervyn, this is Ethan Wainwright. Ethan, I'd like you to meet Ambrose Mervyn, our CEO." I decided not to bring up the Merlin issue. It was enough to expect him to believe that magic was real without throwing in the fact that the company was run by a legendary enchanter.

Ethan shook hands with Merlin, then I introduced him to Rod and Owen. Rod wasn't quite as friendly to Ethan as he'd been to me when they were first recruiting me, but I imagined that he only really poured on the charm for women. In contrast, Owen wasn't nearly as shy as he'd been with me. He was in full-on professional mode, still soft-spoken and reserved, but able to be direct and articulate. Fortunately, Ethan had been too busy being freaked out Friday night to notice them, and even if he had, I'm not sure he would have connected them to the odd events.

We all sat around the table, then Rod asked, "Would you like some coffee?"

Ethan cleared his throat. "Yes, please." A mug instantly appeared in front of him, and he jumped. "Oh, boy. Wow. Yikes. You didn't do that with mirrors, did you?"

"That is just the smallest of demonstrations," Merlin said. "I understand Katie has already told you the basics."

Still staring at the coffee mug, Ethan said, "Yes, magic exists, but it doesn't affect me, and you need a lawyer."

"Very well, then." Merlin then launched into the same briefing I'd heard during my first formal interview. It was funny how much of that information I now took entirely for granted. Ethan seemed to be absorbing it all. He asked good questions, even though his face remained pale and his eyes were wide. I had a feeling he was going to come through this okay.

When Merlin finished, Ethan shook his head. "You know, I find all of this incredibly hard to believe, but I'm not sure I can come up with a simpler explanation."

"Occam's razor," Owen said softly. "The simplest explanation is most likely to be correct. Just imagine the resources it would require to play a prank this elaborate, and what would we have to gain?"

"Meanwhile, doesn't this explain a lot?" Rod added. "Doesn't it make you feel better to know why you've been seeing things? You're not going crazy. You're not working too hard. You simply see a reality we don't let others in on."

"I can't believe it took me this long to notice," Ethan said with a nervous laugh. "That says a lot for my powers of observation." He took a deep breath and grasped the edge of the table until his knuckles turned white. "Okay, I'll believe you until I have good reason not to. Magic is real, but it doesn't work on me, which is why I see things I'm not supposed to. It makes a strange kind of sense. Now, Katie says you have a possible intellectual property dispute?"

Owen leaned forward, clasping his hands together on top of the table. "Yes, we have a former employee who's gone into business for himself, competing with us. In most cases, we wouldn't have a tremendous problem with that, but this situation is dangerous. We're very careful to make sure our spells can't be used to harm others. He's selling spells designed to cause harm. We're worried that if he's successful, it will unleash darker magic on the world, the kind of magic we've tried hard to suppress for generations."

"And he's basing what he's selling on work he did while he was employed here?"

Owen nodded. "He was on my staff in Theoretical Magic. Most of what we do is study the ancient texts, looking for spells that could be updated for use in the present. He found some spells that were darker in nature than we normally deal with. He worked on developing practical applications for them, but when he presented them as potential products to the board, they declined to pursue commercial production. When we found out he was still working on these projects, we dismissed him."

"Was he working on these projects on company time, using company resources?"

"Yes. All of his work was based on a spellbook we own."

"It's not information he could get any other way?"

Owen shook his head. "We have the only existing copy."

"Do we have a case?" I asked.

"It's hard to say based on only this information," Ethan replied. "I'd have to take a closer look, and even then, it's not particularly clear-cut. The fact that your company declined to commercialize his work when given the opportunity shades things somewhat, but then there's also the fact that he was using company resources. And then it might ultimately be up to a judge or jury. But that doesn't mean we can't take action. You can sometimes get a favorable result just by sending a carefully worded letter. A lot of people back down when they see the letterhead."

"You could write such a letter?" Merlin asked.

"That's what I spend a good amount of my life doing."

"So you're willing to take our case?"

Ethan smiled for the first time that day. "I couldn't pass it up. It's too fascinating."

"This won't cause a problem for you at your firm, will it?" I asked.

"I have my own firm. If I want to take a case, it's my business."

Merlin looked supremely satisfied. "Very well. You can discuss your fees with Mr. Gwaltney. Mr. Palmer can give you access to all the information you need. He's also your best resource for any questions you might have about magic."

Ethan pulled a Palm Pilot out of his breast pocket. "Let's see, I have tomorrow afternoon open if you'd like to meet then."

"I'll work around your schedule," Owen said. A business card appeared in his hand, and he handed it to Ethan.

"Okay, you just pulled that out of your sleeve, didn't you?"

Owen grinned. "Actually, I did. Stage magic is a hobby of mine."

That was news to me, but then I remembered that I knew nothing about Owen's personal life other than that he liked baseball and opera.

"That seems like a weird hobby for a real wizard," Ethan remarked, and I had to agree.

"It's fun," Owen said with a shrug. "But what I'll show you tomorrow has nothing to do with sleight of hand."

Rod made a show of shoving his sleeves up, then his business card appeared in his hand. "And here's my card. Call me to discuss your retainer."

Ethan slipped his Palm Pilot back into his pocket. "I suppose I'll see all of you tomorrow afternoon." They shook hands all around, then I walked Ethan to the exit.

"Are you going to be okay?" I asked.

"Yeah, I think so. In fact, I feel better than I have for a while."

"That's good to hear. I wouldn't want to think you were going around the bend. We need you too much."

"This stuff that's going on, it's that bad?"

"They're afraid this is the first step in a possible magical war. It opens the door for magical people who want to use their powers in a darker way, and that makes life riskier for everyone. If we stop it now, we may be able to prevent a lot of suffering."

"Then I'd better do a damn good job." He started to go, then paused and turned back. "I realize you didn't exactly have dating on your mind when you had me get in touch with you, and I know our date isn't going to make the hall of fame—at least, not in a good way—but would you be interested in trying again? This time, I promise not to have a nervous breakdown."

I hesitated. I did like him, and he was cute. He was also the most normal man I knew. But did I really want to date him? This didn't seem like the best time to mix business with pleasure. "Can we talk about it once the immediate crisis is averted?"

"That gives me plenty of incentive for getting this done right, and soon. I hope I'll see you tomorrow when I come by."

"I'll try to at least drop by and say hi while you're here."

"It would be a good idea for you to be there when Ethan comes by this afternoon," Owen said as we walked to the subway station the next morning.

"Why's that?"

"It'll help him feel more comfortable. He's going to see things that are beyond his imagination, and it'll help to have someone he knows and trusts nearby. You're an anchor to him, someone he knows is real."

"I'll see if Mr. Mervyn needs me for anything, and if not, sure, I'll come down." I was more than a little curious about what Idris had been working on before he was fired, and this would be a good way of finding out.

At the same time, I thought this was the ultimate evidence that Owen had no romantic interest in me. If he were interested, would he want me spending even more time with a guy he knew I'd gone out on a date with—even if my reasons behind that date were strictly business? While Rod had shown the slightest hints of jealousy upon meeting Ethan, Owen had been friendly, in his reserved sort of way.

I grinned then. "Magic tricks, huh?"

He laughed. "Yeah, card tricks, coin tricks. I have quite the collection."

"Everyone needs a hobby, I suppose."

"What's yours?" It was the closest thing to a personal question Owen had ever asked me.

"I like to cook. I don't have time for it often, and my kitchen here is pathetic, but it's fun to see what I can make out of what I have available. I grew up on a farm, so we were always working with fresh produce in season. I also love to bake."

"That's interesting. I'd love to try some of your cooking some-time."

"This time of year, I get baking urges. I'll have to bring in some bread and cookies to share around the office."

"I'm looking forward to it."

That afternoon, I headed down to Owen's office just before two. His desk was piled with books and papers. "Is that all your stuff on Idris?" I asked.

"Yeah. I'm missing just one thing." He was rummaging through a filing cabinet. "There it is." He added the file he'd just found to the pile. Just then the crystal on his desk glowed and Hughes's voice said, "Mr. Wainwright to see you, sir."

"Thanks, Hughes. I'll be right down."

I went with him to meet Ethan, but before we got to the door of the R&D department, I stopped him. He must have spent the morning digging through bookshelves and cabinets, for his hair was rumpled and his tie was askew. I straightened his tie, then brushed his hair out of his eyes. "There, that's better," I said.

His ears turned red. "Thanks."

But he was right back to professional cool as he greeted Ethan and escorted him up to R&D. He gave a perfunctory tour of the department on the way back to his office. Ethan's eyes drank in every detail.

While Owen talked, I compared the two men side by side. Ethan was half a head taller than Owen, and both had slender builds, but Owen's shoulders were a little broader, proportionally speaking. He looked sturdier than Ethan. Owen was all sharp contrasts—nearly black hair, very fair skin, dark blue eyes—while there was something almost blurred about Ethan. His hair was brown, with the slightest hint of silver showing at the temples, and his skin had more color to it than Owen's did. His eyes were a silvery gray that barely showed up as a color. He wouldn't stand out from any crowd unless he tried, while Owen was likely to draw anyone's eye, unless he was making an effort to hide.

Oddly enough, I got the sense that their personalities weren't all that different. They were hitting it off well enough, so well that I wasn't sure Ethan really needed me to be his anchor. Today he was taking the magic in stride.

We got to Owen's office, where Owen gestured us toward the chairs facing his desk. "Would you like some coffee?"

"Is it going to appear out of thin air?"

"I'm afraid so."

"Brace yourself," I warned. "But you do get used to it."

A mug appeared in Ethan's hand, and he only flinched a little bit.

"Katie?" Owen offered.

"No, thanks. I'm good."

Owen leaned against his desk, facing us. "Well then, I suppose we should get down to business. First, do you have any questions about what you learned yesterday?"

"Maybe one more demonstration, to prove to myself I didn't imagine all this."

"Okay." Owen took a quarter out of his pocket and held it in his right palm. He waved his left hand over it, and the quarter disappeared. Then he opened his left hand to reveal the quarter. "That was sleight of hand." He held his left hand palm up with the quarter in it, then the quarter rose to hover an inch over his palm, flip over, and land back on his palm. "That was magic. Can you tell the difference?"

Ethan frowned. "For one thing, I can't tell how you did it. For another, I think I felt something, like a charge."

Owen nodded. "You did."

"But I'm supposed to be immune to magic."

"You can still feel the energy at work. Everyone does. Most people just write it off as a shiver up their spine or static electricity. It's amazing how good the human brain is at rationalizing things it doesn't understand."

"Yeah, I spent the past year thinking that fairies were making a fashion statement and that elves had seen *The Lord of the Rings* too many times," I said.

"You know, I think I'm ready to believe you," Ethan said. "So what do you have on our case?"

Owen handed him a file. "This is Phelan Idris's employment record. I was careful to document everything, every assignment, every reprimand, every performance evaluation."

Ethan flipped through the file. "This is very thorough. Did you know he was a troublemaker from the start?"

"I had a feeling. No evidence, though. I just knew that I'd need documentation someday." He scratched his ear and looked embarrassed, although for once he didn't blush. "I have a touch of precognition—not enough to be a real seer, just the occasional flash of insight. This time it proved useful."

"Can I take this?" Ethan asked.

"They're copies. Go ahead."

Ethan slipped the file into his briefcase. Owen handed him another file. "These are the projects he was working on while he was employed here. I've made copies of his source material."

"And you have the only known copy of this source material?"

"On the bookshelf over there."

Ethan stuck that file in his case, and Owen handed him yet another file. "This is my analysis of the spells he's marketing. I've highlighted the comparisons where I think he lifted work he did while he was here. His work here forms the core of these spells. Without that work, he'd have nothing."

Ethan frowned as he studied these. "I have to admit that this makes very little sense to me. I'll have to rely on your notes. They seem pretty extensive. Anyway, our goal is to just get his attention. I should have enough to go on."

"Let me know if you have any questions or if you need anything explained. You have my card."

Ethan closed his briefcase. "Anything else I need to know?"

"That should do it, unless you have questions along the way."

"Then I should be able to get a letter drafted by the end of this week. Should I send it to you for review?"

Owen nodded. "And I can get it in front of Mr. Mervyn."

"Then I'll talk to you later this week."

I walked Ethan to the exit. "He seems nice enough, not at all what you'd expect of a wizard," he remarked.

"What would you expect of a wizard?"

"Oh, I don't know. More mystery, I guess. Maybe more intimidation and power."

"You haven't seen him really working." At least, not that Ethan knew of. It was best that he didn't know who was behind the shenanigans at the restaurant.

"To be honest, I'm not sure I want to. I'm comfortable with this level of involvement. I don't think I'm ready for full immersion. I don't know how you do it."

"It's easier than you'd think."

On Thursday afternoon there was a tap on my office door, and I looked up to see Owen. "Hi, there!" I said. "Can I help you with something?"

"I just got Ethan's letter draft, and I want you to take a look at it before I show Mr. Mervyn."

"I'm no legal expert," I warned him.

"Neither am I. Maybe between the two of us, we can tell if this makes sense."

The letter was full of legal mumbo jumbo that was less intelligible to me than the spell Owen had made me read. "I have no idea what this says, other than that the gist of it is that Idris has to stop using his stolen spells and pay restitution to the company, or something like that. It seems legitimate enough to me. Do you think Mr. Mervyn will understand it?" I wasn't sure a guy who'd spent a thousand years asleep was going to grasp the intricacies of the modern American legal system.

"You'd be surprised."

We went together over to Merlin's office and gave him the letter. He read it carefully, making the occasional "hmmm" sound. It looked like Owen was right. He did know what he was reading. He must have spent his free time studying every reference book he could get his hands on, or maybe he'd discovered the Internet.

"This is excellent work," he said.

"You know about law?" I had to ask.

"Remember, the Romans hadn't been too long gone in my day. Your modern legal system has its share of similarities to their law. Please tell Mr. Wainwright to go ahead and send the letter to Mr. Idris. And then we'll see what happens."

It didn't take long to get a response. Within two hours I had a call from the lobby that Mr. Wainwright was there to see Mr. Mervyn. I met Ethan at the top of the escalator. "What is it?" I asked. He looked flushed and out of breath.

Merlin joined us a second later. "You've had a response?"

"He wants to meet."

eighteen

"Trix, get Owen up here," Merlin instructed before turning to head back into his office. Ethan and I followed him. "So, he wants to meet?"

"Yes, sir. I made it clear that I could get an injunction and tie him up in court for the foreseeable future. That could eat into his potential business dealings. Now he must want to get all of this out of the way."

"Do you really think he'd want to negotiate?" I asked. "I mean, he doesn't seem like the kind of person who'd much care what the courts say."

"Everyone cares what the courts say, if it means you're out of business," Ethan said.

"No, I doubt he wants to negotiate," Merlin confirmed. "I imagine he's as tired of playing games as we are."

Owen arrived then, panting and disheveled from what must have been a sprint up to Merlin's office. "What is it?" he asked.

Ethan explained, "I heard from Idris. He wants a meeting."

"Already? That letter must have been more powerful than I realized."

"Let's just say my C and D letters are my own brand of magic."

We gathered around the table, and Ethan pulled out his Palm Pilot, then brought up a document. "Here's the gist of it. He wants to keep this out of the mundane legal system—I suppose that's your word for nonmagical things. But he also wants us to get out of his way. He wants a meeting to hash all this out, but not around a conference table. He said something about the 'good old-fashioned way,' and that you'd know what that meant. We get to pick the place."

"He's challenging us to a magical duel," Owen said, his eyes grave.

"You still do those?" Merlin asked.

"Not often, at least not officially. They're as frowned upon in our community as the sword or pistol kind is under mundane law."

"Don't look at me," Ethan said. "My game is legal briefs at ten paces. I'm just the go-between here. I'm supposed to get back to him with a location within an hour. The time is set for sunrise tomorrow. And only four people are to come per side, no creatures. Only humans."

"Then that's not technically a duel," Owen remarked. "A duel implies two people. But details were never Phelan's strong suit."

"You're going to fight a duel?" I asked, not sure whether I should believe what I was hearing. "Isn't that kind of archaic?"

"I'm more than a thousand years old," Merlin said with a wry smile. "I'm the very definition of archaic. I might as well live up to it. Are you in, my boy?" he asked Owen.

Owen went pale. "I've never done this sort of thing before, not seriously. Just what they taught us in school."

"You're our strongest. I can't think of anyone who'd be more up to the task."

"Wait a second, you're more than a thousand years old?" Ethan asked, lagging somewhat behind the conversation.

I leaned over to whisper in his ear. "He's Merlin, the real one. I'll explain later." He stared at me, then at Merlin, then back at me, and I nodded to confirm it. He shook his head in amazement.

"If we get to select the location, we might as well make it one to our advantage," Merlin continued, ignoring Ethan's question. He raised a hand, and a large book flew off the shelf to land on the conference table. He leaned over the book, stroking his beard as he studied the page. Then he pointed to a spot. "There, that seems to be the area of weakest magical influence in this region."

I came over to the book and saw that he was pointing to a spot on the southern New Jersey coastline. Ethan joined us. "Yeah, I would have guessed that the Jersey shore was pretty nonmagical, especially this time of year. The place should be more or less deserted." He bent to look closer at the map. "Hmm, Wildwood. We went there once on vacation when I was a kid. Very kitschy. The boardwalk is nice, though. It has a good amusement park."

"But why are you choosing a nonmagical area?" I asked. "Don't you need something to draw on for power?" I remembered what Rod had said about the need for a power supply.

"That will weaken him more than it weakens us," Merlin said. "We have a secret weapon." He turned to look at Owen, who appeared uncomfortable. A couple of bright spots formed on his cheeks, then spread over the rest of his face.

"I can probably outlast him," he said softly. That must be what Rod had meant about Owen being particularly powerful. He didn't need to draw on other energy sources as much as others did. Or something like that. One day I was going to have to get that physics of magic lecture from somebody.

Then Owen's lips turned up in a mischievous grin. "Let's meet at the amusement park. That will keep us out of sight so we won't have to worry about masking while we're fighting, and it gives us something to work with."

"It'll give him somewhere to hide, though," I pointed out. "Do you really believe he'll stick to the rules he set out?"

"That's why you'll be there, both of you," Merlin said. "We'll need our legal counsel, of course, upon the outcome of the battle, but it will be very handy to have a couple of immunes on our side. I doubt that's something he'll have."

"And we can work with that." Owen was really getting into this. It was the most enthusiastic I'd ever seen him about anything. "He may bring extra people and mask them, but we can make him think we've got a few other things on our side." He grinned, and a wicked gleam formed in his eyes. "It's all about the sleight of hand."

"So, we get back to him," Ethan said, "tell him he's on, and we'll meet at the boardwalk amusement park in Wildwood, in front of the roller coaster, at dawn. Does that work for everyone?"

Merlin nodded. "Please let him know we accept his challenge, according to his terms."

"Is there a phone I can use?"

"My office," I said.

While he went to make the call, I thought of logistical matters. "That's about a three-hour drive from here. My roommates and I once drove down to Atlantic City, and this is even farther. We'll need to leave pretty early in the morning—more like the middle of the night— to get there on time. That means we'll need a car, or do you guys have magical transportation?"

"That would be unwise, as we'll need to save our energy for the fight itself," Merlin said.

"Okay then, we'll need a car. I still have a license, so we can rent one." I was looking forward to getting on the open road. That was something I missed from Texas.

"I have a car," Ethan said as he came back to the office. "No need to rent one. We should leave by two in the morning, to give us plenty of time to get there, scope the place out, and get situated. Oh, and he did agree to the location. We're definitely on."

Merlin looked satisfied. "Good."

"This isn't to the death, is it?" I asked, suddenly nervous.

Owen shook his head. "No, it shouldn't be, not unless he refuses to surrender when he's clearly beaten."

"You sound awfully confident."

He shrugged. "I am. I've gone up against him before, though never in so formal or so serious a fight, and he's never given me any problems. But if we are clearly beaten, we'll surrender so he doesn't have to kill us."

"And what then?"

"Depending on the outcome of the fight, I'm sure we'll work out an agreement regarding what spells he's allowed to produce," Merlin said. "We win, he stops using these spells. He wins, we have to let him."

"Maybe we should bring back dueling," Ethan mused. "It would really unclog the court system, and thin out the ranks of lawyers."

"We'll all need our rest, so everyone should go home and pre-pare," Merlin said.

"I can pick everyone up, depending on where everyone is," Ethan said. "I live in Battery Park City."

"My home is in this building," Merlin said.

"Katie and I live near each other," Owen put in. "She's off Four-teenth, and I'm in Gramercy."

Ethan fed all our information into his Palm Pilot, then we ar-ranged pickup times and places and headed out. The thought crossed my mind that we could have tried to find hotel rooms in the area so we wouldn't have to drive all night, but by the time we all got home and packed for an overnight stay, it would be rush hour, so it would take us about as much time to get out of the general metro area as it would to make the whole drive in the middle of the night, and in the off season, finding a hotel room late at night might be a challenge.

I ran into Owen at the subway station. He looked tense but excited. "Are you really up for this?" I asked him while we waited for a train.

"I think so. I know what to do, but I've never had the chance to try it."

"And you're really more—" I searched for a word I could use safely in public. "—capable than he is?"

"Apparently so. People are gifted in a lot of areas. This happens to be mine." He shrugged. "Maybe it's genetic."

"Were your parents like that?"

"I don't know. I never knew them. They died when I was a baby. At least, I think they did. I don't even know who they were."

As usual, a train showed up just as things were getting interesting, and a crowded subway train wasn't the place to get into a conversation about someone's mysterious origins. If Owen was an orphan, that could explain some of his awkwardness around people.

He walked me home from the subway station, saying he didn't want to take any chances, then we said we'd see each other very soon. I went upstairs and laid out an outfit for the morning. I wasn't sure what one should wear to a magical battle—not even Gemma the fashion maven would have an answer to that—so I went with warm, comfortable clothes that were still businesslike—a black wool pantsuit with a gray sweater underneath and low-heeled short boots.

I knew I should go to bed early, but I was too wired to sleep. Instead, I baked cinnamon rolls. Cooking always relaxes me, and I had a feeling all of us could use some sugar in the morning. The rolls were rising when my roommates got home. "What are you up to?" Marcia asked when she saw the flour-spattered kitchen.

"I have to go on a very early road trip for work in the morning."

"Ah, sucking up to the boss with some goodies, huh?"

"Or impressing the cute guy?" Gemma teased.

"Mostly just sorting out my thoughts," I said, although they were both partially right. "I can switch beds with you for the night, Marcia, so I don't disturb you when I have to get up and go. It's going to be god-awful early."

"What kind of business trip is it?" Marcia asked.

"Just a meeting my boss is going to."

"And he's too cheap to spring for a hotel room. Typical. He is driving with you, though, isn't he? He's not putting himself up in luxury for the night?"

"No, he's driving with us. It was a last minute thing, so we couldn't get rooms."

"Is that cute guy, the one you were talking about, going to be on this trip?" Gemma asked. She has a one-track mind.

"Yeah. Actually, there will be two of them." I hadn't yet told them Ethan was working with my company, so I decided not to try to work that in right then. It would get too complicated to explain. Come to think of it, "complicated" was a very good word for my life.

I set Marcia's alarm for one, and when it woke me, I started the coffeepot while I dressed, then filled a couple of thermoses. I had a feeling we'd need plenty of caffeine to keep us all going. I'd just made it to the sidewalk when a silver Mercedes pulled up. The passenger window rolled down and I saw Merlin's face. "Good morning, Katie," he said, looking perkier than any thousand-year-old man had a right to look at that time of the morning.

I climbed into the backseat, then Ethan took off. We turned off onto a narrow, tree-lined side street, where Owen waited on the side-walk. He wore a black, double-breasted greatcoat over a dark suit, which was somewhat incongruous with the pillow he had tucked under one arm, like a child heading off on a family vacation. I scooted over to make room for him in the backseat.

And then we were off. "I brought coffee," I said. "Does anyone want any?"

"Oh, bless you. You're an angel of mercy. Black, please," Ethan said. I poured some into a travel mug and passed it up to him. He turned to Merlin and said, "I can see why you hired her."

"Anyone else?"

"No, thank you," Merlin said. "I must confess I haven't developed a taste for this coffee you drink."

I turned to Owen, but he was already sound asleep, his head resting on the pillow he had wedged against the window. I didn't see how he could sleep at a time like this, but it was good that he could. We needed him at his best that morning.

An hour into the drive I was wishing I'd brought my own pillow. Not that I thought I could sleep, but there wasn't much else to do. In the front seat, Ethan and Merlin talked quietly. It sounded like Merlin was giving Ethan a Magic 101 lecture, answering all of Ethan's questions. I would have liked to listen in, but they spoke too softly and I didn't want to risk waking Owen by asking them to speak up so I could hear. It was too dark in the car to read, even if I had brought a book, and I couldn't see the scenery outside in the darkness.

It was still dark when we pulled into a parking lot near the board-walk. "Looks like we made good time," Ethan noted. "But if we'd left later, something surely would have come up."

"I made cinnamon rolls, if anyone wants breakfast," I said.

"You aren't an angel, you're a goddess," Ethan said. I passed rolls forward for him and for Merlin. Ethan took a bite, then said, "You made these, yourself? Look out, Sara Lee."

"You cooked for us?" I jumped when I heard Owen's voice, then turned to see that he was awake, blinking sleep out of his eyes.

"Yeah, would you like some coffee and a cinnamon roll?"

"Yes, please. I take it we're here?"

"With plenty of time to spare," Ethan said as I handed Owen a mug and a roll.

"After we refresh ourselves, we can get the lay of the land," Merlin said.

I got a roll and some coffee for myself. The nearly sleepless night was already catching up with me, in spite of a bad case of nerves. "These are wonderful, Katie," Owen said, his voice sounding very close to me in the darkness of the backseat. "You're a good cook."

"Everyone needs a hobby," I said, glad he couldn't see me blushing.

After we finished our breakfast, we got out of the car and walked toward the boardwalk. The sky was just starting to turn gray on the eastern horizon, and a light fog forming near the ground gave the deserted boardwalk a ghostly quality. Merlin unlocked the public restrooms so we could all recover from the long drive. I touched up my lipstick before heading back out to join the men. A girl just couldn't face a magical battle without her lipstick.

We walked together toward the amusement park. If this had been a movie, it would have been one of those slow-motion power shots, our coats swirling around us as we strode purposely through the fog toward our destiny. As it was, we all felt a little cold and damp, so we clustered together tighter than we normally would. I noticed that the men had closed ranks around me, and I wasn't enough of a feminist to mind all that much. If they wanted to protect me from the scary bad guys, I was totally on board with that plan. Never mind the fact that I was probably safer than Merlin and Owen were from whatever was likely to happen.

A gate sealed off the amusement park's pier, but one touch from

292 | Shanna Swendson

Owen and it opened soundlessly. In the pale early morning light and the fog, the amusement park looked like something out of a Scooby Doo cartoon, very eerie and haunted. I halfway expected to find the evil caretaker wearing a rubber zombie mask. Only bits and pieces of the giant roller coaster broke through the fog, looking like sections of a railroad to nowhere.

"Do you think he's here yet?" Owen whispered.

"I'm not sensing anything," Merlin replied. "You two"—he indicated Ethan and me—"keep your eyes open for anything unusual, anything you don't think should be there."

My heart pounding in my throat, I scanned the empty amusement park, then did a double take when I saw a darker shadow up in the rigging that supported the roller coaster track. "There's someone up in the coaster," I said.

"I see it, too," Ethan said.

"I don't see it," Owen said, frowning. "And I suppose that answers my question. He's here."

"How, exactly, do you define sunrise, anyway?" I asked. "It's getting light, but the sun isn't up."

"For our purposes, it's sunrise when the sun is clear of the horizon," Merlin explained. I looked to the east and saw that only the topmost part of the sun was showing. We had some time to go. "But if they attack, we fight back, no matter what time it is."

I saw movement out of the corner of my eye. "Look out for the guy on the coaster," I warned.

Owen barely lifted a hand, and the man up in the coaster flew back against the iron bars, seemingly held there by invisible cords. "I don't think he'll be a problem," he said mildly. "Let me know if you see anything else."

"How did you know where to hit?"

"If I know something's supposed to be there, I can feel it. Invisibility's no good once you know someone's there."

That was good to know, and it explained how Owen had snagged that intruder, back when all this had started for me. "I don't see anything else," I said as I strained my eyes for anything odd. There was more light now, and the sun was halfway above the horizon.

"Something's in motion, nine o'clock," Ethan said mildly. He was really getting into this. I forced myself to turn calmly in that direction and noticed a man high up on another ride.

"Got him," Owen said, just as calm as Ethan. "Let me know if he moves."

"We should take our positions," Merlin said. "Katie, watch our backs."

I didn't like having to turn away from them, even though I knew there was more security in facing away from one another. I just liked the visual reminder of having three men who were strong in various ways nearby. I wished the sun would get it in gear and finish rising so we could get this over with.

And my wish was granted, sooner than I expected. Four men came striding out of the fog, coming from the ocean end of the pier rather than from the boardwalk. "They're here," I said softly. Our whole group turned, and Owen and Merlin stepped forward, leaving Ethan and me behind them.

Our opponents looked like something out of a Matrix movie, all swirling black trench coats. I could practically hear the movie soundtrack swelling with the kind of ominous throbbing bass line that makes your seat vibrate. They moved slowly, relentlessly, toward us, the fog parting around them like it knew they were trouble and wanted to get as far away as possible. The fog had a good idea, as far as I was concerned. I realized that the throbbing bass line in my imaginary movie soundtrack was actually the pulse roaring in my ears. I was a simple farm girl from Texas. What was I doing here?

Then they got closer, and they looked more like what you'd see at a Matrix-focused science fiction convention. I would have laughed out loud if I hadn't been afraid it would break my side's concentration. These guys might have the wardrobe, but they needed to work on their intimidation. Then again, in this game, appearances had nothing to do with it. Owen wasn't exactly the sort of person you'd guess was a powerful wizard if you saw him on the street.

Not that I had the slightest idea what kind of person I might see on the street and assume was a powerful wizard. But these guys definitely weren't it. If we'd been in Silicon Valley, I would have pegged these guys for the founders of a software start-up. I supposed, in a way, that's what they were.

I assumed that the one in front was Idris. He was about Owen's age, but much taller, even taller than Ethan. He had a lanky beanpole build, all arms and legs and not enough grace to make use of his height on the basketball court. His trench coat sleeves struck him just above his wrists, and even though he was facing away from the sun, he wore dark shades.

His three sidekicks were even less impressive. One wore surplus military fatigues that didn't fit him well. Another was short and squat, with a belly hanging out from under his black T-shirt. The fourth actually looked physically intimidating, but his face had the blankness of a mindless thug. I wasn't sure how he was going to play a role in a magical battle.

With their side in jeans and fatigues, and the MSI team all in suits, this looked for all the world like a classic renegades versus establishment battle, but I knew Idris and his people weren't fighting for creativity or freedom, only greed and power. For once, the ones in the suits were the good guys.

The tall guy stepped forward. "So, Owen, here we are again."

"Hello, Phelan," Owen said mildly, like they'd just bumped into each other in line at Starbucks. I was right about which one was Idris.

"You had to dig up Grandpa here on my account? What a laugh. I thought you were supposed to be hot stuff."

"Try me." Owen's voice was full of ice and steel.

"I'm only here to advise on strategy," Merlin said. "My advice was to get you out of the way."

"What's wrong, can't handle a little competition?"

"Competition is fine. Misuse of power is an entirely different story," Merlin replied. "We don't use our abilities for personal gain, especially not at anyone else's expense. That's part of the code."

"I never signed on to that code."

"Obviously," Owen said dryly. "And the sun is now up. I have an appointment this afternoon. Can we please get this over with?"

Idris opened his mouth to reply, but he was already sailing backward to land against the nearest lamppost. His cohorts likewise went flying. My hair felt like it was standing on end from all the power in the air. Ethan and I both stepped aside to get out of the way, even though we were supposed to be immune to the spells flying around.

The magical battle wasn't anywhere near as spectacular as you'd think from the movies. It wouldn't take much in the way of special effects to depict it. It was more of a silent battle of wills. I waited for someone to conjure up a dragon or at least a snake, but it didn't seem to work that way. They weren't even using wands that had sparks flying from the ends. Once Idris and his cronies righted themselves, the fight seemed to be all about them throwing spells and Merlin and Owen deflecting them. The strategy was apparently to just let the bad guys wear themselves out against Owen's presumably greater resources. I wondered if Merlin had similar strengths. He was, after all, Merlin.

I felt a tingle, then caught movement out of the corner of my eye. One of the guys who'd been hiding was making his move. "Owen, look out," I called. He turned just in time to deflect the surge of energy the guy threw at him, then he immobilized that guy the way he'd done the one up in the roller coaster.

"Cheating, Phelan? Doesn't that indicate a lack of confidence?" Owen said to his opponent.

"Or lack of morals." Idris sounded out of breath. Then he suddenly whirled like he was defending himself against an attack, leaving his back open for Merlin to hit him with something that temporarily paralyzed him. I hadn't seen anything attacking him, and I realized that the attacker must have been one of Owen's sleight-of-hand tricks. Idris brought extra people and used magic to hide them, while Owen was conjuring up imaginary attackers to distract Idris.

The henchmen gave up trying to fight directly with magic, and soon just about everything that wasn't nailed down—and a few smaller things that were—was flying through the air at Owen and Merlin. I ducked beneath a bench but still tried to keep my eyes open for even more treachery. A trash can flew through the air toward Merlin, but Ethan jumped in to pull him to safety. It did hit Owen, striking a glancing blow that sent him to the ground before he waved a hand and flung it toward Idris.

I didn't know enough about magic to have a sense of how the battle was going. Owen looked a little battered from the barrage, but was otherwise unruffled. Merlin looked like he was out for an afternoon stroll. Meanwhile, the other guys gasped for breath, all red-faced and sweaty.

Merlin pointed in the direction of one of the henchmen, and the man froze in his tracks. He sweated and strained, but apparently no longer had the strength to free himself. That was one out of the way. Owen similarly pinned another one. Now we were down to a more fair two-on-two fight—if we counted the official combatants. I suspected the bad guys had a few more tricks in reserve, and Ethan and I were still there. If it came down to it, I supposed I could contribute a few catfighting skills. I'd grown up with older brothers, so I could hold my own in a dirty brawl for a little while.

But for now it seemed that Merlin and Owen had the situation more or less under control. The air crackled with power that gave me goose bumps. I felt like I was caught in the middle of an electrical storm. A visibly weary Merlin finally disabled the remaining sidekick, while Idris and Owen were locked in a standoff. They stood about six feet apart, Idris with his arms stretched out in front of him, Owen with his hands at his sides. I was sure I could see the power glowing between them. Now Owen was beginning to fray around the edges, but he still looked better than Idris did. Idris resembled those people they show on the news crossing the finish line after a marathon and promptly collapsing.

It seemed like it was just a matter of how long either of them could hold out. The last one to collapse would win the fight, and I'd put my money on Owen. I'd never before seen a full demonstration of what he could do, but now I could tell for sure that he was more than just a pretty face.

He seemed to have it more or less in the bag. Idris was wilting, backing away. But he was also smiling, which was not right for the situation. Now I got nervous. I looked around for a looming threat and saw nothing.

Then I looked again, and something was coming out of the east, flying through the sky, zooming toward Owen so rapidly that it became clearer to me in a fraction of a second. At first I thought it was a gargoyle like Sam, but it was some other kind of winged creature. I would have to find some mythology books if I was going to stay in this line of work.

"Owen, look out!" I shouted.

nineteen

s it got even closer, I could see that the flying thing looked like a cross between a pterodactyl and a really, really ugly woman. Was this a harpy? It didn't matter all that much at the moment because it was right on top of Owen, and I hadn't managed to yell in time to give him a chance to react while he was still fighting off Idris. Neither he nor Merlin seemed to see it. The thing grabbed his shoulder with its claws, and that gave Idris a chance to catch his breath. Merlin jumped in to keep Idris occupied, but the thing still had a hold on Owen.

Whatever it was must have remained veiled, for Merlin couldn't seem to figure out what to do about it. He waved a hand in its general direction, but it did no good because it squirmed around so much, dodging whatever Merlin sent its way. That couldn't have been good for Owen's shoulder. Then Merlin had to turn his attention back to Idris to keep him from launching a magical attack on Owen. Owen struggled, and the bird thing jerked about like something was hitting it, but it didn't let go. I was sure the thing was going to eat Owen alive at the rate it was going.

It looked like it was up to me to save him. I didn't have magical powers, an MBA, or a boyfriend, but I did have the ability to see what was really in front of me, which gave me an advantage here. I also had a pretty good right arm. I scrambled on the ground for something to throw and found a small, softball-sized chunk of cement that had been broken off of something larger during the fight. I picked it up and threw for all I was worth, mentally blessing the brother who'd insisted on teaching me to throw a baseball. He would have been proud of me. I hit the thing square between the eyes, making it release Owen.

Owen fell to the ground, clutching his injured shoulder. Blood flowed from between his fingers. Merlin immobilized the creature, which must have lost its veil when I stunned it. Owen got to his feet shakily, then let go of his shoulder and pointed a bloody hand toward Idris. Now he looked mad, really and truly angry, and I understood at last why he was held in awe. He was the nicest guy in the world, but you did not want him as your enemy. The air around Idris glowed, trapping him in a magical field. He struggled, then finally collapsed, and the field dropped. He raised his hand like he was going to try another spell, but I didn't feel any surge of power along with it.

Then he took off running along the pier. Owen moved as though to chase him, but then swayed. Ethan leapt into action, giving chase. Before long he brought Idris down with a flying tackle that would have made any football coach proud.

It appeared to be over.

Merlin, Owen, and I made our way over to where Ethan had Idris pinned. Merlin looked exhausted, but he managed an impish grin as he said, "Mr. Idris, have you met our attorney? Now, Mr. Wainwright, if you're through sitting on Mr. Idris, I'll need you to draw up some documents. Miss Chandler, please see to Mr. Palmer."

We made an odd procession on our way back to Ethan's Mercedes, with Ethan frog-marching Idris, a very smug-looking Merlin alongside them. Owen, increasingly pale and shaky, followed, me supporting him. His left sleeve was now soaked in blood, and it appeared that he'd used up all his power resources and had tapped into his physical strength as well.

Ethan spread his legal documents out on the trunk of his car, while I made Owen sit on the backseat. I listened to all the legal mumbo jumbo while I peeled the bloody layers of coat, suit coat, shirt, and undershirt away from his injured shoulder. "You're lucky you went with the power suit today," I told him. "Otherwise, this would have gone a lot deeper." The claw marks weren't deep enough to cause serious damage, just enough to be painful and draw blood.

"It was one of my favorite suits," he said plaintively. I tried to ignore the fact that the suit covered a very nice build. He hadn't been lying about his gym habit.

From the back of the car I heard Ethan's voice in lawyer mode. "So, what you're agreeing to is that you will cease marketing any products based on your work done as an employee of Magic, Spells, and Illusions, Incorporated. That removes any products you have already released from the market, as well as affecting any future products you may produce. Now, if you'll just sign here and initial here."

"Use this pen," Merlin said. "It makes the contract binding in more than a legal sense."

"You're kidding," Ethan said. "Could I get a set of those for my practice?"

Owen winced as I dabbed the claw marks with disinfectant from the first-aid kit Ethan had in his trunk. "Sorry about that," I said. "But you have no idea where those claws have been, and you don't want an infection."

"No, I don't. Go on, do what you have to."

He gritted his teeth as I finished cleaning the wounds, then bandaged them and pulled his bloody clothes back up over his shoulder. I took off my own overcoat and wrapped it around his legs. He looked a little shocky, and I didn't want to leave him exposed.

"Now, if you're quite through humiliating me, could you release my people?" Idris asked.

"It's worn off by now," Owen told him.

"This isn't over, you know, Palmer. I'm perfectly capable of creating my own spells."

Owen didn't rise to his bait. "I'm sure you are."

"You're just lucky your girlfriend here has a good arm."

Owen turned pink in spite of his ashy pallor, but his voice remained even. "She also has a good eye."

"And a nice ass, but you're going to need a lot more than that next time. I have things up my sleeve you haven't begun to imagine." He gave us a mocking bow and salute. "Until next time." Then he turned and stalked away, back to the boardwalk.

"What an asshole," I said before I realized I'd said it out loud.

"That's putting it mildly," Ethan chimed in. "He's even worse than some of the lawyers I know, and that's really saying something."

"Do you really think he'll come up with something else?" I asked nervously.

"I'm sure of it," Merlin said. "That type doesn't give up easily. And worst of all, I believe he's out more for a sense of power than for material riches. He'd thoroughly enjoy being the one to trigger a magical war."

"Then we'll have to find a way to stop him."

"It'll take him a while to develop something on his own," Owen said. "He was never the most original thinker. That should buy us some time to prepare."

"We'll have to rally our people once more. We've grown complacent, from what I can tell," Merlin said. "The last challenge of this magnitude was about thirty years ago, according to the archives I've seen. I'll have to study how, exactly, that challenge was met."

"So this sort of thing happens often?" I asked.

"About once a generation seems standard. There's always someone willing to try to cause widespread trouble, and then the good people have to find the will to fight it."

"Things seem to work that way in the real world, too," Ethan remarked. "Shall we hit the road?"

"Do you have a towel or something?" I asked. "He's going to bleed all over your leather seats."

In addition to the first-aid kit, Ethan did have a towel, along with a spare blanket. My mother would love him. She never left the house without being prepared for a weeklong expedition into the wilderness. We got Owen settled in the backseat with a towel under his wounded shoulder and a blanket draped around him. "We'll get you to the healer as soon as we get back to the office," Merlin assured him with a gentle pat on his good shoulder. "It's a pity I didn't bring any of my potions with me. I wasn't anticipating physical injuries."

"I knew he'd cheat, but he took it further than I expected," Owen said with a weak smile.

I passed around more coffee and cinnamon rolls, then we headed off, back to the city. I couldn't wait to get back, or at least get out of that ghost town. I was sure it was a cheery place in the summertime, but now it was full of empty motels and skeletons of plastic palm tree trunks, their artificial fronds in storage for the winter. Before we were out of town, Owen was already asleep. I tucked the blanket more securely around him, then settled back in my seat for the ride to New York.

I don't think I'd ever been so glad to see that skyline looming ahead of me. We went into the depths of the Holland Tunnel, then emerged on Canal Street in the refreshing combination of weirdness and normality that was Manhattan. It was good to be home. Then I realized that was the first time I'd truly thought of New York as home.

Ethan took us straight to the office and said he'd be back in a little while, after he got the car parked. By this time it took both Merlin and me to get Owen up to Merlin's office. The initial shock had worn off enough that he was really feeling the pain now, and that, combined with the morning's exertions, had left him weak and shaky. We got him onto Merlin's couch, then I had Trix call for the company healer while Merlin got a painkilling potion into him.

While the healer tended to Owen, Merlin pulled me aside. "You did very good work today, Katie."

"Thank my brother Frank, who really wanted me to go out for softball."

"Not just that, but you kept a clear head in a frightening situation that would have scared many people."

"It scared me," I admitted. "But I thought if anyone could handle it, you two could. I mean, come on, you're Merlin. How can they beat that? And Owen's not so bad, either."

"He is a truly remarkable young man." Merlin's face grew thoughtful and his eyes were solemn as he watched the healer working on Owen's shoulder. "Quite remarkable." A shiver went down my spine at his tone of voice.

Ethan came in then. "Is he going to be okay?" He gestured with his head toward Owen.

"It appears so," Merlin said. "And now, I would like a word with you. I have a proposition to make." The three of us moved over to Merlin's conference table and sat down. "I'm not sure if we can fight the rest of our battles in the legal arena, but I'm coming to see where the law is a great power in this place and time, and it's a power we need to harness. We also have great need for people with immunity to magic. We can only hope that we find both in the same person.

Would you be interested in a more permanent position here, Mr. Wainwright?"

Ethan blinked. "You mean, you're offering me a job?"

"How would you like to be our corporate attorney?"

"I'd be honored. I'd have to rearrange some things at my practice, but I've got a partner who'd be up to moving into a more substantial role. I'm not sure I could come over on a full-time basis, but perhaps we could work out a retainer?"

"Whatever you think is best, but I would like to be able to call upon your expertise whenever it's needed."

"I'd like that, too. After this, the usual software cases are going to be boring."

The healer finished with Owen, who came over to join us. He carried his left arm in a sling and he still looked pale. The blood on his shirt didn't make him look any better. "Apparently, I'll live," he said dryly. "I suppose I need to worry about what we should do next."

"I've asked Mr. Wainwright to serve as our corporate counsel on a more permanent basis," Merlin said.

Owen nodded. "Good idea."

"And I'd like to form a task force to address this issue." It sounded like a certain ancient wizard had been reading contemporary business books. If he brought up quality teams, I was going to run screaming. "I can begin working with the greater magical community to build a coalition. Meanwhile, we need to find other avenues of fighting this battle. Mr. Wainwright will provide the legal angle, Miss Chandler will lend her marketing and communications expertise, and Mr. Palmer will focus on the magical aspects."

His voice grew firm. "We will not—we can not—let the likes of these destroy the foundations of a way of life I built more than a millennium ago. I would rather there be no magic left in the world than to let people like that subvert it. I hope it doesn't come to that. We won't let it come to that."

I felt properly inspired, and a little scared at the same time. There was something to be said for blissful ignorance. But would I have been happier with no idea about what threatened my world? At least this way I stood a chance of doing something about it. There weren't too many problems in the world where I could make a meaningful impact.

"But we'll start work on that Monday morning," Merlin said. "For now, all of us need to rest. Thank you all for your efforts this morning."

Ethan headed out first, then Merlin told me to make sure Owen got home safely. I decided this was no time for frugality and had Sam hail us a cab. Neither of us spoke as we sat together in the backseat. Owen looked beyond exhausted, but the healer had said he would mend quickly. He just needed rest.

The cab pulled to a stop on Owen's street, in front of a row of elegant town homes. Owen tried to insist that I stay in the cab and have it take me straight home, but I shook my head. "No, I'll walk from here. Besides, with the one-way streets, it's quicker to walk than drive."

We watched the taxi drive away, then stood there for a moment. "It's been quite a day, hasn't it?" he said after a while.

"That's an understatement. You were incredible there. I had no idea what you could do. I'm still not sure I have that good a handle on what magic really is."

He turned pink, which I took as a good sign, as it meant his color was coming back. "You weren't so bad yourself."

"Just a lucky throw," I said with a shrug, even as I felt my own cheeks grow warm.

There was an awkward silence, and I wondered if I should say good-bye, or if there was something else that needed to be said between us. In books and movies this was always the part where the battered, wounded hero expressed his true feelings for the heroine. But in real life I imagined that when a man was as battered, wounded, and exhausted as Owen was right now, all he really wanted to do was go to bed—alone. That meant saying good-bye was my best course of action. "I'll see you Monday. You take it easy, okay?" I said, turning to leave.

I'd barely taken a step before he said, "Katie?"

My heart throbbing painfully in my chest—now I really knew what they meant by heartthrob—I turned back around.

He looked me straight in the eye, something he so seldom did. "Thank you. I owe you my life."

I wondered if there was something in the magical community where he was now obligated to me or required to grant wishes. I wanted to make a flippant remark to that effect, but he was so serious. He was also pretty heavily drugged, come to think of it. It wouldn't be fair to ask him to follow sarcasm. "You're welcome," was all I said. That was probably the extent of the confession of true feelings I'd hoped for.

He smiled. "Needless to say, I'm glad you took the job offer."

"So am I." And as I said it, I realized I meant it. I'd refused the opportunity to leave, but I hadn't thought much about whether I was glad this chance had come my way. Now I couldn't imagine my life without Owen, Merlin, Rod, and all the others in it, without understanding why I saw such strange things. Sure, it complicated the rest of my life, and I hated not being able to tell anyone about everything happening to me, but that was a small price to pay to be part of something so truly incredible.

"Have a good weekend," he said softly, still looking me in the eye and not blushing at all.

"You, too!" I called out, then cursed myself. I doubted he'd be having much fun. "Get plenty of rest," I hurried to add before I turned and headed home.

So, that was that. I convinced myself once and for all that Owen wasn't interested in me as anything other than a friend. That wasn't the end of the world. I could cope with having someone like him as a friend, and at least he wasn't chasing every other woman in sight, getting into a miserable relationship and then complaining about his girlfriend to me, like so many of the guys who'd just wanted me as a friend had done in the past. After this morning, I wasn't so sure I really wanted to be more than friends myself. He was gorgeous, nice, kind, brilliant, and all that, but I wouldn't in a million years place him at my family's dinner table for Thanksgiving. That kind of power was frightening. I could only imagine what he'd do if my brothers picked on him, which they were bound to do.

The phone was ringing as I opened the door to my apartment. It was Ethan. "I was just making sure you got home okay. And Owen, too."

"I just left him at his place. He swears he'll be fine."

"That was something else this morning, wasn't it?"

"Yeah, I guess it was. Sorry you got thrown in the deep end so quickly. I at least had the chance to ease into things."

"Well, now I know I'm not crazy. Or am I?"

"Don't ask me. If you're crazy, then I'm just as nutty."

He laughed. "Nice to know I'm not alone in this. Anyway, I wanted to see if you would like to try that date thing again, and I promise not to freak out on you. I'd assume that fewer weird things would happen this time."

"Don't count on it. Ever since I got caught up in all this, things just seem to keep getting weirder. It comes with the territory. But now you know more what to expect." Then I thought about his date offer. He wasn't Owen, but I'd decided that Owen would have to remain a nonissue. Meanwhile, Ethan wasn't bad at all. He was cute, nice, funny, and smart, and he was just like me in so many ways. It might be nice to be with someone who saw the same things I did but who wasn't likely to make things appear out of thin air. I could definitely take him home, and lawyer was a job title my parents would understand a lot better than wizard. "As for dinner sometime, that sounds great," I said at last. "But would you mind if we wait until next weekend? I'm not sure I'm up to anything but collapsing right now."

"How does next Saturday sound?"

"It sounds good."

"Great. I'm sure I'll see you around the office, so we can firm things up next week."

After I got off the phone, I took a long, hot shower. It was nice not to have to worry about two roommates who also needed to get into the bathroom. Then I dried my hair and got dressed. In spite of all that had happened already that day, it was still early afternoon, and I was too wired to nap. I got out of my jeans, put on some work-appropriate clothes, and headed to the subway station to go back to the office. If I stayed at home, I'd just think. At work, I could get things in order so Monday wouldn't be such a pain.

In the middle of the afternoon the platform wasn't nearly as crowded as during rush hours, but it was far from deserted. There were a few tourists, some students in outfits that made them look weirder than anything I'd seen in the halls of MSI, and a street performer. There was a fairy I recognized vaguely from work waiting for the train as well, but I just nodded to her and focused my amused staring on the students, who were definitely sacrificing fashion and good looks to youthful rebellion.

Finally, a train arrived and we all got on board. I was lucky enough to get a seat, so I pulled my book out of my bag and read. As the train made its way farther downtown, I heard a chicken squawk and looked up. That same chicken man was making his way through the subway, trying to pass out flyers. This time I shared an "only in New York" look with the fairy seated across from me, then went back to reading my book.

Sometimes, this city is really weird, and most New Yorkers have no idea how weird it can get.

About the Author

Shanna Swendson has written category romance novels (as Samantha Carter), radio scripts, marketing brochures, annual reports, newsletter articles, and too many news releases to count. She has been a finalist for awards given by organizations ranging from *Romantic Times* magazine to the Dallas Press Club. She lives in Texas but loves to play Southern belle in New York as often as possible. *Enchanted, Inc.* is her sixth published novel. Visit her website at www.shannaswendson.com.

About the Type

ITC Berkeley Old Style, designed in 1983 by Tony Stan, is a variation of the University of California Old Style, which was created by Frederick Goudy. While capturing the feel and traits of its predecessor, ITC Berkeley Old Style shows influences from Kennerly, Goudy Old Style, Deepdene, and Booklet Old Style, all of which were also designed by Goudy. It is characterized by its calligraphic weight stress, and its x-height, now described as classic, is smaller than most other ITC designs of the day. The generous ascenders and descenders provide variations in text color, easy legibility, and an overall inviting appearance.